Liz's Road Trip

BERNADETTE MARIE

5 PRINCE PUBLISHING

Published by 5 PRINCE PUBLISHING & BOOKS, LLC

PO Box 865, Arvada, CO 80001

www.5PrinceBooks.com

ISBN digital: 978-1-63112-312-2

ISBN print: 978-1-63112-313-9

ISBN Hardcover 978-1-63112-314-6

Cover Credit: Marianne Nowicki

08192023

For Stan,
Because of you,
I've been living my greatest adventure.

Acknowledgments

T,N,G,J,S and A,
I cherish that you are my adventure!

Mama and Sissy,
Oh, the adventure we're having.
I'm glad that we're on this adventure together.

Cate,
Who knew that we'd still be learning so much?
Thank you for digging in and being my girl!

Marianne,
Your design gave me inspiration. Thank you for sharing your
talents and making me look good.

Whitney,
There is nothing better than hearing it all come to life. Your talents
are amazing.

My Beloved Readers,
Thank you for coming back time and time again. I hope that you
will enjoy Liz's story, and come back for the next.

Also by Bernadette Marie

At Last

THE ROM COM MOVIE CLUB

The Rom Com Movie Club - Book One

The Rom Com Movie Club - Book Two

The Rom Com Movie Club - Book Three

FUNERALS AND WEDDINGS SERIES

Something Lost

Something Discovered

Something Found

Something Forbidden

Something New

THE DEVEREAUX FAMILY SERIES

Kennedy Devereaux

Chase Devereaux

Max Devereaux

Paige Devereaux

STANDALONE TITLES

The Happily Ever After Bookstore

Liz's Road Trip

THE MATCHMAKER SERIES

Matchmakers

Encore

Finding Hope

THE THREE MRS. MONROES TRILOGY

Amelia

Penelope

Vivian

THE ASPEN CREEK SERIES

First Kiss

Unexpected Admirer

On Thin Ice

Indomitable Spirit

THE DENVER BRIDE SERIES

Cart Before the Horse

Never Saw it Coming

Candy Kisses

ROMANTIC SUSPENSE

Chasing Shadows

PARANORMAL ROMANCES

The Tea Shop

The Last Goodbye

HOLIDAY FAVORITES

Corporate Christmas

Tropical Christmas

Date for Hire

Mistletoe Memories

Liz's Road Trip

The End

The inhale is sharp, just as the last three have been. As I hold my grandmother's hand, fragile, pale, and cold, the inhalation doesn't expel.

I hold my own breath as the nurse holds a stethoscope to my grandmother's chest, listens, and then gives me a controlled nod.

Gran is gone.

The breath I've been holding on to comes out as a sob. My vision is clouded with the tears I've been holding back.

Gran died in hospice. I've sat by her side. This isn't a surprise. Nevertheless, here I am, unable to breathe through the sudden grief that takes hold of my heart and squeezes. The pain is nearly intolerable.

For the first time, Gran is in a room and the mood isn't lifted. She was the kind of woman who lit up a room when she walked in. She loved everyone she ever met, and she loved me the most.

A hand comes to my shoulder and rests there. There is no need for words. The condolence that comes from Grace's touch gives me the calm I can't give to myself. This is what the love of a best friend can give you—peace when you have none.

I suck in another sob. Since Gran came to live with me when I was ten, after my mother died, I've talked to her every day. Even on mornings when we didn't have breakfast together, we had coffee while we talked on the phone. I'll never have coffee with Gran again.

Grace sits down in the empty chair next to me. "Can I get you anything?" she asks softly, touching my leg as if to let me know she's right there.

"I don't know," I say on another sob.

"I'm going to give you some time. I'll go get some tea. You could use a snack too," Grace says, and I'm grateful she's here with me in the middle of the night.

I nod. I long ago lost what time it was. I've been sitting in the hospice room for days, only leaving to go home and shower—and cry. Grace has kept me fed and hydrated, and I owe her for that. Someday, I'll be able to repay her, because this too will be her reality. It's all of our realities. For some of us, it comes at a young age. For others—well, they're the lucky ones who get entire lifetimes with their parents and grandparents. That isn't my reality.

The grief squeezes my heart again.

Grace follows the nurse out of the dark room, and they disappear. The night closes in around me, and I let the tears fall freely. My hand is still clasped around Gran's.

Am I supposed to talk to her? Am I just supposed to sit here until I'm ready to walk away? What's the protocol?

It's been twenty years since I sat with my mother as she died. The ten-year-old me cried, yelled, and they'd pulled me away from her—my mother.

It feels the same, deep inside, as I hold Gran's hand. I want to scream and yell, but what good does that do? Gran is gone. I am alone.

I wipe the back of my free hand over my wet cheeks. I will cherish being here with Gran at this moment of her death as much as I will the past twenty years together.

Gran was more than a caretaker. She was a confidante and a

teacher. When I was young, she volunteered at the school for everything. When I went to college, she took the opportunity to travel, since I wouldn't go anywhere unless we drove. She even wrote articles for the local papers from time to time, and she introduced me to the woman I now work for at a local magazine. I've never met anyone who wasn't taken with her, and I always understood how lucky I was to have her as my grandmother.

She was always my cheerleader, excited when it was my time to shine, and when she disciplined, she tried her hardest to be a hard ass, but usually she caved.

That very thought makes me chuckle through my tears.

Looking down at the woman who was bigger than life, the tears are back. A sickness, which I've become very familiar with, stirs in my stomach. It's the lack of sleep. The lack of food. Too much coffee. Stress of the unknown. All of it mixing in my stomach. It threatens to turn me inside out. At times, it does. Other times, it's been my strength to carry on—to just get out of bed in the morning.

Now, at this moment, I don't know what to do with it.

Gran had been sick for the better part of a year. She'd stopped traveling a few years ago, stopped going out all together a year ago, and stopped talking to her friends as her body got weaker. It was as if she'd been dying all this time.

Her mind was sharp, but her body succumbed to cancer, just as my mother had when I was little. It scares the shit out of me to think that someday this might be my fate, too.

Grace walks back into the room, a cup of tea in each hand and a roll of Ritz crackers in the pocket of her sweater.

She looks at where my hand still holds my grandmother's, and I can see the sadness resurface in her eyes. Grace has been around Gran as long as I have. I know she feels this loss as deeply as I do.

"They say to stay until you're ready to go. No hurry. I have tea for you and some crackers. I'll take my tea out into the hallway," she offers, but I shake my head.

3

"Don't go. Stay here with me." My voice is weak, and so am I.

Grace nods, sets the cups on the tray behind us, and takes the open seat again.

Needing her more than I ever have, I reach my free hand to Grace and she takes it and holds it in hers.

Sitting between these two women who have loved me through every up and down, I bounce between acceptance, graciousness, anger, love, bitterness, and the cycle continues. Grief is a weird and vicious monster, and this is just the start of it.

"There's a lot to do now," I say, clearing my throat.

"We'll work on that later. Whatever you need from me, I'm here," Grace promises, and I know that's true. There has never been a time when Grace hasn't been part of my life, and this is no exception.

"I'll need your help," I plead.

"And you know I'm here. Tonight, when you're done here, we'll go home and get some sleep. You can make the phone calls you need to make in the morning, and then we can go through her plans and get her funeral situated."

I laugh weakly, shaking my head. "She doesn't want a funeral. Not a traditional one," I say.

Grace leans her head on my shoulder. "You'll do right by her. You always do."

I owe Gran everything. In the final act of getting to do something for her, I will make sure she's honored.

Swallowing hard, I look at the frail woman in the bed. This isn't the way I want to remember the woman who raised me since I was ten. I want to remember the vibrant woman who sang songs and made up stories. I want to remember the woman, who, no matter how old she was, turned men's heads. I want to remember the woman who stepped into my world and gracefully eased me into going on with life without my mother.

However, the image before me is seared into place now.

"Cosmo," I nearly shout out the name as I sit up straight in the chair.

Grace nods slowly and smiles. "I've been taking care of him. He's fine. He's got food, water, litter, and I hid some snacks around the house. I even turned on the TV."

I ease back in the chair. Yes, Grace has always taken care of me, especially when I can't think straight.

"Thanks."

"My pleasure."

"I hate that cat," I say weakly and Grace laughs loudly, and then covers her mouth.

"You do not. And I wouldn't say that in the presence of your grandmother."

"Oh, she knows," I admit. "And she also knows I'll take care of him."

Grace grins at me. "That cat is going to be your saving grace."

I roll my eyes, and then my shoulders. "You know what's wrong with you? You're always so damned optimistic."

"Someone needs to be. Your pessimism is stifling."

I pucker my lips so I won't smile, then I rest my head on her shoulder and sit there for just a little longer.

We sit in the dark room, in the middle of the night, in silence, for just a bit longer. I know that when I walk out of the room, that's it. This is the last time I'll see my grandmother. The last time I'll touch her. The moment is suspended in time as long as I sit here. I'm just not ready to say goodbye.

WATTS Calling

Cosmo paws my lap as I sit on the couch, surrounded by piles of tissue. I haven't stopped crying since I got home.

I hadn't walked through the door until nearly eight o'clock that morning.

Once I'd found the courage to leave Gran, there were forms to fill out and questions to be answered. I don't know what I would have done if Grace hadn't been there with her level head.

To be honest, I would probably still be sitting there with Gran. Grace gave me the courage to leave.

I brewed a pot of coffee when I got home, put on my pajamas, and sat down on the couch, where I've been sitting for hours. I don't even have the TV on.

Cosmo knows something is amiss. Not only is he at my house, but Gran's been missing from him for the past few weeks.

He'd probably like to see Grace about now, too.

Thank God she'd taken it upon herself to take care of him. My mind certainly wasn't on his wellbeing. I suppose that's why I've never considered having children. I can't even take care of a cat.

It's nearly two o'clock in the afternoon now, and I have no

ambition to do anything else but wallow in my sorrow with the cat.

I run my hand over his golden fur and the tears come again. "You goofy cat. You're all mine now," I say and the cat responds with a purr, as if he'd have it no other way. "What are we going to do?"

Resting my head back against the couch, I let myself sink into the sobs that come. I know it's only been a few hours, but I would have thought the tears would have all dried up by now.

It's just that I've been taking care of Gran for a long time. She raced to my rescue when I was a child, and when I returned from college, we took care of one another. The past few years, I've taken care of Gran as her health began to decline.

Every day I spent time with her. If she had an appointment, I took her. If she wanted to spend time with friends, I'd either drop her off or stay and play Scrabble or cards.

We had TV shows we watched together, and no one interrupted her soap opera watching. She'd talk about those people as if they were real, though I never considered that her mind really thought they were. Actually, she often commented on the writing of the shows and how she would take the storyline. It humored me.

Now, well, I feel useless, as if her death is my fault. I know that's not true, but I can't help but think that if I'd taken better care of her—

I startle when my phone buzzes on the coffee table. I pick it up, and just seeing Grace's name brings peace to the ache in my chest.

Did you shower? You promised me you'd shower, the text reads.

I wrinkle up my nose and type back the same lie I would say to her face.

Yes, I showered.

Did you eat? Grace responds.

I actually look around the room for proof that I've eaten, because honestly, I don't remember.

The truth is, I don't think I have eaten yet.

Yep, I reply. *I've eaten.*

There's a beat before the next text comes in.

You're a big fat liar. I'll be over in an hour. Is Cosmo okay?

That makes me laugh. I swear I hate this cat. Grace swears I don't. But she knows I'd never let anything or anyone hurt the damn thing.

Gran took a trip to Florida years ago and came back with him. All she said was that a friend gave him to her. She loved this crazy cat. She loved him as if he were her best friend.

Cosmo moved out an hour ago. He just couldn't take me being his one and only now, I text back.

Grace sends a gif of a woman facepalming and shaking her head.

You're a piece of work and I love you. I'll be there soon.

I toss my phone to the side. Cosmo is completely unfazed by it all.

I run my hand over his fur again, and I won't admit this to Grace, or to Cosmo, but it does offer me peace to pet him. Was this why Gran had him?

I let my head fall back and I close my eyes. Lists fill my head.

Lists of people I need to call.

Lists of places I have to go to finalize plans.

Lists of things I have to do to put Gran's life to rest.

I have lists of items I'm missing for my job—and that's still important. If I want to be paid, I have to work.

I groan, and it's enough to have Cosmo lift his head and give me a disapproving glare before returning to his nap on my lap.

My hand, by its own will, I'm sure, continues to stroke the cat. I close my eyes and let the heaviness of the day wash over me.

I have to assume that I had just fallen asleep by how hard I startle when the old-time phone ring has me jumping up from my seat. Cosmo hisses at me and jumps down as I jump up.

That ring tone belongs to my grandmother.

I mean, it's her phone.

Shit, where did I put her phone?

It takes me a moment to realize that I put it in my purse. I kept it charged, just in case. I mean, I was the only person who would call her on it, and she hated to use it, but here it is ringing.

By the time I pull it from the bottom of the bag that collects everything from my life, it stops ringing.

I scroll to the missed calls, assuming that it would tell me that there was a spam call or something. I'd been very specific with her that she wasn't to answer any call from numbers that weren't in her contacts. The last thing I'd needed was her getting sucked into some scam because she didn't understand what it was they were saying, or because her heart was too big and she felt as if those who were less fortunate deserved what she had.

The Caller ID was a Florida number, and it was in her contacts. It came up with the name *WATTS* only. The picture of the contact is the front of a house with stucco exterior with an arched entry and an ornate wooden front door.

I wait a moment for a voice message to come in, but instead the phone dings in my hand.

Hey, Doll! The pool boy says hello. The front tree died, so I had it taken down. How's the cat?

I blink hard and reread the text. *Hey, Doll!* What in the—

The doorbell pulls me from the message.

When I pull open the door, Grace is standing on the other side with a bag of groceries.

"What's wrong?" she asks as she pushes by me, drops the groceries, and shuts the door.

"My grandmother just got a call and a text from Florida."

"Did you tell them what happened?"

"Not yet. I figured it was a solicitor, but..." I turn the phone to show her.

"Ooh-la-la," she sings, and humor lights in her eyes. "Gran was keeping a guy on a leash?"

"Seriously? You're kidding about this?"

"Liz, relax. Whoever it is, they're obviously not close to Gran. They would have known she was gone by now."

"I haven't told anyone," I say, looking at the message again. "It just happened. I need to get my head wrapped around it first."

"Well, anyone who was close enough to her would know she was eighty-five, and has been out of touch for the past month—the past year, really," Grace says.

I consider that. Gran had all but isolated herself with me in the past year as she grew weaker from the cancer. She stopped going to the senior center and playing cards with friends. Friends stopped calling because at some point she told them to.

"What if this person has been taking advantage of her?" I ask.

Grace picks up the bags again and narrows her eyes on me. "How?"

"Money?"

"Has she had money going out? You take care of her books."

"Me and her financial advisor," I say in consideration, "and no. I haven't seen money going out."

"Then maybe she hasn't cut herself off from everyone. There is a man in Florida, that calls her doll. I think it's sweet."

I tend to think it's a little creepy.

Gran hasn't been to Florida in the past six years. So whoever this person is, they must be very out of touch.

I startle when Gran's phone begins to play music. I look down and see that an alarm has gone off. It's titled *Call WATTS*.

I silence the alarm and look up at Grace, who is wearing a wide smile.

"Ooh-la-la," she says again with a laugh, but I think the whole thing is going to make me sick.

The Text

Because Grace is the kind of friend every person should have, she fed me and waited for me to shower. She made sure I had meals for the next day, and before she left at ten o'clock that night, after we'd watched a marathon of *Friends,* she left with the promise that she'd be back the next day.

Grace had been my salvation since childhood, and nothing had changed. She'd been my friend since elementary school. She'd been my friend when my mother had died. Other kids didn't know how to act around someone who'd lost their mother, but Grace didn't treat me any differently. Every day that Grace came over to play, she was sent to our house with something in a casserole dish or something sweet baked and wrapped in foil. Not only did Grace take care of me at that time, her mother took care of Gran and me, too. Grace is one of those people that if you have one in your life, you never let them go. You can't afford to let them go.

Cosmo leans back and stretches on my lap. He knows something is wrong with me. Though this cat has been living with me for a month, and has been around me for years, he's never given me this kind of attention.

I can't decide if he's looking for answers. Does he have the answers? Does he know Gran isn't coming back? Is he just trying to comfort me?

I run my hand down his back. "Who was she, Cosmo? What did I miss?"

Seriously, I think he understands me. Cosmo turns his head to look up at me for a moment as if he's annoyed I've asked him such an obvious question.

"I know. I should have known her better. I should have taken the time to get to know her. I'm a horrible granddaughter."

Cosmo stands on my lap, makes a circle, and sits back down.

"No," I say aloud to myself. "I wasn't a horrible granddaughter. I was a girl who had lost everything, and Gran came to take care of me. She didn't make me move to Florida. She moved here."

The tears are back and I just let them fall.

When I need his comfort most, the stupid cat moves the moment my tears roll from my cheeks and land in his fur. I can't blame him, I guess.

Gran left her life in Florida and moved to Colorado so that my life didn't change any more than it already had. No ten-year-old is prepared to lose their only parent. But then I guess no 65-year-old is prepared to suddenly raise a ten-year-old, either.

Again, Gran's phone dings, and I scramble to pick it up from the coffee table.

Hey Doll! Joe says you hadn't been feeling well when he spoke to you last. Are you doing okay? I'm getting worried about you. Reach out, won't you? I have a new chapter for you. Give Cosmo my love.

The text was from WATTS again. *And who the hell is Joe?*

Curious, I scroll through Gran's contacts.

DR. KNOTT

LIZ

LIZ'S FRIEND GRACE

MONEY GUY DICK
MONEY GUY TOM
MONEY GAL VAL
WATTS

Seriously, why have I not gone through Gran's phone more often? First of all, there are only seven people in her contacts? She has three money people? Does that mean she has the name of bankers or financial advisors? I mean, I know Dick is an advisor. I have his information in my phone too. But who are the other two? Why does she need that many financial advisors?

WATTS is the person that keeps calling her *Doll*, so I assume WATTS is a guy—maybe?

I thought I knew this woman. What kind of secrets was she keeping from me? A man in Florida? Financial advisors I didn't know about? What kind of finances did she have that she needed to be advised about?

Scrolling back to the text screen, my thumbs hover there for a moment. *Doll*—they'd called her *Doll*. It's getting to me.

Who is this? I text.

Those annoying bubbles pop up, then go away. Then pop up again.

I did text Betsy, right? is their reply.

How do you know Betsy?

The phone rings in my hand. All I can do is stare down at it. WATTS is calling.

I don't answer, and after four rings, it stops.

Then the phone buzzes again.

Who are you? They ask. *Why don't you answer if you have Betsy's phone?*

For a moment, I feel as if I'm in a horror movie where the person stalking me can see me. I know that's not true. First of all, WATTS is in Florida—or so says the caller ID. Second, I seem like the stalker.

13

Why do you want to talk to Betsy?

Cosmo jumps back up on the couch, only this time he scares the bejesus out of me and I yelp. Of course, in return, I scare him and he runs off. "Damn cat," I mutter.

Betsy is a friend. Is she okay? I'm worried about her. Who is this? Is this Liz?

I actually stop breathing.

Shit! Whoever this is, they know my name. I look around the room as if someone will appear from behind the closet door. Then, I jump up and close the blinds completely and double-check the lock on my door.

Finally, I have to take a breath. My heart is racing and I don't like this feeling. Okay, I could just turn off her phone and leave it off. If it was only me and Gran in the world, well, then I can be the one that knows she's gone. No one else needs to know.

Then again, someone reached out to her and was checking in. Obviously, I'm not the only person in Gran's world.

How do you know Liz? I respond.

Seriously. I need to know Betsy is okay. If this isn't Liz, who is it?

Maybe the texting is stupid. I should call WATTS.

No. I'm too afraid. Of what, I don't know. But the only way they would know my name is if Gran told them, right? They knew Cosmo too. In fact, not only did they mention the cat twice, they used his name.

My thumbs twitch over the screen. *It's Liz.*

Thank God! They send back.

Where is Betsy? They text again.

Liz, is something wrong with her?

Can we please just talk on the phone? My fingers are starting to cramp.

The texts come in one right after the other. And then, the phone rings again.

WATTS is calling.

Again, as if he's trying to comfort me, Cosmo jumps back up

the couch and settles in next to me. My body is shaking. My breath is labored. My heart is racing.

I have no idea who WATTS is, but they know me.

"Hello?" I say as I answer the call. My voice is shaky.

"Liz? Is this Liz?" The voice on the other end is male, and it's not as old as I'd expected. "Hello?"

"Yes, sorry," I stammer. "This is Liz."

He lets out a sigh. "I'd recognize your voice anywhere," he says.

"How exactly?"

WATTS chuckles. "You're her outgoing voicemail message."

"Right," I say, realizing that I did record her message when we got the phone. "And who are you?"

"Mark. Mark Watts."

Okay, now WATTS has a real name, but I still don't know who the hell he is.

Cosmo meows next to me loudly, and Mark laughs.

"Is that Cosmo?"

I look down at the cat. Seriously, what does this cat know?

"Yes."

"Give him a pet from me and tell him his old friend Mark says hello."

Cosmo meows again.

"He says hello back."

"Right," Mark chuckles. "So, how is your grandmother? I'm going to assume she's not well if you have her phone. Or maybe I'm just jumping to conclusions. She usually calls me every Sunday," he continues. "She hasn't spoken to me in a month."

"I'm sorry, who are you?" I ask again.

"Mark. Watts." He breaks down his name and says it slowly, as if I didn't catch it at the beginning of the conversation.

"I mean, how do you know my grandmother? How do you know me?"

He's silent for a moment. I almost think he's disconnected the call, but then I can hear him breathing.

"You don't know who I am?" he asks.

"Should I?"

"I would have thought you would."

"Why?"

"Because I live in your grandmother's house."

The First Secret

"Hello?" Mark says, when I fall silent.

"What do you mean you live in her house? Who the hell are you?" My temper is flaring now, and I want some damn answers. "Don't touch anything. I can't believe you're calling me, and—"

"Liz," he says my name firmly. "Calm down."

"Calm down? Calm down?" The second time I say it, I'm not calm. "Listen, I don't know who you think you are. But to call me the day my grandmother dies and tell me that—"

"She's gone?" Now his voice breaks. "Oh, Liz," he says, nearly sighing. "God, I'm so sorry."

My bottom lip trembles, and I bite down on it to still it. There are tears in my throat now, and I make some strangled sound when I breathe. "She passed early this morning."

Mark blows out a breath, and I swear I can feel it come through the phone. "So she *was* sick?" He emphasizes *was* as if he'd had that conversation with Gran and she'd denied it.

"Yes," I say, and then find I want to tell him more. "Cancer," I blurt out the ugly word. And then as if that wasn't enough, I say it again. "Cancer."

"An actress to the end, huh? She never mentioned it."

This sets me off. I have no idea who this jack-hole is, and he's acting like he knew my grandmother intimately enough that she might actually tell him things?

"What did you mean that you live in her house? Your phone number comes up as Florida."

"Well, yes," he says. "I'm in Florida."

"Then how do you live in her house?"

"Her house here," he says this slowly, just as he had his name. God, that's starting to piss me off.

"She lives here," I confirm.

"Betsy Evans? Elizabeth Cassandra Evans?" Mark rattles off her full name and sickness washes through me.

This man is phishing for information and I'm feeding it to him. God, I'm so stupid.

I sit there for another moment.

"Liz? Are you still there?"

I want to tell him to take the shortcut to hell, but instead, I slide my finger over the screen and disconnect the call. Then, I turn off Gran's phone.

I don't know why people feel the need to prey on those who have just lost someone, but that's what he's doing.

Yes, my grandmother once lived in Florida.

Yes, my grandmother visited Florida whenever she vacationed.

But when my mother died, Gran packed up her life and had it shipped to my house to live with me. She'd let me open the unlabeled boxes, one per day.

It was like a little gift to each of us. She'd have a little bit of her life in our house. I'd get to open a box and not know what was in it. She'd moved in piece by piece, so I wouldn't be overwhelmed. For a few weeks, it got us through.

Mark Watts telling me he lives in her house, well that just pisses me off.

Gran's little house—the house my mother and I lived in, which is in Colorado and not Florida, and is only a few miles away from my condo—now sits without Gran. It'll be something I have to tackle, in time. But today, on the day my grandmother died, I'm not going to do anything, but sit and mourn with her cat.

Her cat, that seems as if he knows Mark Watts.

Shit! Maybe I should call him—

My thought is disrupted when my own phone begins to ring.

Surely word will get out on its own. I expect that my phone will begin to blow up soon with condolences. Even though Gran cut off contact with her friends, they were still her friends. They're going to call.

But when I pick up my phone off the coffee table and look down at the ID, the number just says Florida.

Coincidence, right?

"Hello?" I answer the phone. Already my voice shakes.

"Liz? It's Mark. We got disconnected."

Anger has me sitting on the edge of the couch. Cosmo jumps down and begins to circle the coffee table. Oh, yeah. He knows I'm mad, and he's feeding off my feelings. He's doing my pacing.

I draw in a sharp breath. "Listen, I don't know who you are, how you know me, why you have my number, or know my grandmother's name. But if you call me again, I'll press charges."

"Liz, can you give me five minutes to explain?"

"What's to explain? You did a google search and now here you are phishing for more information about me and my grandmother. Well, buster, she doesn't have anything. Okay? So if you're looking for money or—"

"Elizabeth," he cuts me off again by saying my full name this time. "I'm going to hang up. But I'm going to text you an address. I want you to look it up. Then, you need to look up ownership. Ask Grace to verify it," he says, throwing my best friend's name in the mix. "When you have the answers you need, you have my number. Mark. Watts," he breaks down his name again, and I swear I'm going to throw my phone against the wall.

As promised, he disconnects the call.

And, like an idiot, I sit there with my phone in my hand and watch the screen.

A few moments later, a text appears from the Florida number. Just as he said, there is an address.

I click on the address and my map app opens. It pinpoints it to an area in Palm Beach.

God, this conman must be good to have connections in Palm Beach?

I change the map to street view and look at the house at the address. It's the same picture as the one on my grandmother's phone. The one attached to Mark Watts' contact information.

The stucco exterior, arched doorway, and the ornate wooden door match the address.

I want to call Mark back and ask more questions. How long has he been preying on my grandmother, I wonder? I need to get into her financial accounts and make sure that there isn't anything going out.

Then again, when did she get numerous financial advisors? And why didn't she tell me about them?

I'll press charges against this asshole if he's stealing from her.

I'm not going to call him. He said I needed to search for the owner of the property. I'm going to do that. When I have my answers, I'll either call Mark Watts back, or I'll call the police.

My palms are sweaty now. I put down my phone and wipe my hands on my pajama pants.

Gran taught me, the forever pessimist, to play the game *What if?* *What if* Mark Watts was a straight up guy? *What if* Mark Watts really knew my grandmother? *What if* Gran still had her house in Florida?

I sit back on the couch and let my head fall back.

I was ten when my mother died. Ten.

She was sick for two years before she died.

What does an eight-year-old understand about a sickly mother? Not a damn thing.

Mom couldn't play with me all the time and sent me to Grace's house.

She slept a lot, and I watched whatever TV shows I wanted to.

The only time Mom and I visited Gran in Florida I'd been six. We went to Disney World, swam in the ocean, built sand castles on the beach, and there were palm trees. That's all I remember. It was a vacation to me—for me.

That's all I remember because the flight home was so traumatic, we nearly died.

I shake that thought from my head. I'm already panicked as it is. I don't need to relive the chaos on the airplane to throw me into a state where I just might need medical attention.

I look at the map again.

Let's be honest. Palm Beach and Orlando aren't right next to one another. So that trip—even if we did stay at Gran's—wasn't about being at Gran's. Not to me.

I remember that we were there for a few weeks and after the first week, I wanted to get back to my friends.

The very thought of what that trip had cost my mother is devastating to me now.

Tears flow freely from my eyes again, and I don't even bother to wipe them away. With Gran gone, am I going to mourn my mother all over again?

I stretch out on the couch and lay my head on the arm. I tuck my hands up under my cheek and they quickly become wet from the tears.

Cosmo jumps up on the couch and settles into me. We're both mourning. All we have is one another. Okay, I have Grace, but she has a life. I can't count on her to always be here for me. She will be, but I'd be an asshole to think her life should revolve only around me.

Unlike me, she embraced finding love and starting a life of her own with a man she loves. Ashton adores her, and luckily, he lets me occupy more of her time than I should.

My eyes grow heavy. All I can do now is pray that sleep will take over, because every single part of me is exhausted. I don't want to think about making arrangements, or where Gran is right now. I don't want to wonder about a house in Florida or if someone is stealing from her. I don't want to hear Mark Watts' voice in my sleep.

But as my body grows heavy, and I can feel Cosmo's deep breathing against my stomach, I hear Mark Watts' voice saying my name. *Liz. Liz. Liz.*

The Morning After

The sun was fully up when I pry open my eyes. Cosmo must have slept in too, because when I reach for my phone, battery life of three percent, after he'd started pawing my chest, I see that it's eight o'clock.

Usually he has me up by five-thirty to feed him. Then, the little asshole takes a nap and I'm fully awake.

I sit up, and Cosmo jumps down, smugly walking to the kitchen where his food bowl resides. He's not even going to give me a moment to pull myself together and go to the bathroom.

Once I get him situated, plug in my phone, and start the coffee pot brewing, I head to the bathroom. One look at myself and I'm crying again.

My face is splotchy, which makes my freckles darken. Yes, thirty-years-old and I still have a face full of freckles. It comes with the red hair, which my Gran and I shared. And that—the hair—is an absolute mess.

It's going to take an hour to get it brushed out.

What else do I have to do with my day?

I'm not planning a funeral for Gran. Not yet. Not until I have her ashes back and I know I can hold my own around other people. Besides, Gran didn't want a church funeral. She wasn't a huge believer in God, and I don't feel right making the last thing that's about her involve a religion, of any kind, which she didn't believe in.

No, right now, she'll come home with me and Cosmo. Though I'll have to put her in a cupboard or something, because that little asshole climbs over everything and will knock her over.

Strangely enough, that makes me laugh, and doesn't that feel good?

Pulling my brush from the vanity drawer, I start the assault on my hair. I'm going to go over to Gran's and start sorting through her things. I guess I need to decide, do I stay in my condo, or do I move back into the house? Both are paid for. One could be income property. Grace will have a better idea of which property would be better for that. She's a real estate agent, and she'd have to manage it for me. I don't know the first thing about leasing out a house or a condo.

From the kitchen I can hear a text ding on my phone. It has a special ding, a doorbell chime to be exact. That means it's Grace.

Still brushing my hair, I walk through the kitchen and look down at my phone. Swiping my finger over the screen, I bring up her text.

Good morning. Are you awake? Are you up? Get up. Get showered. Eat!

I'm stupid to think I'm alone now that both Mom and Gran are gone. Even though she's married, I'm still a top priority to Grace. I'll never—ever—be able to repay her for that.

I'm up, I reply. *Brushing out my hair. Having coffee with Cosmo.*

Eat! she texts back.

I smile down at my phone. *Yes, ma'am.*

I have a showing at noon. I'll come over later.

I rest my hip on the counter and chew on my bottom lip while I contemplate that. *Meet me at Gran's. I'm going to try to find all of her important paperwork.*

Does she have a will? Grace asks.

Maybe. I don't know.

For a moment I think about my conversations with Mark Watts from the night before, and how he mentioned Grace by name too.

If I send you an address, can you look up an owner?

Sure.

I search for the address, but before I can send it to her, Grace shoots another text.

I have to go. I'll get it when I get to a computer. EAT!

God, I love her.

No hurry. I'll see you later, I say, and then copy and paste the address into the text. Let's see what Mark Watts is all about.

The shower wakes my body and clears my head. It's a good thing too, because when I get out of the shower, I have three text messages. They're all condolences from people who have learned of Gran's passing. No doubt Grace has told a few people, after all, she sat with me until the wee hours of the morning. Then she spent the rest of the day trying to take care of me. People were going to know Grace was missing from her life, and they'd ask questions. And since our lives have been intertwined since we were six, she knows the same people I do.

I might think I'm alone in this world, but I have friends, co-workers, people I'm friendly with. But Gran was my world. That ache isn't going to go away any time soon.

Wrapped in my towel, my curls air drying, I send back texts of thanks to those who reached out. But it's the Florida number that catches my attention.

I know I promised not to text again, please forgive me. There are people asking if Betsy's arrangements have been made yet. I know it's all fresh, but I thought I'd ask so I could tell them. Honestly, most of them are too old to travel, but they'd like to send condolences. Let me know. Mark.

The simple ending with his name squeezes at my heart. Okay, maybe this man, who seems to know a lot about my grandmother, is on the up and up. And who were these people in Florida?

That tremble in my lip is back, and damn if the tears don't just start up again. But this time, they're self-deprecating. I should have known her life better. She traveled back and forth to Florida to visit people for years. Did I ever take the time to ask who they were? No. I was so self-consumed with my own life, and feeling so sorry for my own self, I never took time to ask.

With my phone in my hand, I scroll through my pictures. I had tagged all the pictures with Gran and me so they were in a folder. I think I knew I'd need them for salvation, and there they were.

Gran was great at taking pictures. Maybe she knew I'd need to piece a life together someday. Mom, she wasn't so good at it. I have pictures of my first ten years, sure, but not as many as I have following her death.

Every picture I've ever found in albums Gran put together on the kitchen table, or stored in boxes, I've taken a picture of and I have on my phone.

Birthday parties, vacations, dinners that I cooked for her, outings we took, they're all here, in my hand.

If it happened that I had a granddaughter that needed me as I'd needed Gran, could I give up my entire life and just move to take care of her? Would I stay when she was grown?

God that hurts.

I've never thought of anyone but myself. It was always about me growing up doing the things I wanted to do because my mom died. I went off to college, paid for with a life insurance policy my mother had, and I got, because she died. I wanted to be the best at my career, because it would have made my mother proud, but she died.

It was great when Gran would travel, and I thought how nice it was she would go to be with old friends. *Old friends.* How inconsiderate I was. Those were her friends. The ones she gave up so she could take care of me.

What an ungrateful twit I was.

It occurs to me that she asked me to go from time to time, but she always knew my answer. I wouldn't fly. There was no way I would get on one of those death traps. She'd stopped asking me to take her to the airport, because just hearing planes fly overhead would throw me into a panic attack that sometimes I would need to be medicated for.

Scrolling back to my texts, I look down at Mark's. Those friends now wanted to know how they could honor her, and here I was, keeping her hostage even longer.

I don't know who the hell Mark Watts is, but she did. His name was one of seven in her phone.

I don't have plans yet. She's being cremated, and she didn't like churches, so...

I choke out a laugh when Mark sends back a gif of the priest in *Princess Bride* with a text that reads, *Religion was not something Betsy found joy in. That is for sure.*

Okay, so he did really know her.

Did she really have a house in Florida? Was this man someone she'd left behind too?

I'll let you know if I decide on a memorial, I text back.

We'd all appreciate that.

Just as I set my phone back down on the counter, it chimes again.

How are you doing?

My throat clogs up with tears. Only Grace would ask me that question, in light of Gran's death. But here, here is a stranger who doesn't know me, and he's asking how I'm doing.

Tears sting my eyes, but they're not falling. That's progress, right?

What do I say? Honestly, I'm a bit of a wreck. I feel a little lost. Knowing I'll never see my Gran again makes me sick.

I'm doing okay, I reply.

I'm always here, he texts back. *Text or call any time.*

Ownership

Gran's house smells of her, and I find that after I let myself in, I have to envelop myself in the air that surrounds me. As soon as I open a window, vacuum, or wash her sheets, that part of her will be gone. I'm actually surprised that it still lingers. She hasn't lived here in weeks.

I realize that even the house feels sick to me. Is that Gran? Is that my mother? Is that me?

Now I need to open a window. I can't breathe, but I'm hesitant. Again, I don't want to lose that little part of her that I have left.

My phone ringing in my pocket pulls me from my thoughts.

The ID says it's the magazine office, and I suppose it's time they followed up on me. It is Tuesday morning. I did miss a meeting. And I have no doubt I'll miss deadlines too.

"Hey, Julie. Good morning," my voice cracks as I try to add a calm tone to the words.

"Liz, tell me what's up. You didn't call in this morning. Things aren't good, are they?" Julie asks, and I decide to walk through the house and out to the back porch. I need that air, but I'm not ready to open a window.

I notice we left dishes in the sink when I took Gran to the hospital weeks ago. I'll tend to those first. She'd be so disappointed to think that anything was left undone.

"Gran passed very early yesterday morning," I say to her, and I can hear her sigh.

"Oh, Liz. I'm so sorry."

"Thank you."

"What can we do for you?"

Again, someone wants to take care of me. Do I do this for others when they're in despair? Am I a horrible friend? Should I have expected this from more than just Grace?

"I'm just going to need some time to work through her estate," I say as I walk out the back door and sit down at the small cafe table Gran has on the porch. "But it won't affect my work. I can still work."

"Of course you can," Julie says. "But you can take some time too, Liz. You don't have to power through this." There's an awkward silence between us for a moment before Julie talks again. "You know, maybe you can use this. It could be therapy of sorts."

"I don't understand."

"Write a piece about going through illness with someone. Then you can write a piece about immediate grief. There are the steps to putting their life in order after the fact. What it takes to go through their things, sell their house, you know, all of that. Maybe it will help someone else down the line."

I hate it. I absolutely hate it. Then again, it would keep me working while I do what I have to do.

"Can I think about it?" I ask, twisting a tendril of my hair around my finger.

"Sure. But give me an answer by Thursday," she says. "Deadline for the next issue is the following Thursday, but we have your piece on the steak house in RiNo, so that buys you some time."

I'd forgotten about that piece. It seems as if I'd written it so long ago—a lifetime ago. One thing about the redevelopment of the once industrial area of Denver is that there is plenty of new activity to write about.

"Thanks, and I'm sorry I didn't get to the meeting this morning. To be honest, it slipped my mind."

"I know, hon. I knew when you didn't log in that something had happened. You've never missed a meeting. If there is anything else you need from us, you let me know."

"Thank you."

"How about dinner? Do you have dinner plans?"

I wrinkle up my nose. "Oh, I'm not much into going out to dinner."

"No," she laughs. "I didn't mean that. Sorry. You'd think since I'm the editor of a major magazine publication, I'd word things better." She laughs again. "I mean, can I send you over dinner?"

I think about the food that Grace brought, but it'll hold for another day. Maybe something from a restaurant would be nice. Surely, Julie isn't going to go home and cook and deliver me a casserole or a lasagna that she threw together or has in the freezer.

"I would really appreciate that," I say.

"Wonderful. I'll send it over tonight."

"Can I text you my Gran's address? I'll be here tonight going through things."

"Sure, hon. Text me and I'll make it happen. Does six work?"

"Six is great," I agree. "Thank you. It means a lot."

"You're very important to us," she says. "I know you need this time, but whatever we can do to help you through it, we're here."

And that is why I work for the magazine that highlights Denver, the Rocky Mountains, and travel around the country. They really do take care of those that work for them.

Julie says goodbye, and I sit on the porch for a bit longer. The yard is nothing but a postage stamp, and my old swing set still sits in the corner, rusting away. I have some decisions to make. Do I want to come back here and live? Other than Mom dying, I have only good memories of this house.

This is where Mom and I made a life together. Grace lived down the street. My saddest days have been spent here, but so have my best days.

Gran made it our home. We painted rooms together. We cooked meals together. We watched TV, decorated for Christmas, had Bunco nights with her friends from the senior center.

Then again, is that all in the past and am I supposed to leave it here?

Do I sell the house, or rent it out, and let other people make their own memories?

Or is this what I can hold on to?

I scroll back to my texts and look at the last one from the Florida number.

I'm always here. Text or call any time.

I click on the contact information, and select edit. I type in the name WATTS. It feels too personal to add Mark or even Mark Watts. Besides, WATTS is how Gran had it in her phone. It's good enough for me to have it this way too.

I go back to the last text and type. *What was Betsy's favorite drink?* I ask, then stand to walk inside.

Trick question, he answers back immediately.

How so? I ask as I pull closed the screen door, but leave the back door open. I need to tend to that sink of dishes.

Before 9, coffee. 9:45, add whiskey. A mimosa mid-day. Dirty martini with three olives in the afternoon or evening. Bloody Mary on Sundays.

My heart squeezes in my chest. Why had Gran never mentioned this man before? He obviously thinks the world of her and knows everything about her.

Another text follows.

And in the case of an Oreo cookie, a glass with two fingers of milk. She won't drink the milk, but it's enough to get all the edges of the cookie moist.

I lean my hip against the counter and smile down at that text. He does know her.

Is Mark Watts an old lover?

Does Mark Watts like the pool boy too, or does he just oversee that the pool boy does his job? And why is there a pool boy?

There's a pool boy because if my grandmother actually owns the house in Palm Beach, there is a pool—obviously.

I blink hard just thinking about it.

If my grandmother owns a house in Palm Beach, then maybe she does need three financial advisors. You don't just have a house in Palm Beach and collect Social Security.

Holy shit!

Does Gran have a pool boy and a house boy? She hasn't been to Florida in years. She pays for this?

I'm torn between the excitement to learn the truth of the mystery at hand and I'm sick to think she's paying for some *man* to live in her house.

My phone rings in my hand. It's Grace.

"Make plans to stay for dinner," I say as I answer. "Bring that guy you're married to too, if you want."

"Gosh, sweetheart. Thanks for the lovely invite."

I laugh and pull open the dishwasher, which is musty, so I close it back up. "Sorry. The magazine is sending over dinner. To Gran's," I specify.

"Ashton isn't home tonight. I'll stay though."

That's even better, I think.

"I got some info for you," Grace says.

I move to the kitchen table and sit down. "What did you find out?"

"Have you looked at that house you gave me the address on? I mean, have you really looked at it?"

"I saw the street view. Stucco. Big wooden door. Palm tree in the front yard. No," I think again. "That got taken out," I say, remembering Mark's first text.

"Anyway," Grace continues, "There is a house and then there is a guest house. This thing is one street away from the beach, Liz. The beach!"

I pull a napkin from the holder, which was Mom's, and I start to twist it between my fingers. "Okay. So, it's a nice house."

"It's worth almost seven million dollars," Grace says drawing out the words.

I swallow hard. That should tell me everything I ever need to know about it.

Gran liked to shop at the thrift store. She was a regular at Dollar World. There wasn't a coupon the woman wouldn't use.

"So, the guy that gave me the address is trying to pull a fast one, right?"

"What guy? Oh wait, the text guy?"

"Yeah."

"Liz, your grandmother owns that house."

I crumple the napkin in my hand and hold it tight. "What?"

"Her name is on that house. She pays the taxes on that house."

"How? I have her check book."

"Do you?" Grace asks. "I'll be there after lunch. I'll bring what I found. I think you're going to need to make a trip to Florida," she says and my body starts to shake.

My grandmother owns a seven-million-dollar house in Palm Beach, Florida? With a pool boy?

I take the napkin and wipe my forehead with it, because I've just broken into a cold sweat. Who was she? Certainly she wasn't the woman I thought I knew.

"Liz?"

"Yeah?" I snap back to the call.

"Go home and get Cosmo. Let's just make a full night of it. I'll pack a bag. I'm curious as hell now," Grace says, and there is a hint of excitement in her voice.

I don't share in that excitement, but this is a mystery that I need to sort out.

"Yeah. I'll do that."

We say goodbye and I continue to work the napkin in my hand.

I need to go home and get the cat, some clothes, and my computer. The next google search I do is going to be on Mark Watts.

The House that Petsy Built

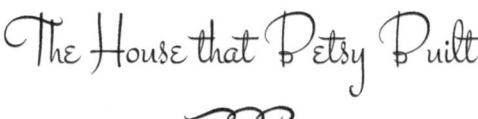

Cosmo prances around Gran's house. He's familiarizing himself with his home again, but he seems to feel as out of sorts there without her as I do.

I decide to wait for Grace to arrive before I go into some deep dark hole involving internet searches. But, I took one of Gran's notepads, and started a list of things we needed to tend to.

I need to find her paperwork. I thought I knew everything about her finances, but obviously, I'm in the dark. She has a will, and I should have thought to have had it in my hand already. Surely she has it somewhere I'll easily find it, though, I should have had the foresight to ask about it when I knew her cancer was terminal.

Needing to occupy myself, I run the dishwasher that still smells musty, and hand wash the dishes that are in the sink. Gran's bed was made the morning I took her out of her house for the last time. I should strip the bed and change it, but why? Who's going to sleep there? I guess I could. Though I have a bed at her house. She'd always left it for me.

I walk down the hall toward my bedroom.

My hand trembles as I turn the knob of the door to my old

bedroom. The blind is pulled, and the room is dark. I flip on the light and look around.

I left this room when I was eighteen and I never came back. Sure, over the years I've spent the night here, but I didn't live in it again. My posters still hang on the walls. My corkboard is still filled with pictures of Grace and I during high school. Thank goodness I learned to stop making duck lips and now keep my tongue in my mouth.

Grace's mother would always roll her eyes at us when we'd take a picture like that. Gran just laughed. She must have known we'd outgrow it.

The pull to keep the house, and keep my room intact is strong. I have time to think about it. I have to remember that. I don't have to clean this out right now. I can mourn her, remember her, and feel her for a bit longer. I just need to search for anything that will help me settle her estate.

As I look at the room, decorated by a child who grew into a teenager, I wonder what that house in Florida looks like. Is it bare and dilapidated? No, not if someone lives there and the pool boy still comes.

But does it have Gran's touch? What do you buy at Dollar World and put into a seven-million-dollar house?

Does Mark Watts rent the house from Gran? Is that why she has other financial advisors?

I pull my phone from my pocket.

I looked up the ownership to the house, I type and lean against the doorjamb to wait for Mark's reply. There isn't one.

I wait a few more moments.

Okay, so he's not sitting here just waiting for me to text him Betsy trivia.

Fine.

I might as well get to finding what I need.

I wander back to Gran's bedroom and stand in that doorway. It feels wrong to move in and start going through her things, but it's necessary. There are accounts that will need to be closed. Life insurance policies that will need to be cashed out. I know she has an address book somewhere too, and maybe it would have details for the people in Florida who want to know the plans, as Mark had asked.

Just past two o'clock, I hear the front door open.

"Oh, Lizzy, I'm home," Grace calls out in her best Ricky Ricardo impression.

"I'm in Gran's bedroom," I call back to her.

A moment later she's standing in the doorway, a grin on her face as she looks at me sitting on the floor surrounded by boxes.

"The lids are on all of those boxes," she says, pushing up her sleeves.

Cosmo pokes his head out from the closet, walks to Grace, circles her feet, and then returns to the closet.

"I'm not ready to open them yet," I say.

"Do you want to know the rest of what I know?" she grins at me.

"Yes."

"I brought beer. Let's have one."

"It's the middle of the day," I say, as I'm a firm believer that you can't drink alcohol before six at night.

Grace blows out a breath. "I'm beginning to think it wasn't your grandmother that was the old lady," she says and turns, then disappears down the hallway.

The very thought of my prudish rules humor me. Hadn't Mark specifically given me my grandmother's drinking schedule?

Before 9, coffee. 9:45, add whiskey. A mimosa mid-day. Dirty martini with three olives in the afternoon or evening. Bloody Mary on Sundays.

Well, if I'm going to do any changing, now would be a good

time to try that on. I might as well drink beer in the middle of the day on a Tuesday.

I push myself to my feet, and carefully step around the boxes, and walk out of Gran's bedroom. Grace is in the kitchen, at the table, with a beer open for each of us, a nacho box from Taco Bell, of all places, and a small stack of paper with a binder clip sits next to the open seat.

She pulls a chip from the pile and guides it to her mouth, her other hand held under it as to catch any cheesy drips.

I sit down in the empty chair, pick up the beer and take a long pull. The papers in front of me detail the house my grandmother owns. The seven-million-dollar house my grandmother owns. I take another long sip of beer.

"The house was built in 1965," she says. "Your grandmother had the house built."

I slowly set my bottle on the table. "That's before my mother was even born."

"Where did your mother grow up?"

Running my tongue over my teeth, I study Grace as she lifts her brows to enhance her question.

"Florida."

"Palm Beach?"

I take another pull of my beer, but it's bitter on my tongue. "I don't know."

"God, Liz, did you ever ask any questions of anyone?"

"Yes. No. Maybe," I shoot out the answers. "You remember I was ten when she died. I didn't think to ask her that."

"You never asked Gran either?"

I purse my lips. "I know Mom was raised in Florida. But after graduation she moved here, went to school, and this is where she landed. This is where I was born. I had my mother for ten years. Eight if you consider how long she was sick."

Grace reaches for my hand. The thing about this friendship is that Grace was there for it. She's one of the few people in the world, that is my friend, who knew my mom. That alone is worth its weight in gold to me.

"I get it," she says. "This just drives home the reason for me to sit down with my parents and ask some serious questions. The more I know..." she trails off and I nod.

I look at the stack of papers in front of me. "So my grandmother built a house in Palm Beach in 1965? When she was twenty-five?"

"Looks like it," Grace says with a smile.

"And now it's worth seven million dollars?"

"Yep."

"But she was never married."

Grace shrugs. "You don't have to be married to build a house." She reconsiders. "Then again, in the sixties you couldn't even have a checking account as a woman. Maybe she came from money?" she suggests and shrugs.

"I can't imagine. Seriously, Dollar World is her favorite store."

Grace laughs, and I know she's thinking that none of this makes sense.

"Maybe that's how you keep your wealth intact," she says. "Well, the point is, the house is in her name. The taxes are current. Why did text guy give you this address?"

I run my fingers up into my hair and comb them through the curls. "He says he lives there."

"Text guy lives in your grandmother's house, which you didn't know she had? There's a story here."

"Ya think?" My voice is filled with irritation, but it's only because I don't know anything.

"If text guy lives there, maybe he rents it from her." Grace suggests.

"What kind of rent do you collect on a seven-million-dollar house?"

The grin on Grace's face is wide. "Do you think that's what she did to bring in income?"

I shrug. "I obviously have no idea what the woman did."

I leaf through the papers Grace brought about the house. Talk about a vacation destination. I can't believe my grandmother has anything to do with this house. Though there are no pictures of the inside, the outside of the house is remarkable.

"You need to find out about the guy. The text guy," Grace says.

"Mark?"

"He has a name?"

Puckering my lips, I forced myself not to smile. For some reason, Mark's texts had brought me a bit of joy in my darkness. Well, once I decided that maybe he did know my grandmother and he wasn't some stalker. Or when he asked if I was okay.

"Yes he has a name," I say.

Her brows raise. "You've talked to him? You're holding out on me."

"I'm not holding out, but yes, we've exchanged texts and I've talked to him on the phone."

"Text and talk? I wasn't away from you but a few hours." Grace shakes her head. "Do you think they were involved?"

I shrug. "I don't know. He doesn't sound all that old. But he did text on behalf of everyone out there wanting to send their condolences, and mentioned that they were all too old to come out here, or unable to come out here. Either way, you get my point."

"Maybe Gran was involved with a younger man," she says and at this point, all I can do is shrug. "So you told him she died?"

"It came out."

"You're going to find out about him, right?" she asks, and I run my finger over the picture of the front of Gran's mysterious house.

"Of course," I say sitting back in my chair and picking up my beer. "But I think I'd better go through those boxes and see if Gran has any information on it."

I take a long pull from my beer, and I can already feel it swimming in my head and my belly.

"This would have been a lot easier if she'd told me these things."

Grace shakes her head and grins at me. "In your next life, you'll know not to be so self-consumed and ask some questions."

The look I shoot her is supposed to be a threatening snarl, but I'm afraid it comes out more like a wince. She's right. Damned are the self-consumed.

Letters

For the first time in my life, luck seems to be on my side. Now let's consider that there is nothing lucky about sitting on the floor of your grandmother's bedroom going through her things. But when you're looking for something that will tell you anything, and you find it in the very first box you open, it's lucky.

Aside from finding the envelope from a lawyer with Gran's will in it, Grace hands me the envelope she found. "It has your name written on it," she says.

As I reach for it, I notice that my fingers twitch.

Scribbled across the front of the envelope in Gran's nearly unreadable writing is my name.

Elizabeth Christine Evans.

I sniff and swallow down the sob that wants to rise up. "Leave it to Gran to use my full name when she's about to tell me something she should have shared while living."

"Your grandmother always did have a flair for the dramatic," Grace says, sitting back on her heels.

That makes me choke out a laugh. Then something Mark said during one of our calls hit me.

"An actress to the end, huh?"

43

Grace is right. Gran was full of flair and drama—always. I assumed she was that way to make my life more fun. You know, the kind of fun you try to give a kid whose entire world has been ripped from her when her single-parent mother dies right in front of her.

My hands shake as I slide my finger under the lip of the envelope and pull out the letter. It's handwritten, and I wonder if I'll be able to read it. Gran never did have the best handwriting, and in her later years, it was almost illegible.

The letter is dated a year ago, around the time she began to fall ill. Or, at least when I knew she was ill. That drama bell rings loudly in my head now. I think Gran had been hiding her true failing health for a while.

I read the letter aloud. What do I have to hide from my dearest friend?

> My Dearest Lizzy,
>
> I'm dying. Oh, the doctors don't know shit, but I know I'm dying. I'm not sad. Okay, I'll miss the hell out of you, but I've had a good, good life.

I have to wipe my eyes because the tears have pooled and I can't see a damn thing. When I look up at Grace, she's wiping at her eyes too.

This might take all day.

> A life well-lived means no regrets. Remember that. When I left my mother's home, she told me that I'd regret my decision. I never did. I had no use for being a mid-western housewife. I had a

big fat life to live, and I did, honey. Boy did I live it.

I rest my back against the wall, and Grace pulls her knees to her chest.

I'm not going to spill all my secrets in this letter to you. You, my brilliant granddaughter, you need to find those on your own.

"What in the actual hell?" I look at the letter and wipe my eyes clear. "Is she sending me on a scavenger hunt?"

"Finish reading. You're killing me," Grace says. "Your grandmother isn't the only person who has a flair for the dramatic."

I snort out a laugh. Okay, that wouldn't be the first time someone mentioned that to me.

Don't bury me in the ground. You know I want to be cremated, and you'd better have done that.

I laugh and wipe my nose with my sleeve. "Sure one of the things we did talk about was the fact that she was vain enough to not want to leave a corpse."

Grace reaches a hand out and lays it on my knee, and I continue.

I'm not to be put on a shelf, or God forbid, forgotten in the bottom of the closet. And, I apologize, somewhere in this house, you'll find the urn of my father.

I pop my head up and see that Grace's eyes have gone wide. She looks toward the open closet and scoots away from it.

I pulled all the boxes from the closet and certainly didn't find my great-grandfather. What closet was he in?

Blowing out a breath, realizing I'll have to search the house, I look back down at the letter and continue.

Take me on an adventure, dear one. Take me home—to Florida.

Again, I look at Grace and now she's smiling. Hadn't she said I had to go out there?

Scatter my ashes there, and along the way. I promise you'll know where to leave me. And, when you get there, Watts can tell you all about your Gran. The Gran you didn't know.

I can't see again. Tears are freely flowing and I'm sobbing. Grace takes the letter from me and finishes reading.

One thing you need to know, my sweet child, is that you were my greatest adventure. I would have loved to have had your mother here for it all, but I've never regretted a day with you. You are the love of my life, and yes, so was your mother. I'm so very proud of you, my Lizzy. Don't waste a day. Life is to be lived, honey. Enjoy the adventure.

Grace's voice cracks with the last line.

All my love, Gran.

Grace sets down the letter and moves until she can reach me. She pulls me in and holds me against her as I sob. She's sending me to Florida to scatter her ashes somewhere, and I have to learn about her life from some man who lives in her house I didn't know she had. What was wrong with that woman?

"Oh, Liz. I don't even know what to say," Grace says as she eases back, and tucks a strand of my hair behind my ear. "This is a crazy way to learn about someone." She lets out a tiny laugh.

"This is just like her," I say. "But I can't go to Florida."

Grace eases back. "I don't think you get a choice."

"I have all the choices. I'm not flying. I don't do airplanes."

"Then you're driving," Grace says, matter-of-factly.

"I can call Mark Watts and get my answers," I say, but then realize he hasn't even texted me back yet. "Gran will never know she's not scattered on some Florida beach."

Grace scoots away from me, her eyes narrowed. "I will be so pissed at you if you don't do this."

"I have a life that doesn't allow me just to drive to Florida."

"A flight is four hours."

"I'm not flying," I reiterate, and I can't believe that she even thinks I'd consider it. She knows what I went through.

"Then write about it. Sell the story to the magazine and write it off. Drive to Florida. Make it business if you have to. But for once in your life, think about someone else."

I feel my mouth fall open and my eyes widen. Did she really just say that to me?

"I'm sorry. What?"

Grace gets to her feet and looks at the mess surrounding us. "I'm serious, Liz. I'm not just being a shit friend. I get that the cards you were dealt sucked. But Gran gave you a good life. She set you on a path to find yourself, and you found yourself right back where you were planted. She's not telling you to leave here for good to find out about her. She's asking you to take her home. Home, Liz. One last adventure. She gave it up to come here and be with you." She points to the letter now shaking in my hand. "She doesn't regret coming to you, but you owe it to her to take her home."

Grace bites down on her bottom lip, something she does when she's said something she regrets. In a moment, I'll have a string of apologies coming at me. I wait.

Instead, Grace turns around and walks out of Gran's bedroom.

I purse my lips and look down at the letter.

Cosmo walks over the papers we have scattered from the box we opened, and he settles in my lap as if he's there to ground me in the situation at hand.

I look into the box where we found the letter. At the bottom of the box is a stack of envelopes tied with a ribbon. Reaching in, I pull out the stack.

Carefully, I untie the ribbon, then stick it down my shirt so that the stupid cat doesn't take off with it. He eyes me coolly, then settles back in.

The letters have postmarks from 1958 through 1970, the year my mother was born, and they are all made out to Genevieve Paige.

The handwriting is male, that much I can tell. Even Gran, with her scribble, has femininity to it. Whoever Genevieve Paige is, she started out in Hollywood, California. In 1962, the addresses float around. One's address is Saint Louis and then there are a handful that are addressed to Genevieve in New York City. After that, the last letter is forwarded to Palm Beach, Florida. In 1965 the letters are addressed to Genevieve at the address Mark gave to me.

There is no name on the return address, and that address is different too on nearly every letter. But, the handwriting is the same.

Gran had her eclectic side, that was for sure. She loved dramatic flair. She loved gossip. There must have been a reason she loved soap operas like she did. And looking at the boxes that I pulled from her closet, and down at the stack of letters in my hand, she liked secrets—other people's secrets.

Do I go through the letters in order? Or should I just read the last one, postmarked July 31, 1970? Or do I even bother? These aren't even Gran's letters.

I pick up an envelope, lift the flap, and then stop. It's as if I can feel Gran around me, and my skin chills.

Lifting the cat from my lap, I set him on the floor next to where I'm sitting, and then struggle to stand. My legs have gone to sleep sitting there.

I gather the letters, pull the ribbon out from inside my shirt, and head out to the kitchen.

Grace is putting away the dishes I'd rewashed in the dishwasher. Watching her flit around Gran's kitchen makes me smile. She could have walked out that front door and gone home in her anger, but she's still here. I don't know what I did as a small girl to find this friend, but I will be grateful for her until the day I die.

The Plan

Grace startles when she sees me watching her. She rips the earphones from her ears and bites out a curse.

"I didn't see you there," she says, setting her earphones on the counter and going back to unloading the dishwasher. "Are those the letters from the box?"

I nod and move to the kitchen table, Grace follows. We each take a seat.

"They're addressed to Genevieve Paige," I say.

"Who's that?"

I shrug. "At some point she's at the house that Mark gave me the address to. Gran's house in Palm Beach."

"Interesting. Maybe she was a roommate?" Grace says as she takes the first letter and looks down at it. "Hollywood?"

"Yeah."

"Where's your laptop? Let's find out who Genevieve Paige is."

I rest my hand atop the stack of letters. "Not yet."

Grace lifts a brow. "Unlimited information at your fingertips, and you don't want to look up the name Genevieve Paige?"

My teeth are already working my bottom lip, and when I taste blood, I know I've bitten too hard. I rub my finger over my lip.

"I'm not ready. I think my head is on overload. I need a moment."

Grace nods and sets the letter on the table. "I get that. This is a lot."

It seems as if it's been a week since Gran died, but that could just be my body that feels that way. I haven't slept and I've hardly eaten in days. I hadn't wanted to miss a moment with Gran when she was in hospice, and now that she's gone, it's not any easier.

I run my finger over the handwritten address on the top envelope.

"I don't know who Gran was," I say. "Now I know she must have been some wealthy to-do. Well, must still be. You don't have a seven-million-dollar house across the country that you still pay taxes on if you're not."

"Right." Grace leans in on an elbow and rests her head in her palm. "So what are you going to do?"

"Just as Gran asked of me. I'm going to take this little adventure to Florida to leave her there."

Even though she's visibly exhausted and doesn't lift her head from her palm, Grace's mouth turns up into a smile, "Good."

"I'll talk to Julie and see about writing about the trip. She already wants me to write about the grieving process, and what it takes after someone passes. It's like a year's worth of articles."

"Steady employment," Grace says.

"Right."

My phone rings, and I realize I have no idea where I set it.

I stand up, walk back down the hall, and find it on Gran's bed. It stops ringing before I get to it.

Picking it up, I notice that it was Mark.

There's a funny calm that washes over me seeing his name there. I have no idea, yet, who this man is, but I know he's part of this journey that Gran is sending me on. He was one of the names in her phone. He's important.

My phone buzzes in my hand with a text from him.

And? is all it says in response to my finding out the owner of the house.

Instead of texting back, I close the bedroom door, sit down on Gran's bed, and call him back.

"Hey," he says, answering the call as if we're old friends and I call him all the time. Not the formal hello of someone who has rocked my world in the past twenty-four hours and that I've never met.

"Hey," I say back as easily as I look around the room I'm so familiar with.

Gran is everywhere, I consider. Her jewelry is still on the dresser. Her dirty clothes are in the hamper. The movie poster she has framed on the wall always seemed out of place, but she'd insisted on having it hung next to her bed.

"So, what did you find out?" His voice has a sleepy gravel to it. I can't decide if he'd been asleep, or if he's sleepy. It's nearly eight o'clock in Florida, so if he's Gran's age, maybe he's headed to bed.

The thought has me smiling and laying back on the bed. He doesn't sound Gran's age.

"Well, I found out you are living in my Gran's house."

"Imagine that."

"What I don't understand is why Gran has a house in Florida. Or a house in Palm Beach, is more like it. I don't know how she pays for it." I'm rambling, but I can't stop. "Do you live in the main house or the guest house?"

Mark lets out a low hum. "You've done some homework. Grace gave you the specs on the house?"

"How do you know Grace?" My voice trembles with the question.

"I knew your grandmother."

"That doesn't answer my question."

"Liz, your grandmother talked about you all the time. All the time," he says again. "I've read your work. I've seen pictures of you. I feel as if I know you."

My heart is hammering in my chest now. I feel as if I might be sick. Who is this man?

"So why don't I know anything about you?"

Again, he lets out a sleepy hum. "I don't know," he admits, and there is sincerity in his tired voice. "Betsy liked a little drama in her life," he chuckles. "But, I didn't think she'd include you in it."

"What kind of drama?"

"Nothing big. Things like owning a house in Palm Beach and not telling her only living relative."

Well, that summed up the drama in my life at the moment.

"Who are you?" I ask, laying back again.

"Mark Watts."

God, there is something about how he says his name that cracks me up. I can't help it. Does he think he sounds like James Bond?

"Yes, Mark Watts, I know your name," I say, smiling up at the ceiling. "I asked who you were."

"Just a guy living in the guest house I guess," he says, in answer to my earlier question, and yet sounding a bit disappointed as if he thought I should have known who he was.

"You have the run of the place and you live in the guest house. Does she have the rest of the place rented out to eccentric billionaires?"

Mark laughs, and it's warm. "Just me. But there is a room for you. When are you coming?"

His words have me wincing. "Why would I come down there?"

"Because you own it now," he says and my breath catches in my lungs.

Shit! I own a seven-million-dollar house in Palm Beach.

Shit! I can't afford a seven-million-dollar house in Palm Beach!

"And," he continues, "I know she wants to be scattered here."

"How do you know that?"

"Because we're friends," he says again.

I don't know who Mark Watts is. I haven't done my due diligence yet to figure that out. Right now he's a warm voice on the end of the phone that knows a hell of a lot about me and Gran. And a flash of jealousy zips through me. I knew she wanted to be cremated, but why didn't I know she wanted to be taken to Florida and he does? I had to get that from a letter?

"You know all her wishes?" I ask.

"I know that she wants to be scattered here. I know that she wants you to do it. And I know you have a room here waiting for you."

I sit back up again. "I do?"

"You've always had a room. But you haven't been here since you were six."

"I was there? At the house?" I'm asking questions as if this guy was there. Was he?

"You and your mom came once."

"I don't remember the house."

He chuckles again. "It's a nice house. Are you bringing Grace?"

"Yes," I say without any other thought to it. Why wouldn't I take Grace? I have to take Grace.

"Let me know when you head out. I look forward to seeing you, Liz. It'll be like seeing an old friend again."

I wish I could say the same thing.

"Mark, were you involved with my grandmother?" I have to know what I'm walking into.

"I live in her house."

"Right. So you and Gran..." I leave it hanging there.

"Are you asking if we were in a romantic relationship?"

I swallow hard. "Yes."

This time when he laughs, it isn't low and sleepy. This time, he's truly humored by my question. "No. There was nothing romantic between me and Betsy. Admittedly, she was my whole world, but not because I was *in* love with her. But I did love her."

"Who wouldn't?"

"Exactly," he says. "Keep me updated," he says and I hear him yawn.

"I will."

"Goodnight, Liz. Sweet dreams."

So That's Mark Watts?

Grace and I eat the dinner that the magazine had sent over, drink wine, and sort through the rest of the boxes in Gran's closet.

There are three boxes that had nothing but my accomplishments in them. Awards and accolades still hang on the wall in my old room, but this box has old school paper articles I'd written, English essays I'd gotten A's on and the teacher had written praises to my writing skills. There is a program from every school production I'd ever been in, and my letter of acceptance into college. Actually, there are four letters of acceptance. Three of which I'd never seen.

Gran had been playing with my future for a very long time. Though all the schools I applied to were local, because I certainly wasn't going to travel to go to school, I attended the school furthest from home. The acceptance letters that I hold in my hand are from colleges that aren't more than an hour away. Gran has been making me take adventures for years. What a sly old woman.

One box has old AVON lipstick containers. Don't ask me what she was doing with them, but at least Grace and I have something to laugh about until we cry.

Then we find the box Gran kept of Mom's things. I put the lid back on that box. That's for another day. I can't even right now.

And at eleven o'clock, we are still crying because laughter that runneth over always brings deep seated tears. Since Grace has been with me during the long nights with Gran, we're both exhausted, and that has made us slap-happy as we go through boxes.

Grace falls asleep on the couch after calling her husband and having a gushy conversation with too many *I love you*s.

It isn't until she's asleep that I realize I haven't discussed our trip to Florida when I get Gran's ashes back. Grace will have to rearrange her schedule. Maybe Ashton would like to go too, I consider.

I'm going to be honest. I don't want him to go. I want it to be me and Grace. But I've already established that I'm an asshole for taking her away from him so much lately. And, he's a decent guy. I suppose having a man with us while we travel by car would be a good thing.

We'll discuss it.

Now, laying in Gran's bed, surrounded by her, and scrolling on my phone in the dark, I decide it's time to figure out Mark Watts.

I'm not ready to plug in the names I've learned in the past day, but I can hear Mark's voice in my head, and I need to know who he is. So, he and Gran weren't romantically involved, but he's someone. He's someone she trusts enough to tell everything to.

I open the browser on my phone. I get the name Mark typed in, and my fingers start to twitch. Do I want to know?

God, yes!

I add Watts to the search, and of course there are numerous Mark Watts. I realize that the phone has customized my search to my location, so I filter it by adding Florida.

There are three Mark Watts that come up in the search.

Mark Watts owns a plumbing company.

Mark Watts is an author.

Mark Watts died six months ago at the age of ninety-six.

Well, I suppose I have my answer, sort of. He's either a plumber or an author.

I look at the information that is given for Mark Watts the plumber. The phone number doesn't match the one in my phone. I'm tempted to call and see if his voice matches WATTS' voice. It's one o'clock in the morning in Florida. What a jerk I'd be.

There is a picture of the plumber. It's an ad. Family owned and operated and all.

This Mark Watts is in his fifties, I presume, and surrounded by said family which includes a wife and kids.

I wouldn't figure that my WATTS is married, though, who knows. Maybe he lives in Gran's house with his family.

Mark Watts the author has different head shots that come up. Mid-thirties, maybe even forty. Some pictures look as if they were taken to make him look mysterious. Others have him looking scholarly. But there is one, and it's candid. It's also poolside and a beige stucco house is behind him.

He writes biographies of movie stars, and in his biography, it says he's based in Palm Beach, Florida.

I can't help myself. At this point, I'm an asshole who hasn't slept but a few hours in weeks, whose grandmother just died, and who is desperate for answers before she treks to Florida to meet a man and spread her grandmother's ashes.

I'm going to text, and he's going to get the text at one in the morning.

So, are you Mark Watts the biography author?

Again, my fingers twitch over the screen waiting for the text to be read. Then I click on the Facebook icon. Nothing. Really? He doesn't have a stagnant Facebook account?

Instagram.

I've hit the jackpot. If that is my WATTS then he's a nice-looking man. Though why my grandmother has a younger man living in the house I didn't know she owned, is beyond me. But, I guess an author, researching old movie stars, would be home all the time and could take care of the property. And maybe Palm Beach is filled with old movie stars living out their years. I just don't know.

His Instagram is filled with photos of him and notable actors from movies of the fifties and sixties. There are a few I recognize that aren't as old, but this guy is usually surrounded by older people with white hair, or no hair, in his pictures. And maybe the people asking about Gran are the people in these pictures.

But Gran never talked about knowing famous people. Seriously, if you know someone famous, doesn't their name drop from your mouth? I mean, I'm asking. I don't know anyone famous.

Yes, the text chimes in my hand and I switch back to my text message.

Really? I text back, both surprised that he's an author and that he's texting me back.

Aren't you a writer? Why are you so surprised?

I sit up in bed, arrange the pillows, and turn on the bedside lamp.

I write for a local magazine, I say. *You know famous people.*

He sends a laughing emoji. *Knowing famous people has nothing to do with the fact that our careers line up.*

I'm not published in book form. He has books. He has lots of books.

I'm envious, I text. *Someday maybe I'll write a book. For now they want me to write about going through this grief.*

This time he sends a gif of a woman waving her finger.

Not even fair, he says. *They should just let you mourn.*

Seriously, I don't know who the hell this guy is to Gran, but having him to banter with is keeping me sane, and that's crazy.

I'm sorry if I woke you up, I text back, and true to form, my phone rings in my hand.

"Hey," I say softly, as if I'm going to wake Grace who is in the living room.

"Hey," he says back in his easy way. "I was awake."

"Why?" I can't help myself. I never stay up late, but the past few nights have certainly been an exception.

Mark chuckles. "I keep strange hours I guess. I do a lot of my writing in the middle of the night."

"What are you working on now?" I ask, truly curious.

"Another biography. I'll show you when you get here."

The comment is so intimate that I forget we're not friends and, in fact, don't know each other at all. But the calm that fills me when I hear his voice, I just don't care that he's a perfect stranger.

"You're sure I'll come?"

"I know you will," he says.

"How do you know?" I challenge. He's been comforting, but I don't want to think that he knows me so well that he can predict my actions.

"Betsy asked you to."

"She did," I say, and I wonder if he knows she's committed him too. Gran's letter said that Watts would fill me in on who she was.

I roll to my side and turn off the lamp.

"How old are you?" I ask, as I settle back into the bed, Gran's sheets pulled up around me.

"I thought that was a question you weren't supposed to ask people," he teases.

"Just women. I'm thirty, by the way," I say, as if it'll coax him.

"April fourth," he adds, and I tighten my hand around the phone.

"You freak me out," I say. "How do you know my birthday?"

"Liz, I know you," he says gently. "Your grandmother talked about you all the time. I was serious when I told you that."

"Then why didn't she ever mention you?"

"I don't know," he says, his voice still soft and patient. "I guess she wanted you to find me on your own."

My breath hitches at that. He didn't mean it in a flirty way, I don't think, but that's how it came across.

"You didn't answer my question," I say, trying to get the flirty out of my brain.

"Which one?"

"Age?"

"How old do you think I am?"

"Seriously?" I ask. "Why won't you tell me?"

"Because if I tell you then our game is over for the night. I enjoy talking to you."

Okay, now that's a little flirty, straight up. "Why?"

"Liz, you seem nice. It's just been nice to banter with you the past few days, at all hours."

Didn't I think that too?

"Besides, let's be honest, you're not over the age of eighty," he continues. "You've yet to tell me to eat better, go find a girl, live a little, or that you need me to pick you up for a doctor appointment."

I actually snort out a laugh when he says all of that. "Is that your real life, Mark Watts?" I use his name as he says it—in that James Bond way. "Helper to the elderly?"

"Living in a gated community of mostly retired, well-to-do people, I tend to be the token *guy*," he says.

"It appears you were that to Gran too, even from this far away."

"Anything for Betsy," he says, and it squeezes at my heart a bit.

"You're not going to tell me how old you are, are you?"

"Is it that important?" he asks.

"Since you're the *guy*, I'm going to assume you don't hit the median age of Palm Beach, Florida, which is seventy."

He laughs. "I'm not seventy."

"You don't look seventy."

"You've seen me?" His voice perks up and I cradle my phone

against my pillow, pressing it to my ear. It seems intimate, but I'm not going to move.

"Instagram." My voice has softened even more.

Mark hums into the phone and my eyes begin to close.

"So that's how you know I know famous people?" his voice has grown lower, softer too. Was he in bed too, I wonder?

"Yes."

"Mark A. Watts, try that one."

"Instagram?" I ask.

"One is professional. One is personal."

"And the personal one will tell me how old you are?" I ask on a yawn.

"You need to go to bed," Mark says, and I realize that my eyes aren't open anymore.

"Fine. Mark A. Watts, I'll find you tomorrow."

"Hey, Liz?" Now his voice is only a whisper.

"Yeah?" My voice is only a whisper too.

"You were here when you were six," he says.

That does have my eyes opening. "At Gran's house?"

"Yes. I was here," he tells me. "I was twelve."

There is a smile on my mouth, and when I think of his voice in my ear, the smile grows wider.

"Good night, Liz," he says, and the call is disconnected.

Mark A. Watts

Grace's eyes are wide and her smile tight as if she's trying to keep it from spreading. Her hands are wrapped around a coffee mug that says *Get your own grandma. This one is mine.* It was something I'd painted for my grandmother, and she'd laughed when I'd given it to her. No matter where I end up, I'll keep the mug.

"I can't believe you've talked to the house boy this much," she says, finally sipping her coffee. "Gran is playing matchmaker from the beyond," she says.

I shake my head and my hair bounces around my face. I should be exhausted, but falling asleep to Mark's voice seems to have soothed me.

"Wait till I tell him you called him a house boy," I say, pushing the hair from my eyes. "And I don't think she's playing matchmaker."

"How old is he?"

I sip my coffee and grin at her as I lower my mug. "Thirty-six, or at least that's the number I've come up with thanks to the word problem he gave me."

Her brows draw inward in obvious confusion.

I shrug. "He said he was twelve when I visited Florida with Mom." Grace is still staring at me. "I was six when I was there."

Slowly, she nods. "So he would have been sixteen when Gran left Florida to move here."

I sit back in my chair, cross my legs up under me, and sip my coffee. "I guess so."

"No one leaves a sixteen-year-old in charge of a house like that. Mark belongs to someone else that Gran trusted. Or, someone came before Mark as the house boy."

"I guess we'll find out when we get to Florida," I say.

"Who is we?"

I blink a few times, because what a stupid question. "You and me."

"I'm not going to Florida," she says, standing and moving to the sink to pour out what's left of her coffee.

"You have to go. I'm not going alone."

"Um, yes you are," she argues. "I have a job that I can't just walk away from on a whim. And I have a husband."

"He can go too."

"You're driving cross-country, Liz. This isn't a day trip. It's not meant to be a day trip. Gran has plans for you, and that doesn't include a tag-along."

I shift again, planting my feet on the ground, but I can't get up from the chair. My legs are numb now, and I'm not sure I'm steady.

"Grace, I need you."

"And I'm here, babe, but I'm not going to Florida. You need to know that it's you and Cosmo on this adventure."

I let out a breath. "I can't take the cat."

"You have to take the cat," she argues as she leans against the counter. "Liz, you're going to get paid to write about Gran's death. So do it with some flair. Write about the process. Write out what you learn. Write about the adventure from Colorado to Florida with a cat. Write about not really knowing the people who raise us, the house boy, the pool boy, and a piece on Palm Beach, Florida," she smiles. "Your whole life you've had me or Gran to walk beside you. Do this for you, Liz. Live this adventure just for you. She set it up to be just you."

I want to be mad. I want to lose my shit on her, but she's right. I get it. I really do.

I need to make this an experience.

The words from Gran's letter replay in my head. *A life well-lived means no regrets. Remember that.*

I hadn't realized Gran had had such a grand life either. But her letter said something different. She was much more than a coupon-clipping bargain hunter, I guess.

I've had a good life, but I haven't had a life well-lived. Thirty-years-old and I understand grief. I have a nice job, a home of my own, and a ride-or-die friend, but where is the life?

At the end of the journey is a guy who likes to talk to me on the phone in the middle of the night, and who knows my Gran in a way that I don't.

What would it hurt for me to take the drive, grant Gran her wishes, and meet the guy?

Of course, I'll also learn about her life well-lived.

I consider that for a moment. I am the age Gran was when she had my mother. In 1970, thirty was considered old to start a family. So, why had Gran waited? What occupied her? Obviously she never did become a mid-western housewife, just as she said she told her mother she didn't want to be.

Mom never knew her father, just as I never knew mine. I have to admit, I just thought that was the way of it. It had never been an issue, even when Mom died. I didn't long for some man I didn't know to show up and take care of me. Gran showed up, that was all I'd needed.

Grace opens the dishwasher and puts her mug inside. "I have to get ready and head to work," she says. "Are you going to be okay?"

"I'll be fine. I'm going to sort through those boxes, and I think I'll call Mark and ask him about doing something for Gran when I take her back."

"So, you're going to go, even if I don't?"

I nod. "I am. You're right. This is my adventure, and she made it that way. *A life well-lived means no regrets*," I quote Gran's letter and Grace smiles at me.

"She's right."

"She always is."

"Ashton has some dinner thing we're supposed to go to tonight. I can get out of it if—"

"Go. I'm okay." I sigh. "I have to learn to do it all on my own now. And I mean that sincerely. I know I'm a grown up, college degree, blah, blah, blah. But, I have to figure out how to do things without Gran right there. I'm going to be fine."

Grace moves to me, takes my face in her hands, and kisses the top of my head. "You will be. I cannot wait to hear about your adventure on the other side of it, Liz."

I don't like the reason behind the road trip, but Gran deserves her last wishes granted, and I deserve an adventure.

"I have a feeling it'll be an epic tale."

Grace gives me a wink as she lowers her hands. "No doubt."

Once Grace leaves the house, I shower, make more coffee, and then I sit on Gran's bed and look around at the mess we've made. I still need to decide what I want to do with her house. I'm not sure I want to live here again. It's not that the house is sad to me. I have wonderful memories of Mom here and Gran too, but it's my past.

My place is mine. I bought all the things inside of it, and I painted the walls. It matters, I realize, now very aware of that *a life well-lived* mantra.

I reach for my phone, which I've left on the nightstand all morning. It's my feeble attempt to be present in the moment, and not to be worried about what's outside these walls. I need to document my feelings at this very moment and put it in my article.

Instead, I open Instagram.

The moment I open the app, I type in the name Mark A. Watts. Now, I'm inviting in the distraction.

There he is, and much less formal. He was right. Professional vs. private Mark is much different.

His professional account is stiff. The photos of him with old Hollywood, and what I'd consider *getting older* Hollywood, don't compare to the pictures of the pool, the palm trees, and the ocean. There are pictures of Mark, in selfie mode, enjoying his surroundings. He has an eye for unique and an eye for simple. And, just from the pictures, I know he appreciates everything—just as Gran did.

Personal Mark isn't clean shaven, often. There's always a day's growth on his face, and he wears Ray-Bans. Most of the pictures are outside. But there are a couple photos taken inside, and his hair is dark, but his eyes are blue.

If he stands with a woman in a photo, he's never touching her. Yet there are a few where he's out with guy friends and his arms are draped over their shoulders.

Maybe he does have a thing for the pool boy.

And that, too, would be living his best life, I think.

But, there is a part of me that hopes he's not into the pool boy—especially now that I've seen this side of him.

Then again, I certainly don't need any complications in my life right now, but I do enjoy the attention he's given me the past few days. Attention probably given to me because he needs attention too. It's been apparent that we both lost Gran.

Those are more feelings I'll need to address. She wasn't just mine to lose.

She left friends back in Florida who want to pay their respects.

She left friends here too, and I need to let them know she passed.

I scroll back far enough in his feed that I come to photos of him and Gran—and a tiny Cosmo.

I straighten on the bed and scroll slowly. These pictures are where Mark Watts and Mark A. Watts intersect. He's with Gran and they are surrounded by the Hollywood elite I'd seen on his other account. And we're not just talking *old* Hollywood, you know, the ones you don't even recognize anymore because they've been missing from the media for thirty years, gone gray, and packed on the wrinkles and the pounds. They are surrounded by influencers and starlets. Of course, these pictures are at least six years old, but Gran is front and center. These *stars* are surrounding her.

I realize I don't know this Gran, and I don't know who Mark is to her.

That's part of the adventure. There's a reason Gran never shared this part of her life with me. There's a reason she never shared Mark with me until now.

I set my phone down and look around the room. I need to make a list of things that need to get done.

The mortuary said they'd call when I could come to get Gran's remains. As soon as I have them, and I find my great-grandfather in the house too, I'll need to grab Cosmo and head out. I have a life to live—and live well with no regrets.

Photo Proof

Julie is on board with all of my articles. I'm not sure I am, but if it gives me carte blanche to travel and write, I take the opportunity. I seize the moment. I live that part of my life with no regrets.

She figures it'll be timely, since the first article will come out the first part of November. Thanksgiving—family—trauma, it all ties together, or so she says.

I haven't been to my home in two days. My focus is on finding my great-grandfather in this house. I've been going through the boxes in Gran's room, and I've been waiting for Mark to text or call. I haven't spoken to him since the other night.

It's stupid to wonder what he's doing, who he's spending time with, what he's writing. I keep considering, he's my distraction, and I need a distraction. After Gran is left in Florida, and I sell the house out there, I guess Mark Watts and I will part ways.

And it's then I realize I've made my decision on the house in Palm Beach, I guess.

Now there's a heaviness in my chest. There is so much to do.

Maybe I should call Mark.

I don't have anything to talk to him about.

He might be my distraction, but maybe I'm just a distraction to him.

Taking the stack of old books Gran kept in her closet, I put them into one of the moving boxes I'd bought that has handles. I didn't see anything inside the books that she'd hidden. These must have just been books she'd had moved and never unpacked. But none of them interest me either.

Looking around the room, I can't help but wonder why Gran kept these boxes close to her. Other than the box with the letter addressed to me, I've yet to find anything important. Okay, the box with every program to every sing-along, musical, concert, and whatnot that I'd been in, that was interesting.

I leave the chaos of Gran's bedroom and walk to the kitchen. Opening the refrigerator, I pull out the blended kale juice I had been working on. My eating and sleeping schedule is out of whack. I'm trying to get my vegetables in any way I can.

On the table is the stack of letters addressed to Genevieve Paige. I haven't googled the name, because I don't want more information in my head.

My phone buzzes on the counter and I pick it up.

Any calm that I have is interrupted and I swear I can feel the blood moving through my veins. This shouldn't happen when I see the name WATTS pop up on my phone screen, but I can't help it. In a few days, this stranger has done something to me.

And, I consider, it's all innocent. I have to keep reminding myself he lost Gran too, and according to him and his Instagram, she was important to him.

When I open my text, I'm surprised to find a picture.

I swear my throat is swelling shut, or clogging shut with the tears that are suddenly rising.

The picture is in front of Gran's Palm Beach house. Or at least the front door matches the contact photo of the door that she had for WATTS.

What has me stirred up is the picture of me, at six, Mom, and Gran.

God, is this man trying to kill me with this? I cover my mouth to hold in my sob.

Where did you find this? I've never seen it, I type. I hope that's what it says. I can't see through the tears now clouding my eyes.

Just wait, he replies.

A moment later another text comes through. There's another picture. Again, it's me, Mom, Gran, and there is an older gentleman with his hand on the shoulder of a pre-teen boy.

Quickly I wipe away my tears. My fingers hover over the keyboard on my phone, but I don't know what to say.

Luckily, he must, because under the picture arrives the text, *I told you I knew you, Elizabeth Evans.*

Is that you? I type back, very aware that's what the text means. I've met Mark Watts.

I just found these in an album that my mother gave me yesterday.

I assumed he was calling me when my phone rang. It's our usual protocol, if you can call it that after a few days of texting and talking to a stranger.

"Hello," I try to disguise the tears in my voice.

"Liz Evans?" The woman on the other end of the call asks.

I clear my throat. I hadn't even looked at the ID. I was just prepared to hear Mark's smooth voice.

"Um, Yes. This is Liz."

"This is Alberta Chavez with the Parker-Peterson Mortuary."

My knees begin to wobble, and I know I need to sit. Sliding down the front of the cupboard, I sit down on the floor.

"Hi," I say, as if we're pals and I'm not just crumbling under hearing the name of this woman's employer.

"Ms. Evans, I'm calling to let you know that we have your grandmother ready for you to pick up."

There's no composure to me now. The sobs come on hard.

"Um, thank you," is all I can manage.

"Would you like to come by today?" she asks, obviously used

to people falling apart when she calls them. What a shitty job to have.

"Yes," I manage. "Yes, I'll come by shortly."

"Just ask for me, Alberta Chavez," she repeats her name, which is good. I'm sure I still won't remember it. "Would you like us to have someone here to talk to you? A counselor?"

And that, too, rattled from the woman easily as if she had to offer that to every person she called who then turned into mush on the other end of the phone.

"No," I say, confident that I can handle this. "I'll be fine. Thank you."

"Should you change your mind, we have someone on staff that can walk you through it."

"I appreciate it," I manage trying to control another sob. "I'll see you soon."

I'm a mess on the kitchen floor of Gran's house, and everything in me hurts. She's gone. I'm here. What I have to do today is pick up what's left of her so I can drive across the country and spill her out.

The sobs come harder now.

I want to throw up.

I want to break something.

I want to be alone—I am, except for Cosmo who is making circles in the kitchen as if he's keeping others away from me.

The only thing I can think to do is call in reinforcements.

Looking at my phone, I scroll, and push the button.

"Hey," his voice is that soft and easy sound that I thought I needed. But when I hear Mark's voice, I crumble. I can't even speak.

"Liz?" He says my name and I slip further to the floor until my cheek is pressed to the linoleum. "Honey, are you okay?"

Honey. The way he says it makes me feel as if I woke up in his arms.

"Liz, what's wrong?" Mark's voice soothes me, just as I hope it would. Well, it begins soothing from the inside, because I'm still sobbing and I can't stop. "Should I call someone?"

"No," I manage. "No," I say again.

He gives me a moment. He sits there, just breathing, and he gives me the chance to pull myself together. I realize he's captive, and can't physically comfort me from Florida, but his silence brings the calm.

"I'm sorry," I say through the last sob that steals my breath.

"No, no. Why? What happened? You're okay?" His voice is filled with a panic that I hear now.

"I can go pick up Gran."

There is a moment before he says, "Oh."

"Do you know what they do when they cremate someone?" I blurt out the question. I know what they do. I've always known. I even investigated it for an article once, but I didn't think about it when Gran said that was her wish. It was just going to be done. And now it was done.

The tears are coming at an uncontrollable rate now. I can hardly breathe, and I certainly can't stand or drive to go get her.

"Oh, baby, I wish I could be there to help you through this," he says and my sobs pause.

Baby. Baby?

I hear it over and over in my head.

This isn't what I should be focusing on.

Why has this pulled me out of the meltdown I'm having?

"Liz?" He's out of breath now. "God, tell me you're okay."

"I'm fine." My breath shudders as I try to take in a full one. "I'm fine."

I hear him blow out a breath and settle. "Good. You really had me worried."

"I interrupted you, didn't I?"

"What? No."

"You're out of breath," I say. My own breath finally slowing.

"I was pacing," he admits. "I can't drive over and help you

through this," he says with a small laugh.

"I should have called Grace, huh?"

"No," he's quick to say. "I'm glad you called me."

I sit up and press my back to the cabinet and collect myself. "So, we've met?" My voice is still wet, but lighter, and I'm willing to change the subject so that I can compose myself.

"We have," his voice is soft again, and soothing.

"I don't remember."

He laughed softly. "You were into the princesses at Disney and the fact that there was a pool."

"I wish I remembered the house."

"You probably thought it was a hotel."

Now I laugh as I wipe the dampness from my cheeks. "Probably. Thanks for sending those. It was nice to see Mom and Gran." I draw in a breath and realize how settled I am just having him on the other end of the phone. "Who is the man with you?"

"My grandfather," he says.

"Did you go to Disney World with us?"

"No," he chuckles. "We only met that night. We had dinner at the house."

"Maybe when I'm there, I'll remember it."

There is a moment of silence between us, and I cherish that it isn't awkward.

"Can Grace go with you to get your grandmother?" he asks.

"I'll call her next," I say.

"When do you think you'll start this way?"

I push my hair back and close my eyes. "I don't know. Let me get Gran and then I can decide. Besides, I have to find my great-grandfather."

"Your great-grandfather? He's still living?"

I smile, and then the laughter grows from that. God, I can't tell him what that means, but the laughter feels good.

"I'll tell you about it when I see you," I say.

"Deal," he says. "Liz, have a good night."

It Would be a Fantastic Flower Vase

Grace has to drive. My emotional stability isn't holding. One minute I'm fine, making a list for my cross-country trip. The next moment I'm a blubbering idiot. And yet, in the next, I'm grinning from ear to ear at hearing Mark say *baby*.

But, when Grace pulls into the mortuary parking lot, there is just silence.

This is it.

Grace reaches for my hand and holds it. "I'm here, Liz. It's all part of the process," she says and I squeeze her hand.

Only the greatest friend would stand with you when your grandmother takes her last breath, and then again when you pick up her urn of ashes. And only because Mark and I have forged some strange friendship in the past week, I won't kidnap her the moment we get back to the car and take her with me to Florida.

"I can do this," I say, and I realize it's not for her benefit, it's for my own.

Alberta Chavez walks us to a small room where the purple urn I'd picked out for Gran sits on a polished wood table.

. . .

ELIZABETH CASSANDRA EVANS

The name, bold on the urn, brings the nerves back and my stomach twists.

Grace takes my hand and we stand there staring at it.

"It's beautiful," Grace says.

"It is. She would have loved it."

My tears aren't falling, and I'm surprised. This is when I thought I'd be a mess. This is where I thought I needed Grace's strength. This is where I suddenly feel some control over the situation.

"I just realized, though, it's useless," I say, still looking at the urn with her name on it.

"Why?"

"She wants to be dumped out." The first laugh hits and I cover my mouth. "What do I do with that thing when I've completed her final wishes?"

Grace looks at me, her eyes wide as if she can't believe I said that. Then she looks back at Gran.

"Well," she pauses and grips my hand tighter. "It would be a fantastic flower vase."

The second round of laughter erupts from me, and I press my head to hers. A flower vase. Gran would love the dual purpose of that.

Alone in the house, with Gran and Cosmo, I sit at the table and stare at her urn. A life well-lived fits into a vase.

There is a profound thought there. First, it's going to be the title of one of my articles. I need to write it down before I forget it.

Second, I have to ponder my life.

What good is a life well-lived? When it ends, it ends. The pauper and the queen both end up the same. I stand from the table, walk to my bag by the door, which waits for me each day as if I'm going to leave Gran's and go home, but I don't.

I take out my laptop, return to the table, and open it.

I open a new document and put in my thoughts on the urn, a life well-lived, and the ashes to ashes junk you hear all the time. I pick up my glass of wine I've poured for myself and contemplate it. I don't drink alone. Gran always said not to.

The thought makes me think of Mark's answer to my question about Gran's favorite drink. She never did drink alone, and now I wonder if back in Florida she was always surrounded by people.

The way I look at it, I'm not alone. I have Gran and Cosmo, just as I always have.

Before I take a sip, I reconsider.

I set my glass back down, pick up my phone, and call Mark.

"Yeah?" His voice comes through the phone in a rush of breath. It's loud enough I startle.

I say, "Hey," in the easy manner that we have that usually turns my insides to goo.

"Who is this?" he shouts.

"Liz," I say, reaching for my glass.

"Right. Right. Hey," he says, and I realize his surroundings grow quieter after he tells whoever he's with to wait a moment. "Hey, sorry."

"I caught you at a bad time," I say, taking a long drink from my wine, and then wincing at the bitterness of it.

"A little bit." His voice is softer now. "Everything okay?"

"Me? Sure. Fine. I'll let you—"

"You're sure it's all fine?"

I can still hear voices, but they're muffled now. So, the man doesn't just wait for my calls at all hours of the night. How silly of me to have considered otherwise.

"Yep, all good here." I steel my voice and drink again.

"Did you get your gran?"

I take a deep breath and run my finger down the side of the urn. "Yep, she's right here."

"Good," he says in the tone I'm used to. "You'll be coming soon?"

"Just have to find my great-grandpa," I say.

"You mentioned that."

"So I did."

"Markey," a woman's voice calls out to him. "The bed. Now," she says and he actually groans.

"I'll be right there," he shouts back.

"Wow, I really did call you at an unfortunate time." I hear the bite in my voice and I'm embarrassed by it. Between that and the wine, my face is on fire right now. "I'll let you go."

"No, wait," he says, keeping my attention, which seems as if that would only piss off the woman looking to go to bed. "When will you know your plans?"

"I don't know. I have a lot to think about."

"Just keep me updated. Her friends here want to have a memorial."

"Right." This trip is for Gran, not for me, I remind myself. I have to remember that even my very best friend in the entire world told me I needed to think of others once in a while, and not myself.

Well, wasn't that what the trip was for? To take Gran home? Take her to the home she gave up for me? Selfish me who needed someone to take care of her and love her? Me, whose mother died, and all.

I swallow down the rest of my wine, and decide right then and there, fuck it, I'm drinking alone.

"Liz?" Mark's soft voice breaks through my thoughts. "I could fly out to Denver and then drive back to Florida with you," he offers, and at that moment I realize my lips have already gone numb from the wine.

"It appears to me that you're a little too busy to worry about that," I say in a tone I don't even recognize. But I'm conflicted now. There's a woman telling him to come to bed, and then there's me, swooning over the word *hey* because I'm desperate for attention. No, he can't fly out here. What's wrong with this man? What's wrong with me? "I'll leave here on Wednesday," I tell him. "Whether I've found my great-grandfather or not. I'll bring the letters. I'll bring Gran."

"What letters?"

Seriously, I didn't mention those? "The letters she's kept to Genevieve Paige."

"*You* have those letters?" There is great interest in his voice.

"Yes. I don't know why she has them. They're not even addressed to her," I admit.

"Markey," the woman's voice says again.

"I'll get to it in a minute. I need to take this call," he tells her.

"Seriously?" she comes back at him.

His hand covers the phone now, but I only hear the words, "I'm sorry."

"Liz?" he comes back to our call.

"Yeah, I'm here. But you're going to have one irritated woman on your hands."

"Why?"

Is this why he lives among the elderly? He's too clueless for his own generation?

"I obviously interrupted an intimate evening," I say. "You don't need to worry about talking to me right now."

"I like talking to you," he says as if he's totally oblivious to the woman directing his attention to the bed.

"You don't owe me anything."

"Nope, but I still want to talk to you."

"You have a woman trying to get you in bed, and you think that—"

"Whoa," he says, and his voice is lit with humor. "Who's trying to get me in bed?"

"That woman?"

"Brenda?"

"She didn't tell me her name when she yelled at you."

He's laughing now, so I pour myself another glass of wine. Fuck him. I'm getting drunk.

"We're moving her," he says. "You caught me in the middle of carrying her stupid bed out of the bedroom."

"Oh," my face heats even more. "You should—"

"I should sit here for a moment and talk to you—my friend Liz."

I swallow hard. "I'm sorry. It's really none of my business."

He hums low. "It's sort of is your business. I mean, you and I are, well, we're working on a project together."

"A project?"

"Didn't you say you have the Genevieve Paige letters?"

"*The* Genevieve Paige letters?"

"Yes."

I look at the stack of letters next to me. "I guess I do. I don't understand why Gran kept someone else's mail."

"What?"

"What?" I repeat. "Who the hell is Genevieve Paige?"

Mark is silent for a moment, so I drink again.

"You're kidding me, right?" he asks.

"No."

"You seriously don't know who Genevieve Paige is?"

This conversation is going in circles, so I polish off that second glass of wine. Still fuck it! I'm on my way to drunk.

"Why should I know who she is?" I ask.

"I'm writing her biography."

"You've written many biographies."

"Well, this is the one I'm working on right now. Betsy was going to send me those letters."

"Great, I'll bring them."

"They're her letters, Liz."

"And that's why I have them, Mark." I punctuate the K of his name to make my point.

"You found them and didn't even google them?"

"I have a lot going on. My grandmother died. I have her sitting in a jar on the fucking kitchen table," my words slur a bit. "I have to think about closing out accounts, fulfilling damned wishes, and driving across the fucking country to drop her off at a damned house I don't even remember—with her cat."

"You're not dropping off the cat," he says.

"I'm talking here," I say, trying to steady myself so I don't sound like some drunk.

"Go on," Mark says, and I swear I can hear him laughing.

"I don't have time to give a care who Jennifer Post is."

"Genevieve Paige," he corrects, and he's not even hiding his humor now.

"Whatever."

"Are you drinking?"

"Maybe."

"Alone?"

"You should go back to your girlfriend," I spit out the words.

"Not my girlfriend, sweetheart."

"I like it better when you call me baby," I say, though I seriously didn't mean to. In fact, maybe I didn't say it. Maybe I just thought it.

"Wow, Liz," he says, still humored. Okay, I said it out loud. Shit! "Betsy always said to not drink alone."

"Well, she's not here is she?" I say, then look at the urn. "Well, she is here, but she can't tell me not to."

He laughs again. "Are you going to be okay?"

"Yes."

"Should I call Grace?"

I purse my lips. "You can't. You don't have her number."

"She's a real estate agent, Liz. I can find it."

Dammit! "No. Don't call her. Let me have my own pity party. I wrote down my notes for my article before I drank wine."

"Good. I'd love to see it when you get here."

"Then I'll show you."

"I look forward to it." The more we talk, the more humored he is by me, and that's pissing me off.

"I'll leave on Sunday."

He doesn't say anything, and I can hear voices again. "I thought you said Wednesday."

"I changed my mind."

"Okay, then. Let's FaceTime tomorrow so we can make plans."

"I can make my own plans," I argue.

"Liz, will you just go to bed, and I'll talk to you tomorrow. I want to know your plan to get here. I want to keep track of you."

"Why?"

"Because we're friends now."

I let out a long breath, and Cosmo leaves the room as if it were offensive. "Don't sleep with that girl," I blurt that out and then cover my mouth embarrassed that I said it.

"She's not my type, baby," he says. I know he said it just to stir me up, and you know what, it does. I'm all gooey hearing him say it, but dammit, he's just being a shit.

"Who is Jennifer Post?"

Mark's laughter warms my entire body. "Genevieve Paige," he corrects again, and I blink hard at the letters. "Google her tomorrow, Liz. Let me know what you find out. Just remember, Gran loved you most."

When we finally say goodbye, I sit and stare at my phone. What the hell did that have to do with these stupid letters that belong to someone else?

Hangovers

I had one more glass of wine before bed, because I could. I'm sure that Grace knew I was completely drunk when she called, but she didn't say anything. Maybe she understood my need for it.

Now, hungover, I'm back at the kitchen table, a pot of coffee next to me for easy refilling. This is more my norm. When I sit down to write my articles, I'm in sweatpants, coffee within reach, and my hair piled atop my head because usually I've just rolled out of bed and gone straight to work.

If I were at home, I'd be in my office. But I'm still at Gran's. It just feels as if this is where I'm supposed to be until I leave for Florida. I guess whatever I find out in Florida will determine if I keep the house there, or the house here.

I've already changed my mind a few times.

When will I know?

With my legs curled up under me, I look at what I've written so far. My hands are wrapped around the coffee mug that says *I'm Not Listening Until This Mug is Empty.*

Gran bought the mug when we were thrift shopping one day.

It was a twenty-five cent find. The purchase now confuses me, since she owns a seven-million-dollar house.

I've started brain dumping. Nothing on the screen is in order, and that's okay. When my head is more clear, I'll take what I've dumped out and start organizing my thoughts into articles for the magazine.

My head is pounding, but I smile at the number of times I've written Mark's name.

Cosmo walks around the legs of my chair as if he's looking for my feet to lay on. I accommodate him, dropping my feet to the floor. He circles again and then lies on them, as if it's his way to keep me in my seat working.

When the FaceTime rings on my laptop, I stare at it. Oh, hell no. I wasn't ready for this.

Cosmo has already fallen asleep on me.

Shit!

I wipe the sleep from my eyes, and cover the camera on my computer with my thumb before I connect the call.

"I wasn't ready for you," I say when Mark's handsome face appears on my screen. Though, admittedly, he looks like he has the same process. Roll out of bed, grab coffee, and start to work. He's had hours to get work done and comb his hair. But the bed head on him is sexy as hell.

"Why can't I see you?" he asks, lifting his coffee mug and smiling behind it.

"That's on purpose. I can't find my sticky note to cover the camera."

"I waited until you'd be up," he laughs. "I'm sure you look amazing."

"I look like I do when I work from home."

"I'm sure that's still beautiful."

Oh, what the hell. I guess he's due a dose of reality when it comes to me. Or maybe it's the other way around, and I need to face my reality.

I move my hand from the camera, and his smile widens.

"There she is," he says in that smooth and easy way.

"Yeah, well, she's hungover," I say running my hand over my hair.

"I'm sure she is," he laughs. "You needed that."

"I always pay for it after."

"Your grandmother has a nice collection of wine in her cellar here. Of course, it's well aged," he offers. "Let's make a plan to share one of her best bottles to celebrate her when you're here."

"Really?"

"Why not? It seems like a waste if we don't use it to celebrate."

"Okay. Let's plan that."

"Done," he says, smiling at me.

I chew on my bottom lip and watch him. "Do you drink from her wine cellar often?" I have to ask. What kind of rein does he have at the house?

"Never. She would have let me. She'd often ask if I tried a certain wine and then let me know she had a bottle if I wanted to try it. But everything in the house is hers. It's not mine to use for my own good. But, I think it would be nice to celebrate her with you."

My lips are dry, and chewing on them now hurts. But I have more questions. "So, you don't go into her house? You stay in the guest house?"

Mark shrugs and pushes his coffee to the side. "I sleep in the guest house, mostly. It's not very big. Really, it was the pool house, if you will."

A pool house. God, who was this woman?

"Then you are in her house the rest of the time."

The corner of his mouth curls up. "I use her kitchen. And, though the house has an office, I usually work from the kitchen, or out by the pool on the patio."

I shake my head. "I can't believe any of that is real."

"You will." He leans in and studies me. I lift my coffee mug as if I'm hiding my face. "You look just like your grandmother when she was your age, don't you?" he asks.

"So I've heard."

"I have a lot of pictures," Mark says, and now that has me leaning in, my elbow on the table and my head propped up in my hand.

"She just left her life there, didn't she?"

"Well," he says, rubbing the back of his neck with his hand. "We've been working on a project together over the past few years. The pictures are part of that."

"Gran hasn't been there in the past few years."

"Okay, well, we've been working on this project for a lot of years," he admits.

"Why did she leave you at the house? Why didn't she just sell it?"

Mark shrugs. "I think she kept it so you'd have it."

"Then why didn't she tell me about it?"

"That flair for the dramatic."

I snort out a laugh and sit up straight. "I really thought she saved that for PTA meetings."

"What does that mean?" His eyes are wide now with interest.

"When I was younger, she'd go to the PTA meetings just to stir up drama."

"Please, do tell."

Without thinking about it, I pull up my legs, and Cosmo hisses at me. I'd forgotten he was laying there, and now he prances off, pissed that I've disturbed him. It won't be the last time today.

"Charlene McKavik, Debbie Wells, and Karen Smith each wanted to be the head gal in charge. You know the type?"

"There is an actual Karen in this mix?"

"Yup." I tuck a strand of hair behind my ear. "Anyway, Gran was loved, as you know. So she was always the PTA president."

Mark laughs. "I can't imagine that at all."

I shrug. "None of it makes sense now. PTA president, Palm Beach homeowner, coupon goddess, and the keeper of other people's mail. I swear I don't know this woman at all." I study the thrift store mug in my hand.

"But, please continue," he says, humored.

"Anyway, she did it so she could pit those three against one another any time she got the chance. She'd create committees and put the least likely one in charge and the other two would lose their shit. The drama was deep. They thought she was their confidante, but she really was just messing with them. The other parents in the PTA got a lot of amusement from it, as did Gran. But poor C-D-K, they worked so hard to outshine the other. I guess it made for better potlucks and school fairs."

"C-D-K? That's what you called them, wasn't it? Your grandmother never used anyone's names. She'd give them nicknames or use initials." He says this as if he's solved a mystery. I suppose in a way he has. He's given me one more nugget of information that tells me he really did know her well.

"What was your nickname?" I swear his cheeks blush when I ask.

"Clyde."

I crinkle my nose. "I don't even understand that."

"She was the Bonnie to my Clyde. We were going to cause havoc in the world," he mused, and looks a little sad when he talks about it.

"How?"

"When I was writing my first few books, she'd try to give me false information. Luckily, I had a professor that said to always triple check your sources. She was quite humored with herself."

I lean in on my elbow and rest my hand on my fist. "What kinds of things did she tell you?"

He considers for a moment. "Kurt McLaughlin, you know, the actor?"

"Um, yeah," I say, intrigued that my grandmother would know him.

"He and Betsy had an on again, off again, thing that became public in sixty-one, I think it was."

"Excuse me?" I sit back again. "First of all, in 1961 my gran was twenty-one. Wasn't Kurt McLaughlin a movie star in the forties?"

"Yup," Mark says, with an extra punch with the P.

"So he was, what, in his fifties by 1961?"

Mark nods slowly, but doesn't say anything else.

"I think I'm going to be sick," I say.

"It was a different time. That just wouldn't fly nowadays."

"At least she was of legal age," I say, trying to comfort myself.

"Oh, baby, by that time, they'd been on and off for years. It was 1961 when it became public."

I let out a groan. "How did she know him, anyway? I get the retirement thing in Palm Beach and those people retired there, but to have a *thing* with a huge star like that?"

"Oh, Liz," he says as if he's pitying me. "She had a life that—"

"I know. A life I don't know about. A life she gave up. I don't know this woman at all," I say looking at her urn.

"But, you do. You know the part that she took the most pride in."

And doesn't that hit me right in the gut?

"So why keep it all? If she didn't want to own up to that life, why keep it intact so I had to find it?"

"I don't know. All I know is she's let me live here and take care of this gorgeous house so that when she wanted to come home, she could. It's been a huge pride job, if you will."

"So you're her house boy?"

"Man."

"Right." I cross my arms in front of me. "What will you do when I sell it?" My tone is snide, because right at the moment, I'm not much caring about her affairs or her fancy house. To me, they're lies. How can I not know this woman?

88

Mark's eyes go wide. "I guess that's something for us to discuss, isn't it?"

"I guess it is."

"Have you googled Genevieve Paige yet?" he asks and I shake my head. "I'll wait."

Genevieve Paige

I'm not humored by him this morning, and I'm sure my face lets him know this. Then again, it's not Mark's fault. I guess, I'm not humored by Gran.

I knew she'd die. No one is raised by their grandmother and assumes that they'll be old together. I knew I'd live half my life without her. What I can't wrap my head around is the fact that in thirty years, I've never heard these names associated with her. I didn't know she went *home* when she went back to Florida. I thought she stayed with friends and sat on the beach. I thought she ate dinner at four o'clock buffets and wore funny hats. What did I know?

I swallow down the lump in my throat when I think at twenty-one, my grandmother had some affair with a man who was not only famous, but in his fifties.

I actually gag. I don't want to know any more.

Mark has moved from his computer and walked to get more coffee. He's in my grandmother's kitchen. I'm in my grandmother's kitchen.

If I turn around to get more coffee, I'll take two steps. He's had to get up, walk around the island, walk to the counter with the coffee maker, and make his way back. Why did she give all of that up?

"I'm waiting, baby," he says as he sits back down, grinning behind his mug.

"Don't call me that."

"You said you liked it when I called you that," he says, and my chest tightens even more.

"I did?"

"Last night."

I scrub my hands over my face. "I'm sorry about last night."

"Don't be. You needed to blow off some steam."

"You didn't sleep with that woman, did you?"

Mark laughs. "You remember that, but you don't remember telling me that you like it when I call you baby?"

I shake my head.

"I didn't sleep with her. She's just a friend," he says.

"I don't have many friends," I admit as if I have to.

"You have me and Grace. I think you're doing just fine."

I *met* this guy less than a week ago, and I've become his friend. I'm comfortable with him. Well, I must be if I told him I liked it when he called me baby. And I did. I also accused him of sleeping with someone, and that was none of my business. That is why I don't get drunk. I can't be trusted.

"You have nice legs, by the way," I say, picking up my coffee, which is cold now.

Mark raises a brow. "You were checking out my legs?"

"You walked through the kitchen in your shorts."

"It's ninety degrees here. Pack for it, by the way."

I nod, and look down into my mug. I stand, walk the two steps to the coffee pot, and pour myself more coffee. When I return, he's grinning at me.

"I can't see your legs in flannel pants," he says.

"It's not ninety degrees here," I say.

"I'll bet they're nice too," he says.

"Now I'm self-conscious," I say and he laughs.

"Don't be. I'll bet you're perfect."

This friendship comes with a lot of flirting. I'm not sure if it's me or him that starts it. Okay, that time it was me, but it's nice. Will we be flirty in person? Are we safe behind computer screens and text messages?

Will it all be different when we're saying goodbye to Gran, our only connection?

"Okay, Liz. Google it," he says, reminding me of my task at hand.

"I'm deathly afraid to now."

"I'm right here for you, baby." He grins when he says it, but I don't correct him this time. This time, it does bring me some comfort.

"Will I get upset?"

"Yep."

"Great," I say, lifting my hands into the air. "Then why do I want to look?"

"Because you want to know."

"Do I?"

"Yes," his voice is softer now. "I'm not going anywhere. I can sit right here on this call all day with you, in our pajamas and bed hair."

Now, that seems downright intimate.

"Fine," I say minimizing the window with his face, but keep it in the corner of my screen.

My hands shake as I type GENEVIEVE PAIGE into the Google search bar. I don't even have to hit the enter key before the name begins to generate items.

I feel tears in my throat. I can't even see the small thumbnail images that pop up clearly. But I can see that they have my face.

The breath in my lungs is harder to push in and out. I feel dizzy.

"You doing okay, Liz?" Mark's voice is calm and sweet.

"I don't understand this."

"Keep looking."

I click on the first image of Genevieve Paige.

It's Gran.

The photo is in black and white, and it's stunning. It's dated 1958, and she would have been eighteen.

I choke when I swallow, and then I cough. Picking up my coffee, I read the caption to the image.

Genevieve Paige, RKO Pictures, The Secretary, 1958.

"She was an actress. That's what you meant, when you said that." I don't even recognize my voice.

"Said what?" Mark's voice is quiet.

"You said something about her always being an actress," I say as I scroll through the other photos.

Mark nods. "She did an RKO picture before they closed up. Then she had parts in some MGM movies."

I'm looking at her, but I can't believe this is my Gran.

"She's beautiful," I say.

"You look just like her," he says, and I lift my eyes from the pictures to look at him.

"I didn't know any of this. None."

"I know. I'm writing her biography. It was supposed to be collaborative, but, well, she hasn't been much help the past few years," he teases.

"Why wouldn't she share this with me? I mean, this is a big deal."

"It was once," he says. "Liz," he let out a long breath, "when she got pregnant with your mom, everything changed for her. Everything. From then on, she just wanted to live a quiet life. That's what she did."

"Why?"

"I think that's for us to figure out together."

I look at the letters sitting on the table next to Gran's urn. "She wanted us to read these—together?"

"Maybe." He chuckled. "She did like drama. I wouldn't hold it against her to have withheld those from me until you could be there with me to read them."

"You don't know who they're from?"

"I have an idea," he says. "But, no. I don't know."

I swallow hard, pick up my coffee, sip, and then sip again. "Can I trust you?" I ask, and I see the flash of maybe anger in his eyes, but it's gone as quickly as it happens.

I make the screen with his picture on it bigger.

Those deep blue eyes are looking right at me. Gran did this on purpose, I think. She put me right in his path.

"Liz, I would never do anything to break Betsy's trust. I owe her too much. But if you think that I might—"

"I don't," I interrupt. "I didn't mean it."

"I understand it."

"Well, Gran is a good judge of character. There's a reason she's kept you around, and a reason she hasn't told me anything about this."

"I wouldn't take that personally. I think she wanted you to have a normal life too, or as normal as she could give you."

"In other words, I'm old enough to handle this now?"

Mark chuckled. "Yeah, I guess so."

"This is a lot to learn."

"There's more, but let's do that together, okay?"

My breath is shaky. I don't know if I want to learn more, but I agree with a nod.

"Can you really leave tomorrow?" he asks and I nod again. "Let's map out your trip, unless you think you can manage a flight?"

"No," I quickly reply. "I can't fly."

"Okay then. Let's make you a road map. I'm anxious to see you in person—again."

Mapped Out

There is a plan, and I hate it. It consists of me getting up at four in the morning to head out.

It's going to take me most of the week to drive to Florida. The thought makes me sick.

Five days in the car, and that's making it so I don't run off the road because I'm tired. I have to think of Cosmo too. He could be a nightmare passenger.

Mark and I mapped out the drive, and looked up hotels along the way. He helped me book rooms, and even decide on places I could stop to eat. I think he's going to be on my phone most of the drive, and I can't say that's a bad thing. I enjoy talking to him—a little too much.

Seriously, I should buck it up and get on a plane, but just thinking about that makes me break out into a cold sweat.

I haven't been on a plane since Mom and I flew home from Florida when I was six.

It was that trip.

My skin begins to heat, and anxiety begins to take over any calm I managed after hanging up with Mark. I remember it, that flight. I remember every single moment of it.

Of course I remember it. I wake up in the middle of the night screaming—still. It causes me to panic when I hear a low-flying plane. It makes me sick when I think of people using planes as weapons and flying them into buildings.

The trauma from that flight is probably why I can't even remember the trip itself.

I try to calm my breath which has become labored just by me thinking about flying.

My answer to flying is always, "I won't fly." There's no more thought to it. I just don't.

But now, in the kitchen, looking at the road map laid out on my on my laptop, and the sheet of notes in front of me, I remember that flight from Florida to Denver vividly.

Mom has her arm around me and the plane bounces around. She keeps smoothing my hair and telling me that everything will be okay and that sometimes the air gets bumpy.

"God put these bumps in the air so we won't go too fast," she says, but her voice shakes. "It'll pass in a few moments."

It doesn't pass.

We will learn later that one of the engines went out on the plane. The oxygen masks deploy, and mom puts hers on and then puts mine on me. She holds me next to her, all the while telling me it will be fine.

Because we were near our destination, we land without incident. Well, without much incident. The landing shakes us all, and maybe that's because we were all in a fucking crash position waiting to die!

There is screaming and crying, but we land. A moment later the plane is surrounded by fire trucks spraying down one of the wings, and they hurry us off on deployed slides from the exits.

A few people stay on the plane, and I see one man with a cut above his eye. It isn't fine for him.

It takes all night to get home, and all the things we brought home from Disney World are ruined from when they sprayed down the plane.

· · ·

When the front door opens, I let out a scream and Grace runs through the house to find me.

"Jesus Christ, Liz," she stands before me panting, her hand on her chest. "What in the hell?"

"You scared the shit out of me," I yell up at her.

"I didn't mean to. I knocked and told you I was walking in when I opened the door."

I'd never heard that. All I could hear was the blood rushing through my ears.

She scans a look over me, assessing me in the kitchen, still in my pajamas.

"It's one o'clock in the afternoon. Have you been sitting here all day?" she asks.

"I've been working," I snap out my reply.

"On your articles?"

"Yes. No. Yes."

Grace lifts a brow and picks up my coffee mug. "This is cold. You haven't eaten anything, have you?"

"I've been working."

She grunts and walks to the refrigerator, setting out to make me lunch.

"Why are you all wigged out?" she asks as she starts to make me a sandwich.

I turn in my chair to look at her. "Mark and I made plans for my trip."

"Good."

"I've been learning about Gran," I say.

"Good," she says again.

"I was remembering why I don't fly."

Now she turns and eyes me coolly. "Oh."

"I just haven't thought of it much lately, and that's a good thing. But looking at this map, and planning this trip, it brings it back."

"Because flying would be easier?"

97

"Yes." I run my fingers over my unruly hair. "This is my life. Fraught with trauma and secrets."

"Give it a break, Liz." Grace turns back to the sandwich, and I stand up to move to her, but I have to hold on to the chair. My ass and legs are numb. I haven't moved in hours.

"Seriously," I say, moving to her finally. "I found out that my grandmother was a Hollywood star who had an affair with a fifty-some-year-old movie star when she was twenty-one."

Grace lifts a brow and looks at me either because of what I've said or because of the speed at which I've said it.

"Oh, that's only the start," I continue without much of a breath. "She *is* Genevieve Paige."

The knife in Grace's hand falls to the counter. "You're kidding me?"

I shake my head. "Mark was working with her on her biography. Oh, and look at this." I move back to the table and pick up my phone. I scroll through his long texts until I get to the picture of us that he sent me.

Grace looks at it. "You, Gran, your mom, and?"

I point to the boy. "Mark."

"You've met him?"

"I guess I have."

The corner of her mouth curls up into a smile. "Gran is setting you up?"

"I don't know. Silly really. Right?"

"I don't know. It's cute. Who's the man?"

"His grandfather."

Grace nods. "Were they involved? Him and Gran?"

My body is heavy again. "I don't know."

"Well, there's a lot going on in your boring and mundane life, Elizabeth Evans," she says grinning at me. "Think of the story this will make some day."

Grace has gone over my map and my travel plans at least three times.

"You have enough money?" she asks.

To that, I wince. "Gran does. Gran has more than enough to get me there, set me up nice, and get me home with a driver if I want one."

She nods slowly. "Okay, but can you access that?"

"I'm on all of her accounts. We did that when we found out how sick she was." I reconsider. "I'm on some of her accounts, I guess."

"And you weren't alarmed by how much money she had?" Grace asks.

"Gran always had money. I just figured she'd never spent anything—ever."

Grace laughs and sits back in her chair. "Well, let's get you packed. What else do you need?"

"I need to find my great-grandfather."

"You haven't found him?"

I shake my head. "He's not in any closet."

"Do you really think he's here?"

"I don't think she would have said that if he wasn't."

"Well then, it appears we only have a few hours to find him." Grace stands up. "We'll pack you up and get your car loaded while we look. Any mess we make, I'll come back and help you clean up when you get home."

"I love you, my friend," I say, and Grace reaches for my hand.

"I'll be here, Liz. I'm your constant. But from what you've told me and shown me today, you're about to have an adventure of a lifetime, and I can't wait to hear all about it when you come back. If you come back."

I wince at that. "If I come back?"

"You might find that a Palm Beach mansion with a good-looking man is right up your alley."

I pull Grace to me and hold her. I don't think I'd have survived without her by my side for all of it. I believe in soulmates, but I don't always think that's reserved for romantic interests only.

"What do I pack?" I ask Mark and he laughs through the phone. "Seriously. I don't travel."

"Liz, just be comfortable," he says.

This is the first time I've been home in days. Standing in front of my closet, I'm looking at all the clothes that just don't seem to mean anything anymore.

"And how long will I be there?" I say it, but it's not really a question, and Mark doesn't answer it.

"We do have a laundry room," he says. "The washer and dryer are new, we replaced them a year ago."

"That'll be helpful since I'll be in a freaking car for a week," I snap out the words.

"I'll buy you a plane ticket."

"No," I nearly shout as I pull a few more shirts out of the closet and throw them on my bed.

"Don't forget a swimsuit," Mark says.

"I'm not wearing a swimsuit."

"Your call," he teases, and it causes me to stop.

"Excuse me?"

He laughs. "Liz, just pack and get here. I'm anxious to see you."

I sit back on my bed. "Really?"

"Yes," he says. "I'm going to call you bright and early in the morning to make sure you're up and ready to go."

"I'll be cranky."

"I'll be prepared," he says, and then a moment passes between us before he speaks. "Liz, I can't wait to meet you again."

Great Grandpa Found

I found him! I found him!

I stare down at my phone and decipher the text from Grace, and then it hits me. She found my great-grandfather.

Instead of texting back, I call. "Where? Seriously? You found him?"

"It would have taken us until we packed up this house to move everything out."

"Okay, where was he?"

"Sending a picture," she says, and a moment later my phone dings in my hand and I switch over to my texts.

Grace has sent me a picture of the corner cupboard of the kitchen with the door open.

"You found him in the kitchen?" I ask, and then those heebie-jeebie chills take over my body.

"Oh, honey, it gets better," she says. "More pictures coming."

I put Grace on speaker, and then scroll back to the texts.

The next picture she sends is from up on the counter looking into the cabinet, which is deep because it's a corner cabinet.

On the very top shelf, all the way to the back, tucked in the corner of the shelf, is an ancient coffee can. Across the front of the can is a piece of masking tape with writing on it.

ALFRED EVANS

1918-1990

"Oh my God! Oh my God! Oh-my-God!" I repeat.

"I told you. We'd never have found him," she says, and I realize I can hear her moving a ladder. "I have no idea how your Gran got him up here."

"What made you look up there?"

"Because I have looked in every nook and cranny in this house, Liz. We couldn't leave anything unturned."

I wince. "What kind of mess do we have?"

"Well," she says with a chuckle. "Let's just say that we can now assess everything in the house and decide what you want to keep when you get home from your road trip."

"I think Gran did that on purpose," I say throwing a few shirts into the suitcase I'm going to take with me. "It's not as if her pile of secrets wasn't enough. Hiding her father in the house is like the cherry on top," I say.

Grace laughs and I look around my bedroom at the mess I've made just trying to pack for this trip I have to take now.

"Maybe you should come over here and help me pack. I'm at a loss," I say.

"Take a swimsuit," she says and I shake my head.

"I'm not wearing a swimsuit."

"Your call," she says as if she and Mark had planned their responses, and hers held every bit as much pleasure in it as his had.

"I hate this," I say, throwing in another shirt, then taking it out, looking it over, and throwing it back in.

"You'll be home before you know it. And, you'll get to meet the guy in the house. Sit by the pool. Go to the beach. Fulfill Gran's wishes," she lets out a breath. "Liz, it's going to be epic."

"I wish you were going with me."

"It's not for me," she says, and I know she's right. But I can't help but to let the anxiety rise through me until it paralyzes me.

"Maybe I should just dump my whole wardrobe in this suitcase," I say, realizing I don't even know what I've even packed.

"If it's made for winter, leave it. If it snows in Palm Beach while you're there, I'll ship it."

"Fine. I'll hold you to that. I'll be back to Gran's in the hour. Feed the cat."

We found my great-grandfather. I have my grandmother. I have the letters. I did pack a swimsuit, though I have no intention of wearing it. The car has gas. Grace's husband checked the tires, the engine, and the oil. Cosmo hates the little crate. I'm pretty sure I'm going to throw up. How is your night?

I want to sleep, but I can't. And, it's only ten o'clock, but I have to be out of the house super early. Sleep would be welcomed.

It's quiet, he responds.

Oh, I don't mean to bother you, I say, worried that his answer means he's enjoying the last bit of peace before I blow into town. God, this has to be like waiting for the circus to arrive. Here comes Liz and her drama to dump her grandmother out, decide she's going to sell the house, and roll back out again.

Is he worried that he'll be homeless?

Why does he live there anyway? A man of thirty-six shouldn't be living in some old pool house. He has to be a slacker—a mooch.

I don't really want to think that. I've enjoyed his company so much in the past week, I want to believe he's something special— someone special, I mean.

Who said you were bothering me? he replies and then sends a picture.

It's the pool draped in moonlight, and I see his legs stretched out on a lounge, and he's holding out a glass of wine.

It's midnight there, isn't it?

Yep! he says. *Best time to just sit out here and think.*

I can't help myself. I have to call.

He doesn't even get out a word. I hear his phone connect, and I say, "What are you thinking about?" My voice is sultry, edging on sleepy.

"You," he says, just as sultry.

I lick my lips, not sure if I should really read into that, but I need the distraction.

"What about me?"

"That's the second time you've said you're not wearing a swimsuit." I can hear the humor in his voice, and the moment is ruined.

"I mean, I don't plan to swim."

"I'm not sure how you'll avoid it. It's hot here. The pool is nice. And, honestly, when you're here, you're going to want to get into the water, sit beside it, just feel its calm."

Tucked into Gran's bed, the lights off, and anxiety keeping me up, I wonder if I'll find that kind of calm there.

"I'm having second thoughts," I say. "Well, second, third, fourth, and fifth thoughts."

"Liz," he says my name, and it's airy in my ear. "You're supposed to be here. Don't overthink it. Come be with me. Let's write this book. Let's write your articles. Let's give your grandmother the kind of send off she deserves."

He's attached more to this trip than I have expected. Is that what he wants? He needs the letters I possess to finish his work? Am I just an assistant?

"I'm not quite as enthusiastic as you," I say. "She's kept so much from me that I'm afraid to learn about who she was."

"She's the same woman you knew. She just lived her life in grand segments, if you will. I don't know much about who she was once she left to be with you," he says. "You don't know who she was when she was here."

I think about the letter she wrote me. *A life well lived means no regrets. Remember that.*

Segments. That's something to consider, I guess. I've had segments too. With Mom. With Gran. Without both.

Grace has been there for all the segments.

Mark is new.

A chill prickles my skin. Maybe Mark isn't a segment. Maybe he's a distraction without a segment.

Will I be disappointed if that's the case?

"I guess we're both about to learn who she was," I say.

"What we know is that she was thoughtful, loving, fun, and full of life," he adds.

He's right. I can't believe this man knew her as well as he did, and yet I didn't know him.

"Liz, get some sleep. You need to start out bright and early," his voice is soft again.

"I guess I'll see you soon."

"Not soon enough."

On the Road

Ashton pushes down the hatch to my Subaru. "Tank is full. Snacks are in your passenger seat. Spare tire looks good. I put the jack where it can be easily accessed and you won't have to unload your car."

I hug him. "Thank you."

Grace wipes tears from her cheeks. "Call, a lot," she says as she pulls me in to her.

"I'm going to be fine."

"You've never driven this far from home without me or Gran. I'm going to worry about you every moment."

"And that's why you're standing in my driveway at four o'clock in the morning," I say, loving that she's here to see me off.

"I couldn't let you go otherwise." She kisses my cheek before easing back. "But, seriously, call me every hour."

"I will."

"Enjoy this."

"I'll try," I say. How can I promise her that I will?

"Let Cosmo have a few hours in the crate. It'll give him time to get used to being in the car."

"Yes, ma'am."

She shakes her head. "Liz, just have fun."

"This isn't supposed to be a fun trip."

"But it just might be," she says winking. "Let me know what he's like."

"I'll be home soon," I say, leaning in and kissing her on the cheek.

Grace moves in next to Ashton and he drapes an arm over her shoulder, pulling her close.

"Be safe, Liz," he says.

I pull open the door, and I can hear Cosmo already hissing at me. With a wave, I slip behind the steering wheel, start the car, and back out of the driveway.

I haven't even gotten to the end of the street by the time my hands begin to shake and tears streak down my cheeks. This is an adventure. A beginning. But when I look at Gran's urn seat-belted in the seat next to me, the bag of snacks next to it, I realize it's an ending too.

I startle when my phone rings. At the stop sign, I put my car in park, and answer my phone.

"Good morning, beautiful," Mark's voice says in a cheerful tone.

"I thought you were going to call me bright an early this morning," I say holding my phone to my ear and putting the car back into drive.

"I didn't want it to seem like I was stalking you."

"Aren't you?" I ask.

"Maybe just a little. But not creepy like."

I laugh at that. "Well, I'm on the road. I'm at the end of my street," I say turning out of the neighborhood. "But, I'm on my way."

"You'll drive through to Topeka?"

"That's the plan, right?"

He snickers. "It is."

"Hold on," I say as I manage to put him on speaker. My

Subaru is old enough, it doesn't have that fancy hands free stuff. But a Subaru is a lifetime car, and I'm going to test that theory. "Have you talked to her friends? Is Saturday a good day for her memorial?"

"It seems to be. There's a shuffleboard tournament at the shuffleboard courts at two that day, but it shouldn't interfere with an eleven o'clock memorial."

"There are shuffleboard courts?" I'm humored by this.

"There are. It's a no nonsense thing down here."

"And do you play?" My voice has lifted with a tinge of humor. It does that when I talk to him.

"It's part of my costume that helps me fit in. I might only be in my mid-thirties, but I can keep up with the seventy and eighty-year-olds just fine."

That warrants a genuine laugh. "I can't wait to see what that really looks like."

He's quiet for a moment. "Can I ask you a favor?"

The smile on my mouth puckers. "I suppose you can ask."

"I know where Betsy wants to be scattered, and I know it's my job to get you there."

"How do you know? Did she ask you?"

"No," he confirms. "I just know, and I guess I just feel as if it's my job to get you there."

"Understood."

"I'd like to be there with you when you scatter her ashes."

For a moment I think his request is humorous, because there hadn't been a time when I didn't think he'd be with me. I'd just assumed that saying goodbye to Gran was going to be our thing—not just my thing.

"Of course you can be there," I say.

"That means a lot to me. Thank you."

I don't know what to say to that.

"Liz, I'll let you concentrate on driving. If I remember right, you have about eight and a half hours to go."

I groan. "Thanks for bringing that up. And I think Cosmo heard you, now he's hissing again."

Mark laughs. "Cosmo, be a good boy for Liz," he says loudly. "And, Liz, call me anytime you're lonely."

I don't want him to hang up, but it's probably for the best as I head toward the highway. Once I'm out of the city, talking on the phone will be a necessity to keep me awake, but for now, I should concentrate.

"I will, and Mark, thanks."

"Why are you thanking me?" he asks.

I can think of a hundred reasons. He's been my rock for the past week, and I don't know this man. But there is a kinship between us that I needed, and I think he needed it too.

"I just appreciate you loving Gran and helping me through this week."

"Oh, Liz." I swear I can hear his smile through the phone. "I can't wait to see you."

For some reason Queen is what's keeping my spirits up for the first two hours. Freddie Mercury begs for me to sing along.

Cosmo has fallen asleep. At the next rest stop, I'll let him out of the crate to freely move about the car. We'll see how he does.

My travel plan takes us into Kit Carson for gas and a necessary bathroom break. When I open Cosmo's crate, he doesn't jump right out at me, for which I'm grateful. There's a part of me that thinks he's being good because he knows Gran is in the car too.

I shoot a text off to Grace to let her know that I stopped and am getting back on the road. She sends me back a picture of a house she's showing. I assume it would give Gran's Palm Beach house a run for its money. If she closes that sale, she's buying dinner.

As soon as I cross the Kansas border, my phone rings.

"Do you have satellite telemetry on me?" I ask as I answer, putting Mark on speaker phone, and Cosmo butts his nose right up to the screen.

"I'm just looking at my watch," he says. "How's the drive?"

"Smooth and easy so far. People are just starting to wake up. The sun isn't a factor at the moment, now that it's up past the horizon."

"And Cosmo?"

I look at the cat sitting next to me, and I run my hand over his fur. He's been my other savior through this, just as Mark and Grace have. "He's doing great."

"I'm glad. He can be mean."

I consider that for a moment. "You know a lot about this cat."

He laughs. "I gave her the cat."

My hand stills on Cosmo's back. "That's where he came from?"

"I got him as a kitten. He wasn't too old the last time Betsy came out here, and Cosmo took to her." He laughed. "Now that I think about it, I don't know if I gave him to her, or if I was told she was taking my cat."

I can't help it. I spit out a laugh. I mean, I have to wipe off my steering wheel with my sleeve, I spit so hard.

"She stole your cat!"

"I think she did. She could get away with anything."

"That's Gran."

He's still laughing. "He might see me and try to scratch my eyes out."

"Maybe. Perhaps I should turn back around," I tease.

"No," his voice has become serious. "I'm kidding. Don't go back."

"I'm not," I chuckle and then realize the mood has shifted.

"There's no turning back now."

"Good. Hey, I gotta run. I'm sure she never told you about Chuck Grove?"

"Of course not," I say, but then I wonder if she did mention people from back in Palm Beach, and I just didn't know they weren't people she knew at the senior center. "I mean, I don't remember."

"Well, he passed a few days after Betsy did. He lived around the corner. His wife passed a year ago. His memorial is in an hour, and I need to be there."

"You're really embedded into that community aren't you?"

"I grew up here. It's normal to me. Everyone is from somewhere else, and they don't get here until they're retired. I'm in my thirties and still the youngest person around. Well, me, Brenda, Finn, and Georgie are the young'ns around these parts," he says with a twang.

I swallow hard, because I remember that Brenda was the woman who was calling to him the night I thought she was wanted him to go to bed with her. I want to ask about his friends, and I suppose there will be time.

"I really have to go. I'll call you in a few hours. But, Liz," he pauses until I make a noise that lets him know I'm listening. "Call me if you need anything at all, okay?"

"I will. Pass along my condolences. You know, from Betsy's granddaughter."

"I will."

The call is disconnected and I have to admit that my mood plummets. I could talk to him the entire drive. How strange is it that I've connected to a man I met once when I was six, more than I have to the people I'm surrounded by in my daily life? I mean I have Grace, and I'll always have Grace, but those I work with, or went to school with, or live next to—I don't know them like I know Mark. It's a very strange thing to me, and I hope when he meets me, he's not disappointed.

So, This is Kansas

I'm going to admit that I'm a bit of an asshole. Yep. I've never traveled much. Once Mom and I got off that airplane, we stayed put. I've driven to Las Vegas, and out to San Francisco and down the coast. I've gone to New Mexico and enjoyed the beauty of Santa Fe. But, after having driven through hours, and hours, and hours of farm country, I'll admit, I thought Topeka would be a 7-Eleven and a motel. And for that, I'm an asshole.

This is a real city. I mean they have big buildings and lots of stoplights. So to all who dwell here, I'm sorry for thinking all of Kansas was nothing but farm. I'm educated now.

I let Siri direct me to the hotel and I check in, leaving Cosmo in the car and hoping to hell he doesn't turn on me while I'm gone.

So, here's the kicker, when I get back to the car, he's crawled into his crate. He's looking up at me as if he knows what we're doing. Seriously, he knows Gran is watching. I'm convinced of this. But something tells me that when he sees Mark, things will change.

Cosmo and I settle into our hotel room just after two-thirty. I have half a day to kill here before I go to bed. Part of me considers just taking a long nap and getting back on the road. But that wasn't in the plan. Mark and I made a plan, and everyone knows where I am on this trip. So, I'll stay.

But, with Cosmo, I'm mostly confined to my room. No exploring for me. And now I think I really do want to look around. I mean, I was serious when I said it wasn't just farmland. Yes, I'm still an asshole.

I order food at four, and Cosmo and I lounge on the bed and watch cartoons on TV. I don't like cartoons, but as much of an asshole as I am for thinking this town was going to be small, there also is nothing to watch on TV.

I'm so engrossed in Scooby-Doo, that when my phone rings, I jump. This must have startled Cosmo too, because he digs his claws into my leg.

"Ow, you creep," I say as I connect the call.

"I thought we were friends," Mark's soothing voice comes through the phone.

"Cosmo just dug into me. He hasn't done that in years."

Mark laughs. "I have a scar from him too. When you get here, we can compare."

The comment has me licking my lips. This is so not good to get wound up like this. This guy is a temporary fixture in my life. I'm going to Florida to uproot him. Does he understand that? Do I?

"So, you're safe and sound?" he asks.

"Yup. We're fed and happy. I'll be back on the road by six in the morning."

"Stick to the schedule. Then I'll know where you are."

I nod and take a tater tot from the bag popping it into my mouth. Cosmo eyes me as if he's wanting one. But that isn't going to happen. The last thing I need is a sick cat.

"Yes, Dad," I say with some sass. "I'll stick to the route and keep my time."

"Seriously, Liz," he scolds. "This is a huge trip. Have you ever driven cross-country—by yourself?"

"No."

"Don't lose focus."

When he'd started this rant about my trip, I thought it was sweet. But I have to admit, there's a bit of annoyance now. I'm thirty years old. I'm not some kid. I'm not some inexperienced adult either.

Well, I guess I am when it comes to traveling.

Still, I can take care of myself, and maybe I should just tell him that.

"God, Liz, I'm sorry for being such a pain," he says, as if he's reacting to the thoughts I have going on in my head. Or, I hope they stayed in my head and I didn't accidentally say them out loud. "Today made me miss Betsy even more," he says. "There we were saying goodbye to Chuck, and everyone was asking about her. She's so missed—by everyone."

I chew my bottom lip and sit up from my stack of pillows.

There's an anxious pulse that moves through me. It's jealousy. There, I admit it. I'm jealous of this man for having a relationship with my grandmother. I'm jealous that people miss her, and I don't know who they are. Why didn't she share these people with me? Why didn't she share me with these people?

The thought shakes me to my core.

Did my grandmother hide me from the rest of the world?

No, didn't Mark tell me that she talked about me all the time?

I hiccup a sob and then cover my mouth.

"Liz?" Mark says. "Hey, are you okay?"

"Yes. I'm fine," I steel myself. "I have to go," I say, and without another word, I disconnect the call.

My hands are shaking, and I don't want him to call back. I can't talk to Mark right now.

So, I turn off my phone. Right now, I need to be alone in my room with my cat. Only this stupid cat can console me now.

Cosmo knows what's going on.

He begins to paw my belly, as if to tell me to lay back, and then he rests on my chest.

"She left you to me, didn't she?" I ask, and Cosmo responds with a meow that was specific to my question.

I shift my attention to the small table by the window. My grandmother's urn, and my great-grandfather's coffee can sit there. I brought them in with us because I've heard stories where a car is stolen and someone's loved one is lost. I couldn't afford to lose her again.

"Why did you never include me in your life? The extra part of your life?" I ask her as if she's going to give me the answers. But, just as she was in life, she was quiet about that.

I wipe my palm across my eyes to ward off the tears.

Maybe she was protecting me. I mean, how was I ever to get to Florida? Gran didn't drive across the country, and I can't —won't—fly.

I suck in a breath, and then clarity washes through me. Finding out who Gran was and why I don't know about it is one of the reasons I'm even making this stupid trip.

I pick up Cosmo and hold him to me as I kick my feet off the side of the bed and place them on the floor. Wiggling free, Cosmo jumps from my arms and back to the bed.

I move to the small box of necessities I brought in which contain the letters. I would hate to lose them too if some took off with my car.

Maybe it's time to read them.

Maybe I should know something about my grandmother that some stranger in Florida doesn't know. I mean, I feel as if I'm owed that. She didn't give him the letters, did she? No. She saved those for me.

"Genevieve Paige, who were you?" I ask as I pull the first letter off the pile. "Why did you exist? Why didn't I know you existed?"

Sitting back on the bed, I open the envelope from 1958, sent to Genevieve in Hollywood.

Dear Genevieve

~~~

1958

Dear Genevieve,

I miss you already. I miss the look of you. The smell of you. The feel of you in my arms. I'm grateful for the photo you gave me. I'll keep it with me always.

I don't know when I'll be able to write again. Right now, I'm awaiting my ship to take me back.

My sweet Genevieve. When the time is right, I'll come for you. I must make this trip first. I love you, my sweet.

Love, O.Z.

I lower the letter. Who in the hell is O.Z.? Was he a soldier? Certainly he wasn't Kurt McLaughlin, which means Gran didn't wait for this guy if she had a known affair with the older actor a few years later.

Considering that, there is an uneasy feeling that moves through me. *The feel of you in my arms*, I reread the passage and choke out a laugh.

I was in love when I was sixteen, and Gran wouldn't have it.

"You'll keep your wits about you and your knees together," she'd said more than once. "Stay true to yourself until you're ready."

When I was eighteen, I moved into a dorm with a girl who ate her boogers. I'm not even kidding. I gained my obligatory freshman fifteen. I lost my virginity to a guy I didn't even care about, it was just something I felt as if I needed to do.

My grandmother left her home, moved to Hollywood, and had affairs with men who were thirty years her senior. Was this man, the one who wrote the letter, an older man? Was he an actor too?

I tuck the letter back into the envelope and put it back on the stack.

I won't read another letter right now. This one has unraveled me a bit. Maybe I'll wait for Mark. Maybe he has the answers. Maybe he knows who O.Z. is.

I pick up my laptop and sit back on the bed again, with my back up against the headboard.

I'm not going to check my email. I'm not going to work on my articles. I am going to search Genevieve Paige. I need to know who she was.

I type in the name, and again, pictures fill my screen that are familiar because they look like me.

Gran was beautiful.

Funny enough, I've never thought I was all that pretty. Cute, sure. Red, unruly hair and freckles. But Gran—oh, Gran wore it with grace.

The photos of her have her hair in curls, as was the fashion of the time. Her make up is beautiful, and in the black and white photos, she's stunning.

Somehow, I'll need to scrape all of these pictures and keep them in a file. I could look at them all night.

She has a Wikipedia page. Who knew?

Genevieve Paige (b.1940 -)

St. Louis, Missouri

Seeing that has me looking up at her urn. "St. Louis, huh?" I look back at the screen.

Genevieve Paige, actress RKO and MGM. (1958-1964)

Below that is a list of the movies she was in. She never had the lead role, but she wasn't just some extra either. Her characters had names.

There was no bio. No parents' names. No mention of my mother. Of course, no mention of me.

Genevieve Paige just disappeared in 1969, the year before my mother was born. And hadn't Mark said that when my mother was born, everything changed for Gran?

Things I do know. She built the house in Palm Beach in 1964. My mother was born in 1970. Between 1964 and 1969 there is a hole. But according to the pictures Mark A. Watts has on his Instagram, she wasn't forgotten.

My next search is for Alfred Evans.

Okay, that gave me a million hits. So I narrow it. The only thing I do know is the name of Gran's parents. I type in Alfred and Bessy Evans.

I get a few hits, but it's not them. It's not until I scroll to the bottom of the page do I find some ancestry site that lists the marriage of Alfred and Elizabeth Evans in 1935.

I shake my head. Well, for being a family with no history, we sure got a lot of use out of the name Elizabeth, and yet not one of us is known by that name.

Alfred and Elizabeth Evans lived in St. Louis, Missouri when they married in 1935. They had two daughters. Alifa, obviously named after their father, who was born in 1936, and Elizabeth, my grandmother, born in 1940.

Another search tells me that Alifa died in St. Louis in 2002—the same year as my mother.

That has me closing my computer. What had Gran gone through that year, losing her daughter, her sister, and gaining a ten-year-old? Maybe that was why she just walked away from her life and started over. She needed a new beginning too.

Cosmo stretches next to me, then readjusts so that he's butted up right next to me.

"You still have me, you goofy cat. I just hope you don't want to stay with Mark. What will I do without you?"

With that, I set my laptop on the nightstand and turn off the light. Tomorrow I will head toward St. Louis, where I now know I need to leave some of Gran, and I think I need to leave my great-grandfather too. I'll set out earlier than planned.

Before I leave, I'll find out where my great-grandmother is buried. I would assume she's in St. Louis. Maybe my great-aunt is as well. I'll take my great-grandfather and scatter him there. I'll leave a bit of my grandmother too.

The very thought has tears welling in my eyes.

Well, this is what she wanted.

Take me on an adventure, dear one. Take me home—to Florida. Scatter my ashes there, and along the way. I promise you'll know where to leave me.

There is a donut shop on the corner, and I figure Cosmo is okay for the twenty minutes it will take me to walk over, get a donut, and a cup of coffee. I leave him some treats in the room.

With my phone in my back pocket, I hold tight to my can of

pepper spray. Even though I would think Kansas is nothing but sweet farmers, the city has me on high alert. Besides, no one expects me to be out of my room at six o'clock in the morning, but I have plans.

I need to find out where Elizabeth Evans, of St. Louis, Missouri, is buried. This is part of the adventure, and I'm not going to miss it.

Back in the room, I study the information I was able to find. I must have relatives somewhere, because after paying for an ancestor membership to some site, I found that Elizabeth (Bessy) Evans was buried in the Bellefontaine Cemetery.

I plug in the address to the cemetery and readjust my route.

"Okay, Gran." I reach out and rest my hand on her urn. "Here we go. The adventure begins, right? This is what you wanted?"

I let out a breath.

"I don't want to leave you anywhere, but I want you to have what you want—Genevieve Paige," I say with a snicker. "God, I miss you. I would have rather have had this adventure with you here. I mean, you, not you in a vase."

Cosmo circles my feet.

"Yeah, boy. It's time to say goodbye to her. Let's go."

The Detour

Cosmo and I are on the road three hours earlier than my schedule has us leaving, but there's something about knowing I'll be near relatives. I've never known relatives. Yes, I realize my great-grandparents are dead, but this is still huge.

I've never had cousins, aunts, or uncles. I had neighbors, teachers, friends.

I guess family is different for everyone.

The Subaru is old enough that I still have a CD player, and I have a CD of the Hamilton soundtrack cranked up. Cosmo has snuggled himself into his crate, and I'm sure I've annoyed him.

An hour into the drive, we've made it to Kansas City. My donut has worn off, and I could use a snack, other than the bag of goodies Grace and Ashton packed for me. I take the opportunity to pull into a Starbucks. Since I have the longer leg of my trip still ahead of me, I order two drinks, one hot, one cold. I also order a protein box and a breakfast sandwich. This is an adventure and I'm living big, right? No regrets.

I pull up to the window and the cheerful woman at the window gives me my total and I pick up my phone to pay with my app.

My phone is off.

Oh, shit! I turned it off when I hung up on Mark last night.

I smile at the woman, who is being quite patient and making small talk while my phone starts up.

The moment it's up, I try to open the app, but the number of text messages that are coming through keep knocking me out of the app.

Again, I smile at the woman whose smile is now straining.

"Sorry about that," I say, handing her my phone to scan.

Once the transaction is completed, she hands me my order, and only then do I remember I still have the cup from the donut store taking up space in my cupholder.

Okay, so things aren't going as smoothly as I thought.

Trying to rearrange my car to accommodate my new drinks, I drop my phone between my feet, and of course, it begins to ring.

The woman in the window is still grinning at me with that forced smile.

Eventually, I take the drinks, managing one of them in the cupholder and the other in my hand. Carefully, I pull out of the drive-thru and to the nearest parking lot. I can't drive all the way to St. Louis with a cup in my hand.

The phone on the floor is still ringing, and now Cosmo has climbed from his crate and is sitting on my console.

"I don't have time for your antics right now," I tell him as I roll down my window and pour out the coffee from that morning. Though, I know some of it has now landed on my car.

I throw the empty cup in the back seat, put the second drink in the holder, and wiggle myself in the seat until I'm able to pick up the phone which has stopped ringing.

But as I manage back into my seat the phone rings again.

WATTS.

Usually I'm giddy to see his name pop up, but realizing I hung up on him last night and neglected to turn my phone on, I'm not as excited to answer this call—but I do.

"Hey," I say in that tone we've used for a week with one another.

"Hey? Where in the hell have you been?" His voice is sharp and angry.

"I'm fine," I say looking down at Cosmo. "We're fine."

"You're on the road by yourself, and you hung up on me, and then turned off your phone. Grace is panicked."

I grip the phone tighter in my hand. "It's nine o'clock here. It's only eight at home. Why is Grace panicked already?"

I can hear him clear his throat. "Maybe because I called her."

"You what? You don't have the right to—"

"Liz, I don't want anything to happen to you."

"You're not my keeper."

"No," he says. "I'm your friend."

And what am I supposed to do with that? "We're fine," I grind out the words through my gritted teeth.

"What happened last night?" His voice has softened now, and once again, I know I was the asshole.

"Nothing," I say, the lie burning into me.

"Liz," he says my name and I close my eyes. Why does it have any effect on me at all?

"Fine. I'm jealous. Okay? I'm jealous that Gran had people in her life that loved her, and she didn't share them with me," I say loudly and quickly.

Oh, God!

A sob chokes me. I knew I was jealous, but until I shouted it in the phone, I didn't realize I was jealous because she didn't share those people with me. I just thought I was jealous that other people loved her.

"Liz," he says my name again, and the sob grows stronger. "Baby, take a breath."

"Don't call me that," I manage, but I can't imagine he even heard it.

"Don't leave the hotel until you're calm, okay?"

For a long moment, I don't say anything. I work to calm myself and catch my breath. Who did I think I was to have this little adventure of just going to the cemetery without someone worrying about me?

And again, I'm an asshole, because they worry because they love me—I mean care. Grace loves me. Mark—he's a distraction.

"I'm in Kansas City," I finally manage and I hear him take a breath. But before he can say anything, I continue, "I found out where my great-grandmother is buried, and I'm taking my great-grandfather."

The phone rings while I'm holding it. Mark is FaceTiming me. I'm not in the mood for this.

I click over the call and look at him.

He's next to the pool with no shirt on. This is too much for me to handle this early.

"You have to fill me in on this great-grandfather thing," he says.

"Maybe you should put a shirt on," I say.

The corner of his mouth curls up. "It's ninety-five degrees in the shade. There isn't humidity in Colorado, is there?"

"None."

"That's what Betsy used to say," he chuckles. "Tell me about your great-grandfather."

I turn my phone so that he can see the coffee can in the passenger side floor in a box.

"She had him in the kitchen cupboard."

Mark lets out a laugh and then stifles it.

"In the same letter where she told me that you'd tell me all about her, she told me her father was somewhere in the house," I say.

Mark's eyes are wide and so is his smile. "She's a piece of work, your gran."

"I'm going to take him to where his wife is buried."

"That's pretty special."

I nod. "I'm going to leave some of Gran too."

Mark blinks hard. "Oh. That's special too."

"In her letter she told me to scatter her along the way too, and I'd know where."

Mark runs his hand over the back of his neck and then pushes his sunglasses up to the top of his head.

"So you learned a little more about her?" he asks.

"I did, and I read the first letter," I admit.

Now Mark leans forward and the phone shifts so that his face is now in a shadow. "You read it?"

"I had to. I needed to know something."

He licks his lips. "Well? What did you find?"

"Gran's letter telling me that she had a big, fat life to live, and boy did she live it—well, I'm learning that my gran was a woman about town."

Mark snickers. "That never changed, Liz."

I wince. "What does that mean?"

"Do you really want to know?"

"No, I don't think I do."

"She was loved, Liz." He grins and slides his glasses back on. "She loved, Liz."

This is more information than I've ever wanted.

"I need to get back on the road," I say.

"Don't turn your phone off again."

I want to tell him not to piss me off, but then again, I guess I did that to myself.

"I won't," I promise and then notice that Grace is now calling.

"I'll see you soon," Mark says. "But I'll talk to you sooner."

The Arch

"Grace. Grace," I say again to stop the rant happening in my ear. "I won't turn it off again. I promise."

"Seriously, having Mark call me scared the hell out of me," she's still ranting.

"I wish he hadn't done that."

"He cares about you," she says, but there is a lifted tone in her voice.

"He's a total stranger."

"Eh, I don't think he is," she disagrees. "Where are you headed? You're on the road too early."

"I'm headed to St. Louis. I found out where my great-grandmother is buried, so I'm going to take my great-grandfather."

"And a little bit of Gran?"

I smile at that. "Yes, and a little bit of Gran."

"But you're not going any further, right? You're staying in St. Louis."

"Yes, ma'am," I say with some snark. "I won't head out for Nashville until tomorrow."

There's a moment of silence between us, so I situate my Starbucks so I can get to it and enjoy my snacks and my drinks.

"Tell me you're having a good time."

I let out a hum. "I've been driving highways for going on two days. I have two more days—with a cat. What kind of fun can I have?"

"Seriously, Liz. I know this sounds dumb, but are you talking to your Gran? Your cat? To Mark?"

I pick up my hot drink and take a careful sip. "Well, I've had a Queen singalong, as well as an Elton John singalong, and Les Mis," I say with a laugh. "Gran and I talked a little last night. And, yes, I've talked to both Cosmo and Mark."

"So you're not lonely?"

"Not yet."

"You're not driving and crying are you?"

I consider that for a moment. "No. I think I'm okay." She doesn't need to know that I have cried. What will that help?

"Good. God, this is good for you," Grace says, and I wonder what kind of strange hermit I was for her to be so happy about me being out on the road. "What do you think will happen with Mark when you get there?"

I take another sip from my cup. "What do you mean? Nothing will happen. Well, I suppose I'll be the hag that makes him homeless."

"You're going to sell the house?"

"I can't afford taxes on a seven-million-dollar house."

"Maybe you can. You don't know what she has yet."

I close my eyes and let my head fall back against the headrest. "You're right. But we know I'm not going to make this trip frequently, so the house in Florida is worthless."

"Unless it feels like home."

Okay, this is the end of this conversation, I think. I put my cup back in the holder.

"I have to get back on the road," I say.

"You're not driving? You're parked? Where are you? Are you in some strange parking lot? You're not supposed to stop along the way." Her voice is tinged with anger again.

"In a parking lot next to a Starbucks in Kansas City. So, I'm going to hang up and get back on the road. I have ashes to scatter, you know."

"Be careful out there."

"Oh, you know I will be."

The thing about not traveling away from Colorado is that I've missed out on the beauty of this country. Sure, Kansas was miles and miles of farmland, but it had a different glow to it. It was nice to find out that Topeka existed.

Kansas City is a metropolis and I decide to start a list of places I want to return to. Somewhere, mid-Missouri, I decide that if I sell a seven-million-dollar house, I would have the funds to take some time to road trip all over the country. Maybe I'd even venture into Canada. I'm quite sure I'll never touch land on another continent, but I'll be content with that, since I won't fly.

Via Siri, who is my new ride or die, I've started a list of places to visit—or revisit.

Kansas City is on my list of places to return to. A drive-by wasn't enough time to really get a feel for the city.

And then there are tears when I drive into St. Louis and see the Arch. Who would have thought it would have that kind of effect on me. But it's knowing that I've never seen it that starts the tears.

Mount Rushmore. Niagara Falls. The Grand Canyon. The Space Needle. I've never seen anything. And my memories of Disney World are marred by the plane ride home.

I have to suck in a breath when I even think of that.

By the time I pull over to plug in the address of the cemetery into my phone, the list of places to revisit is long.

Yeah, it's time I step out of my comfort zone and chase that well-lived life.

The very thought of Gran's words surge through my body, and I turn to her urn.

"God, you made me leave home," I say to her. "You knew I'd never leave if you didn't make me. You're a sly old woman," I say as I laugh. "And Mark is the prize at the end?" I ask, and then lower my phone.

What made me say that?

I know Mark is a temporary distraction this week. He just fell into that role, whether he knew it or not.

I swallow hard. I don't need to think about Mark, except to know that he's at the end of the route, he has answers to the mystery that is my grandmother, and he'll be homeless soon.

That hurts me a little. I don't want to displace him, but what is a thirty-six-year-old man doing living in someone else's house anyway? And he doesn't expect me to keep it, does he? No, he's too smart for that.

Maybe he can move in with Brenda.

And, that has a heat moving through me that makes me sick. I didn't mean it when I thought it. God, I can even fight with myself when left alone.

Siri guides me to the cemetery, and as I pull through the entry, there is the strangest sense of energy buzzing through me and the car. I'm among family here, and that's what I'm feeling. I have Gran. I have her father. And her mother is here.

Shit! I forgot to look for her sister. I need to find her sister before I drive any further. I need to know where she's buried too. They all need to be together. I'll save some of my great-grandfather for when I find her.

I shake my head as I pull up to the building that houses the offices for the cemetery.

There is something demented about me having multiple deceased people in my car. Not only am I talking to one of them often, I'm going to randomly disperse them. Maybe I should take up writing mysteries and thrillers instead of fluff pieces for a magazine.

I'm starting to get a bit slap-happy in my own company. I'll call Mark when I get back on the road. Or when I get to my hotel. Yeah, that's a better idea. I'll let the crazy take over until I'm locked into a hotel room.

I leave the comfort of my car, which now smells like stale coffee and potato chips, and walk into the building to inquire about the grave site of my great-grandmother. By chance, I ask about my great-aunt, and when the man behind the counter plugs in her name, I find that she's buried right next to her mother. Now that is a lucky break.

Back in my car, I drive through the small lanes between sections of the cemetery looking for the numbers that the man in the office gave to me.

On the far side of the cemetery, under a large shade tree, I find them. I'll bet in the summer, when the trees are full of green leaves, the grass is lush, and fresh flowers adorn the headstones and small gardens, this place must be beautiful.

Now, in late September, it's turning brown, and the breeze that blows through is cool.

Leaving Cosmo in the car, I carefully balance both Gran and Great-Grandpa Alfred in my arms and walk toward the headstones marked EVANS.

I'm shaking.

My mother is buried in Golden, back in Colorado. Gran put her there so that she'd be near to us. Now I wonder if she belongs in this cemetery in St. Louis.

I reconsider. Gran's life started here. Mom's started in Florida.

131

Only now I understand what Palm Beach, Florida is and where my mom started.

The thought resonates even more.

When we were together, Mom and I, in our little house, things were hard. I wonder now if she always owned the house. Did Gran offer help? Was Mom just doing everything on her own, because that was the woman she was?

Why didn't I ever consider these things before I was standing in a cemetery, about to dump the ashes of my great-grandfather out into the grass.

I walk to the graves and stand there looking down at them. I have never met anyone from Gran's side of the family. When I say it was Mom, Gran, and me, that's no lie.

Carefully kneeling down in front of the headstones, I set Gran and her father down on the ground and ease back to rest on my heels.

For a moment there is a calm, but then a near violent need to get sick washes through me before it settles.

This is the beginning of letting Gran go.

I am alone in this world. I close my eyes. I think I'm begging for my mother's energy in this moment. I need her. I shouldn't be doing this alone. She should be here.

But then I consider. If she were here, I wouldn't be doing this. This entire situation would be different.

If Mom were here, would Gran have died with me holding her hand? Would Mom have been there instead? Would Gran have been in Florida and not in Colorado?

"I don't want to say goodbye," I say aloud and a breeze blows through the near empty branches of the trees.

Then I realize, I don't have to do this alone.

I pull my phone from my pocket and click on the contact.

The Cemetery

"Hey," Mark's voice carries that ease that I need to make it through this step in my trip.

"Hey," I say back, but that's when I crack.

I'm surprised I have tears left. I really would have thought they'd be gone after having cried so much in the past week.

"Everything okay?" he asks, but I'm guessing he knows everything isn't okay. I'm calling him—again. Crying—again.

"I'm at the cemetery."

"Oh," his voice is soft. "And you called me?"

"I'm feeling very alone right now," my voice breaks. "A week ago, I was holding her hand. Today, I'm going to begin to leave her in places I didn't know existed."

I hear him chuckle, and I'm confused by that.

"You're laughing?"

Mark sighs. "No, baby, I'm honored," he says.

My knees are hurting, pressed into the hard ground. I readjust so that I'm sitting on the ground. There's a dampness on the grass, and I can feel it soak through my pants. But I just don't care at this moment.

"When I open this urn, I start to leave her. She won't be with me anymore," I say.

"Liz, she's always with you. You're part of her. She's part of you."

My jaw is trembling. This is why I called him. I realize he's an author, and maybe he's just making words sound beautiful, but it's working.

"You asked to be part of this," I say.

"I did," he agrees.

I look down at my phone and hit the FaceTime button. A moment later he's there, looking up at me.

"You're working?" I ask, because his hair is a mess, he's in an old T-shirt, and I can tell he's at the kitchen island.

"I am."

Licking my lips, I study him. He's so familiar to me, as if he's been in my life forever.

"What are you writing?"

The corner of his mouth turns up. "Don't laugh, okay?"

But that has me laughing. "I promise."

"You already laughed."

"But I didn't laugh at what you were going to tell me, yet." I smile wide, and inside I'm so grateful that again, he's defused the moment for me.

"I'm writing a romance."

My eyes are wide, and I'm trying not to laugh, but a little something squeaks out. "You?"

"Why not me?"

"I don't know. You write non-fiction."

"You write about restaurants and hotels," he counters. "You could write romance."

"I would never," I say.

Now he laughs. "We should write one together. We can take all of Betsy's escapades and turn them into romances."

I wrinkle up my nose. "Oh, hell no." Then I reconsider what

he's saying. "Is that what you're doing? Are you writing her romance? I thought you were writing her biography? Genevieve Paige's biography," I correct.

"Liz, I'm writing this for fun. It has nothing to do with Betsy's romances." His voice is sincere, and didn't I decide I can trust this man? Why, I don't know. But I know I can.

"Why romance?"

"Best-selling genre out there."

I bite down on my cracked lip. "Is it all sexy?" I'm nearly whispering, and he rolls his eyes. "What?"

"Do you know that's why I would never tell anyone that I'm doing this. Ever."

"Why tell me then?"

Mark grins. "I like you. I trust you."

"You don't know me."

"Don't I?" he says so matter-of-factly that it makes me hold my breath before I speak.

"No."

"I think I do. Besides, I write it under a pen name."

"Don't want to own up to it?"

His lips pucker. "I'd own up to it just fine. But, here's where that women's power comes in. I can't sell romance under my own name. How's that for an admission? When I put a woman's name on it, it sells."

"You've written more than one of these," I say, realizing that's what he's telling me.

"So?"

"You have, haven't you?"

"Yes," he says with a nod. "Constance Frost."

"I've read her! I've read you!" I'm shouting at the phone in the quiet cemetery as if I've forgotten what I'm doing. "She doesn't write white hot sexy stuff."

"What does she write?" he asks as if he's amused by me.

"The good stuff—I mean HEA and sweetness with just enough spark to make you hot."

His smile returns. "But you wouldn't have bought it if it said Mark Watts on it."

I let my gaze soften. "I might have if it said Mark A. Watts," I tease and I swear his cheeks blush.

"Liz, you're sitting in a cemetery," he says as if he has to pull me back to reality.

"I am," I say, reminding myself as well. The mood shifts. "I'm not ready for this."

"You'll be okay. Remember it's what she wanted."

I nod. He's right. Gran asked for this. She wanted to be taken back to Florida and left along the way. She said I'd know where, and here I am.

"Her sister is buried here too," I say.

"The whole family will be back together."

A sob sticks in my throat. I need to save some of Gran and take her back to Mom. And when I think about it, this is my whole family too—sans Mom.

What kind of life were Mom and I given to only have one another and Gran? Mom didn't know her dad. I don't know mine.

"Liz?" Mark's voice pulls me from my thoughts.

But I have Mark, I think, looking down at my phone and into his kind eyes. I don't even know this man, but I have him.

"I'm okay," I say, because I know he's wondering.

My breath shudders as I draw it in. It's time.

I look around and find that there aren't any people at the cemetery on a Monday, midday. No funerals are being held. No one is visiting. Fate has left me alone to do this, with Mark on my phone.

I take the coffee can with my great-grandfather and I study it.

"I'm sorry you've been hidden in a cupboard for all these years," I say as I curl my fingers around the lip of the lid.

But before I pull the lid off, I stop. "What if Gran doesn't want to be with her father or her mother," I say aloud, but really, it was meant for myself.

"Why wouldn't she?" Mark asks.

I set the can on the ground and pick up my phone so that Mark and I are eye to eye.

"What if he was a bad man? What if she didn't like her mother? What if her sister was a horrible person?"

Mark is smiling with his eyes, even though his mouth hasn't turned up. "And enter what I know," he says. "Though your grandmother's parents weren't excited about her wanting to leave for bigger and better things, and admittedly, they didn't talk for a few years while she figured things out, Betsy had a good relationship with them."

"She did?"

"She did," he confirmed. "Her sister as well. They were close."

"If they were close, why did I never meet my great-aunt? I mean, she died the same year Mom died. There were ten years in there for Gran to—"

"And how many times did you see your Gran?" he interrupts my rant.

I have to consider his question. The past twenty years of my life have been just me and Gran. Is he asking because he knows and he's proving a point?

"Not too often, I guess," I admit. "Here and there. I talked to her on the phone a lot. She wrote letters and sent gifts."

And now that I consider those gifts, they were always boring and useful. She was helping us out.

"Do you want me to tell you more?" Mark asks and I'm not sure I do want to know more. In fact, I contemplate hanging up and turning off my phone again. But then that's not what this journey is all about.

"What do you know?"

Goodbye Grandpa

Mark begins to walk through the kitchen and then out to the patio where he sits down in a chair by the pool. He slides on his sunglasses, which he must have picked up as he walked through the kitchen.

"Your mother ran away to Colorado," he says.

"She went to college," I correct.

Mark shakes his head. "She ran away."

"That's not what I was told."

He shrugs. "What Betsy told me was that she followed a guy out there."

"My father?" My question sounds more hopeful than I mean it to be.

"No." His answer is simple, and it crushes me a bit.

"So she ran away with just some guy?" I don't even know the women who raised me.

"Maybe we should talk about this later."

"Maybe we shouldn't be talking about it at all."

"Liz," he says my name almost as if it's a warning, but with kindness.

"I mean, maybe this should have been said to me long before

this. Maybe you shouldn't be the one to tell me this at all. Maybe—"

"Liz," he interrupts me. "Do you need to know more than that you're loved? Was there ever a time in your life that you didn't know that? Honestly?"

I swallow hard. "No."

"Then what does it matter what got them to where they were?"

"I'm sorry."

"New rule. No sorries. We're in mourning," he says adding himself to what I'm feeling. "It's going to be rocky right now. But I hold no ill will to you, and I don't think you hold any toward me. And I know for a fact that you don't hold any toward your grandmother and your mother. I just know stuff. I had an opportunity to get to know Betsy because she wanted me to. You have to remember that it could have been anyone she chose to write her story. It happens to be me, because she trusted me with knowing. And, thanks to her believing in me, I get to be part of this with you."

"And that's not a burden to you?"

Mark takes off his glasses and looks into the phone, as if he's looking into my eyes. "No, baby," he says again, and it's as normal to me as when he says my name. "It's an absolute honor to get to go through this with you."

"Okay. I'll calm down," I promise, but even as I say it, I know it's a lie.

I set the phone by my knee so that Mark is looking out toward the headstones. I can't worry if he can see everything. The only way that's going to happen is if I hold the phone, but then I can't do the task.

And, I have to admit that I don't want to spill my grandfather all over the place, and I certainly don't want any on me.

I set the coffee can on the ground in front of me, and carefully lift the lid. The thought that the can in front of me has been sealed since 1990 creeps me out. Why hadn't Gran buried him or spread him? It wasn't as if she were taking care of me yet, I wasn't even born.

Was this can in all the things that they shipped to Gran when she moved? I certainly don't remember opening a box and finding it when we opened the boxes that were shipped.

Maybe—well—I don't even know what to think. All I know is that Mark said Gran was good with her family. So I'm going to leave him with his family. Seriously, being part of the ground where his family is buried has to be better than being in Gran's cupboard.

"Hold on," I tell Mark, and then set my phone flat on the ground with him looking up at me.

I stand and walk toward the tree. There is a big piece of fallen bark, a small twig, and a few rocks at the base of the tree. I collect them all and walk back to the headstones.

"What are you doing?" Mark asks.

"I can't just dump him out right here. He'll just be ashes that'll blow away."

"Isn't that the point?" Mark asks.

"Doesn't feel right," I say as I take the bark and try to clear away some of the grass near my great-grandmother's headstone. When that only works so much, I take the stick and repeat the process.

Mark says nothing as I dig a little moat around both headstones.

"There," I say, setting the stick down and picking up my phone.

"The sky is nice there," Mark laughs and I realize he hasn't seen what I've done, and he didn't make any comment at all, so I turn the phone around so he can see my work.

"If I pour him in there and then cover it up, then he's with them. Right?" I ask.

"Does it bring you peace?"

"I think it will."

With that, I set Mark back on the ground, but this time propped up with the rock so maybe he can see what's going on. Then, I open the can, and with my lips pressed tightly together, as if that'll keep my great-grandfather's ashes from going into my mouth, I pour him into the moat I've created around the headstones.

When the can is empty, I move the dirt back into place. I pull up grass, and find more rocks to lay on the ashes. I'm probably making a horrible mess, but I feel better about it.

Picking up the phone, I look at Mark, and he's smiling.

"I need one more thing," I say and then set him back on the ground, but this time I hear him calling after me.

I hurry back to my car and pour out the last of my cold drink from Starbucks. It was mostly the last of the ice.

I take the stack of napkins they'd given me and I wipe out the cup until it's clean and dry. Hurrying back to the graves, I feel a new sense of commitment to my project.

"What are you doing?" I hear Mark ask as I kneel down next to the phone.

I pick up the phone and look at him now. "Gran needs more care," I say.

Propping Mark up on my great-grandmother's headstone, I sit flat on the ground and put Gran's urn between my legs. The lid doesn't come off easily. In fact, I have to break the seal with the small knife on my keyring. But when it does start to move, my heart begins to hammer.

Though, it's not because I'm dreading the task. I'm not worked up as I was when I'd arrived nearly an hour ago. No, now there is a sense of pride in what I'm doing. I'm fulfilling final wishes. I'm putting a family back together. I'm doing this on my own, and there's a sense of accomplishment.

I look at Mark, who is focused on me. Even though he's there, it doesn't take away from what I'm feeling.

When the lid is off, I take the Starbucks cup and fill it. This is the part that I will leave of Gran.

I carefully set the cup to the side and close the urn.

Then, in the part of my moat, next to both headstones, I fill in the hole with Gran.

I'm not crying. It feels so good to do this and not cry.

When the cup is empty, I cover both areas with the rocks that I collected and I sit back, picking up Mark and showing him what I did.

"It's what she wanted," I say.

"You did right by her, Liz. I know she continues to be proud of you," he says, and that's when the tears start.

Recover and Relax

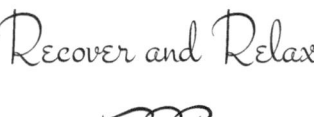

Meditation was something that Gran believed in. She said it saved her many times. It wasn't until I was in my final year at college that I understood what she meant by it.

When I was little, we would sit in the living room and meditate —or Gran would meditate and I would sit next to her, legs folded, and one eye open watching Gran because I couldn't imagine why meditation was helpful.

Now, legs folded under me on the plush bed at the hotel, Cosmo on my lap, I sink into the meditation.

The soothing music plays from my phone, and I know it's a big no-no, but I bought a candle at Walmart and I have it burning. I swear I'll extinguish it and keep an eye on it. I'm not *that* asshole.

With every breath I inhale, I add a grateful memory of Gran. I'm grateful she came to me. I'm grateful for the care. I'm grateful for the memories. I'm grateful for this trip. That thought needs a few breaths, but I am.

Twenty minutes later I let out a steady breath. My heart is calm. My body is calm. And what I did today feels good.

I turn to pick up my phone and it rings in my hand, causing that calm heart begin to race.

There is a flood of mixed emotions as I look at Mark's name on my phone.

"Seriously, you just killed twenty minutes of quiet meditation," I say.

Mark laughs. "You're the one that had your ringer on."

"I guess that's on me then," I say as I lay back on the bed and Cosmo readjusts next to me. "What are you doing?"

"Still writing. I'm on a roll," he says, and it causes me to smile, knowing he's writing a love story. I don't know why that surprises me, but it still does. "What are you doing?"

"I just told you. I was meditating."

"Do you like pedicures and massages?"

I sat up, pissing off Cosmo who hissed at me and jumped off the bed. "Why?"

"It's a simple question," he says with a lift of humor in his voice.

"Yes. Of course," I say.

"Good. And I have to assume you have nothing left to do today? No hot dates? No sneaking out and flying to New York next?"

"I don't fly," I snap.

"I need to remember that," he says, no doubt because I've been fairly adamant about it. "I scheduled you a massage and a pedicure in the spa there."

"There is a spa here?" I ask with some enthusiasm.

Mark chuckles. "Remember, this is a nice place."

"Yes, I remember." I was planning on making reservations at Holiday Inn and Mark reminded me what my grandmother was worth, financially, and that fell to me now. I could afford this whole trip on my own, but I don't need the man to know everything about me.

"You made me appointments?" I ask.

"I did. They're in an hour. Does that work for you?"

I look around the room. Cosmo found a spot on the floor to relax in the last bit of sunlight coming through the window.

"It does work for me," I say.

"Good. It's paid for, and don't let them pressure you for a tip. I took care of that as well."

"Mark," his name comes out as a sigh.

"You need this. Your grandmother would want this for you," he says.

"I appreciate it."

"My pleasure. You won't have quite the need for adventure heading into Nashville tomorrow," he teases.

"Like hell I won't. Have you been to that hotel? I looked it up. It's huge."

Mark laughs. "You have a Gaylord Hotel in Denver, don't you?"

"Well, yes, but I haven't been out there. When it opened that assignment went to someone else."

"You have my promise that I'm going to fly out there and take you to the Gaylord of the Rockies hotel there. We'll go when they have their Christmas set up."

"Why do you know so much about that?" I ask as I swing my legs off the side of the bed.

"I read the magazine you write for. You should find the article."

"Smart ass."

"Enjoy your evening, Liz."

Mark's treat was amazing. My toenails are a bright pink, just like Gran would wear. And when I fell into bed, my muscles were like butter.

Though the entire experience messed with my head, because the dreams I had that night after my massage were explicit.

As I load Cosmo into the car, I'm still thinking about the dreams—yes, dreams. Mark and I seemed to have needed each other all night, according to what I can remember.

Even thinking about it, again, my skin is warm.

It's a good thing I have a few more days before I see him, in person. I can't have the thoughts of what we did while I was asleep interfere in the mission I'm on.

Besides, it's not like that with Mark. He's just the guy on the other end of the phone, who looks amazing without a shirt.

Shit!

I shut the hatch on my car and rest my head against it. It's the lack of company I'm keeping. That's what this all is about. As soon as I get in the car, I'm calling Grace, and she's going to talk to me all the way to Nashville.

Ashton is about to get a call. I have been on the road for over two hours, and I can't get hold of Grace. She's not answering my calls. She's not answering my texts. And she busted my chops?

When the phone rings with Grace's ring tone, I nearly throw it across the car because I grab it so fast.

"Where have you been?" I begin my assault on her, just as she had done to me.

"Nope, you don't get to do that to me," she says calmly, and it's a bit disappointing. I expect to hear tears or lots of commotion behind her. Grace never ghosts me.

"Sure I do. I need you."

"And I needed some time for myself this morning," she says unapologetically. There's something wrong with her voice, but I can't decide if she's mad, sad, indifferent—it's just not normal.

"Were you showing a house?" I ask.

"No."

"Did you forget your phone?"

"No."

"Are you mad at me?"

Grace lets out a breath and clicks her tongue. Yep, she's mad.

"Do you remember that conversation we had just a few days ago about you being selfish?"

With one hand on my phone, I grip the steering wheel tighter with the other. "Yes," I say, realizing that the word selfish has been thrown around a lot in a week. But my answer is firm, and I won't argue with her.

"This is one of those moments where it's not about you."

There is a heaviness in my chest, and I'm worried that something bad has happened.

"Grace, what's wrong?"

She lets out a little laugh. "That's better."

"Seriously?"

"Sweetheart, there's nothing wrong. Are you driving?"

"Yes."

"How long have you been on the road?"

"Two hours," I say with some emphasis as if she will understand that I needed her company to settle my mind.

"Call me back when you can pull over," she says as if she can't actually read my mind which needs her comfort. I think she's losing touch with me.

I look at the signs I'm passing on the highway. I can pull off in two miles. But her needing me to pull over is freaking me out.

"Two miles. I can pull over then," I say.

"Call me back."

"Can't you just talk until then?" I ask. I don't want to let her off the phone. What if I get off the highway and she can't talk again? What if something is really wrong, and she's trying to hide it from me? I can't let her go.

Besides, I needed her, and now I have her. She's my warm blanket in a storm. My comfort food when I'm blue.

"Fine," she resigns. "How was your night last night?"

Now I let out a little laugh, and I'm grateful that we're going to get to talk about what I need to talk about. "Mark arranged a massage and a pedicure for me."

"Liz! What's going on with that guy?" Her voice has lifted now.

"Nothing. But, something. He's comforting. He's—he's a friend, I guess."

"I don't know. It seems like so much more."

I can feel the heat rise up my neck, because I'm about to tell Grace about my dreams—because there was more than one, and they were X-rated for sure.

"Listen, I don't know him. I'm under no misguided perception that he's someone who is going to be part of my life for the long term."

"But..."

"I had a dream about him last night. Actually, I had multiple dreams about him."

"Liz!" she's shouting through the phone. "Tell me all about it."

"I only have a mile left."

"You're impossible. Was it sexy?"

"Yes," I draw out the word in a warm growl.

"Oh, Liz. Tell me everything."

My laugh comes easily now as I check my mirror and begin my exit from the highway. Her excitement about the conversation is what I've needed for the past two hours.

"I don't have anything to base this on."

"You don't need to. You know his voice. You've seen his face.

The rest of it is inserted into a fantasy. Was he good? Was he attentive? Did he rock your world?"

I snort a laugh, which always makes us laugh harder. "Yes!"

"Thank God!" Grace is so loud I have to move the phone from my ear.

"Hold on," I tell her as I focus on turning and driving toward the McDonald's that is just down the road. When I'm safely in the parking lot, I put the car in park, and make sure my doors are locked. "Okay, I'm parked safely."

"Finish your story first."

I let out a groan. Best friends are pains in the ass. "We were in my hotel room. We both had massages, and then we dropped the sheets, kissed, and the rest is one hot, sweaty memory."

"You're a freaking writer. Can't you give me more than that?"

"I don't think I can," I say, and the smile on my face is so wide, I'm nearly sure the dream was actually real. I can still feel it.

"Fine. But you're safe and parked?"

"I am."

"Okay. There's a reason I couldn't get to your call."

Grace's voice has changed, and the smile I've been holding is gone.

"Grace, what's wrong? Are you sick? Are you dying?"

"You're pathetic. Why do you go straight to that?"

"I don't know. Because two weeks ago my grandmother was alive and yesterday, I left part of her in a cemetery in the dirt."

"Oh, Liz." She's sympathetic.

"Just tell me what you have to tell me. My hands are shaking."

"I'm pregnant. I'm pregnant!" she shouts.

"Oh, God!" I'm actually screaming in the car and Cosmo has hidden himself back into his crate. "I scared the cat," I say on a loud laugh. "Are you happy?"

"I'm so happy. Ashton is beside himself."

"I can't believe it. I'm so happy for you."

"I knew you would be."

149

I can't tell if she's crying. And if she is, is she happy, or did the realization just hit her as it did me? With Grace being pregnant, everything changes. For me, I will no longer be the most important person to her. I mean Ashton can come and go, but I still get Grace. A baby is going to change that.

My throat feels as if it's closing.

Don't be a selfish asshole, I remind myself. This isn't about me. For once this has nothing to do with me.

"Grace, I really am happy for you. You're going to be an amazing mother."

"Thank you. And you're going to be the best auntie ever."

And just like that, those fears are gone. Of course she'd let me be part of it all. But as we finish our call and I start back toward the highway, I'm dying to call Mark and tell him the news. Or maybe I'm just dying to have someone make it all about me.

Music City

It takes me an hour on the highway to decide to call Mark. I needed to compose myself.

I'm still uneasy with Grace's news. I am happy for her, but it's that kind of happy when your friend gets the job you really wanted. Not that I want a baby, ever, but it's selfish, I know. I'm worried it'll change my friendship with Grace. However, I know it will only change if I change. If I let that baby be the reason I back away from Grace, then that's on me. I wouldn't do that to her. Grace is my everything and always has been. A baby is just an extension of that everything. I need to remember that. I mean, she got married, and I didn't lose her.

God, I'm pathetic.

Cosmo moves through the car, and I think I should really make sure he's always in his crate. First of all, he scares the shit out of me when he just appears at my arm. Then there is the safety issue. I really would be devastated if anything happened to him.

He settles in next to Gran's urn. I continue to believe he knows she's there.

"Just a couple more days," I say to Cosmo as I reach for him and run my hand down his back. "Then, I guess we'll figure out what we do from there. But one thing is for sure, it's you and me."

He answers back, as he does now. We're pals. I promise not to say I hate him again, because I never did.

The thought that Mark might want him back crosses my mind. He is Mark's cat. What do I do then? Surely he won't demand that I give Cosmo back. I mean, he was Gran's.

I pick up my phone and click on his contact. The phone rings, and for the first time, I hear his voicemail message.

"It's Mark. If you do this right, I'll talk to you soon."

I'm irritated that I got the message, but I laugh at it, because what more do you have to say nowadays? I think I'll consider changing my message. Then again, I use my phone for work, so if I don't identify myself as a writer for the magazine, some people won't leave messages. So, I'll go on being envious of the house-sitting biographer, friend to the elderly.

That makes me laugh, too.

Maybe I'll tell him he should consider adding that to his outgoing message.

I put my phone back, and the sadness of disappointment lands heavy in my chest. I really wanted to talk to him.

The final two hours of our trip to Nashville are quiet. Cosmo has been sleeping next to Gran, and I finally turned on a podcast to hear someone talk.

Three full days on the road, with two more to go, it's lonely.

But the things that have come in and out of my head have been therapeutic.

Between calls with Mark and Grace, I've learned a lot about myself and Gran. I've even learned more about my mother than I wanted to. Aside from clerks at convenient stores, or those in drive-thru windows, or at front desks of hotels, I haven't talked to anyone else. It's been me and Cosmo—though, we've had some good conversations.

I wonder if I could be that person, who just jumps into a car and travels the country.

Then I rethink it.

I get to make this trip again, sans Gran. No, I don't think this is for me. I'll keep making notes and plans to go back to certain places, but I don't think I can just travel around by myself. I'm lonely, and doesn't that sum up the state of my life?

God, here come the tears again, just as I cross over into Nashville.

I'm cursing Mark in my head for not being there to talk to, because now I've delved deep into myself and admitted that I'm lonely. Yes, I'm the lonely thirty-year-old orphan with only one friend, a remote job, and a cat.

I have a cat.

I look at Cosmo. He's no help in fixing my mental state right now.

I'm tired. That's it. I'm tired. Driving for hours is exhausting and I don't know how truck drivers do it. Then again, this trip wasn't supposed to be fun. Aside from the cemetery, I haven't stopped for anything else. Of course, the massage and pedicure were nice. Does Mark understand what I'm going through? Is that why he did that?

"Stop it!" I shout to myself in the car. I'm tired of my own thoughts.

Cosmo lifts his head and hisses at me, and I actually feel guilty for waking him.

I drive until Siri directs me to the hotel, and as I pull into the parking lot, I'm overwhelmed by the size of the building.

"Seriously?"

I lift my sunglasses to the top of my head.

"Cosmo, we're going to get lost in here."

He's perched up on the console as if he wants to see the next adventure. I've already searched out the restaurant I want to eat at. There are a few shops in the atrium that I want to look through and get something for Grace. I've ruled out the boat ride down the river inside the hotel because that seems lame, but at the same time, there's a freaking river with boats in it at a hotel.

That makes me laugh as I park.

Cosmo is cooperative so we can get inside, but the moment I finish the long trek to our room, having had to stop and ask for directions twice, he's out of the crate and checking out the room. He's tired too, and unfortunately, this is all he gets to see. I'm not one of those people who will take their cat out to eat with them.

I texted Mark, who hasn't texted or called me all day, to let him know I safely made it to the hotel.

Where are you going to eat? he replies.

Old Hickory Steakhouse, I say. *I kinda feel like not being in sweatpants for an hour.*

You'll enjoy it.

I sit on the edge of the bed and look at the casual texts. Does he know how much I missed him today? Do I want to actually admit that?

You've been here?

I ask, feeling some kind of kinship with him over that. Or maybe it's knowing I'm where he's been?

It's silly to get this wrapped up in him. I met him once. I have to remember I've been around him before. But the fact that I don't remember at all confuses me.

Yes. Let me know what you think.

That feels like the end of our conversation.

I made reservations for the restaurant, not that they can't get in a single woman who could sit at the bar. But I did it anyway. Then, I gave them the name Genevieve Paige.

I don't know what made me do it, but the joy that is

resonating through me makes me giggle. Did Gran feel giddy being someone else? Was that part of the charm of a stage name?

When I slide into my dress, and slip into the only high heels that I own, I feel different. I leave my hair down, but curled. I'm going to let the freckles be free, and not cover them with makeup, as I would if I were going out for business or on a date.

This feels good.

God, I love being Genevieve Paige.

Headed to dinner? Mark texts.

I am.

And because I'm feeling alive and flirtatious. I take a selfie in the full mirror and send it to him—to which he never responds.

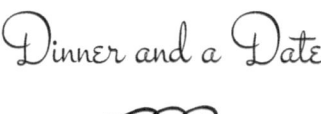

Dinner and a Date

Cosmo isn't as excited to be left in the room as I'd have hoped. He's hissed at me. Scratched me. And then he dumped out his food.

Okay, I might reconsider my feelings for this cat.

But, as I grab my purse and phone, still irritated that Mark has said nothing about my dress, Cosmo settles in and ignores me as I leave the room.

The hotel is so large, it takes me twenty minutes to get to that side of the property. When my phone rings, and I see that it's Mark, I silence the ringer. Nope, he doesn't get to interrupt me since he went silent after I sent the picture.

But, he calls again.

I silence it again.

On the third time, I finally answer. "What?"

"I like 'hey' better," he says. "Why aren't you taking my calls?"

"I'm going into dinner. Can I call you later? Or I'll see you in two days," I say, as if I can go two days without talking to this stranger who has become my lifeline.

"You made reservations under Genevieve Paige?"

His question has me stopping my walk toward the restaurant.

"Are you stalking me? How do you know that?"

He laughs easily. "I know all things Genevieve Paige."

"Well, I don't. And I think the fact that you called the restaurant and—"

"Your face gets red when you're mad," he says and my heart begins to hammer in my chest.

"Where are you?"

"By the way, you look beautiful in that dress."

Now I know he's toying with me. I sent him a picture of the damn dress—which he hadn't commented on until now.

"Okay, you're just being a jerk," I say, starting to walk toward the restaurant. "I sent you a picture of the dress."

Again, his laugh comes through the phone. "That you did. But you didn't tell me you'd smell so good."

That has me stopping again, and I realize that I heard that in my phone and from behind me.

Without turning around, phone still to my ear, I say, "I have to go."

I disconnect the call, tuck my phone into my purse, and then turn around.

He's standing there.

Mark A. Watts is standing there.

When he smiles, those blue eyes flash. His dark hair seems longer than before, as if I really know, and he has the shadows of a beard. He's dressed in jeans, a suit jacket, and tie. God, he's freaking gorgeous, and he's standing there.

Suddenly the surprise of it all melts into irritation and anger.

"What are you doing here?" My voice is not filled with that joy that should accompany seeing him.

"No hello kiss?"

My skin heats.

"Ah, your cheeks redden at that too," he says, his grin widening.

"You're stalking me."

"Actually, I thought I was being a good friend and showing up to give you some company."

I have to think about that. This is supposed to be a nice surprise. It is a nice surprise. I'm out of sorts. I'm dizzy.

"I need a minute," I say.

Mark nods. "I'll let them know we're here. Don't ditch me, okay?"

I mean to nod my acceptance of that, but I'm not sure I do.

I hurry toward the bathroom I saw walking to the restaurant. I duck in, pull my phone from my purse, and call Grace.

"Hey, Liz. What's—"

"He's here," I blurt out the words before she's done talking. "He's here."

"Text guy?"

"Yes!" I shout but in a loud whisper as if the bathroom is flooded with people trying to hear my phone call.

"What are you going to do?" Okay, now she sounds as panicked as I feel.

"I don't know. I'm freaking out."

"Liz, calm down," she says, but her voice is still shaking too. "Okay, you were going to him anyway. So, he shows up. Why did he show up?"

"He said to give me some company."

"Aw," she sighs. "That's sweet." Now her voice isn't shaking. Why isn't it shaking?

"You're not helping. What do I do?"

"Have dinner with him."

"What if he's a psycho?"

Grace clears her throat. "Um, you're headed to his house. Well, Gran's house where he lives. Did you think you wouldn't be staying close to him?"

"I'm not going to sleep with him."

"I never said anything about that. What's wrong with you?"

"I'm scared."

"Why? Gran liked him. She liked him enough to leave him in her house and he knows all the juicy stuff about her."

And that's why Grace is my best friend. She's right, and in the moment of panic, I couldn't remember that.

"Okay."

"Go eat dinner with him. Get to know him. But you still have your own room. You don't have to share it with him."

"Right."

"Live that life, Liz," Grace says, and its calm resonates with Gran's words.

When I hang up with Grace, after she gives me another little pep talk, I tuck my phone into my purse, and look into the mirror. My freckles are dark now, and I wish I had put on foundation.

I walk back to the restaurant, but Mark isn't standing there. I walk to the desk.

"I have reservations for Genevieve Paige."

The man nods. "I've just seated your guest. Follow me."

I wrap my hand around my purse, gripping it as if it's my lifeline. As we approach the table, which happens to be in a dark corner, Mark stands, and the Maitre d' heads back toward the front of the restaurant.

"Hey," he says, and my mouth goes dry hearing the word and staring at him. It has that same calm that grounds me when he calls.

"Hey," I say.

We don't move to sit, or move toward one another. I'm staring at him, and he's doing the same to me.

"I'm sorry for acting so strange," I confess.

"I wanted to surprise you. I guess I didn't think about how you'd take it." A crease forms between his brows, and I know he's concerned that he crossed a line. Maybe he did, but now that he's within reach, I think I'm glad that he's there.

"You did surprise me."

159

His gaze moves over me. "You're certainly not six anymore," he laughs. "That sounds bad."

"No. It's okay. I still don't remember you at all."

"There's no reason you should," he says holding out his hand, which I take. "It's very nice to meet you in person, Elizabeth."

No one calls me Elizabeth, but as the name slips from his lips, mine part, but I can't speak.

My hand is still gripped in his, and he eases toward me.

"I feel as if we're very old friends," he says, his voice soft, yet filled with gravel as he draws near.

"Me too," is all I can muster.

"I'd really like to hug you."

I'm afraid to hug him. I've built him up in my head and here he is. What if I hug him and it feels wrong? What if I hug him and then can't move from him? I don't want to appear needy, but what if touching him makes me need him more?

"Thank you," I blurt out the words and his smile widens.

"For wanting to hug you?"

"No, no." I shake my head, feeling the curls I put into my hair bounce around my face. I close my eyes tightly, gather myself, and take a breath. "I'd love to hug you."

Mark moves in and pulls me toward him. His arms come around me, and as my head comes to his shoulder, I think I could cry. I'm not going to. I can't do that. But, oh, his hug is everything I dreamed it would be. And I've dreamed of his hugs.

I wrap my arms around him and feel—just feel.

The heat from his body is soothing, and the smell of him intoxicating.

For the past week and a half, his words on the screen of my phone, his voice when he calls, and even his disheveled look when he FaceTimes me gives me a peace that even Grace can't give me. Now, wrapped in his arms, I could die happy. Why is it that this man can piece me back together, and yet, this is the first time we're near one another—well, as adults?

His breath is at my ear. His chest, firm beneath mine moves with that breath. I could stay here all day—all night, just feeling this comfort. His texts, his calls, they'd been enough until this very moment. I'm so freaking screwed.

As he eases back, his bristly cheek brushes mine.

We stand there for a moment too long, silent, and awkward.

The server approaches the table with a bottle of wine and two glasses.

Mark steps back as the server sets the bottle and the glasses on the table and then retreats.

"I took the liberty to order wine for Genevieve Paige," he says with a wink.

I wrinkle my nose. "I guess it's a sign that we should celebrate her."

"It most certainly is."

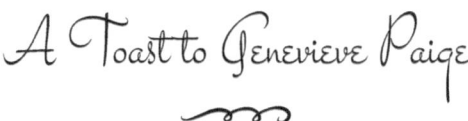

A Toast to Genevieve Paige

Mark pulls out a chair for me. I don't think a man has ever done that for me.

"Thank you," I say softly as I sit down, and then he takes his seat.

His hands move right to the wine bottle, and he pours me a glass, and then one for himself.

It surprises me when he sniffs the wine in his glass and swirls it. Does he really know what he's doing? Then he holds it out toward me.

"To Genevieve Paige. To her glorious life that brought us together," he says.

"To having a big fat life to live and enjoying the adventure," I say, and the line between his brows deepens. "I'll tell you later."

Mark nods as he taps his glass to mine then sips.

I finally sip, then lick my lips as I set down my glass. Mark is watching me, and it makes my skin warm.

"What made you decide to join me?" I ask as I pick up the menu.

"I would have flown out to drive the whole way with you." He picks up his menu, but he doesn't look at it. "Besides, I was getting the feeling that you might be lonely."

"Cosmo and I are doing just fine. Besides, Gran is with us."

His mouth curls into a smile. "Well, if you're not lonely, there's another flight out in the morning."

Unable to concentrate on the menu, I set it down and pick up my wine. "Since you're already here..."

Mark does the same, putting down his menu, and picking up his wine, still smiling. "Actually, I was jealous that you were getting to have this adventure without me."

"Jealousy, huh?"

"You might as well know, I'm petty," he says before sipping his wine, grinning from behind the glass.

"Well, I can guarantee that you have nothing to be jealous about."

"Sure I do. You've spent the last twenty years with Betsy."

Because I don't know how to take that, I set my glass on the table, I take my napkin and set it in my lap, gripping it between my fingers.

"And that makes you jealous? My mother died, that's how I got Betsy."

Mark's eyes go wide. Okay, that was a little snotty, but what is he trying to tell me?

"Liz, I didn't mean—"

"I know. I'm sorry." I lift my napkin from my lap and wipe away my lipstick. "I don't know how to handle this relationship you had with Gran. I don't understand the relationships she had that she didn't let me in on. I sat at my great-grandmother's grave yesterday, and I didn't even know anything about her. Grace is pregnant, and that worries me. And I'm afraid you'll take Cosmo from me."

His smile is gone, but it lingers in his eyes. "That's a lot to process for one person."

"And I need to write this all down so I can get paid," I say, trying to defuse what I've just spit out so that maybe it doesn't sound as crazy as it feels.

Now he smiles as he moves from his chair, across the table, to the chair next to mine. He reaches for my hand and folds it into his as if touching one another is normal—and it feels normal.

"Part of this journey was so you could find out about the relationships your grandmother had, even with me. Remember, you're learning who she was." He pauses. "That's really great news about Grace. And I promise I won't take Cosmo from you, but I do want to see him."

"You'll see him."

"I know." His thumb brushes over my knuckles. "Are you okay that I'm here? I really just wanted to have a few extra days with you, in person."

"Yeah, I am," I say. "I'm just not good with surprises."

"That would have been good to know," he says, looking down at our joined hands. "I don't want you to think you're going through this alone." He lifts his eyes to meet mine. "You're not alone."

I could get lost in those eyes and those silky words.

We're friends. I need to remember that over the past few weeks he's called me to check in on me. He's asked how I am. He knows things about Gran that I don't—and I guess I know a part of Gran he doesn't. There's a reason we're together on this journey.

And there it is.

We're on this journey together.

I reach for my wine, but my hand shakes so I withdraw it. I don't know who this man is to Gran, but I'm here to learn.

I lift my eyes to meet his again.

I don't know who this man is to me, but there's some excitement in the unknown.

A life well-lived means no regrets. Remember that.

"Thanks for being here," I say and Mark's smile widens.

"There's nowhere else I'd rather be."

I think in that moment I could lean in and kiss him, but the server comes back to the table to take our orders, and we each ease back and pick up our menus.

He's not here for me to fall for. He's not here for me to get confused over. He's here because we have a friendship given to us by Gran. I need this friend.

I'm grateful for this friend.

I'm not one to order dessert, but Mark is. He's assured me that dessert is living his life to the fullest.

And because he's a new friend, he shares his dessert with me. Truth is, this is a good meter of our friendship. A stranger would have either not ordered dessert when I said no to ordering one, or they would have ordered two just to not be alone in their indulgence.

A ride or die friend, like Grace, would have ordered dessert and stabbed my hand with a fork if I tried to take a bite.

The new, and considerate friend, Mark, ordered one dessert and asked for two forks. He's not beyond sharing. Gran knew that, didn't she?

Mark cuts a small bite of the cheesecake with his fork and lifts it to his lips. "What are your plans for the rest of the night?"

I'm focusing much too hard to keep the expression on my face neutral. Him asking that has my mind going straight to that dream I had. It's a bit too real now.

"I was just going to go back to my room and hang out with Cosmo."

Mark nods. "Have you been reading more letters?"

I take a bite of the cheesecake. "No. I decided to save those. I need to concentrate on the drive."

"Right. Well, I was thinking we could get a car and head downtown."

"I have a car."

His grin widens as he cuts another bite. "But if we have someone drive us, we could have a few drinks."

I press my lips together. I don't want to smile at the invitation. Gran's words ring in my mind. I could play this multiple ways. I could go back to my room and give him a time we'd leave in the morning. Or, I could go downtown with this man who has already had an effect on me, in every way, and enjoy my night. I could have a few drinks, maybe dance, maybe...

"Well?" he asks drawing me out of the thoughts I'm having.

I pull my bottom lip through my teeth. "I think I'd like that."

The Reunion

We decide that before we go downtown, we'll stop in to see Cosmo. The walk through the atrium and toward my room is innocent, but it feels like that walk back home after a first date. The kind of moment where there's an energy in the air that pulses with your heartbeat.

Every once in a while, our arms brush, but we only walk next to each other, keeping our hands to ourselves.

"When were you in Nashville last?" I ask as we turn down the hallway toward my room.

"I was here last year. I did book signings for a biography that I wrote on Jimmy Bellevue."

"Gran loved his music."

"She introduced me to him. Well, by then it was via phone calls and emails, but she made it happen."

As we stop in front of my door, I turn to study him, again. "I wish I knew she did things like that. I just don't understand why she seemed to keep two lives."

"There's a reason she didn't want you to know about Genevieve Paige, and I assume that's why she kept it from you, even if she continued to live it, the slightest bit," he says.

"I just can't imagine what it was that she didn't want me to know."

"You had an absolutely normal life, minus losing your mother at such a young age," he says with a tilt of his head in consideration. "I think that's what they wanted for you."

"They?"

"Your mother and your grandmother."

That small statement says a lot to me. "Is that why my mother ran away? Because of who her mother was?"

Mark reaches out a hand toward me, brushing away a curl that has made its way to my cheek. The movement is so intimate, I actually lean in, as if he were going to silence me with a kiss.

"This was my job, right? I'm supposed to tell you all these things."

I moan something that is my agreement, but the anticipation still grows for that kiss.

"Your mother hated your grandmother's fame," he says, lowering his hand from my hair. "When you were born, your mom and grandmother weren't even on speaking terms."

That feeling of anticipation now turns into something else that squeezes around my heart.

"I didn't know that."

"I know," he says. "I'm here to fill in the holes."

"That's so fucking selfish of them," I say warding off tears that threaten. "They should have told me this. This isn't your job."

"I don't mind," he says placing his hand against the door, next to my head. "I want to be your friend, Liz. I want to know who Betsy was when she was just being Gran."

"Why?"

"Because she meant something to me too."

"Why?"

Mark chuckles and eases back. "Do you remember the picture I sent you of your visit? The one with my grandfather and me in it?"

"Yes."

"Grandpa was involved with Betsy," he says, and I ease back against the wall because my knees have gone soft.

"Involved?"

"Involved." He stands and slips his hands into the front pockets of his jeans. "I moved in with them when I was twelve. Into the house in Florida, shortly before you came to visit."

"My head is spinning."

"Why don't we go inside?"

I search his eyes for proof that I can trust this man, who now I understand was a grandson, of sorts, to Gran.

I take the card for the door out of my purse and hand it to Mark. He presses it to the lock, and because he holds it together better than I do, he eases the door open, aware of blocking the entrance in case Cosmo decides to take off.

We step into my room and let the door close behind us.

I realize I left my room in a bit of shambles. The bag with my clothes in it is open and scattered on the bed. There are four different drink cups on the small table, and a bag of snacks. Cosmo's litter has a scent from the bathroom, but Mark doesn't seem to be put out by it.

Then, from out of a dark corner, Cosmo makes his entrance and moves straight for Mark's feet.

"Hey," Mark says in that easy tone, crouching down and putting his hand out for Cosmo.

Cosmo studies him, then moves to Mark's hand. This man has already made a move on my cat, because Cosmo steps right into his arms and Mark picks him up and stands.

"You're much bigger than you were when I brought you home," he says, nuzzling his face into the cat's fur. "Do you remember me?"

Mark's voice has gone soft and sweet.

Cosmo nuzzles his head against Mark's chest and looks

content. He doesn't usually let me pick him up. He'll cuddle up to me, but on his own terms.

Then again, maybe I'm just jealous over that damn cat.

"I think he remembers you," I say.

"Maybe." Mark runs his hand over Cosmo's back. "It's nice to see him again."

While they reunite, I take a moment to stuff everything back into the bag on my bed, and pour out the drinks I've left on the table.

When I notice Cosmo walking around the room, I look up at Mark, standing with his back against the wall, watching me move around the room.

"Should we head out?" I ask.

"If you're still up for it."

"I think stepping out of my comfort zone and going out is exactly what I need."

"That's out of your comfort zone?"

I nod. "Completely. I don't go out unless I'm with Grace. I certainly don't take an Uber anywhere. And, well, I'm already out of my comfort zone having a man in my hotel room."

Mark stands straight, putting his hands in his pockets again. "I didn't mean to impose on you."

"You didn't. I want you here. I want to go out in public with you. I want to get to know you."

The corner of his mouth curls up. "You do?"

"I do. You've been a great comfort to me. I'm looking forward to going through those letters and learning about Gran. I can't wait to see the house, and I guess I'll make it a point to get all of my articles written while I'm there." I press my hands to my cheeks because they're warming. "It seems as if our lives are more intertwined than I had thought. And if I've learned anything from this trip, Gran's death, and Grace's recent frankness, it's that I'm selfish and not a lot of fun."

"I think you're fun."

I laugh at that. How could he possibly think that, except that when we do talk, I seem to be a little more laid back. Maybe he brings that out in me. I'm willing to feel that out.

"Well, let's find out. Order up a car and let's see what this town has to offer."

His smile is wide now. "Okay."

"You do have your own room don't you?" I ask and then realize that very question makes me sound dull. But I don't assume he's come to meet me in Nashville for motives other than those he'd said—to keep me company on my drive.

"Of course I have my own room. I have one in Georgia, too," he says, and I'm grateful for this man—whoever he might be to me now and in the future.

The Dance

Lower Broadway is everything I thought it might be. Pictures just don't do it justice. I have to admit, I feel like a fraud. I'm a lifestyle writer. I write about restaurants and events that happen in Denver —in Denver! There's an entire world beyond my square little state. But having rooted myself where I'm safe and comfortable has left me blind to what is around me. I know I'll never see Europe, or Hawaii. There's no way I'll get on an airplane and travel to see the glory elsewhere. But maybe if this road trip with Mark works out, maybe we could travel together. I mean, he obviously travels to learn about the people he writes about. I could write about the places.

My phone dings in my hand and I look down at the text from Grace.

Well? You went radio silent. Did you have dinner? Is he decent? Is he hot? Call me and tell me all about it. Or are you too busy?

Grace adds a GIF of a woman pumping her arms in the air in celebration.

"You're grinning," Mark says as the Uber driver pulls up in front of Tootsies.

"Am I?" Even my voice is grinning, and I hear it now.

"You are."

Can't call now. We're going bar hopping downtown. I'll call later, I text back as Mark tips the driver and we climb from the car.

I drape my purse across me and look up at the lights of the buildings that surround me. Music pours out of each door.

"It's Tuesday. Why are there so many people out on a Tuesday?"

Now he's grinning at me. "Tourist area. Are you going to tell me what you were thinking about."

I want to. I will.

I hold out my hand so that he takes it. "Buy me a beer. Let's talk after that."

Mark takes my hand and links our fingers. The rush that it gives me is nearly equal to the anticipation of the kiss I never got.

I want to live this best life. I want to make Gran proud. I want to know what I've missed out on, both with Gran, and this big world around me.

The music drums through me as Mark pulls me through a doorway and into a bar where people are dancing and singing. He has to yell our order to be heard, and I'm alive.

When the bartender hands Mark two beers, he turns and hands me one. He moves in close so that he can talk right into my ear.

"Do you want to sit or walk around?" he asks.

I'm so overwhelmed I don't know what to do. I'm trying to think of the last time Grace and I went anywhere that was this loud. Seriously, do I ever go anywhere?

"Let's walk around a bit."

He nods, and then takes my hand again, just as he had outside. Our fingers are linked, palms pressed together, and it tethers me to him as we walk between the people.

We find a high-top table and stop, resting our beers atop it, and take in the music.

"We'll have a beer here and then go around the corner to Warner Wright's place," he says, leaning into me.

"I didn't know he had a place." I'm familiar with the man's music, but no more than what I hear on the radio.

Mark nods. "I wrote a tell-all book on his step-mother and he had me up to celebrate it, on the down low," he says with a cheeky smile.

I inch in closer. "Who's the most famous person you've ever met?"

He puckers his lips in thought. "Met as in sat down and had a drink with? Or met as in crossed paths?"

The fact that he has levels of meeting someone is impressive.

"Both."

"Well, once while I was at a golf course with my grandfather, when I was young, I got hit in the head by a wayward ball which was hit by someone who was playing with, or behind, Bill Murray."

"You talked to him?"

Mark shook his head and took a pull from his beer. "I don't think he really knew what was going on. And the fact that I was star struck probably helped me forget about the headache I had."

"Okay, who do you know personally?"

"Besides Betsy?"

"I'm still not sure she was famous, just easy with an alias."

"Ouch," he says tucking in his grin. "You don't have any idea how famous she was."

"Nope, but that's why I'm drinking. I figure it'll hurt less, for the night anyway."

"She was a good person, Liz."

"I know. I know that better than anyone. I know that Betsy Evans was a good person. I don't know anything about Genevieve Paige."

He regards me for a moment, takes another sip of his beer, and cups his hands around the bottle when he sets it on the table.

"This is a hard question. Everyone I know *was* famous. Most of them could walk into the supermarket and never be recognized now, but they all once were tabloid fodder."

"So no one is more famous than the other?"

"The only one that comes to mind, who you'd probably know right away is Bridget Bloom."

I wrinkle my nose and think of the childhood star that graced most of the made-for-TV movies, aimed at teenagers, when I was younger.

"You knew her?"

"Oh, yeah," he says taking a long pull from his beer.

Assuming I'm going to learn a little something about Mark Watts, I take a long pull from mine as well.

"Just a passing through kind of know her? Or really know her?"

His eyes narrow. "She portrayed the high school cheerleader until she was about twenty-six."

"No kidding?"

"She was always older than her roles. So, most of the people who were enthralled with her were thirteen-year-old boys, or forty-year-old men."

"That makes my stomach churn," I say. And I wince when I think of Gran having an affair with a fifty something man when she was barely an adult. I drink until my beer is nearly empty. When I can breathe, I look back at Mark. "Where did you fall?"

"I was only a few years younger than she was. Flavor of the summer? Someone who didn't much care for the limelight? I had the right connections, but was perfectly normal?"

"You dated her?" I ask, putting the pieces together.

Mark chews his bottom lip. "Yeah. I dated her."

I can't decide if I was more shocked to learn about Gran, or the fact that this man, who has my number in his phone and calls me often, who was holding my hand, bought me dinner, and now a beer, dated a movie star.

"Wow," is all I can say before I finish off my beer.

"I was young and naïve. She was, well, not really my type."

My curiosity is piqued with that. "What's that type?"

"I'm not a party boy. I'm not fond of PDA for publicity. I'm not just one of many."

It takes me a moment to put that all together and pull out what's important there.

"This is as close to clubbing as you go?" I ask.

"Yes."

"Other than the shuffleboard club."

"It's the only club I can appreciate," he says smiling.

"You're not one to parade around hoping to get photographed for publicity?"

"Hence the reason I rarely go further from the pool house than the kitchen."

"You're far from home, Mr. Watts."

"I'm not being tracked down at the moment, Ms. Evans."

Now I'm smiling at him. He waves down a server for two more beers.

"As for the not one of many?" I ask.

"I believe in relationships. Even if it's casual sex."

I wrinkle my nose. "I don't understand that."

"I mean if you're seeing someone, you're with that one person. It's a relationship. There are boundaries and rules that I think should be unspoken, but in this day and age you need a damn contract."

I nod, but it's more just to keep up.

"And if you're just casually having sex, meaning, oh I don't know, friends with benefits, then you make that clear and when one or the other finds someone, you back off," he says.

"Was that what was happening with you guys?" I ask as the server brings our beers.

Mark takes a long pull from his full bottle. "No. I thought I was in a relationship. I thought I was the calm to her storm. I don't know what I was to her. Just a pit stop, I guess. It was short-lived. It's a story I don't like to talk about, but she was the most famous person I knew."

I blink hard a few times. Admittedly, I'd forgotten what led us to that admission.

"I don't do casual," I say as if he needs to hear it.

"That's good."

"Is it? Did Gran do casual?"

Mark lifts a brow, and I begin to drink down my beer. I'm going to need to be more drunk if I ask questions like that and want answers.

"Would you like to dance?" he asks instead of answering. I'm grateful for this, but then wonder if that was my answer—his avoidance.

Mark takes my hand, and we each take our beers. The dance floor is crowded and I don't know how to dance like these people around us, but that doesn't seem to be what Mark has in mind anyway.

He wraps his arms around my waist, and I wrap mine around his neck, dangling the bottle from my fingers. I can feel his bottle on my back.

The music is thumping at a much faster pace than what we're dancing to. Maybe he hears something in his head I can't hear.

The speed at which I drank my one and a half beers, and the swaying, is causing my eyes to close. I press myself against him.

"I'm glad you're here," I say as I feel his grip around me tighten.

"So am I."

"I've really valued your friendship since Gran died."

"I hope I haven't been bothersome."

I chuckle, and let my cheek brush his unshaven one. "Not in the least."

"Liz, I want us to be friends. I think we need one another."

I close my eyes tight and then ease back just enough that I can take a drink from my bottle.

"I think we can be friends," I say, but there is disappointment dripping in my words.

One of his hands moves up my back, and I lean further into him. Friends, I repeat to myself. And then again, suddenly, casual sounds so good to me.

Elevator Rides

Warner Wright's bar was much smaller than the others, but it, too, was packed. I'm not going to lie, I was disappointed to find that he wasn't in the building. That would have been fun to have rubbed elbows with a celebrity, since it's part of Gran and Mark's life that I haven't been privy to.

I'm on my third beer, and second shot. I'm glad we took a car because I couldn't have driven. That's a lie. I would have driven, because I wouldn't have even had one beer. I'm living in the moment, and that's what Gran wanted right?

It feels good.

"You're grinning again," Mark says as we watch the band on stage from a bench against the wall. His shoulder is pressed to mine, and so is his thigh.

I lift my head and keep grinning. "I'm having fun."

"I'm glad." He blinks slowly, and I'm aware he's had as much to drink as I have. "I'm having fun too."

"I trust you," I say, and his brows draw in.

"Was there any doubt?"

I rest my head on his shoulder. "No. I don't think there was."

"Maybe we should head back," he says on a tired breath. "You did a lot of driving today. I did a lot of flying. And we have a long drive tomorrow."

I lift my head. "One more dance?"

"Anything for you, Liz."

Mark manages to stand before I can. He holds out his hands to ease me to my feet. I let myself fall into him and his arms come around me.

I love the smell of him and the feel of him against me. I'm so screwed.

Mark was just a voice or a string of words in text on my phone. But I knew the first time I saw his face, he'd be easy to enjoy. That dream I had about us, that still messes with my head. But being in his arms, I know I want to make something of this strange friendship.

But then I still don't know everything about him. Don't I need to know everything? He lives in Gran's house. My house. He'll hate me when I sell it. He'll hate me if I decide to live there. He'll hate me if I start to rent it out.

Deciding that I want to smell him more, hold him against me, maybe make my dream come true, I grip his hand harder as he leads me to the dance floor.

A life well-lived means no regrets. Remember that.

No regrets.

Was that Gran's tool for success? No regrets?

I swear it's as if a light goes on in my head.

I'm so afraid of losing everyone, that I don't have anyone.

I don't want to regret missing anything, so I don't do anything.

He pulls me in close, again, the music not matching the slow grind we're putting ourselves through.

"We don't have to leave early in the morning. Since I'm with you, I won't worry about where you are," he says in my ear because our cheeks are pressed together.

"Okay," is all I can manage because in my head I'm undressing this man with no regrets.

I breathe him in, and I swear he's doing the same to me.

I want this man. I want everything about this man in my life.

We stop swaying. Now we're just holding one another on the dance floor.

"Let's get a car," he says and I nod.

Mark holds my hand as we walk out of the bar, and outside as we wait in silence for the driver to pull up. Once inside, our hands link again, as if we hold hands all the time.

The driver, a native to Nashville, feels the need to fill the silence in the car, but in the back seat, Mark and I are shifting flirtatious, anxious, drunk glances between one another.

Every once in a while, I have to close my eyes, because I'm drunk. It's not even sorta drunk. I'm drunk and the world sways.

But the *living life to its fullest with no regrets* mantra of my grandmother resonates in my head. Drunk or not, I'm taking this man home. This man, who in less than two weeks has become my new ride or die friend—my fantasy.

I let out a breath, and when I look at him, he's chewing on his lip. Is he thinking what I'm thinking? Does he know what I'm thinking?

When the hotel comes into sight, I feel my lungs clog up, but it's from anticipation, not fear. Mark's grip tightens on my hand— oh, he's thinking what I'm thinking.

As soon as the driver stops the car, Mark and I scramble from opposite doors. He tips the driver, and we hurry through the lobby, across the atrium, down the hallway to the elevator. It's when the elevator opens, it all begins.

I step inside and press the button. Mark steps in after me. The door closes.

I'm not sure who moved first.

All I know is we collide in the middle, and now my body is pressed against the wall of the elevator. Mark's mouth is on mine, and I open to his kiss. Drunk or not, this kiss heats me from my core and makes my head swim.

The elevator comes to a stop, there aren't many floors, and we step back from one another, but quickly reach for one another's hands as if we might lose the other on the walk to my room.

The hallway seems smaller somehow, but maybe it's because we're hurrying and our bodies bounce against the other's.

I walk past my room, and Mark pulls me back with a laugh.

The tug to my hand throws me off balance, and I crash into him, and against the door.

The laughter takes over as I fish my key card from my purse.

"Hurry, Liz," his voice is hot and breathy in my ear. His chest is pressed to my back, and his arms wrap around me.

I finally manage to push open the door, and it slams at our backs as we push ourselves up against it.

I've never wanted anything—anyone—this much.

I drop my purse to the floor, not even considering that my phone is inside, until it hits the ground. But I can't pull from his possession, nor do I want to.

Mark's hands grip my skirt and begin to gather the fabric until it's high around my waist. Then he cups me, and I can feel the heat that has pooled there.

His groan against my neck undoes me, and I need to get him out of his clothes.

"Liz," he moans my name into my skin, nipping my throat.

I reach for his belt and manage to unhook it, just as I feel the paw of our mutual friend on my toes, and his fur on my legs.

Mark steps back as if he's been pushed.

We both look down at the cat that has interrupted us.

I realize I hadn't left a light on in the room, and panic rushes through me. Did Cosmo make a mess? Did he leave me small presents throughout the room? What was that going to cost me?

I reach for the switch on the wall and turn on the lights.

Mark and I both wince from the sudden brightness.

Cosmo is still wandering between our feet.

Mark rakes his fingers through his already mussed hair. His eyes are glassy, his lips swollen from my kisses.

I raise my fingers to my lips, realizing they tingle from his whiskers.

Cosmo moves into the bathroom and straight to the litter box.

I ease myself against the wall and press my hand to my head, and the other to my stomach.

"Stupid cat," I say, and Mark laughs.

"Maybe he's genius."

I try to focus on Mark's face, but it's hard. "How's that?"

He moves to me and presses his hands to the wall on either side of me, resting his forehead to mine.

"I'm going to go to my room."

I push him back, and he wobbles before getting his footing.

"Fine. Go."

"Liz," he sighs, and it twists me up just like it always does. "This isn't smart."

"Sure. Sure. I'm Betsy's granddaughter. You should stop."

"That's not what I mean."

I move from beneath him and walk into the room, where that stupid cat has pulled all my clothes from the bag.

"Go. You said you were going," I say sitting down on the bed and falling back on it.

"I just mean—"

"Just go." I assume I'm shouting. It's loud in my head.

I let my eyes close, and I feel the sob in my chest. Maybe I'm crying. I'm so mad.

All I hear is the door closing behind him.

Road Tripping

Even though it hurts, I'm up.

The phone ringing and Grace's face on my screen could be looked at as a godsend, or sheer annoyance. I'm willing to give her the benefit of the doubt.

"You didn't text me last night," she scolds before I even say hello.

"I'm a grown ass woman. I don't have to check in." I don't even recognize my voice.

"Are you doing a walk of shame? Or is it a walk of *Oh-my-god?*" she laughs.

"Shut up."

"I will not. You've never taken a trip like this, so I'm going to keep checking in on you. Ashton wants to make sure the car is okay, too."

"The car is fine."

"So, tell me all about it—about him."

I close my eyes, my head still resting on the pillow, and Cosmo is snuggled up next to me.

"He's delightful."

Grace lets out a groan. "Delightful? What the hell, Liz? That makes him sound eighty. He's not eighty, right?"

"I showed you a picture of him."

"Right. But when he got there, was he eighty?"

That does have me laughing, and then wincing because it hurt so much. "No, he's certainly not eighty."

"Oh, is he in bed next to you? Please tell me he's in bed next to you."

"He's not in bed next to me."

"I'm so disappointed," she says, and I think, that makes two of us. "Why isn't he in bed with you?"

"He has his own room."

"No sparks? God, I was really hoping there would be sparks."

I laugh at that. "Oh, there were sparks. And then when he decided to go back to his room, there was some anger."

"You kicked him out?"

"No, he left. I know he left in good conscience because we were both drunk, but I might have been a bit too childish about it."

"Liz..." she scolds.

"What? I'm not used to meeting guys and just jumping into bed with them. That was out of character for me."

"You could use some character building, and I'm saying that out of love."

I'm not so sure she is.

"Listen," she continues, "call me along the way. Let me know you're safe, okay?"

"Okay."

"I mean it. Don't make me start hunting you down. And, Liz, enjoy the hell out of this. You're on an adventure of a lifetime and you deserve to have fun."

It's more like an adventure to end a lifetime, but I'll keep that to myself.

"I love you," I say to her.

"I love you, too," she replies and Cosmo lets out a loud meow and Grace laughs. "I love you too, Cosmo," she says before we disconnect our call.

I texted Mark at eight o'clock and told him that I'd meet him by the car. I think the only blessing from last night was that I never got up from that spot on my bed.

Cosmo let me sleep until seven, when he finally woke me up for food.

I managed a shower, but it hurt. I have no makeup on. My hair is piled on top of my head loosely, because any tighter and I'd cry.

My eyes are swollen, so I'm not taking off my sunglasses no matter what.

I've already had Tylenol, and I'm waiting for it to work on the pounding in my head, but it's taking its time.

Leaned up against my car, I can hear Cosmo's protest through the open windows. The fresh air is helping the sickness in my stomach, and the coffee in my hand is my fuel.

At almost nine o'clock, I pull my phone from my pocket to text Mark again, but the whistling has me looking up.

He's walking toward me, a duffle bag over his shoulder, a cup of coffee in each hand, and a baseball cap shielding sunglass-clad eyes.

"Good morning, beautiful," he says as he walks to me and holds out one of the cups. "I guess you have one, but something tells me, we'll need a few of these this morning."

I narrow my gaze at him, from behind my own sunglasses. "Why are you chipper?"

"Why shouldn't I be?"

Oh, I can think of a million reasons. The fact that he walked out on me last night is the reason *I'm* not chipper. So why should *he* be?

I take the cup, and now I have one in each hand, which seems to be my downfall because when he drops his bag to the ground, steps in, easing so we're nearly pressed together, I can't move.

"You're beautiful," he says looking down at me.

"You're still drunk."

Mark shakes his head. "Perfectly sober. Slight headache."

"You're an asshole."

Instead of being offended, he laughs. "I sober easily."

Obviously, I don't.

He lifts his hand to my face and brushes back a wayward lock of hair. Then he lowers his head and gently brushes a kiss across my lips.

"Let's try this again," he says, hovering just a breath from my mouth. "Good morning."

I'm confused. He walked out on me after having pushed my dress up around my waist. And now he's kissing me?

When his lips press to mine, with more intent now, I accept the kiss. In the few hours I was asleep, I missed his lips. It's stupid. I want to be mad—I am mad—but I still want that connection to him.

He eases back, setting his hand on my waist. "Everything okay?" he asks.

"No."

That's enough to have him stepping back from me, wrapping his hands around his cup.

"Okay, what's wrong?"

"What's wrong?" The assault begins. "You walked out on me."

"Liz, I was being sensible."

"Sensible? I let my guard down and trusted you to—to..." I sound pathetic not knowing what I'd really expected except sex.

Mark moves in again. "We were drunk. When we take this to the next level, I want to remember it. I want to be present in all of it. Me leaving last night was the hardest thing, but it was the right thing."

"Right for who?"

He smiles. "For us."

Moving in until his body is pressed to mine, he lifts his hand to my cheek and holds it there.

"You said something last night, and I kept thinking about it. You're Betsy's granddaughter."

That has me shifting away from him and opening my car door with one finger, since each of my hands are wrapped around a coffee cup.

"Liz, stop," he says.

"What? I'm okay to kiss and to fondle, but not to take to bed?"

"I don't want to just take you to bed."

"Right. Because I belong to Betsy."

"You don't belong to anyone," he says and then obviously rethinks it. "I mean you're your own woman. And if you want to sleep with a man, you get to do what you want."

"Except with you."

"You're impossible," he says picking up his duffle bag and walking to the back of the car.

"I'm impossible?" I ask as he opens the hatch and throws his bag in the back.

"Yes. You're not even listening to me. So why bother?"

"I'm listening. I was going in with no regrets. I was part of that decision last night. You walked out."

"And I told you why."

"Because of my grandmother."

"No. See, you're not listening."

I set the coffees in the cup holders in the car and walk to the back with my fists on my hips. "Tell me again."

Mark sets his coffee on the roof and backs me against the car. Both of his hands come to my face now and he lowers his mouth to mine. I'm drowning in him again. Why can't I pull away? Why don't I want to pull away?

My arms come around him as he slides one hand to the nape of my neck, the other down my side to my waist. As his tongue slips through my lips, I ease against him. Is he doing this to confuse me?

When he pulls back, I realize my eyes are still closed behind my sunglasses.

"You are Betsy's, so you deserve more care," he says softly and I open my eyes. "You deserve my attention—all of my attention. You deserve to be cared for. You deserve to be treated special. Living a life with no regrets doesn't mean no respect." His hand comes back to my cheek and I look up at him. "I didn't leave because I didn't want you. Quite the contrary. I want all of you, and I don't want you to regret a single moment."

My lips part with a sigh.

I straighten. "I don't regret what happened."

"Good," he says softly.

I lick my lips because my mouth has gone dry. It's sweet that he wants to shower me with all this attention.

But in this moment, everything makes sense to me.

We're fooling ourselves thinking this is about taking chances and not regretting the decision. I'm lonely, so of course I'm attracted to this man, but we're only means to one another's end.

He needs me for his book.

I need him for answers.

This little game Gran is playing forces us together, but this isn't romance. Anything that happens between us will never work.

I steady myself, my back still braced against the car. "I appreciate the care you are extending to me."

Mark's eyes scan over me. "But?"

I swallow hard, somewhat embarrassed that he can read me this well. "But, maybe it was for the better," I say even though it's bitter on my tongue. "I mean, we were thrown into this weird situation. I don't know you. You don't really know me. We have Gran in common, that's all. We're mourning. I have so much to do to finalize her life," I say and wince at the words.

Mark steps back and runs his hand over the back of his neck before reaching for his coffee on top of the car.

"I get it," he says. "Give me your keys."

"Why?"

"I'm taking the first leg. I think you could use a little more sleep."

I purse my lips, but pull the keys from my pocket anyway and hand them to him.

Without another word, he takes his coffee from the top of the car, and walks to the driver's side, climbing into the car.

I take a moment to collect myself. Regret is a funny thing. I didn't think I'd regret *not* sleeping with the man. And now that we're trying to be open and clear on things, I regret that this thing between us can't be anything. We live thousands of miles apart and the only thing we have in common is a love for my late grandmother.

I'm about to rock Mark's world by selling the house he lives in, and he's about to shake mine up by sharing what he knows about Gran.

Maybe it's the hangover.

Maybe it's just being a sensible adult.

Either way, it hurts.

I walk around to the other side of the car and pull open the door.

Mark is wiping at his eyes and quickly puts his sunglasses back on.

"Is that Betsy in the back seat?" he asks.

I look in the seat behind me where I have Gran's urn belted in.

"Yes," I say as I climb into the car.

Mark draws in a deep breath. "I wasn't quite ready for that realization."

I watch him as he starts the car and adjusts the mirrors.

We're both hurting, and now I know that it's only going to get worse.

Turkey Sandwiches

In the three and a half hours to Atlanta, Mark and I have mostly driven in silence.

I'll admit, I slept on purpose. I couldn't take it.

Maybe I was wrong to stop his advances. He was being sincere, and God, all I want to do—well, is him.

"You good to drive from Atlanta to Valdosta?" he asks as he pulls off the highway.

"Yeah," I say.

"We'll eat first. Maybe walk around for a bit."

"That sounds nice," I say, and I'm surprised when he reaches for my hand, lifts it to his lips, and kisses my fingers.

"I'm sorry," he says, sliding his fingers through mine.

I blink a few times, mostly to make sure I'm awake. "Why?"

"I was so excited to have you with me that I crashed your road trip. Then, I didn't even consider that you're mourning. You have work to do while you're on this trip, and all the things you have to do in Florida and back home in Colorado. Betsy didn't have a simple life. There are accounts and houses and plans," he says and then draws in a deep breath. "That's a lot for you, and I shouldn't have made it worse."

I'm not sure how to reply to that. Not only is none of this his fault, but shit, he just made me realize how much there is to be done for Gran. We're going to have to work together. I'm going to need to remember that I need his help. And in return, I have the letters for him for his research.

My job is to finish Gran's life. His job is to make sure it's never forgotten.

Mark pulls the car into a lot and I look around. There is a restaurant on each corner and small shops line the streets.

"They serve a great burger," he says, pointing to the restaurant across the street. "They also have sandwiches and salads, too," he adds.

"I think that sounds good."

"Then, I want to take you somewhere. Is that okay?"

The fact that he's still wanting to spend time with me helps heal that ache in my chest.

"Of course."

Mark cracks the windows on the car slightly and I open Cosmo's crate. I swear the cat nodded at me as if to say, *Go, I'll be fine.*

We walk toward the restaurant side by side, but Mark doesn't reach for my hand. I must be desperate, because I turned the man away, and yet, I'm heartbroken I'm not walking hand in hand with him.

I'm going to need some therapy over this. Hell, I've been in therapy since my mother died. I should know how to handle this. But, in my defense, I've never lost my grandmother, inherited a seven-million-dollar house, and had a man thrust into my life that I can't keep my mind off of.

I don't date. I don't do relationships. I've never considered marriage, and I don't want kids. I'm the kind of professional woman who is fine with working from home, going to the occasional office mixer or Christmas party, and yes, once in a while, having a nice night with a man. Being with Mark is different, and I'm not in tune with that yet.

I need to write all of this down for my next session, when I get home—after I live in Gran's house with this man.

I steady myself with a long exhale, but I keep it as quiet as possible so Mark doesn't hear it.

When we reach the front of the restaurant, Mark opens the door for me and I step into a world of scents that have my stomach growling.

"I forgot to eat breakfast," I say.

"This is a good hangover cure," he says.

"You've been here a lot?"

"Quite a few times," he admits as we walk to the counter. "The burgers are a bit greasy. So, if your stomach isn't quite right yet, you might try something else."

"I'd actually rather have a turkey sandwich."

He nods. "You can't go wrong there either. They do have potato and macaroni salad, but the fries are those big steak fries that are amazing in ranch dressing."

I can't help but smile up at him. "You *have* been here a lot."

Mark grins, places his hand at the small of my back, and we walk to the counter.

I order my turkey sandwich, and fries with ranch. I mean, how could I not?

Mark orders the hamburger, and I eye him coolly. "Your stomach is okay?"

He shrugs. "I can recline on the drive. You're driving the rest of the way," he says and nudges me in the arm with his elbow.

They give us a plastic number and we sit down at a table by the window.

Outside I see people moving in and out of the small stores. Tourists, maybe, exploring what Atlanta has to offer just outside of downtown. I can see an old theater marquee down another street, the kind that would once be illuminated in florescent lights and big letters added underneath with the name of the show playing. I wonder if it's still a theater, or if it's been turned into something else.

Most of the stores are the kind you find in quaint little towns. Candles. Fudge. Souvenirs. There's a bookstore next to a coffee house, and a bar on an adjacent corner.

"This is a cute spot," I say, twisting off the top to my soda bottle and taking a sip. The liquid fizzes down my throat and bubbles come right back up, causing me to cover my mouth to stifle the burp, but it feels so good after last night. "Sorry."

He's grinning at me, but he doesn't seem put off by that.

"Yeah, this part of town just went through a revitalization. They cleaned it up, preserved some, tore some down. You know the drill."

More than anyone, I think. I lived in a part of Denver that used to be affordable housing and commercial properties. Now it's new builds next to hundred-year-old houses, mixed in with high-rise apartments, and little bars and restaurants that once never would have been there.

"Have you always lived in Palm Beach?" I ask, because I guess I should know the guy that I wanted so badly to sleep with last night.

"Mostly. Mom is in Orlando, that's where I was born. Dad," he shrugs. "Dad was in Orlando with us. Moved to Houston. Did some living in a van in Montana, and then Seattle. Last I heard he was in Oregon. Still in the van."

"You don't talk to him much?"

"Not much. Don't get me wrong. It wasn't as if he up and left me. I mean he did. He was a nomad. Passing through here. Passing through there. Mom was a homebody. So it didn't work out for them, or us. They get along. I always heard from him growing up and he'd always visit on his own time frame. It was just how it was."

I can't help but think how similar we were in that aspect. He had a dad that he knew, but he didn't know him. I didn't even know the name of my dad—that's a lie. His name is Sam. Mom never was sure of his last name.

"And you went to live with your grandfather when you were twelve?"

He nods as the server brings our food and sets it down in front of us on red trays.

Mark thanks him, and slides him a few dollars. I don't know if he wanted me to see that or not, he'd done it in such a manner I could have easily missed it. Then again, the kid that delivered the food is so surprised, I would have noticed his face, and certainly caught the excited, "Thank you."

Mark turns to his tray and begins to arrange his food. "I did," he says, answering my question. "Mom was dating a guy, and it was serious. But, the guy was not a huge fan of kids."

"And she still kept the guy?"

He shrugs. "For a while. But I knew to get out as fast as I could. He treated Mom okay, I never saw anything there that would make me think otherwise, but I needed attention, and neither of them could give it to me. Grandpa said there was room with them, so I went."

I picked up one of the fries, nearly too hot to hold, but I dragged it through the ranch, and then bit into it, sorry that I had.

It burned, and I sucked in air through my teeth to try and cool it.

Finally, I managed. Picking up my soda, I opened it and took a sip.

When I'd recovered, I picked up another fry and held it in my fingers. "He lived with Gran then?"

Mark nodded. "He did. They'd been together for a few years. Grandpa was a screenwriter. I think that's where I got my desire to write. I used to sit with them when they wrote. I just picked up on it."

Did he even know he'd just laid on a shit ton of information?

"I don't remember Gran living with anyone," I say before biting into the fry I held.

"Until you guys came out to Florida, I don't think your mom and grandma talked much. That was a moment of coming together, if you will."

"I didn't know that either. Well, not until you'd mentioned it to me."

"Grandpa said your mom was fine with him. Maybe even a little jealous that he doted on your grandmother, and no one doted on her—your mom."

That hurt, but it was probably true.

Mark bit into his fry. "Anyway, she was a grandmother to me, and Grandpa loved having me there. I made a few friends, though, like I said, there weren't a lot of kids around."

He picked up his burger and held it. "Betsy always said she'd love to have you with us, but your mom wouldn't have it. She'd run from what Betsy had, and who Betsy was, and there was no bringing her back."

"So when Mom died, why didn't Gran pack me up and move me?"

He set the hamburger down. "Your mom asked her not to. She wanted you to have an average and normal life. Liz, your grandmother wasn't just a retired actress shacking up with a screenwriter in a big house in Palm Beach. Genevieve Paige disappeared, in person, in the early sixties. Then, G.E. Paige, emerged."

I pick up another fry and lower it again. I lift my soda to take a drink, but put it back down too. Then, I wipe my mouth with the napkin on my tray.

"G.E. Paige?" I ask.

"You know the name, right?"

"G.E. Paige wrote the biggest movies in the sixties and seventies. Didn't they write some of the early rom coms of the eighties too?"

The corner of his mouth turned up into that smile that absolutely undid me every time I saw it. "The writing team of G.E. Paige and Tom Watts."

It all fell into place in that moment. My grandmother was a fucking Hollywood icon in multiple avenues—but to me she was the dollar store, bargain shopping, keeper of her father's ashes in a coffee can, cat lady. God, I missed her.

Learning Opportunity

"That's why you know all of those famous people," I say as Mark and I walk down the street. "Because of Gran and your grandpa?"

His hands are in his pockets, and I wonder if that is to keep from me grabbing hold.

"They knew a lot of people," he says in that charming way that says, *Yes, I know a lot of famous and rich people,* but that keeps the, *I'm a normal man who writes biographies and gave up my cat,* sort of tone.

"I can't believe she could keep all of this from me."

"She did what your mother asked. But if I'm honest about it, I think she liked it. I think she liked stepping away from all the limelight. She never was one to be changed by it."

"Really? My grandmother owns a seven-million-dollar house. I know she's had her share of lovers and moved around. You don't think she was changed by it?"

Mark chuckled. "But that came with who she was anyway, not her stature. The names of the men were just more notable because of who she knew."

"Are you saying my grandmother was just a slut?"

The word hurt to say, but Mark grinned at it. "No. I'm saying she was a forward-thinking woman. And I think women who are confident in themselves and enjoy the pleasure of men are incredible."

"I'm not sure how I'm taking that."

"I mean, since the beginning of time, men who have multiple partners are studs. Women have always been looked down on for it. It's crap. Sure, I believe in relationships. I believe in marriage even though my parents didn't. I believe in a steady home, whether it be in Palm Beach or Denver. Your grandmother did nothing wrong. She accepted herself and was confident."

"Well that sounds better the way that you say it than what I think."

"Am I to believe that she raised you to be closed off to all of that?"

"You didn't know Betsy as Gran, remember."

"Not in the same way you did. You have to remember, she was sleeping with my grandfather when I met her."

"Oh-my-god!" I can't help but sound childish. It was a horrible thought.

Mark laughs from deep within now. "What did she have to say about sex to you?"

"I don't want to have this conversation on some street corner in Atlanta."

"Here. There. What does it matter?"

There's a bench in front of the candy store, and I have to sit down. This is how it's going to be, isn't it? One thing will lead to another. We will each get the parts of this journey when they are presented.

He will learn about Gran. I will learn about Betsy.

This, well, this wasn't what I thought I'd learn today.

Mark sits next to me. I run my hands down my thighs, and he takes advantage of the movement to take my right hand and thread his fingers with mine.

"She didn't like my high school boyfriend, so to say she kept me close would be an understatement." I look at our joined hands and ease against the back of the bench. Mark has this way of making me relax, no matter what.

I continue, "You'll keep your wits about you and your knees together, Gran would say." I enjoy watching Mark's face shift from smiling to surprised. "Stay true to yourself until you're ready, she'd add."

"And that worked?"

I let out a snort of a laugh. "Yeah. C'mon, who wants to disappoint their grandmother? She was right. I stayed true to myself until I was ready."

His mouth worked from smile to pursed. "I gotta know. When were you ready?"

"When were you?"

"When I was thirteen," he says, grinning.

"You had sex when you were thirteen? Where did you find someone to do that?"

"Wow!" He laughs even harder and squeezes my hand. "You think that's what I meant?"

"It wasn't?"

"No. You asked when I was ready."

I shake my head and give him an eye roll. His comment was worthy of it.

He kisses my fingers again, just as he had in the car. "I was a late bloomer, but then again, like I said, there weren't a lot of girls my age hanging around in the neighborhood."

"So, how old was she?"

His lips pucker. "You assume I went older?"

"I'm banking on it."

"Actually, you already know. Twenty-six."

"Holy shit! I was right?"

"It was Bridget Bloom," he confirms, and I remember our conversation about them dating. "I was twenty. She was twenty-six." He wipes his free hand over the back of his neck. "She was in town for the winter, staying with her grandparents, and basically hiding out. It didn't last long. But it was something for a month." He grins. "Luckily, I could always grow a beard. I looked older."

"She didn't know you were twenty, did she?"

"She did not."

"Did you ever tell her?"

"We weren't going to be a permanent fixture, so I didn't see the need."

"You're a romance novel just waiting to be written," I say, and his face becomes more serious.

"Are you going to write it?"

I'm a bit taken aback by that. "Maybe I will."

The grin out of the side of his mouth twists me up again.

"So tell me, oh blessed granddaughter of Genevieve Paige, G.E. Paige, and Betsy Evans, when were you true to yourself?"

Again I shake my head. This man.

"College. When I was eighteen."

"Someone special?"

I wince. "No. It just felt like the right time."

"You're not really going to hold your grandmother's life against her then, are you?"

"I'm feeling a bit childish now."

Mark shrugs. "You should always be unapologetically Liz. Betsy was unapologetically Betsy. There was the fancy part of Betsy. The shoulder-rubbing, queen of words, multimillionaire. And then there's the woman with a cat, a dollar store addiction, and a granddaughter that she's so freaking impressed by, that she tells the local boy about her granddaughter every Sunday when she calls."

I look up into his soft blue eyes and he's smiling at me.

"Who told you she had an addiction to the dollar store?" I ask.

"It was easy to figure out when she'd call me on Sunday and tell me about her week, which always included multiple trips to the dollar store."

I study him for a moment. "She'd call you every Sunday?" I ask.

"Every Sunday since she left Florida."

I think about the day she died and he'd called. Then I remember that the alarm on her phone went off, and it was titled WATTS. How could I always have missed that she called home on Sundays?

"How long were they together?" I ask.

Mark draws in a breath as if it helped him remember. "I think I was nine or ten."

"When did he die?"

"Six years ago."

I cross my legs and rest our linked hands on my knee. "Six years? That would have been the last time Gran went to Florida."

"Yep. When she stole my cat."

I laugh at that. "She asked me to go with her."

"I'm sorry you didn't."

"I didn't know why she wanted to go. And, I won't fly. I can't fly. I couldn't go."

"She was different when she came out for Grandpa's funeral. I think I knew it would be the last time she'd return."

"You've always lived in the house then?"

Mark shrugs again. "I'd actually moved in a few months before Grandpa died to take care of him. I'd moved out for college. When he needed me, I moved home."

"Why didn't Gran move back when I went to college?"

"Liz, you still needed her. She felt as if she owed it to you, but not as if you stole her life and made her stay. She wanted to be with you, to be a part of your life. In all the years she and Grandpa were together, they never talked about marriage and forever. Even if they were perfect together. So when she left, he stayed, they talked on the phone often and once in a while Betsy would help him work through some scripts he was writing."

"Tom Watts," I say his grandfather's name, and tears begin to well in my eyes. "She used to talk about him, but I thought he was just someone she knew from the senior center. I didn't know who he was to her." I wipe at my eyes.

"My statement about her being an actress till the end, stands."

I chuckle and squeeze my eyes close. When I open them, I look at him. "When did she ask you to write the book?"

"She didn't. Grandpa did and Betsy went along with it. It's been in the works for over a decade. We started it when she'd come to visit. Then it was phone calls and letters."

"Thank you," I say, and Mark's brows draw in.

"Why?"

"For keeping alive a part of her that I didn't know about. I couldn't have given her that."

He bats his eyes as if they too were going moist. "The world needs to know her."

"I think you're right."

Mark stands. Taking my hands, he pulls me to my feet. "C'mon. I want to show you something."

Marquee

This time as we walk down the street, we hold hands. I'm not sure when it all changed for me in the past few hours. In the parking lot in Nashville, I knew I couldn't let him touch me again, or kiss me. But now, there's comfort in it.

Gran had lots of relationships, and the woman I knew was never broken—except when her daughter died. Mark and I will always have a relationship. Sex or not—romance or not—we are forever connected through Gran.

We walk until we reach the theater I'd seen from the restaurant. The marquee is even more magnificent than it appeared from across the street.

"Why are we here?" I ask.

Mark leads me by my hand to a small display window near the elegant gold-plated framed glass entrance doors.

Without a word, he points to the display.

Inside there is a photo of Gran and Tom standing next to an old movie camera. The lapels on Tom's jacket have me laughing. That and his sideburns, which scream that the photo is from the seventies.

Gran, who would have been in her thirties, and already a

mother, has long red hair. It's stick straight, so I know she'd had it ironed out. Not only did we share the red, we shared the curls too.

She has on a pantsuit, and though it was very modern in its time, I'm quite sure she has matching ones in her closet back in Colorado, which only makes this secret life of hers so unbelievable. Anyone who was a starlet, used to being in front of a crowd, and rich wouldn't still wear those kinds of clothes.

Next to the photo is the movie poster of *Thief of Reality*.

I'd seen the movie once in a college film class. To be honest, I don't remember the premise of it, except that it had a Pontiac Trans Am, and Mom always loved those cars.

I swallow hard because my throat is clogging with tears.

"Their names were on the test I took in college for the film class I took. I remember writing the names Paige and Watts." I laugh. "I got half credit because I hadn't filled in their full names."

"You remember that?" Mark wraps his arm around my shoulders and pulls me to his side. "This one was filmed here, in Atlanta," he says. "It opened the theater after renovation."

I look into the lobby from where I'm standing. "Did they renovate it in 1976, and that was it?"

"Pretty much," he laughs, and it warms me.

"Thank you for sharing this with me."

"I come here whenever I'm in the area. Just knowing this picture is here makes me happy—they were happy."

I turn to face him. "Were they?"

"They really were."

I drive and Mark sleeps for the hour from Atlanta to Macon. He stirs as I pull off the highway.

"Why are we stopping?" he asks. "Are you okay?"

I smile, looking back where Cosmo has settled himself next to Gran in the seat.

"I'm fine. I saw a billboard for some stores in Macon, and I thought I'd like to drive through. Do you mind?"

He lifts his sunglasses and wipes his tired eyes. "I don't mind. I'm as free as a bird until Saturday."

The comment has my shoulders tightening. Saturday. I'm going to meet all the people Gran never shared with me—beyond Mark and Tom.

I pull my lips in between my teeth. I'm not going to cry. This is what this road trip is all about. Making it to Florida to say goodbye to Gran.

"Liz, that light is red," Mark's panicked voice has me slamming on my brakes. He turns to look at me. "You okay?"

"I'm fine," I say, clenching my jaw. *Pull it together, Liz,* I scold myself.

I drive into town, following the signs to the shops that had been advertised. I park in a lot and turn off the car. Resting my head back against the seat, I take a few moments to collect myself.

Mark turns in his seat, and even Cosmo moves up through the seats and into Mark's lap.

"I'm sorry," I say. "You said Saturday, and I remembered that we're going to say goodbye to her." I look in the back seat, and so does Mark.

"I didn't mean to—"

"It's not you. This whole trip has me mixed up." I wipe at my eyes.

"We'll be home soon and then we can take our time."

"That's not my home," I say and my voice shakes. "I don't belong anywhere but back where I'm from. Everything I'm heading to is a mystery to me. A secret kept."

"Liz—"

"I know. I know, this is stupid. I shouldn't get worked up about it."

"You have every right to get worked up about it. But regardless we have to get there and fulfill her dying wish. We're a team, Liz. You and me. We're all either one of us has. You and me," he repeats.

"I'm miserable."

He chuckles. "Because of me? Because of this drive?"

"Because she's gone, and I didn't get to know this wonderful other side to her," I shout, then clamp my hands over my mouth.

"Baby," he says and I reach for him, planting both of my hands on either side of his face. I pull him in and press my trembling lips to his. He covers my hands with his and deepens the kiss.

I need him. I need this man and I'm going to push him away with my crazy. I need him to help me honor my grandmother. I need him to help me understand the part of her I never knew. I need everything he knows about Gran, Mom, and me. I need to understand the relationship our grandparents had and know that Gran was loved.

I need this man to love me.

"It's okay," he says with his lips still brushing mine. "It's okay to hurt. But I'm here, baby. I'm here."

I ease back and push up my sunglasses. Wiping my palms over my cheeks, I don't even care what I look like sitting this close to him sobbing. "You said they were happy."

Mark wipes away a tear I missed, keeping his hand on my cheek. "Betsy and my grandfather?" I nod. "They were. They were very happy."

"Why didn't they ever get married."

Mark barks out a laugh and gathers my hands in his as Cosmo moves from his lap to mine.

"Your grandmother never wanted to be married. She had her chances. Men proposed. Grandpa even said he'd asked once or twice. She didn't want to be a wife. Grandpa had been married, and it didn't end well. So he figured if she was happy, and he was happy, they didn't need marriage."

"But they were together until..."

Mark nods. "When your mom called and said her cancer was terminal, and she only had weeks left, Betsy packed up, kissed us goodbye, and took off. She called and told us what to pack, and we shipped it."

"And your grandfather stayed in the house?"

"At first I think we thought she'd bring you home. When she made it clear that she wasn't going to do that, she asked Grandpa to stay and take care of the house. When he died, she asked the same of me."

"What happened to him when she left? Your grandfather," I add.

"He was a miserable old man," Mark laughs. "But he kept working. He wrote up until a few years before he died. They still worked together. He'd send her things, and she'd give him input, but G.E. Paige disappeared, just as Genevieve Paige had."

"Did he ever get involved with anyone else?"

Mark shakes his head. "It was only Betsy. She came back at least once every year. You'd be at camp or spending the weekend with Grace or other friends. She came more often when you went to college. They had an epic long-distance relationship," he says, humored by it.

"I'm glad she had him, and you."

"I'm glad we had her too."

Cosmo moves so that he paws at my chest. I ease back and hold him against me. "I think he needs to get out for a bit."

"Do you have a leash for him?"

Now I burst out a laugh. "No. We should get one."

"I'll put him in my hoodie for now. Hopefully he won't be a jerk and claw his way out."

The hoodie works until we find a leash at a quaint little pet store, which also happens to have some specialty cat toys which Mark spoils Cosmo with. There is an ice cream store, and while Mark waits with Cosmo, I buy us a chocolate shake for us to share.

We walk down the street and look into each of the shops. We'd only just eaten in Atlanta, but the pizza restaurant smells amazing. I'm going to remember to come back through on my drive home.

At the end of the street is a two-story building with a plaque that says *Bridal Mecca*. It had a store for everything a bride would need to plan a wedding. But there is an Italian specialty store among the bridal themed businesses, so we walk in.

Mark buys me a beautiful scarf, something he thought Gran would have enjoyed. It was handmade in Lucca, Italy, and he says he'd remembered Gran talking about her European travels.

"There are journals at the house. They're yours. You can travel with her, and know exactly what she thought about the different places she saw."

Finally, I feel as if there is some hope in my heart. I'll never see Italy, or anywhere that I can't drive to. Gran is going to transport me there.

Mark takes my hand, and we lead our shared cat down the street and back to the car.

Back to Work

Mark took the cat with him to his hotel room, and I have to admit, I'm having a hard time focusing. Cosmo has been my working buddy for months. Sitting down to write out my next article without him on my feet or my lap hinders my creativity.

I have my notes from the first few days of my journey. Somewhere between Kansas and Missouri, I had taken the time to dictate my feelings over losing Gran. That grief piece that Julie wanted will need to be scaled down. Although, I wonder if I should hold on to it. I have days that are better than others. And much like Mark, when I see her urn in the car or on the table next to me, it hits different every time. Saturday, there will be people who want to say goodbye to her that I don't even know. There will be tears from people that knew and loved her, and I'm going to have to handle that.

I haven't been to the house yet. I haven't read the rest the letters. I don't know all of the stories about her relationship with Tom Watts.

I don't know what Mark has compiled for his book.

And I haven't gone home without Gran yet—after I let her go.

Grief hasn't even hit yet, I realize—and that begins my article.

Well? Did you sleep with the guy yet? Grace's text is accompanied with every curious and surprised emoji there is.

Is that all you care about? I reply.

Along with the news I gave you the other day comes the reality that pregnancy hormones make you horny and feel unattractive all at the same time. So, yeah, it's all I care about.

I chuckle as I look at the phone and then at the work I'm doing on my laptop. I know she knows there's so much more to this trip, but her lightheartedness makes me smile.

No news, but we're "friendly." I type in and add a GIF of a guy seductively, or creepily, raising his eyebrows.

Hmmm. Fine. Keep it all to yourself. But, when you get home, I'm going to want details. And I mean ALL the details.

I promise, I reply. *I'm working on an article now. I'll text you tomorrow.*

My head has been down for the past hour as I type away on my computer. I can feel the tension in my shoulders, but I'm on a roll. I'll write about grief once I process it, but Julie's article is about knowing that grief hasn't even settled in me yet. I add the story about the letter and Gran's last wishes.

I'm into my second article when there is a knock at the door.

There's a moment of being startled, a second of annoyance, because I'm working and in the zone, and then there is comfort in knowing that on the other side of that door just might be the sexiest man I've ever known—and he likes me.

Luckily it's the cat and the sexy man, who has a coffee in each hand.

"I thought you could use a break," he says as Cosmo walks into the room to check it out.

I grip the front of Mark's shirt and pull him through the door, shutting it by pressing his back up against it and taking possession of his mouth. His hands are extended out, still holding the cups, but it doesn't hinder his ability to participate in the kiss.

When I can't breathe anymore, I step back, and he grins. "I don't remember the last time I've been greeted like that. Tell me it wasn't just because I come bearing coffee."

"That's iffy," I say with a wink, and eye each cup until he holds one out to me.

"How's it coming?"

"I changed directions on my angle for my articles," I say, walking back to the table by the window where I have my laptop open and my pad of notes. There are also wrappers from miscellaneous snacks I've been eating since I got to the room.

"What's your angle now?"

I lift my eyes to him. "About how grief comes in different stages. I grieved when Gran died. I grieved finding her letter. I have grieved multiple times on this trip, but I've also had a hell of a time, which I think was her point. But it's also been a bitch of a trip. I haven't met the people who loved her yet and also will mourn her, and I haven't set foot into her house yet."

Mark gives me a slow nod as he lifts his cup to his mouth and sips his coffee.

"That's a lot to think about."

"It is. I wrote an article on the hotel in Nashville and added a review of the restaurant. I sent it with some pictures I took when I got there, and she was happy to have a travel piece. Well, not happy, but satisfied. I told her my plan for the articles, and she seemed to be okay with my shift."

"Then I suppose it's been a successful afternoon then," he says, stepping closer to me.

I could easily get used to the kind of distraction that Mark Watts is to me. But, I have to remember it's temporary. Even when I move back home, he might still be part of my life, but it'll take planning. That doesn't always work out. But for now, as Gran had said, I'm living my life to the fullest on this trip, and I'm not going to have any regrets—I swear it.

"Your choice," he says, twisting one of my loose curls into his fingers. "We can go out and get dinner, or we can order in."

"I'm exhausted. Order in?"

"I think that sounds perfect." He eases in and nips my lips with a kiss before retreating toward the nightstand where the room service menu sits open. "I know we're under a time crunch tomorrow, and we need to get to Palm Beach so we can get settled and ready for Saturday, but do you mind if we stop in Orlando?"

"Needing a Disney fix?" I tease and he shakes his head.

"I want you to meet my mom."

Just as I'm about to take a sip from my coffee, he hits me with that? Is he kidding?

"You want me to meet your mom?"

"I do."

I set my cup on the table. My hands are shaking. God, when was the last time I met a man's mother?

"Will she be okay meeting me?"

Mark sits on the edge of the bed and flips through the menu. "Why wouldn't she be okay with it? She loved Betsy. She'll love to meet you too."

"Does she know she's going to meet me?" I ask, walking to the bed and sitting next to him.

He hands me the menu. "She knows where I am. She knows who I'm with."

"That didn't answer my question." I raise a brow.

"No. Mom is one of those people that if I tell her I'm coming to see her, she talks me out of it."

"Why?"

"She's a bit of a hermit. As much as my father is a nomad, Mom is the opposite."

I study the menu and hand it back to him. "Club and fries."

"Can't go wrong with that."

Mark calls in the order. Cosmo has curled up on his blanket in the corner. And we sit quietly—on the bed.

"How much time do you need to finish up your work?" Mark asks, reaching for my hand and lacing our fingers together.

I know this is new, but I've never held hands with someone and it makes every nerve in my body tingle.

"I sent off an article for the next issue. I have solid footing for the next. I suppose I could close up shop for the night," I say smiling, looking down at his thumb brushing the side of my hand.

"Good," Mark says, turning and lifting his open hand up into my hair and pulling me back onto the bed with him. "We have some time before dinner gets here to make out like randy teenagers."

I smile against his mouth as he presses his lips against mine, and takes me under.

That Florida/Georgia Line

Mark hadn't gone to his own room until midnight. Though it would have been easy to have him never leave my bed, we'd agreed, when his hand had grazed my bare stomach and Cosmo jumped up on the bed, that having the cat in the room with us was just a bit too much. We decided that we'd revisit the randy teenage thing when we got to the house and could shut the door on the cat.

And because it had been so late when he finally left my room, we opted for a later start time to head to Orlando.

This time, it was me walking toward him with coffees in hand, and a bag of pastries hanging from my fingers.

"You are a sight," he says, the corner of his mouth turning up.

My hair is braided, I'm wearing shorts, because it's starting to get warmer the further south we travel, and because I'm living with no regret, I didn't put on a bra this morning and I might have a little jiggle to my walk. Notably, when you order coffees from a twenty-year-old barista with air-conditioned, cold-hard nipples, you get the pastries for free.

I hand him the bag and one of the cups. He takes them, but he's scanning a slow look over me.

"Are you trying to kill me?" he groans.

"And you ask me that why?"

He groans again. "Because, Elizabeth, you know I want to touch you, and you're not exactly concealed."

It's my turn to give him a crooked smile and a side glance as I walk around him and climb into the passenger seat of the car.

Before I get situated, I look in the seat behind me to make sure everything is in place. Both of the back seats are empty except for Cosmo's blanket.

"Where's Gran?" I shout as I frantically put my coffee cup in the holder and he does the same. "Where is she?"

"She's in the back. I secured her in a box and—"

"No. No. She rides in the seat. Get her," I'm shouting, and now I'm shaking as I climb from the car because I have to get to her.

"Liz, I thought it was a better idea that we—"

"You don't get to think. You don't get to decide. This is my road trip. Not yours. Gran should be up here and not in some box." My voice grows loud enough that Cosmo hisses at me from his open crate. He didn't even come to help me fight my fight.

"I'll go get her," Mark says in an easy tone. "I'm sorry."

My breath is labored. My chest hurts. My hands are shaking.

Mark opens the back of the car and a moment later he comes around the side, opens the door behind me, and sets Gran in the seat. With care, he buckles the urn into the seat and closes the door. And to his credit, he pulls me into him instead of walking around to the other side and ignoring my feelings.

His hands move over my back as my cheek presses to his shoulder.

"I didn't think," he says, placing a kiss to the top of my head. "I mean no disrespect."

"I can't do this, can I? I can't let her go like she wants me to," I sob.

"You can't hold on to her in a cupboard either," he says. "She

216

knows that one first-hand, and this was her way of telling you that wasn't what she wanted."

"Shit," I mumble the curse into his chest before lifting my wet eyes to look at him. "I'm sorry I got so worked up."

"It's okay."

"No, it's not."

Mark brushes his thumbs over my cheek and wipes away the tears. "It is. She was your world, Liz. But look around you, there's so much more. And I'm here for you now."

And although I could argue that this thing with us is temporary, and I could take the mood in a totally different direction, I take in a deep breath and silence those thoughts.

We both know it's a temporary fix to the mourning we're doing.

I might as well let that be part of my well-lived life and not worry about what's going to happen next week, or the week after.

Mark likes podcasts about the silver screen years. I suppose that makes sense since he's written so many books about it.

Until we crossed the line from Georgia into Florida, it was something to keep our minds off of my temper tantrum, my lack of a bra, or what lays ahead for us.

But I did notice that with every sign we pass that says Orlando, Mark tenses a bit more.

When the podcast finishes, we sit in silence until I decide to ask some questions.

"How did Gran and Tom meet?" I ask, and I notice that Mark's shoulders ease a bit. He's working up this visit with his mother in his head, I can tell, because he's distant. This is an all too familiar sign to me. I do the same thing to myself.

"Grandpa stalked her," he says easily, but I cough out a laugh.
"He stalked her?"

"Yep. He was always a screenwriter, even when Genevieve Paige was gaining speed in Hollywood. When he'd learned that she'd retired to Palm Beach, he showed up there."

"She retired there when she was in her twenties," I remind him.

"Imagine how many times she turned him down over the years."

"Why would she turn him down?"

"Because she was young and living that amazing life," he says.

"Seriously?" I ask, turning in my seat. "Were they together even before my mother was born?"

"Oh, no," he laughs. "He didn't catch your grandmother until your mother was a teenager. Betsy had many suitors, so Grandpa went on and got married."

Mark readjusts in his seat as if he's stretching his back a bit. Driving for hours on end is miserable on your back and ass.

He continues, "Years later, he came at it as a working relationship, and Betsy bought into that and the duo of Tom Watts and G.E. Paige began."

"What does the E stand for," I ask, and then hold up my hand. "Never mind. I can't believe I even asked."

Mark chuckled. "I can't imagine, *Elizabeth*."

I shake my head. It's not as if my mind isn't filled with a million other things.

"What made them finally get together?"

Mark adjusts in his seat yet again. "Well," he winced, "my grandmother left him and filed for divorce."

And that made me wince too. "Because of Gran?"

"Yeah. Your mom was a junior in high school. Betsy and Grandpa's private relationship became accidentally public." He chews on his bottom lip. "It had been going on for a few years, and they got sloppy."

I sit back in my seat and press my hand to my stomach. "I'm sorry I asked."

"You would have learned about it. That's my job, remember?"

I nod and turn back toward him as Cosmo makes his way between the seats and hops into my lap.

"Okay, fair is fair. Ask me something about Gran that you don't know."

Mark puckers his lips as he considers. "You told me what kind of PTA president she was, but what kind of mother to a teenager was she?"

I blink hard. Of all the things, this is what he wants to know?

I have to think. Obviously she was a much different mother to me than she was to my mother. I never had the urge to run away —ever.

But then my situation was different. She was my guardian, but she wasn't my mother. She was my grandmother, and I was a girl who watched her mother die when she was ten. That changed a lot of shit in my life.

I run my hand over Cosmo's back. "I had a curfew—always. She made it a point to know all my friends, though I didn't hang out with anyone other than Grace. She was PTA president, and she volunteered enough around the school that I wouldn't be surprised when she'd just show up. She was attentive. She showed up to every concert or play I had. She asked about homework each night, and she proofread my essays. She let me sleep late on Sundays, watch what I wanted on TV, and always kept Oreos in the cupboard because I loved them and my mother had never let me have them. She was full of love for me, and she always made sure I knew. Only now I know she was living some secret life."

Mark shakes his head. "Nope, that doesn't play into your answer."

"Why not?"

"Because it doesn't answer the question. You answered my

question before the secret life thing. Now I know what kind of guardian she was for you."

"Fine. Is that what you thought?"

Mark shrugs. "I suppose it all fits the bill of the Betsy I knew."

I purse my lips and study him. "Did she mother you?"

"Oh yeah," he says with a chuckle. "She would have been my guardian, if you look at it like that, from the time I was twelve until I left for college."

When he says it like that, I find it hard to breathe. No wonder this man wants to be part of saying goodbye to her. He and I have had the same journey.

My mother died, and Gran stepped in and raised me. Mark went to live with his grandfather when he was twelve, and Gran was there in those formative years for him as well. And yet, I didn't know he existed until that day that WATTS came up on Gran's phone.

"So," I choke out the word, because this has become an emotional topic. "What kind of mother was she to you?"

The grin on Mark's mouth is wide. "Much different."

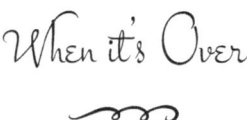

When it's Over

Cosmo stretches on my lap, and then puts his head up on my shoulder, forcing me to hold him against me. This stupid cat is so smart. He's grounding me.

Mark scratches the scruff that has grown on his face over the past few days as he contemplates. His lips tighten and I assume he's holding back the big smile that wants to break through.

"I had Oreos too, but then again, I just had to tell the housekeeper what I wanted, and she made it happen."

"Housekeeper?"

"I lived in the seven-million-dollar house," he reminds me.

"Right."

He runs his tongue over his teeth. "I didn't have a curfew. Betsy and Grandpa traveled a lot, so I was alone often. She bought me my first car, and taught me to drive a manual shift. She spent many, many nights in lounge chairs by the pool just listening to me as I talked about my mother, my father, feeling isolated and suicidal," he says and instinctively I reach for his hand.

Mark shifts a look my way and smiles, but it's weary.

"They traveled less then," he admits. "She got me some

guidance, got me involved in a writing community, she took to heart that I was in need of a steady home."

He pulls his hand back from me and wipes at his eyes. "She made sure I had a decent relationship with my mother, and if my dad breezed through town, she facilitated visits that left me with good memories. As an adult, I know she was making sure his visits didn't cause me any mental harm by just dropping in and out of my life."

He reaches for my hand again, and our fingers thread together. Cosmo, needing to be the center of attention, lays himself over our clasped hands which rest on the console.

We both chuckle.

"Anyway," he continues. "She knew she'd lost your mom. I mean, her focus on herself and her career caused the rift between her and your mom. Your trip to Florida when you were six was an olive branch trip, if you will. They mended that rift, and Betsy became part of your life after that. All the while, she was taking the role as my guardian, and trying to not make the same mistakes with me. When your mom died, and she packed up and took off, she was damned sure she wasn't going to isolate you in your time of need. So, she cut off the rest of her life and raised you."

"But then you lost her."

"I was almost on my way out the door. I was a senior in high school when she left," he admits. "I had a good head on my shoulders by the time I left for college. I had writing scholarships. I had a girlfriend who went to college with me," he says and jealousy zips through me. "Mom was single again, so I spent a lot of time with her. My life was in a good place when she left."

Cosmo saunters off and into the back seat.

Mark gives my hand a squeeze. "She did the best she could for all of us," he says. "She was a different person when she was raising your mom. She was a wiser person when she was raising me. And stepping away from everything when she raised you, was exactly what you needed."

"I would have thought that if she was proud of raising you, she would have told me about you."

Mark shrugs. "I think she needed you to know you were the only person in her entire world. You needed that."

"I could have shared."

"Could you have?" he asks, and I pull my hand out from his. "I mean it, Liz. You lost the only person in your life, and gained a new one. One that you knew, but not as well as you should have. Tell me that if she showed up and said, *well, I have this other kid*, you would have accepted that?"

"I'm not shallow."

"I'm not accusing you of being such. I'm saying that at ten, you needed her support one hundred percent. I wasn't around that much. She called me every week, just as she did until she died. I wasn't her responsibility, I never was. But she took me on. I knew that."

"Did you? Did you know you weren't hers? I don't think you did."

"You're turning around what I'm saying."

"She cut off everything to take care of me. She gave up her whole life. We're on this fucking trip because she wasn't open with me."

"Because she sat with me by the pool for years hoping I'd get up the next morning and live this life I was given. Do you think that maybe that crossed her mind, Liz?" His voice is rising and even Cosmo has retreated to sit in the back with the bags and boxes now. "I think that she gave you everything so that for a little while, you'd have everything. And now you have me."

I pull my sunglasses from my face and stare at him.

"Are you just some replacement?"

"No."

"You just think that she's dead and now I have to put up with you?"

"Put up with me?" he spits out the words. "Is that what you think?"

I ease back in my seat. "No."

"Good, because even though this is the strangest way to get involved with someone, I'm grateful as hell that Betsy sent you into my life. I know she was thinking that we'd both need someone now, and I'm glad as hell for it."

I turn my head to look at him, and my heart settles a bit. "I guess it can only get better from here, right?"

The corner of his mouth turns up in that half grin. "I know you have a lot of things to think about when we get to Florida. The house. Understanding who Betsy was to everyone else. Going home." He reaches for my hand again and laces his fingers between mine again. "You do what you need to do. I'll be okay in the end."

And in that moment, I realize that as afraid as I am to get my heart broken when I leave Florida, he's already resigned to it. He knows I'm here to sell the house and get out of Florida for good. We're both going to send Gran off in the way she wanted. I'll give him what he needs for the book, and he's holding up his end and telling me about the Gran I didn't know.

We're holding hands.

We're kissing when we can.

We're sharing this journey, and we both know it has nowhere to go.

"Will you still text me, no matter what happens from here on out?" I ask as he takes the exit off the highway.

"Of course."

"I mean, in the past week, knowing you're on the other end of the phone has meant the world to me. I don't ever want to lose that."

He gives my hand a squeeze before pulling his away so that he can maneuver through traffic. "Liz, no matter what happens between us, or after Palm Beach, we're connected. I don't want to lose that either."

Mom

Mark's mother doesn't live far from where we exit the highway. He parks the car outside a modest apartment building and sits silently.

"Maybe we should just keep going," he says.

"You don't want to see your mother?"

"I'm just rethinking it." He takes my hand, holds it in his, and studies the connection. "Last week when I was here, it was one of the first times I came and it was planned. Mom and I had a very nice talk, and she sent me home with those pictures I sent you. But it's not usually like that. I'm here for just a bit, and then it becomes awkward. I don't want it to be awkward for you too."

"Why would it be?"

"Because all of this is awkward." He lets out a tiny laugh. "Mom loved Betsy too. Maybe I should say, Mom learned to love Betsy. Who wouldn't? I'm actually grateful for that, because she could have been nasty about her. But Grandpa was happy, and that made my mom happy, no matter how their relationship came to be. But Mom's moods shift so quickly. She'll be happy to see me, but then she'll spend the entire time apologizing for the state of the apartment, or she'll tell me how tired she is and she'll need to rest soon."

"She's depressed."

"Severely. She's also medicated and goes through therapy. It's why her marriage didn't work out," he admits.

"Why don't you move her to Palm Beach? To the house?" I ask. His mother needs him.

Mark studies me. "It's not my house."

"It should be."

He shakes his head. "Let's not talk about this. Mom is fine. I make sure she's fine. I don't know how she'll be today."

"She knows you're with me?"

Mark nods and lifts my fingers to his lips, brushing a kiss over them. "I told her I was going to you and driving back with you."

"Okay. So she knows who I am."

"She knows your Betsy's granddaughter. And, she holds a bit of a grudge because Betsy left us for you."

"Maybe you should just go alone."

"No. Even when Betsy left, Grandpa loved her. I think he always knew it would have an end. But talk about a long-distance relationship that worked, for the most part."

I shake my head. "I was too young to worry that she was lonely. So, it's interesting that she wasn't."

He kisses my fingers again. "And I know, even apart, I'll never be lonely again either," he says and his words resonate through me.

I have to be very careful with this man. He's a master of words, but so am I. It's nothing for either of us to say something that takes hold, or something that can hurt to the core. But in this moment, I want to believe his words.

I take a few minutes to put on a bra and comb my hair before we step out of the car.

Mark tucks Cosmo into the crook of his arm. There's no leaving him in the car in this heat.

Tammy Watts lives on the third floor of an apartment building that has as many full-time residents as it has vacation rentals.

Her door has a fall wreath hanging from it, and a gnome in the front window.

Mark taps on the door. We'd held hands walking up the stairs, but as we walked toward her door, his hand slipped from mine. I know not to take it personally, but everything inside of me is conflicted at this moment.

The door opens slowly and a woman with wiry blonde hair peeks out. "Markey" she says lovingly before she closes the door, unhooks the chain, and then opens the door again.

She pulls Mark to her, and he kisses her on the cheek.

She looks at the cat. "I thought you gave away this cat," she says running her hand over Cosmo.

"I did."

His mother notices me standing there and steps back from Mark. "Who is this?" she asks, looking at me.

I take a breath to introduce myself, but Mark steps to the side. "Mom, this is Liz."

"Betsy's granddaughter?" she looks at him for confirmation instead of letting me answer.

"Yes," he says, smiling at me.

"You were just a tiny girl when I met you," she says to me. "I'm sorry to hear about your grandmother."

"Thank you," I say.

"Can we come in?" Mark asks. "It's ninety out here."

Tammy chews her bottom lip, looks inside, and then back at Mark, and then at me. For a moment I don't think she's going to let us through. "Yes, of course," she says, but still stands in the doorway for a beat as if she's reconsidering her answer.

When she steps inside, Mark looks at me to make sure I'll follow. I do.

The apartment is cool, and for that I'm grateful. The blinds are pulled closed, but Tammy makes quick work to open them all, and turn off the TV. She studies her surroundings.

There are magazines stacked on the end tables. Plates and glasses are scattered on the coffee table as if that's where she eats all the time.

There are a lot of plants, but I'm not sure how they grow in the dark.

"Sorry about the mess. I don't get visitors often," she says.

"The place is fine, Mom," Mark says and looks at me.

I'm still standing near the door, then again, it's not a big place, and Mark is only a few feet away. He motions to the chair nearest me to sit, so I do.

Tammy sits on the couch and begins to stack the plates and glasses in front of her. Mark sits on the couch with her, and Cosmo, the smartest cat on the planet, I have decided, sits obediently on Mark's lap.

"Why are you here?" Tammy asks, obviously resigning to the fact that she's not going to get the room clean by sitting right there. She scoots back on the couch, her hands folded in her lap and her back erect.

"We were driving through on our way home. I thought it would be a good chance to stop and say hello."

Tammy nods. "That's right." She looks in my direction. "How has your drive been?"

I smile, my own posture stiff, just as hers is, and my hands are folded in my lap. "It's been good so far. It was nice to have company the last part of it. Cosmo doesn't say much," I say, and that smart cat lifts his head and gives me a damn nod.

Mark chuckles. "You could come down with us for the memorial. It's tomorrow. It's going to be small."

Tammy's eyes go wide. I think mine do too. I hadn't expected him to invite his mother to drive the rest the way with us.

It doesn't matter, but...

"Oh, no," Tammy says shaking her head, and pressing her

hand to her chest. "No. No. I can't go. I have..." she trails off and never finishes. "I couldn't go."

"Well, the invite is there. If you want to come later, I can get you a ride."

She continues to shake her head. "No. Thank you though," she says and her tone is soft.

"No problem. You haven't been down to see Grandpa in a while. You'll have to come by."

Her brows draw in. "Markey, it's not like he'll know I'm there."

"I'm just saying. He's buried under that tree. Just like he wanted. It's a nice place to sit."

"Well, he paid top dollar for the space too," Tammy says, and then her lips flatten. "And I've already been there."

Silence falls between us all, and Mark finally reaches for his mother's hand. "We should get back on the road. I'll come back up in the next few weeks and we can go to dinner."

"Call first."

"I'll make plans, I promise."

When he stands, I follow. Tammy looks up at both of us, studies us as if she knows something has transpired, and then she stands.

"Again, I'm sorry for your loss. I'm sorry I can't be there," she says to me.

"Thank you." I don't know what else to say.

Mark leans in and kisses his mother on the cheek. "I love you. I'll call you when we get there."

"Okay," Tammy says, and then we head for the door.

The heat hits like a wall when I step out of the cool apartment. Actually, I welcome it.

Mark steps out and hands me the cat before he reaches for his mother and pulls her to him. "I love you," he says softly. "I'll be back soon."

The Final Drive

The car is hot now, so we sit for a moment to let it cool. We don't say anything. Cosmo has found refuge on the floor in the back seat where the vent blows cold air directly on him.

Mark reaches across the console for my hand, linking our fingers.

"I'm sorry. That had to be uncomfortable," he says. "I just needed to check in on her."

"There's no need to be sorry."

"I knew she wouldn't come with us for Betsy's memorial. But I had to ask."

I rest my other hand on the steering wheel, for something to do with it. I get the drive into Palm Beach. "Did she not like Gran?"

Mark shrugs. "There's always that consideration that her father divorced my grandmother because of Betsy. I can only imagine that is something you don't get over. And then her own son would rather live with Betsy than with her," he says of himself. "Though she loved Betsy because she brought joy to her father and her son, Mom would keep her distance."

I understand that. "It's good that you make time for her."

"She won't move to the house, and I've asked."

I turn in the seat toward him. "Does your grandfather own half of the house? I've never considered it."

"No," he says quickly. "The house was all Betsy's. She had it built. She paid for it. They didn't put their names on anything together except movies."

I lick my lips. "If your grandfather was such a name in the industry, he was well off, right?"

"Sure."

"Why does your mother live in a tiny apartment?"

Mark presses his head back into the headrest. "He didn't leave her anything," he admits.

"Oh. Does she have siblings?"

He shakes his head. "Just her, but he didn't want his fortune to just be squandered, or the next guy in her life to walk away with it because she wasn't paying attention."

Scrubbing his free hand over his face, he lets out a long breath.

"I got everything," he says. "But I told her that he didn't have anything left after his care. He asked me to."

"But you take care of her, don't you?"

He nodded. "She gets a nice check every month, and she thinks it's an investment that Grandpa put together for her."

"So you lie to her?"

"As far as I'm concerned it is an investment. Grandpa invested in me. I invested the money. I invest in her."

"You have his fortune and you live in my grandmother's house?" It comes out even more snide than I'd anticipated.

"I run the house. We talked about that."

"Gran never was coming back to it. Your grandfather died. You have his money. Why does she have this fucking house?"

Mark blinks hard. "It's for you."

"Me? She didn't even tell me about this and I'm supposed to believe that she left a stupid house for me across the country, away from everything I know?"

"Yes."

I pull my hand from his, buckle my seat belt, and shift the car into drive. "I'm selling the house."

"You haven't even seen it."

"But I should just keep it because? Do you know what it costs to pay taxes on a house like that?"

"Yes," he says surely. "I do. I pay them, Liz. You think I live there for free? I pay the expenses and the taxes. It's what I do to live there. My job has been to keep the house for you, and that's what I did."

"That's a stupid job," I say, and I bat my eyes because they're filled with tears and now I can't fucking see the street.

I stop at a stop sign and throw the car in park. "I can't do this. I can't drive."

"Fine. I'll drive."

"I want to go home."

He reaches for me again, but I pull away. "You haven't even gotten there yet."

"It's all going to fall apart when I do."

"What's going to fall apart?" he asks, because he seems to be keeping his wits about him.

I don't know what to tell him. I'm afraid.

I don't want to love the house. I don't want to leave Grace. I won't fly back and forth, and I can't make this drive all the time. I don't want to leave Gran, even though she's asked me to. And I fucking think I'm falling in love with this man, and we both know that whatever is going on between us is only comfort during our mourning. We both know.

Someone behind us honks their horn.

"Can you get far enough to pull over?" Mark asks.

"I'm fine," I say, shifting back into drive and rubbing the tears from my eyes.

This is like ripping off a Band-Aid. I just need to get it over with.

The drive is three and a half hours of silence. In that time, Mark has held Cosmo and petted him, pulled out his computer and written something, and now he is scrolling through his phone as if he's looking for something.

Conversation would be nice, but then again, why would he want to talk to me when all I can do is scream and yell over that house I haven't seen yet?

"Do you have any food allergies?" he asks, finally looking at me.

"No. Why?" The question is out of left field.

"I'm ordering groceries. I haven't been home the past few days, and I'd been waiting until you were closer, so the fridge is a bit bare. I was going to order them to have them delivered about the same time we get there."

"I can go to the grocery store myself," I say defiantly.

"Okay, when? We're going to get to the house around six. Betsy's memorial is tomorrow at eleven. And though I have catering for that, we can't go that long before we eat."

The tears are back and I'm on the fucking highway. What is he doing to me? I see an exit, so I take it. He doesn't even ask why.

I pull into the nearest parking lot and put the car in park before I get out and walk to the back of the car.

The temperature is even hotter, and the air is so thick I can't push it through my lungs.

Mark is at me a moment later.

"What's wrong? Liz, what's wrong?" he asks again since I wasn't quick enough with an answer.

"I can't do the memorial."

"Why?"

"I can't say goodbye to her."

"You're not saying goodbye. Her friends are."

"Friends? She didn't even tell me about these friends. I'm not privy to them, so why should I..."

I stop when he pulls me into his arms.

Our flesh is hot, the pavement is hot, and the air is sticky. But I hold on to him for dear life.

"We'll say our own goodbye, when it's time, Liz," he says softly in my ear as traffic on the highway buzzes past us. "We get to take all the time we want."

I want to argue, but I realize I only want to argue because it's the only thing I can control.

"You organized a memorial. I didn't help you," I say, easing from him and wiping at my eyes.

"It's just what I did. I hope you don't think I was stepping on your toes."

I shake my head. "I know we talked about it, but I didn't even consider it."

"Well, it's planned. It's paid for. And it's going to be well attended. Do you think you'll be okay?" he asks, wiping his thumb over my cheek, brushing the tears away.

"I'll be okay, if you're with me."

"I don't ever plan to be anywhere else, but with you," he says, and I take it for what it means in that moment.

In that moment, he'll be by my side.

But deep down, I have to wonder if it means more.

Home

After my meltdown on the highway, Mark drives the rest of the way. My heart begins to beat rapidly when I see the first sign for Palm Beach.

"How much further?" I ask, and Mark smiles.

"About six miles."

I feel as if I'm about to meet someone I've never met. I'm nervous. I'm excited. I'm mad. I'm sick.

I pull down the visor and look in the mirror. At least I have a bra on, I consider.

I take a moment to pull my hair from the knot atop my head and rake my fingers through it. Red curls knot up, but I keep working on it until I get it to lay a bit. With the humidity, I can already tell that this is going to be something I just have to deal with. My hair will be piled on the top of my head until I go home.

I never wear a lot of makeup, but today my face is bare of even mascara, and my freckles pop.

I can feel Mark watching me, but I don't care.

Gran would have had on a full face of makeup, her hair would have been done, and she would have been dressed in some pantsuit that was twenty years old, but it would have looked nice. The least I can do is have my hair combed.

Mark exits the highway and starts toward the ocean.

My palms are damp.

I've been here, but I don't remember.

Part of me will remain here.

Cosmo moves between the seats and perches on my lap, as if he wants a better view.

Mark chuckles and that has me looking at him. No words are spoken, but he takes my hand again, until we come to a huge gate and Mark stops to type in a code.

"It's a gated community?" I ask.

"Yes."

"This is so out of my league. I literally have a homeless shelter two blocks from my place in Denver."

He chuckles. "Just so you know, they busted a house about a mile away a few months ago because it was a crack house."

"Here?"

"Where there's money, there's crime too."

Mark drives through the gate as it opens.

As we begin to pass houses, or walls that hide houses, I look for something familiar, but there is nothing.

Mark slows the car, and then I see it. This house has a big hedge, but the archways are familiar from the picture of WATTS' profile.

"This is it?" I ask.

"Yes," Mark says as he turns into the drive and in front of the house.

There is nothing familiar to me about this house, again, other than the front door which I've seen in pictures. I can tell where the tree was taken out just a few weeks ago. But the house, no, this isn't my house.

Mark parks in the circular drive right in front of the front door.

"This is it," he says, watching me look at the house.

"I don't remember it."

"You were little."

"It doesn't feel homey."

He nods as he opens his door. "You haven't made it home yet. Let's go inside and see what you think."

Mark climbs from the car and shuts the door while I still sit there looking up at the house.

Cosmo paws the door as Mark comes around the side of the car and opens it.

Cosmo jumps from the car and prances to the front door.

"He remembers it," Mark teases.

He holds his hand out to me to help me from the car. I take it and stand. He moves to stand next to me.

"It's all yours," he says.

"It's not real to me."

He turns to me, his hands on my hips, but he stays just far enough that we're not pressed up to one another. It's just too hot.

"Will you promise me something?" he asks, and I look up at him. "Give this a minimum of a month. Stay here. Feel it. Help me work on her book. One month, and then make your decision."

Chewing on my bottom lip, I look back at the house, and then back at him. "A month is a long time."

"And you have a job that allows it. You also have the funds to not worry about the job," he reminds me. "But I'm asking for a month. Give me a month."

And that changed everything, didn't it? *He's* asking for the month. What happens in a month? We decide that without Gran we are just two people who knew her in different times of her life? We finish his book, and then the need for me is over? I sell the house and he has to find somewhere to go? Where does he go?

"Liz?"

I blink and look back at him. "A month?"

"Take a month before you decide. I'm not asking you to make a life here. I'm asking you to take a month to make your decision."

"Okay," I agree, and that smile curls up the corner of his mouth.

"Thank you," he says, stepping in and pressing a kiss to my lips. "Ready to go in?"

"Yes," I say, but then tug against him as he takes my hand and starts for the door. "Wait."

I turn back to the car, open the back door, and take Gran's urn from the seat. If I'm going in, she's going in.

Mark has the front door open, and he waits for me. Cosmo has taken off into the house already.

My legs feel heavy as I carry Gran through the front door of the house she built. I can't help it, I'm crying.

It doesn't smell like her house in Denver. The white marble floor, light walls, and the glass table that adorns the entryway aren't warm—Gran was warm.

Mark closes the door behind us.

He moves in next to me.

"I don't remember it," I say.

"Then it's new to you. It can be anything you want. Remember that. It's yours to change too."

I can't decide if he's stating the facts or hoping that I'll change things if I stay.

"There's an office we can put her in. I don't work in there, but it's where she and Grandpa would work. I keep the door closed, and Cosmo won't get in there."

I nod and follow him into the house.

The floor plan is open, and light. I smile thinking how different the houses are. Of course, Gran moved into my house when she arrived in Colorado. In the past ten years that she's lived in the house alone, she's changed a few things, but not many. Understandably, while I was living there, she changed nothing. She wouldn't have wanted to upset me.

Mark walks toward a set of glass French doors and pushes them open. This room is completely outdated, and I wonder if he keeps this as a museum of sorts.

The air is musty, and the blinds are drawn.

"This is where they worked, huh?" I ask.

"Yes. I don't come in here often. You can still smell Grandpa's cigars. The smoke is embedded in the paneling."

"She let him smoke in the house?" I ask, humored.

"She smoked in the house too, so—"

"She what?"

Mark's lips press together. "She didn't smoke around you?"

"No. No!"

Now he laughs. "Interesting. So she smoked *not* around you."

"Gran didn't smoke."

"Oh, baby, I can't imagine that she didn't smoke. The woman always had a cigarette in her hand. She smoked when I talked to her on Sundays."

Gran's urn begins to get heavy in my arms. "Well, I guess that explains it. Since I didn't know she talked to you, if she smoked on Sundays, then I never saw her do it."

He nods slowly as if my logic makes sense. I'm completely in denial, and I know it.

I walk to the desk, which is covered in scripts, books, and notepads. There's an old desktop computer in the center.

I set Gran's urn on the desk.

Lifting my head, I look around the room. On one wall there are photos, and on the other walls there are movie posters.

I walk toward one of the movie posters that catches my eye. It's from the movie *The Secretary*, Gran's movie at RKO. Her face is only familiar because it looks like me.

Mark moves in behind me, his arms slipping around my waist as he presses up against me.

"You look just like her," he says.

"I was just thinking that."

"You're both beautiful."

I turn in his arms. "I guess I'm about to find out about all of this."

"That's the plan."

"Lovers, a movie career, she broke up your grandparents' marriage, and she smoked. This version of Gran is so different."

Mark presses a small kiss to my lips. "For the record, Grandpa was the one who broke up his marriage. He's the one at fault."

I shrug at that. I'm not sure I buy that, but okay.

I move from his arms, but take his hand and walk to the other wall.

Tears well in my eyes when I see pictures of me on this wall. Baby pictures, and old school pictures. At some point, Mom must have reached out to Gran when I was really little.

I notice that these pictures aren't just Gran's. There are pictures of Tom Watts, Tammy, and a young Mark.

There are framed collages of Gran and Tom on vacations, with Mark at all ages, and with others that I recognize only because they're celebrities. But the photo that moves me the most is a picture of Gran and Tom casually sitting together on the sofa holding hands, each with a cigarette between their fingers which are wrapped around a drink. It's so out of place for me, but somehow, it all looks normal.

Well, it's just one more thing I didn't know.

"You were a cute kid," I say to Mark.

"Were?"

"Oh, I think you're cute now too."

He turns me into his arms again. "Cute?"

"Handsome? Sexy? Which would you rather?"

His eyes have gone dark, and he licks his lips. "Each has its place, I guess."

"Maybe you should show me around the house," I say, even though I'm enjoying being in his arms—this I'm familiar with.

A Place for Liz

The white marble floor flows through the entire house. There is a formal living room where two Academy Award statues sit on a shelf. On the shelf below it, there are three shuffleboard trophies, displayed with equal pride.

"You did say shuffleboard was a big deal," I say to Mark as I look at the prestigious awards.

"One is Grandpa's. One is Betsy's—the Oscars that is," he says. "The shuffleboard trophies are Grandpa's only."

I turn to look at him. "My grandmother has an Oscar?"

He nods. "She does."

"*Thief of Reality*?" I ask, noting the movie poster we saw at the theater in Atlanta.

Mark shakes his head. "*Long Road to Paradise.*"

I cover my mouth with my fingers. "She has that movie poster hanging in her bedroom."

He smiles at that. "She had me send it to her."

Again, our lives are entangled. I remembered having to go to the post office to pick up the package for her. I had been home from college at that time, she'd had knee replacement surgery and couldn't drive.

I draw in a breath.

Mark takes me through the rest of the house. The kitchen, of course, is familiar. I've seen it when Mark walks through on our video calls in his shorts.

There is a formal dining room, and a family room, but it looks more like a screening room.

As we walk through the house, Mark opens blinds, and lets the last of the sunlight in. Every so often, Cosmo darts in front of us, as if he too is familiarizing himself with the house, again.

I can see the pool just outside. The house is U-shaped, and the pool is the centerpiece of the back yard.

Mark opens a bedroom door and turns on the light.

This was Gran's—and Tom's, I'm sure.

I step in. It doesn't feel of her either. I consider that she left this space twenty years ago, and Tom would have stayed until he died. It's just a house, and this is just a room.

"There are two more bedrooms," Mark says, taking my hand and walking me to the other side of the house.

"I thought your room was in the pool house."

"It is," he says as we walk down the hallway, passing an outdated bathroom along the way.

He stops in front of the closed door. "This one has been waiting a long time for you."

Mark pushes open the door, turns on the light, and steps out of the way.

I step into the pink room, complete with a canopy bed. I move to the window to open the blinds. The room feels as if it needs the light, which is dimming outside.

The dresser has photos on it in silver frames. There's a picture of me as an infant. Others are of when I'd visited when I was six, and one that I remember vividly.

I pick up that frame and study it. "Gran came out and stayed with us for a bit," I say running my finger over the glass.

Mark finally walks into the room. "You were eight. It was the first diagnosis your mother got."

I lift my eyes to meet his. "She went on vacation. Gran stayed with me."

He shook his head. "She had surgery to try to remove the cancer," he says. "Betsy stayed with you."

I have to sit, so I move to the bed and lower myself on it. I should have known that. Did I really need to be that sheltered?

"Why this room?" I ask, looking around.

Mark sits down next to me. "They didn't know what would happen. When Betsy returned she and Grandpa planned for you to join us. They set this up for you."

Tears well in my eyes. "I loved pink when I was little."

He nods. "She knew. She knew you wanted a canopy bed. You liked Snoopy, and you'd only eat chicken nuggets."

I sniff back the tears and laugh. "I haven't eaten a chicken nugget in years."

"That's too bad. That's all I ordered with my groceries," he teases as he nudges me with his shoulder.

I look around the room that was saved for me. "So if she went through all of this, why didn't she bring me here?"

Mark places his hand on my thigh and brushes his fingers over my skin. "You were two years older. You were established where you were. Two years later she understood just how devastating your mother's illness was, and she became disconnected here. I think that knowing her only daughter was dying, and that you'd be hers, it was a chance for her to leave everything behind."

"Including your grandpa—and you?"

Mark clasps his hands together. "It felt that way at first. Until your mom was really bad. Then Betsy would call and cry. She wanted us. She wanted you. She wanted your mom to survive."

"I still don't understand why she—"

"It was the best thing, Liz. All of this," he says looking around the room, "this wasn't her life. You were. Another year later, she was with you, and Grandpa started forgetting things. A few years later, he forgot more and more. One time she came to visit, and he didn't know her at all."

He wipes his hand over his mouth.

"I knew this would be hard for you to hear," he says. "I didn't consider it would be hard for me too."

I stand and replace the photo on top of the dresser.

"When do the groceries arrive?" I ask.

"Another hour."

I hold my hand out to him. Mark takes it and stands.

"I think there's one more room you haven't shown me," I say.

He moves so that he's pressed against me, his arm wrapped around my waist. "Liz Evans wants to see my bedroom." His breath is in my ear.

"I said there was a room you hadn't shown me."

"Oh, I heard you." He brushes his lips down my neck. "I really want to show you my room."

I place my hands on his shoulders and ease back just slightly. "Maybe, just maybe, we should save that for after her memorial." I swallow hard.

"I can save it for as long as you want," he concedes, but eases against me again. "But I don't want to. One month, Liz. Give me a month. You. Me. This house. The book. You. Me."

Out of Place

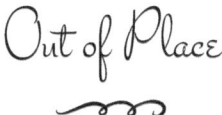

Even with the sun down, it's hot.

The groceries arrive and Mark begins putting them away and making us something for dinner. I decide to unpack the car.

Unpacking the car gives me time to think about the house. Not so much about what I want to do with it, but where I fit in it.

There is a room for me, but the room is for eight-year-old me.

Gran's room wasn't really Gran's room. Sure, she and Tom shared it, but that had been over twenty years ago. Tom had lived there until he died six years ago. Since then, it's sat empty.

Though, I would assume, Gran was the last one to sleep there when she'd come for Tom's funeral.

The house is dated, yet right in time with the area, I suppose. Glass. Marble. Shiny and clean—all but the office which appears to always stay closed up.

I pull everything out of the car and lay it in the driveway. Clothes, essentials, snacks, Cosmo's items, and of course the box of things that were Gran's, such as the letters, all sit on the ground now.

My car is old and dirty.

My shorts are old and somewhere I've dropped something on my shirt.

The humidity has my hair going in all directions.

I'm tired.

"Hello," a voice calls from the end of the driveway, and then I see a man walking toward me.

He's in a pair of blue shorts and a white polo shirt. Even with the sun down, he's wearing a visor.

In the glow of the lights from the house and driveway, I can see that he's leathered tan, which is a stark difference to his head full of white hair.

"There's a lot of activity going on here," he says flashing a bright white smile. "You must be Betsy's kin?"

Kin?

"I'm her granddaughter."

"The one from Colorado? Elizabeth?"

So everyone knows me? "Yes."

"I'm sorry to hear about Betsy. Man, she was a pistol." He chuckles. "Funny that she hasn't been around here for years, but she always was, you know what I mean?"

"I think so."

"Mark's taken good care of the place. He's really at home here, even without his grandfather." The man walks closer, looks at the piles I have on the driveway, and then back up at me. "So you're moving in now?"

"No," I say, shaking my head. "She wanted to be left in Florida. So I'm just here to finalize her wishes and sell the house."

He nods slowly. "Oh. I didn't realize..." He holds out his hand to me. "I'm Ken. I live down the street."

I shake his hand. No need to tell him my name. He already knows it.

"Well, it was nice to meet you," he says. "I guess I'll see you at the memorial tomorrow. Mark's been working hard on getting everyone together to say goodbye. It was nice to meet you, granddaughter of the amazing Betsy."

The man on the driveway shook me up. The whole neighborhood has expectations of me? Gran hasn't lived in this house for twenty years, but it is expected to stay in her family? It doesn't even make sense.

I combine boxes and items so that I can easily carry them into the house. When I open the front door, the scents fill my nose.

I have no idea what he's making, but just by the aroma that is filling the house, I know he's much more competent in the kitchen than I am.

It takes me two trips to carry everything into the house, but after realizing that the people driving around the neighborhood are either in golf carts or in cars that are so expensive, I've never actually seen those models in Colorado, I wonder if there's somewhere we can hide my car. Aside from there being a lot of motion in the house, I can only assume they all saw us coming from miles away.

Shutting the front door behind me, I carry the last box toward the kitchen where Mark has set the small kitchen table, which overlooks the lit swimming pool.

"That's a pretty sight," I say as I set the box on one of the empty chairs.

"I'll often sit in here in the dark late at night and write. The glow of my computer and the pool lights give off a good vibe."

"Maybe I'll have to try that."

Mark carries two plates to the table and sets them on placemats. There are two glasses of wine, and he's lit a candle.

"Is this how you set up dinner for all your house guests?" I ask.

"The last house guest I had was my mother."

"She's stayed here?"

He nods. "Once in a while I can convince her to spend a few days down here. She does really well, but then one day she gets antsy and wants to go home."

He pulls out a chair for me and I sit, then he joins me.

The meal is simple spaghetti, shrimp, and tomatoes with a garlic sauce, accompanied by a gorgeous salad. I say simple because I can identify everything.

"You don't impress women with this set up?" I ask, taking my napkin and placing it in my lap.

He puckers his lips as he picks up his wine. "There is a purpose for this house—but it's not to woo women."

"I think you missed out."

Mark takes a sip of his wine and sets it back on the table. "Okay, here's my question for you. Do you want a relationship with a man based on his home or who he is?"

I pick up my fork and move my noodles around. "Point made."

He picks up his wine again and sits back in his chair. "Tell me about the men you've dated. I'm curious."

Twisting pasta around my fork, I lift a bite to my lips. "I don't date."

"Don't, but have?"

"Sure, but—"

"Then tell me about the men you've dated."

I take my bite and use that moment to think about men I've dated.

Lowering my fork, I pick up my wine and sip.

Mark is watching me over the top of his glass, grinning from behind it.

"Josh was a banker who was boring. We went out on six dates, but it never went anywhere. Kirk was a private security guard, ex-military. He was much too serious and couldn't talk about his job. We didn't have much to talk about then." I sip my wine again. "I dated Ben the longest, two years, but we had different ideas on what the future was going to hold."

"What was his idea?" Mark asks, sitting forward and finally taking a bite of his dinner.

"Marriage and kids."

A line forms between his brows. "And that's not what you want?"

I shake my head. "I have lost the two most important people in my life to cancer. I also don't know anything about my father or my grandfather. I don't know what genetics I possess, no matter what DNA kits I've sent in. I don't wish to pass that on to children."

He nods as he chews, and then he sips his wine again. "DNA doesn't affect marriage."

"It does if one the partners in that marriage wants kids."

"Right."

"Do you want kids?" I ask as I lift my wine to my lips. The liquid moves because my hands shake asking him that question.

Mark shrugs. "I've never set out to find someone to have kids with. Much like you, I have a father who can't stay still and a mother who locks herself in her house. I'm not sure what kind of mental stability I can offer a child. But, if I found the right person to share a life with, I'm not impartial to marriage."

"I've never been around a marriage," I say. "Grace is the only married person I've been around. Okay," I reconsider, "and her parents."

"I've been around an amazing relationship," he offers, and I know he's talking about Tom and Gran.

We sit quietly for a few more minutes, enjoying the meal he prepared.

He eyes the box I sat on the chair next to me.

"What's in that box?" he asks.

I finish my bite and look at the box. Reaching my hand inside, I pull out the stack of letters I promised to bring him.

Handing them to him, I notice that his eyes go wide. He wipes his mouth and pushes his plate back.

"Holy shit. The letters," he says, running his fingers over them as if they're priceless.

"I told you I'd bring them."

His attention is no longer on me. I'm not sure what these letters possess, but he's forgotten all about me for the moment.

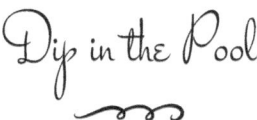

Dip in the Pool

I decide to stay in Gran's bedroom. Mark had it cleaned last week when we planned out my trip, though he'd always had the housekeeper clean all the rooms, minus the office.

The bedding is new and there is a new flat screen TV that hangs on the wall above the dresser. There's an ensuite bathroom, and a luxurious tub, which I've decided to take advantage of after such a long trip.

Cosmo has taken up residence in one of the chairs in the bedroom, and since he's been so good throughout the trip, I don't even make him get down. He deserves the space.

Just as I plug my phone in to charge, it rings.

"Hey, mama," I say to Grace as I sit down on the bed.

"How is it? Is it amazing? You're never coming back, are you?" she starts.

"I don't belong here."

"Liz, you've only been there a few hours."

I lay back on the bed. "Ya, and I feel like some country bumpkin walking into the Plaza."

Grace chuckles. "And now you're there with text guy—how's that?"

I shrug. "I gave him the letters and haven't spoken to him since."

"You don't think that's all he wanted, do you?"

I have to give that some consideration. "No. I don't."

"Tell me you feel safe or I'll catch a flight tonight."

Surely, she knows I'm smiling at that. "I'm completely safe. Just very tired. I'm going to sink into this enormous tub."

"That sounds nice. I know tomorrow is going to be hard. Remember that I love you," Grace says, and my eyes sting with tears.

"I love you too."

"And even though I love you. Don't think you need to make the trip back right away. Give it some time."

I don't tell her about agreeing to stay for a month. I will, but right now, I'm still processing that myself.

We say goodbye, and I try to keep my mind off of the fact that I'll have to make that trip again in reverse. Having noted some of the things I want to see going back, I'm already focused on trying to make it a vacation of sorts. If I don't focus on that, I'll just be miserable.

As the tub fills, I sort through my clothes that need to be washed, and I'll tend to those this weekend. Hanging up the dress I chose for Gran's memorial, I run my hands over the fabric. It's the dress I wore to Grace's bridal shower. Gran and I had gone shopping for something special for both of us. When I'd gone to pay for the dress, Gran bought it for me. She wanted me to have something I could wear for special occasions, and she wanted it to be a gift from her on a day we spent together.

Now here I am looking at it on a hanger in Gran's closet. I'm not sure this is the kind of special occasion she was considering when she bought me the dress.

.   .   .

253

I step out of Gran's room later that night and walk toward the kitchen. Marble flooring would never cut it in Colorado, with the coolness of the floor on my feet, but I didn't even consider putting on my scandals. I'm in a loose tank top and a pair of loose shorts. It's warm enough, I may have to discard them too.

September in Colorado, we walk that fine line between having the windows open at night for cool, fresh air, and needing a sweatshirt to keep warm. I'm not sure I'm cut out for heat and humidity.

I open the refrigerator to pull out flavored water. Closing the door, I lean up against it, and that's when I notice the lights are on in the pool house.

Once I had handed Mark the letters I'd brought, he'd been lost in them. He hadn't invited me out to *his place*, but I need to be with him. Maybe I just need to know that those letters aren't the only reason he'd met me in Nashville. I mean, he'd had days to ask for them.

When I open the patio door, I notice the soft glow in one of the lounge chairs just outside Mark's door. As my eyes adjust, I see him look up at me.

"Hey," he says in that easy manner that I'd quickly become accustomed to.

"I didn't notice you out here. I was just going to say goodnight."

He turns his wrist to look at it, and when he does, his watch illuminates. "Yeah. I guess it has been a long day. We have a lot to do tomorrow."

I ease down in the chair next to his. "So, this is your process, huh? Sit by the pool to work in the dark?"

"Yeah, but I think you knew that," he says with some humor.

Admittedly, I did know that. "What are you working on?"

"I'm going through my notes."

"Did the letters help?"

He turned his face to me. "You didn't read them?"

"Only the one. It was enough for me at the moment. I wasn't the steadiest of people when I left home this week."

"I've only read the first three. There are sixteen."

I surely would have thought that he would have zipped right through them.

"And?" I say.

"And, I'm matching up dates. Betsy liked to tell stories. I have found that some of her *things* don't add up. So I double check everything."

"Are you saying my grandmother was a liar?"

I can see the whites of his eyes as they go wide. "Heavens no. I would never say that. Let's just say that there was a lot going on in those eighty years. I think she just mixed up information."

Mark closes his laptop and turns his body so that our knees touch. "Maybe on Sunday we can sit and go through the letters —together."

For some reason, being included in that decision sends a warmth through me. "I'd like that."

"Do you have everything you need for the night?" he asks, resting his hand on my knee.

With him this close to me, I know I don't want to be alone in the house tonight. I'm sure if I asked him, he'd let me stay in the pool house with him.

Instead, I take his hand and link our fingers. "Ya know, I think I'd like to take a swim."

His mouth curls into a smile. "You specifically said, you weren't going to wear a swimsuit."

I stand, move to the edge of the pool, and turn back to him. Lifting the hem of my shirt I pull it up and over my head. My hair, still damp from my bath, falls over my shoulders.

"Liz..." Mark's voice is low as he growls out my name.

Tucking my thumbs into the waistband of the shorts, I lower them from my hips and let them fall to the ground.

"You're right," I say, my voice deep with need. "I did say that."

Mark stands.

I look at the water behind me and step off the side of the pool, my body slides into the water, and I come up with a screech.

"Oh, God! This is freezing," I say on a gasp with a laugh, covering my breasts with my arm, and then dropping it when I notice him looking at me. His grin is sexy, and I'm sure he's containing laughter. But, honestly, I thought it would be warmer. "Are you going to join me?"

His grin softens, and he wipes his hand over his mouth, pulls off his T-shirt, and then begins to unbutton his shorts.

"You should never swim alone," he says, but there is a crack in his voice.

I lick my lips watching him slip from his shorts. "I couldn't agree with you more."

Mark jumps into the water and swims toward me. But now, I'm rethinking this. Why is it now that I rethink this?

We're in Gran's house. There are neighbors.

I look around and realize the yard is built so that no one sees into the yards of the houses.

He continues to swim toward me, until I've backed myself against the edge of the pool, and he stops.

"Feeling guilty about seducing me in your grandmother's pool?" he asks. There is still gravel in his voice, but it's lit with humor.

"Maybe."

"Want me to get out?"

"No."

"Want me to get closer?" There is no humor now.

I swallow hard. "Yes."

Mark dives under the water, and when he surfaces, he's right in front of me. His hands skim the outsides of my thighs before he wraps his arms around me and presses his body to mine.

The water makes me feel less exposed until I feel his erection against my stomach.

His lips part as if he's going to say something, but what would we say?

Two weeks ago, I didn't know this man existed. Now, he is my existence.

Mark cups the nape of my neck, and my eyes wander to meet his.

"I want to touch you, Liz." He lowers his mouth and skims his lips over mine. "Can I touch you?"

"Yes," my voice quivers.

"I want to explore you," he says with his mouth still on mine. "Can I explore you?"

"Yes."

My body floats against his, and I anchor my leg around his waist to hold me still, but it only pushes us closer together and he moans.

"God, you're trying to kill me," he groans into my mouth as he kisses me, reaching around me and gripping my ass, pulling my heat to him. "We need to get out of this pool," he says.

"Why?"

"I can't do what I want to do to you in here." His mouth skims my throat before he eases back from me and swims toward the stairs.

I watch as he climbs from the pool, his body lit by the lights coming from the pool house.

He grabs a towel from a shelf by his door. Wrapping it around his waist, he grabs another and moves toward the edge of the pool.

Pushing myself up on the edge of the pool, I climb out, take the towel, and begin walking toward the door of the pool house.

"C'mon, Watts. Let's see what you've got."

Earth-shattering

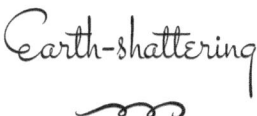

From the moment we walk into the pool house, and Mark shuts the door behind him, we are lost in one another.

He is at me immediately, pulling off the towel, gathering me to him, and hiking me up around his waist as he feasts on my neck.

Laying me on his bed, his perfectly made bed, he does what he said he wanted to do. He touches me, explores me, makes me feel things I have never felt with any man before.

He has touched every inch of me and he has made me light-headed with his tongue.

When I think he should be tired and giving in to sleep, he touches me again, and then lets me have my turn exploring and touching him.

By the early morning hours, I know his body as well as I know the keyboard on my computer. The scent of him now surrounds me as he spoons up behind me and I'm wrapped in his sheet. We've made a dent in his box of condoms.

Only a slight gleam of moonlight flows in through the window, barely illuminating the room.

"You need to go to sleep," he whispers against my ear.

"My body is still buzzing from all the attention," I say.

"Ya, if I'd known it was going to be that good, I wouldn't have left your room the other night," he teases.

I roll to face him. Our legs threading together as our arms wrap around one another. "You didn't think it was going to be that good?"

Mark pushes a strand of my hair from my forehead. "I had no doubt about it. I knew I was feeling something deep, I just wasn't sure you were."

I sigh as his hand glides down my arm until our fingers link. "I knew there was a connection after our second call," I say. "You were important."

"Really?"

I lick my lips and study his face in the shadows. "I went to bed that night hearing your voice say my name."

He smiles and pulls me just a little closer. "I think I should feel really bad about all of this."

"Why?"

"You're Betsy's granddaughter."

"And you're Tom's grandson," I counter, grinning at him. "I don't see the problem."

"I'm supposed to take care of you."

That has me easing back. "Take care of me? I don't need to be taken care of."

His hand comes to my shoulder, gently, but as if to keep me in place. "I just mean..." He lets out a breath. "I didn't mean it that way. Betsy always prepared me for when she'd be gone. She wanted me to be there for you because she knew you'd need someone."

I move from his embrace and pull the sheet around me as I climb from the bed. "It would have been nice if she'd have discussed these things with me. I feel as if she thought I was so fragile I couldn't be told. So, send her other *kid*? Send the kid I didn't know anything about?" I spit out the words as I gather the sheet up so I can walk.

"Liz..."

"I'll talk to you in the morning. I can't even right now," I say as I move through the space and to the door.

"Liz..."

His voice breaks through the silence again, but I keep walking. Tomorrow I say goodbye to my grandmother with strangers. I don't need him telling me he was set up to be my caregiver, because if he was, well then, fuck!

I pace around Gran's bedroom, the sheet still wrapped around me and Cosmo purposely ignoring me.

I like this man. I really like this man.

Falling to the bed, I lay back and try to breathe.

I don't want him to have used me for his project. I don't want to think that he's trying to warm me up to keeping the house, so that he has somewhere to live.

I miss Gran so much that I can't even think.

Sitting back up and hopping off the bed, I open one of the dresser drawers and take out another tank top and a pair of sleeping shorts. My others are still sitting poolside.

I slip into them and then leave the bedroom, walking to the office. Opening the door, I turn on the light. Moving to the desk, I pick up Gran's urn, and carry her back to the bedroom. I need her with me. I don't know that I can fulfill her final wishes.

My room is flooded with sunshine and my head pounds as if I'd been binge drinking. I know that it's from lack of sleep because I swear I didn't get but ten minutes of rest.

I can smell coffee, which means that Mark is up. Or I assume that it's Mark. I don't know how this house runs. Maybe there is an entire staff in the kitchen. I don't know anything about anything.

Kicking out of the sheets, I set my feet on the floor and stand. The marble is cold, and it gives me a chill. I guess I might need to invest in a pair of slippers.

Pulling a sweatshirt from my drawer, and slipping it over my head, I walk out to the kitchen, Cosmo is right on my heels as if maybe I've kept him captive too long in the bedroom.

Mark looks like I feel. I'm guessing he didn't get any sleep either.

He's in a loose pair of shorts. His hair sticks up all over, and I wonder if that was from a restless night, or if I did that with my fingers in his wet hair after our swim.

"Hey," he says, and it still sends tingles over my skin.

Mark lifts his mug to his lips and sips his coffee. There's something comfortable about standing in this space together. But I don't want it to be comfortable. It's temporary.

"Want some coffee?" he asks.

"I'm going to need it," I say, walking toward the counter where he's already turned to pour me the coffee.

He turns and holds out the mug, but his eyes scan over me.

"Are you feeling okay?"

I take the mug and step back. "Oh, I look that bad?"

"I'm just asking. It was a rough night, and it shouldn't have been."

Taking a sip from my mug, I lean a hip against the counter. "It was probably a mistake. I should have kept my head about me."

Mark shakes his head. "It wasn't a mistake. We both know that."

"I should get ready," I say, easing from the counter.

Mark reaches for my arm and moves in to me. "Hey, I know today is going to be hard. I'm going to be there for all of it. I'm going to be there after too. Don't push me away." His hand moves from my arm and slips around my waist, his fingers touching the skin just below my sweatshirt. "I want to be part of your life, Liz. I want to still be important."

I swallow hard. "You are important."

"That's all I want."

"But we both know this thing between us, it's temporary. We need to keep that in mind."

Mark shakes his head. "You're the only one putting an expiration date on it. I don't plan on going anywhere."

In the state of mind I'm in, that should have pissed me off, shaken me up, made me retreat. But today, of all days, I guess that's exactly what I need to hear. I'm alone. I'm all alone.

My jaw begins to tremble and my eyes well up with tears.

Mark sets down his mug and moves to me. He takes my mug and sets it on the counter before he pulls me into his arms.

"Liz, this thing between us is more than this trip. So much more," he says against my ear. "So much more," he repeats.

I can't even argue. I need this man.

Remembering Betsy

There are people at the small club house at the golf course when we arrive. Mark laughs and takes my hand.

"Well, this is no surprise," he says.

"For who?" My voice shakes.

He takes my hand and kisses my fingers. "Remember, she touched a lot of lives. Betsy was—well, loved by every person she ever met."

"Except your grandmother," I say, because I needed to.

Mark laughs. "You're right. She wasn't a fan." He keeps his eyes on me for a moment. "You're going to be okay. They're going to want to hug you and share stories with you."

I nod. "Okay."

"I'll be right by your side the entire time. There's a nursing room near the bathroom, if you need to escape."

That has me laughing. "A nursing room? As in a breastfeeding room?"

"Yes."

"At a golf course in a retirement community?"

Mark grins. "Yes. Brenda fought to have it put in when she was pregnant."

I have to press my hand to my chest. The name alone makes me anxious. "She has a kid?"

"Three of them."

I blink hard. "Oh," I say, remembering that she was the one that he was helping move when I thought he was sleeping with her. "Who else will be here?"

"Finn and Georgie." He grinned. "Georgie was Betsy's name for him. His real name is Jeff."

"God, now you're just confusing me."

"You're going to do great."

"I don't want to do this."

He kisses my fingers again. "This is for Betsy, remember. You can do this."

I let out a slow breath and then turn in my seat, pull down the visor, and open the mirror. I study myself. My hair is done, I have on makeup, and my freckles are concealed. I have on the dress Gran had bought for me for Grace's bridal shower, and a pair of her diamond studs in my ears.

Closing the mirror, I look at Mark. "You'll be right next to me the whole time?"

"I promise."

I give him a nod. "Let's do this."

Mark carries Gran into the club house. I wasn't sure I could walk and hold on to her.

When we walk through the door, the conversation stops. Mark smiles and begins to say hello to everyone, by name.

He sets Gran on the table next to three different pictures of her. One of Genevieve Paige. One of G.E. Paige. One of Gran that was very recent, but not one I'd ever seen.

The photos aren't labeled, I just know the time frames in which they'd have been taken—well, I know them now.

Those who have already shown up, move in around Mark,

placing a hand on his shoulder, some one-arm hug him, others just stare at Gran's urn.

They console him, and he thanks them.

Then he turns and reaches for me. I hesitate before I take his hand.

He introduces me as Elizabeth, Betsy's granddaughter.

A woman, at least ten years older than Gran, tan, short, and in a dress she might have bought in the eighties, moves to me and takes my hand from Mark. She clasps it between her two hands which are adorned with bracelets and a ring on each finger.

"Liz, right?" she asks.

"Yes, Ma'am."

"Millie. You call me Millie."

"Millie," I say.

"Your grandmother," she paused. "Oh, that Betsy. She and Tom, well, they were good together. He loved her till he died."

There just wasn't anything I could say to that.

Millie continues, "Betsy and I were at RKO together. She was a looker. Kurt McLaughlin was taken by her. Well, everyone was," she says patting my hand. "You'll be happy here."

A man moves in behind Millie and guides her to a chair at one of the tables that is set up.

Mark wraps an arm around my waist. "Millie was at MGM, not RKO. She doesn't remember that. And, McLaughlin snubbed her advances."

"Really, she must have been closer to his age," I whisper back and Mark snickers.

"She was married, too."

"Is this how this neighborhood works?" I ask.

Mark leans in closer to my ear. "Exactly. Do you see why I have to double check facts?"

I nod as another man moves toward us.

. . .

For the next hour and a half, dozens of people talk to me about Gran. Some of them knew her in her prime as Genevieve Paige. There are some who knew her and Tom. One man cried because he was in love with her, but there was Tom. He still seems to hold a torch for her.

I met Brenda, Finn, and Georgie—whose name I was reminded was Jeff when Mark called him by the nickname that Gran had given him.

Even though Brenda moves in and hugs Mark, placing a kiss right on his lips, I can see that it means nothing to Mark other than friendship. For that I am grateful.

Mark points out Bridget Bloom's grandfather, who is wheeled in by a nurse. He takes a moment next to the photos of Gran, placing his hand on her urn. Then the nurse pushes him toward me, and Mark is sure to wrap an arm around my waist.

I can't help but scan a quizzical look over the nurse. She looks like she might be dressed up for Halloween—short skirt, heels, and all. Mark's fingers digging into my side make me think he's had the same thought.

"Betsy was a looker," Bridget's grandfather says to me, holding my hand between his paper-thin skinned ones. He runs his thumb over my knuckles, as if we were having an intimate moment. Then he says, "You look just like her."

I smile down at him, hoping I look gracious, but inside I'm a bit grossed out by how he's looking at me.

"Thank you," I say trying to pull back from the man, but he's stronger than he looks.

"Maybe we can do lunch if you're staying," he says, before the nurse whispers something in his ear. He lifts his head, nods, and lets go of my hand. "It's bath time," he whispers, not so quietly as the nurse pushes him toward the exit.

I set my jaw and turn into Mark, who wraps his arms around me, as if I might sob. But we both know that it's just the need for a moment to gather our wits about us.

"Oh, God," I whisper into his ear trying not to laugh.

"I know, baby. I'd better keep you close. I don't want you to leave me for the neighbor," he teases against my temple.

He holds me close a few more moments so that we can compose ourselves.

With the shuffleboard tournament happening soon, many of those who had come say their goodbyes head out. The food Mark had catered had been picked over, the guest book had been signed, and now Mark and I stand in front of Gran. I rest my head on his shoulder and he has his arm wrapped around me.

"This was nothing like I thought it would have been," I say, only now feeling the tug of tears as I look at her photos. "I've been a wreck thinking about today."

"The neighborhood is a little self-centered," he says softly, as if the room were still filled, and with a bit of annoyance.

"Gran didn't belong here," I say, surely.

"Betsy was different. So was Grandpa. But, Liz, they still were retired Hollywood elite."

I lift my head and turn to him. "I think I'm starting to understand. Gran needed to stay with me." I look back at her pictures. "Sure, I needed her, but she needed to leave this."

There was a peace to my heart saying that aloud.

Gran wasn't false.

Okay, even in my head that sounds wrong. Aren't I chasing the truth of Elizabeth Evans, Genevieve Paige, G.E. Paige, Betsy Paige —Gran? Maybe I mean false of heart. Identity crisis—be damned.

The Calm

Mark's life is much more than taking care of the house and sitting at the kitchen counter writing books.

The memorial was much easier to navigate than I thought it would be. I suppose the fact that it was just a gathering of people who once knew Gran, and hadn't even seen her since Tom died, and since there was no sermon or anything, that had helped. Many of the stories I was told weren't of the woman I was raised by, and sometimes, I wasn't even sure they were true.

As soon as we walk into the house, Mark's phone begins to ring. Brenda wants to plan dinner with everyone, including me. Joe, the neighbor down the street, needs a ride to the shuffleboard tournament. And Bridget's grandfather's nurse has called to see if I'm available for a dinner. Mark winces at that call. He informs her that I'm seeing someone and it's very serious.

We share a moment when he says that. I know it was to get the woman off the phone, but settles in me. I like hearing it. I'm equally afraid of it.

I opt to stay home while Mark takes Joe to the tournament. I'm exhausted from our night together, and my lack of sleep after my tantrum. And even though the memorial wasn't as emotional as I had built it in my head to be, it was draining.

Sitting by the pool, my sunglasses and bathing suit on, I indulge in an audio book. I have a permanent smile on my mouth listening to the latest Constance Frost book, and knowing that when the character describes being touched by her lover, those are my lover's words.

My skin is pink from the warmth that the book is giving me, and not just from the sun beating down on me.

I close my eyes and let myself be sucked into the story. When her lover skims his fingers up the inside of her thigh, I close my eyes and imagine when Mark did that to me.

Soon, I'm biting my lip, my thighs squeezed together, legs crossed at the ankles, and the image in my mind is so vivid.

I'm so inside my own head, I don't hear Mark walk through the patio door. I didn't hear him walk toward me. I wasn't even aware of his presence until he touched me and I came up right off my chair, ripping my headphones from my ears.

"Shit!"

Mark moves back and lifts his hands as if to block his face from any retaliation that might happen.

"I didn't hear you," I shout.

"I know that now," he says grinning at me and lowering his hands. "What are you listening to?"

"Nothing," I say, setting my phone and earphones on the small table next to the chair.

"Liar," he counters.

I pull off my sunglasses and squint up at him. "If you must know, I'm listening to the newest Constance Frost book."

Mark crinkles up his nose. "Dear Lord, no."

"Yes, and I just got to the first good part."

"In the airplane?"

My wide smile was enough to have him shaking his head. "Money, Liz. It makes a lot of money."

"I'm not judging you."

"No? You should see your face."

I stand from my chair and move into him. His hand settles on my waist. "Actually, I was comparing."

"That's so much worse."

I take his hand and place it on my chest. "It made my skin hot," I say.

"You're sitting in the heat."

Biting down on my lip, I shake my head. "This isn't from the sun. It's knowing that you've touched me just like your character is being touched."

Mark steps in closer to me, taking his fingers and slipping them under the strap of my bathing suit. "I thought you said you weren't going to wear one of these," he says in a low growl.

"I did say that." I reach for his shirt, the same one he wore to the memorial, and unbutton the top button. "Maybe, you should take me out of it." I unbutton another button.

"Are you sure that's what you want to do today?"

I nod slowly. "I want you to make me feel like the character in your book."

"They fall in love in my book," he says slipping the strap from my shoulder.

I swallow hard considering that, but try not to react.

"Take me to your bed, Mark Watts. Don't make me beg."

The air conditioner whirs all the time, but I'm grateful for the cool room. Midday in Florida, even the first of October is so much hotter than any day in Colorado.

Mark is wrapped around me. We fall asleep after I coaxed him into taking me into his room and having sex. It'll be interesting to read Constance Frost's next book, I humor myself with my thoughts as Mark stirs.

"What time is it?" His breath is warm against my neck.

"Almost three."

"Aren't we living the life of leisure?" He shimmies his body even closer to my back, and his arms grow tighter around me.

"Don't you live like this every day?"

"No." He kisses my shoulder. "I'm busy driving old men around," he teases. "Actually, I spend a lot of time digging into their lives. The other part of my time is giving Constance Frost something to write about."

The calm that the afternoon in his bed has brought me is now prickling sparks of irritation. I start to wiggle from his grip, but he holds on tighter.

"Don't do it, Liz," he says, effortlessly still holding on to me.

"What? I'm naked in your bed and I don't get to be called baby?"

"Oh, baby," he says with a raise of his brow, "you're naked in my bed because I want you here and because you asked to be here. So settle down."

I stop moving, but my breath is now labored. Mark moves close to me again.

"I'm not going to fight you," he says. "I know what set you off. I know what I said. And I know what I meant. No need to get all worked up."

I set my jaw and squeeze my eyes closed, then open them. Finally, I turn in his arms, so that we are pressed together, chest to chest.

"Okay then, explain."

Lazily, Mark opens his eyes and looks directly into mine.

"Constance is a mix of all the lives I study every single day," he says brushing his fingertips over my hip and down my thigh and back. "Your mind went right to me doing this with people all day, didn't it?"

I purse my lips and furrow my brow. "Fine. Yes."

"You're caught up in the romance, but you're only thinking of the sex. Sex sells, Liz. That's why I write it."

"I'm not sure what that says about your character."

He pulls his head back and scans a look over me. "You, baby, were enjoying the sex part. You were at ease. You were in a different place. You weren't thinking about what you went through this morning."

I open my mouth to speak and then close it. What could I possibly say to that?

"Constance writes about people falling in love. And just because I've never done it before, it doesn't mean I don't understand it. And it's fiction, Liz. I'm not some playboy using your grandmother's house for my own pleasure. I would hope you know that by now," he says, his hand still low on my hip.

"I do know that," I admit. "I'm sorry."

"I just don't want you to run away after every time I touch you. You're going to give me a complex."

We both chuckle at that, and I press my forehead to his. "Will you write this into your next book?" I ask.

"No," he says quickly.

I ease back and study him again. "Not memorable enough?"

"Not for anyone else," he says, brushing his fingers up my side, over my arm and shoulder and into my hair. "This is just for us. I get you all to myself."

I'm not even going to ask what that means. I'm going to let that just settle me. Mark wants me all to himself, and I don't feel in my heart like he's just using me to stay in Gran's house. I honestly feel a connection with this man, which is only going to make the rest of the month more confusing.

Breakfast

At breakfast, at Gran's kitchen counter, the stack of letters, tied with the ribbon sits between us. We don't speak.

I had read the first letter, and I was conflicted with feelings that I harbored for my grandmother. Mark has read three of the letters, but he knew more about Genevieve Paige than I did, so maybe none of it was a surprise to him.

"You know, if we just burned these, she'd just be Gran," I say, laying my hand on the stack of letters.

Mark's eyes go wide and he draws in a breath, then settles before walking around the counter, pulling open a drawer, and handing me a lighter.

My eyes widen as I stare at him. He'd let me do it. He'd let me burn everything he'd been waiting for.

My heart hitches. This man.

"Whatever you want to do, Liz. They're your letters," he says.

I shake my head and he sets the lighter on the counter, not putting it away, as if to give me the same choice later if I need it.

Mark moves back around the counter and sits back on his stool, turning so that our knees touch.

"I'm not in this for the knowledge that I don't possess. Betsy was an amazing woman. She was a kind grandmother, a loving partner to my grandfather, a talented actress, and a phenomenal writer. I'm in this because she asked me to be your guide. And, Liz, I'm so much more than that."

I study his face. "What are you?"

Mark lifts his hand to my cheek and holds it there as he watches me. "I really hope I'm someone special to you."

I chew my bottom lip and nod. "You are."

The corners of his mouth lift into a smile. "Good, because you —you'll never leave me," he says with his voice cracking as he takes my hand and places it over his heart. "You mean something to me, Liz. You really do."

The pessimist in me goes right to the fact that this man, though a writer, is just an actor too. When I sell this house, which means nothing to me, by the way, he'll be on his own. I will take that away from him and move back to my life. I can't live in Florida. There is no part of me that wants to stay here.

But when this man touches me or talks to me, everything in me comes to life. If he were acting, that wouldn't happen, would it? Then again, I can listen to his books, written under a pseudonym and which are fiction, and my entire body tingles with just his words.

"How much of Gran's book do you have written?" I ask.

"Most of it." He eases back, but links our fingers on both hands. "She agreed we could talk about her move to Hollywood, and Genevieve ends with her move to Florida. There is no mention of you or your mother. And there are only a few chapters of her working under G.E. Paige with Grandpa."

I'm not sure how to process what he's told me. But I have to remember that the book isn't about Gran, it's about Genevieve Paige. I'm not being cut out of her life—I don't exist in Genevieve Paige's life.

My head is spinning with all the information and we haven't even opened the letters.

"I want to read it," I say.

Mark nods. "Absolutely."

"I want to write the introduction."

His eyes go wide and he smiles again, but only with one side of his mouth—that grin. God, that grin.

"O-kay," he draws out the word. "Liz Evans is going to write the foreword to the book?"

"Yes."

"Granddaughter, Liz Evans?"

I pull my lips in as I consider. "She didn't want that, did she?"

He shakes his head.

"Maybe as journalist Liz Evans."

"O-kay," he says again. "Your call."

"I read the first letter. What does this fill in for you?"

Mark looks at the stack of letters next to us, and then back at me. "There was a man in her life that changed everything for her." His brows draw in. "Again, not your mother's father, but someone very important. I only speculate at who he is, but I think because of their relationship a lot of things would have changed in the world."

"In the world?"

"Yeah," he says on a sigh.

"I can't imagine anything else will shock me at this point. I just have to compartmentalize Gran from Genevieve from G.E. and whoever else I find my grandmother to be."

Mark moves in and kisses my cheek. "Do you want the book first? Or do we read the letters?"

"Can you wait?" I ask. "If I read the book first, I mean."

"I was going to let you burn them," he reminds me. "I'll always be here to finish what Betsy started, but nothing is more important to me than you, Liz. I want you to know that."

"I don't think you'll always feel that way," I say.

"I think I will."

Mark gives my hands a squeeze, stands, and walks toward the

doors that lead to the patio. I watch him walk around the pool and into the pool house.

I turn and look at the letters.

She gave it all up for me, and in what should be seen as a selfless act, and it was, I wonder if it was Gran running away. Betsy Evans existed only as the guardian to two lost souls—Mark and me. She was the PTA president and a volunteer with the theater department, and liked a bargain. She loved playing cards at the senior center. Betsy Evans didn't rub shoulders with movie stars or have grand affairs. She had a cat, who I haven't seen in a bit, so I need to go find him—though I'm sure he's curled up in that chair in Gran's room.

Betsy Evans had a daughter named after her, and a granddaughter named after her too.

This clarity seems to settle me. Suddenly, I'm all in on helping write the book about Genevieve Paige. I want to know all about her, because she wasn't my grandmother.

When Mark comes back with his laptop, he hands it to me. "Take all the time you need," he says.

"What will you do?" I ask and he chuckles.

"Joe needs a ride to the grocery store."

"He doesn't have his groceries delivered?"

Mark laughs. "No, he's a hands-on guy. I usually do my shopping with him."

"What would this community do if you ever left?"

Mark shrugs. "They'll figure it out," he says, and I wonder if he's resigned to the fact that he won't live here much longer.

The Book

I found that I was most focused in Gran and Tom's office, though the air is stuffy. Sitting at the desk, elbows situated for balance, I read, and read, and read.

Mark took Joe to the grocery store and back home, where he then helped the man put away the groceries, clean the bathroom, and prep his dinner.

I don't know if that is a normal day with Joe, and everyone else carved out time with Mark too, or if he's giving me time to read about the life of Genevieve Paige.

She was a dancer. Her mother had paid for dance lessons for her and her sister by taking in laundry. Genevieve's father was a pharmacist who wanted his daughter to do the honorable thing of settling down and starting a family. He was quoted, in later years, to have said he was proud of his daughter as she was very talented.

I pursed my lips at that. Would he have been so proud of her if he'd known she was going to keep him in a coffee can in a cupboard for twenty years?

I chuckle at the thought.

When I hear the door to the house open, I take off my glasses, lean back in the office chair, and kick my feet up on the desk. Mark comes directly to the door where he leans up against the jamb and looks at me.

"I don't know how I feel about you in here so casual," he says, and I can't read his face. It hovers between amusement and annoyance.

"It seemed appropriate."

He nods slowly. "How far did you get?"

"I've read it twice now. You've been gone all day."

His eyes are wide. "You've read it twice?"

"Don't be so shocked. Gran always kept me in books. I never questioned her ability to buy me any book I wanted," I say chuckling. "Anyway, I read fast."

"I guess. So, are you stunned? Sad? Confused?"

I shake my head. "This wasn't Gran," I say. "Genevieve left Missouri for bigger and brighter stars."

"And the Kurt McLaughlin era? How do you feel about it now?"

I drop my feet to the floor, pick up my pen from my notepad, and tap it to my chin. "No less disgusted. Confused as to why it happened while some other man is writing her love letters. And there is still some ick factor in knowing that my grandmother had lovers on the side of every relationship—minus the one with Tom."

"They were made for each other."

I smile up at him. "What a gift you had to be part of that."

He smiles back. "I know that now."

Mark moves from the door to stand in front of me. I set the pen on the desk, and he takes my hands, pulling me out of the chair. He turns me, sits in the chair, and then pulls me down on his lap.

With an arm around my back to hold me in place, he lifts the other hand up into my hair taking out the clip and letting my hair fall. I lick my lips and watch his eyes darken from playful to lustful.

"Liz," he says my name, and it's deep and hot.

"Yes?" I nearly whisper the word.

"I want to be wherever you land," he says trailing his fingers down my throat and over my collarbone.

"What does that mean?" I've closed my eyes because they've become heavy, and my voice is airy as he touches me.

"You're more important than any house or any book," he says running his finger under the fabric of my V-neck, touching the swells of my breasts. "Liz, I need to tell you."

"Tell me what?"

He stops touching me and there is a pause. I open my eyes and he's staring up at me.

"I need to tell you that I'm in love wi—"

I don't let him finish. I bolt off his lap and adjust my shirt.

"Stop. Just stop," I'm nearly shouting. My hands are shaking and that feeling I was just immersed in while he touched me is now just trails of ache.

Cosmo saunters into the room and jumps up into Mark's lap, but he sets the cat back on the ground and stands.

"Don't just let this go, Liz. We're both worthy of—"

I actually cover my ears with my hands. I don't want this right now. I know he says I'm the one putting an expiration date on what's going on between us, but I just can't listen to him profess whatever he thinks he feels right now.

"I can't do this right now," I say, lowering my hands. "You have to understand."

"I don't."

I contemplate that. "I need to mourn her. I need to process all of this. I need to understand what I read today. I need to help you put a tidy little bow on that project, but then who is going to read it? No one. Because no one knew Genevieve Paige," I'm shouting again.

Mark licks his lips. "Everyone knew her."

"No. She was in the background of everything. She wasn't the first name on the marquee. She didn't have the leading roles. How is it that I didn't even know she existed until I found these stupid letters?"

He moves to me, taking my hands, and I let him. I don't want him to waste his words of love on me, but I do need him.

He links our fingers and looks down at them, before raising his eyes to me.

"The book doesn't matter. The only thing that matters is carrying out Betsy's wish. And maybe the book was only to occupy my time and to introduce you to her. It's what she wanted."

"And it's worth your time to put into it?"

He nods. "It most certainly is. She believed in me, Liz. She believed in you, too. That's why you're tasked with all of this. Each of the phases of her life meant something to someone. The letters tell us about the other part."

I look at our hands, still joined. I travel my gaze over the man who I know intimately now. He's right. Gran had phases, and we were both a part of a different phase.

The memorial hadn't helped me say goodbye, as I thought it would. It hadn't been sad. It had been more of a spectacle of the people who knew her through those phases of her life. It was proof that she was missed and loved. But it wasn't sad.

When we take her from the urn and set her free, that will be sad, I know that. It is going to jumble all my emotions, and I know that's why I'm picking these stupid little fights with Mark.

What does it matter if he tells he me he loves me? Grace says it. Even Ashton says it. Julie says it at the end of meetings when she hugs me. "I love ya, doll. You're the best," she says.

Love didn't have to mean anything more than someone loves you being around them in that moment. Mark and I are going to have a lot of moments in the month that I promised him.

"I'm going to go for a swim and clear my head," I say. "Then, I'm going to take a shower."

Mark nods. "Do you want me to start some dinner? Have you eaten since breakfast?"

I give that some thought. "I haven't, and that would be lovely."

"I'll do that then," he agrees.

I step in closer to him, wrapping my arms around him, and his arms instinctively come around me. "After dinner, let's read those letters. I'll help you finish her story," I promise.

The corner of his mouth turns up, and a bit of me turns to goo on the inside.

"I'd really like your help, Liz. I don't think the book can be completed without you."

Back to the Letters

~~~

1958

Dear Genevieve,

I am home, but this isn't home without you. I wish I could have stayed in America. I would have given everything up to be with you.

Perhaps in time I can convince my father to let me travel to bring you here. I know that it is not done, but why not? We'd have everything here. Wealth, the fame that you seek, and we'd have each other.

I dream of you, my sweet. I'll be back to you soon.

I hope you are well, my love. I'll write again soon.

Love, O.Z.

. . .

Handing the second letter to Mark and taking the third, I was surprised by how little the man had to say. So far all I knew was O.Z. was not an American.

1958

Dear Genevieve,

I hope this letter finds you well. I was dismayed to see your face in a newspaper this week in London saying that you were there for the premiere of your movie.

If only I could have you write to me so you could tell me when you travel. I would have loved to have seen you. I did stay to watch your film, and you should have had the lead, my dear. You're much more radiant than any other starlet.

I miss you, my Genevieve. My father has me meeting a family in Egypt next month who has a daughter. I have told him about you, and he says I'm forbidden to go back to America. But I am my own man. I will come for you, my love.

Love, O.Z.

I lift my head, knowing this is as far as Mark has read as well. We're on even ground here.

"O.Z. came from some wealth. Do you get that too?" I ask as I hand Mark the letter and he rereads it.

"If it's who I think it is, he was."

I hold up a hand. "Don't tell me who he is. I'm looking forward to finding out."

He grins at me. "This isn't freaking you out?"

"Yes, no, a little." I pick up the fourth letter and pull it from the envelope. "I'm trying very hard not to condemn my grandmother for this exuberant life she was having. But I have to keep putting it into perspective that this wasn't Gran's life. And without my mother, Gran never would have left Florida, and she would have been hightailing it around here in a golf cart at her age and she'd probably be involved with Joe."

That made Mark snicker. "Joe is gay."

I grin. "He was married to a woman though, wasn't he?"

Mark lifts a brow. "Four of them."

"How old was he when he came out?"

Mark gave it some thought. "Sixty-five?"

"I feel for him. I wish he could have lived his best life like Gran did."

"Who says he didn't?"

I lean in on my forearms. "And why does Joe call you to help him with all his grocery runs and errands?"

Mark leans so that we're nearly forehead to forehead. "I'm the cutest in the neighborhood."

I hadn't expected him to say that, and I let myself laugh fully. I couldn't disagree. Mark is the cutest in the neighborhood, and aren't I the lucky one to have caught him and made him all mine?

But the moment I think it, it sticks in my chest. He might tease me about that expiration date, but it has one, this thing between us.

I amended my thinking and I look at the letters. Maybe Gran was having a momentary relationship with O.Z. just as I am with Mark. But Mark knows I'm leaving. I'm not sure O.Z. knew Gran would keep moving on.

. . .

1959

Dear Genevieve,

It's now been six months since we professed our love to one another and I'm miserable. My father has sent me to Egypt to meet a woman. I told her I was in love with you, and that I would be returning to America to be with you, and she ran out of the room crying. But my father has stranded me here with this family with hopes that I will woo their daughter. I don't plan to do that, but I want to be honest, my dear. I have told them about us, but my father says it isn't real.

I will return to you, my sweet.

My beautiful Genevieve, I have deposited money into that account we opened in your name. I will continue to do so until I can send for you, or I can return to you. Keep me in your heart, my dear. And when I can, I'll write again.

Love, O.Z.

"Why did she keep these?" I ask, holding up the letter and handing it to Mark? "I know nothing about the mighty OZ, but he's whiny."

Mark pulls in his lips as if to not smile.

I narrow my eyes on him. "He is whiny, isn't he?"

"You told me not to tell you anything about him."

"I just don't understand what Gran saw in this guy."

Mark shrugs looking down at the letter. "Did you miss the part where he put money into an account with her name?"

"Do you think she was in it for the money?"

"Struggling actress," he says flatly while reading the letter.

I don't want to buy into that, but okay, I suppose.

1959

Genevieve,

My love, my letter will be short. My heart is broken. I have seen a news reel where you are intimate with Kurt McLaughlin, who is married. Might I remind you that you, too, are married!

"What?!" The word comes out so loudly that Mark startles. "She married the guy?"

Mark takes the letter from me. He hasn't gotten to the fourth letter.

There is no smile, instead, his brows knit as he reads the rest of the letter.

"Give it back. I didn't finish it," I say, holding out my hand.

He shakes off my request finishing the letter before handing it back to me wide eyed.

Genevieve, we took vows. We promised ourselves to one another. I have been sending money to the bank account and I am holding up my end of our marriage even though my father does not recognize it as binding. Please tell me that what I saw was wrong. I will be returning to America soon. I will come for you.

Love, O.Z.

I toss the letter into the center of the table and rest my head in my hands. Who was this woman?

Mark reaches for me, and I give him my hand. "This woman..." I say, letting it hang there.

"Was nineteen when this letter was written," he reminds me.

"I had a zit on my forehead when I was eighteen that was there for three months and I couldn't make it go away. I had the same Subaru when I was eighteen, and I had a line of Mickey Mouse antennae bobbles," I say, and I'm not sure he understands, but he gets the gist.

I pull my hand back and run my hands over my head. "I was eighteen. I did eighteen-year-old things. This—" I pick up the letter and shake it. "This is beyond my comprehension."

"Liz—" he says my name on a breath.

"I know. I know. It was a different time. But I don't know who this was."

"And that's why you're learning about it now. Now when she can't argue your feelings and she can't stop you from feeling them. She wanted you to know it all, and here you are."

He's right. That's what this has all been about.

I pick up the next letter and steel myself before I open it. I'm not sure what I'll find in the rest of the letters, but it sure isn't Gran. Gran was a different person entirely from Genevieve Paige.

Mrs. O.Z.

~∽∽~

The next three letters are the same. They had come in rapid succession, well, as far as international mail did in the late fifties.

O.Z. was moving around, trying to escape this father of his, and he gave Gran—Genevieve—addresses. She must have written back to him, as the eighth letter read much differently.

1960

My Beloved Genevieve,

Your letters remain with me as I travel and speak on my father's behalf. I knew that you would be true to me, as you'd promised to be.

I actually snort out a laugh and Mark lifts his head. He'd brought out his laptop and was making notes from the letters. I wave off his interest, and go back to the letter.

*My wife would be pure to me, which is why
you are my wife. I couldn't have waited until this
was all sorted out to have you. I shall come for
you in a few months. We will announce ourselves,
and then we will have a proper ceremony. We will
have many children.*

*The bank account is growing fuller, and you will
not need to work in those movies anymore. You will
be like the Princess of Monaco, and will bring
beauty and grace to my family. I will write again
soon.*

I love you, my princess.
Love, O.Z.

I didn't know what this man was talking about, and the more I read his letters the more I considered that he resembled some internet creeper that I often found I had to block. But I think that maybe my grandmother lost her virginity to this guy, and he weirds me out.

I toss the letter to Mark and open the next. He only briefly looks up at me when I do so. His fingers have been flying on his keyboard. These were the missing pieces to his puzzle. To me, they are like reading a bad romance novel. Seriously, I wouldn't be surprised if the last letter was in Gran's handwriting and said, *Gotcha!*

1961

Genevieve,

It has been a long while since I have written, but things have changed. I'm sure news has arrived in America of the passing of my father. I now must step into his shoes.

I had long wanted you to come here and live with me, but as time has gone on, I see that we cannot have that. I am sending this letter to your home in St. Louis, as I know you will be going there for Christmas.

Your family will be there to comfort you when I tell you that I am to be married to the woman from Egypt that I once told you about.

I'm sorry my sweet. I know you wait for me, and I must tell you this. This marriage is of duty, and in my heart it is only you, my princess.

I will continue to send money, and in another year, I will come to America, because no one can keep me from doing so. I will come, and we can be together. Once I am established in my role, I will send for you, and I will divorce so that we can finally be together. Wait for me, my sweet Genevieve.

Love, O.Z.

Again, I throw the letter on the pile and Mark looks up.

"Ick, just ick," I say, and Mark grins.

"Not impressed?"

"I hate that it's all one sided. I mean, I have no idea what Gran was doing during these times, but—"

"I do."

My lips part. I hadn't even thought about that. "You have her side."

He shrugs. "I have her stories from this time," he says, and I realize that I read the book he'd put together, up to this point.

Gran was just living her life, taking lovers, making big decisions. She had made some silly eighteen-year-old decision that put this man in her path, and he just continued to come around.

"I think she'd fallen in with this guy and couldn't get out, if you will. I mean, hell, obviously this is a one-sided love affair," he says.

"Obviously."

"How many more letters?"

"Three," I say.

"I think I know where they're leading, but I want to make sure."

"Do you want to share that with me?"

Mark purses his lips and shakes his head. "No. I rather enjoy watching you process all of this."

"You're an ass."

"And you love me," he says nonchalantly as he looks back at his computer screen, but I sit and watch him.

He didn't mean that. I don't love him. I care for him. I'm enjoying him. I shake my head and pick up the next letter. I'm no different from my grandmother, I decide. Therapy—I'm going to need more therapy.

1963

My Genevieve,

I recently saw a TV program, and you were in it. I would call, but it can be traced. This seems safer, for now. I know it's been years since I have written, but I think of you every day. My wife is pregnant with our third child. I have fulfilled that part of my father's plan, but I would rather his heirs have your red hair and sparkling green eyes.

The reason for this letter is to tell you that I will be in New York. I know you are there, on Broadway, and I will come to you. We will share a night together, my love. I miss you.

Love, O.Z.

Yuck. There are only two more letters, and God, I hope we learn something worthy. Gran owes me for this. Why did she keep these? No one needed to know about this guy.

1963

My Love,

Our time in New York was everything I dreamed it would be. You will forever be my one true love.

O.Z.

. . .

So, my grandmother had no scruples. Sure, she'd been dragging this guy along for five years or more. He has a wife and children, but why not meet up with him in New York? If this had been my life, she would have slapped the shit out of me.

I pick up the next letter.

"Last one," I say.

Mark holds up a finger as he finishes the letter I had just tossed at him, and then he makes notes.

"Read it aloud," he says. "Then I'll show you what I have."

I wrinkle my nose. "I'm not sure I want to know any of this."

"I think you do."

I pick up the last envelope. It's postmarked 1970. Seven years from their night in New York. New York must have not been so stellar if they went their separate ways. Then again, maybe he just started calling. If he did that, at least I don't have to read about it.

When I open the envelope, there is nothing but a newspaper article inside.

The Death of a Prince, the article is titled. I swallow hard. *Prince Omar Zaki is dead at thirty-two.*

I lift my head. "Prince Omar Zaki?"

Mark nods and turns his computer to face me. "I was right. This is who she'd been involved with. I just didn't have confirmation, and she wouldn't tell me directly."

"Oh, because it's much more fun to find out this way," I say rolling my eyes.

"Well, at least we got to find out together," he says.

"I think I could have gone my entire life without knowing that my grandmother strung some middle eastern prince along for years, and had an affair with him while his wife was pregnant." I shake off the feeling.

"But it does answer a lot of our questions."

"Does it now? And which questions would those be, because I

feel as if I have wasted my entire afternoon reading these, and now I just feel dirty."

Mark is watching me as if I have missed the whole point. And if I did, I almost don't care. To him these letters were important. To me, well, I think I should have burned them.

"Remember how you asked how a supporting actress could afford to build a house in Palm Beach at the age of twenty-five?"

My eyes go wide. "No."

"That bank account he filled? Yeah, she took it and bought the house."

I slap my hands over my mouth. "My grandmother is a prostitute," I say quite loudly and Mark snorts out a laugh.

"Your grandmother was married to a prince, who, basically paid her off for her silence if you will."

"Or did she steal the money?"

"It was her money. Her name was on the account."

"Not his?"

Mark shook his head. "They would have found that if Omar Zaki had put his name on it, wouldn't they?"

"Scandalous," I say on a laugh.

"In the most delicious way."

Soberly, I sit up straight and look at him. "I don't want that in her book," I say.

"Liz, this whole book has been waiting on this moment. I've been waiting to find out who he was and where the money came from."

"I don't like what it says about her."

Mark blinks hard. "Are you kidding me?"

"Not in the least. The book does not go to press with O.Z. in it."

"It's the only way this thing will sell."

"You said that wasn't important. You were doing this for Gran."

He purses his lips and closes his laptop. "I appreciate your opinion, but I won't honor it. The book is between me and Betsy. Not you and me."

"I'll sue."

"You can't. I have the proof I needed."

I bite the inside of my cheek. "She doesn't deserve this. I don't want her name to be trashy."

"Liz, she asked me to write it, and she asked me to wait to have all the information."

Cosmo walks around our feet, as if he's a child trying to calm his fighting parents. "If you print it, it goes as an unauthorized biography. She's not here to argue."

"You're being a bit too harsh about this."

"I'm in the driver's seat, Watts. There's not much you can do about it."

A Life Well-Lived

Mark left last night after our fight. He took Cosmo with him, and he didn't come back.

I slept in Gran's room, with her on the nightstand, and we had a long talk.

I told her I didn't think it was fair for me to find out about her like this, and that I was pissed. She didn't have anything to say to that, of course.

When the night got too hot, I went out to the pool and sat on the steps in the shallow end. I thought about what Mark had said about not swimming alone, even though it was sexy talk at the time, but under the circumstances, I figure he's right. So I don't swim.

At midnight I text him.

You didn't have to leave, is all I say, but it goes unanswered. At one o'clock, I text again.

Let me know Cosmo is okay.

To that I receive a photo of Cosmo on a chair and I recognize it as one of his mother's chairs.

He'd gone to Orlando. Well, there was no need for me to stay up—he wasn't going to come back any time soon and pick a fight with me, which is all I seem to be looking for.

So, I text Grace.

I should have known that I wouldn't get a text back, instead she called me, frantic.

"Are you okay? Tell me you're okay," she says the moment I answer the phone.

"I'm okay."

"Well, you shouldn't be. You should be dead if you're calling me this late."

"It's ten o'clock there. Seriously, you're already saying that's late?"

"Liz, I'm pregnant. Do you know what my body is going through? I'm sick all the damn time. I'm tired. I'm irritable. It's like having full-time PMS but no cramps yet. I've been in bed for two hours. So what the hell is wrong?"

I look around the room and think of the house, which is now mine and how I plan to sell it. But after having Grace lay it all out, I'm not sure I want to go back.

Okay, that's a full out lie to myself. I hate Florida. I want to go home.

"I'm sorry," I say to her, which was something I'm not going to say to Mark.

"Fine. You're sorry. Now why are you texting me?"

"He left."

"Who?"

"Mark," I nearly shout into the phone.

"Right. Right. Text guy."

"He's not just text guy," I argue.

"No. He's not. He's the man you're in love with."

"Excuse me?" I want a fight, I guess I got one.

"Oh, give me a fucking break, Liz. For the past two weeks, all I have heard about is text guy. Then he shows up in Nashville. Now you're sleeping with him. Now you're picking fights. It's love. This is doomed to be a marriage."

"You're out of your mind," I counter.

"I am. Because I'm fucking pregnant," she shouts back. "What did you pick the fight about?"

"Who says I started it?"

"Because you start every fight, Liz. You can't stand to not have it all about you all the time. Well, there are a lot of people in the world, and guess what, some of us have feelings. So, text guy must have some too."

I chew on my bottom lip. "He's going to write the book about Gran, even though we found out she was married to some middle eastern prince who sent money and she bought this house, and—"

"Liz," Grace's voice is low in my ear. "You do realize I have no idea what you're even talking about."

"Gran isn't who I thought she was."

"How nice. Please tell me that she had this amazing life and did amazing things. What more did she do?"

"She wasn't the woman that raised me, that's for damn sure."

"How lovely to have multiple lives," she shouts into the phone again.

"She was married to some prince who had to leave, I guess to go take over his kingdom."

Now Grace snickers on the other end of the phone, and I realize it sounds stupid.

"But she still had affairs with older, married men. She had an affair with the prince guy when he was married. He gave her the money, and she bought this house. Seriously, all the pieces just don't add up."

Grace snickers. "And to think, she gave it all up to raise a spoiled little brat like you."

Grace's words rattle through me, and then my body begins to shake, and the tears roll down my cheeks. I hit the speaker on the phone and drop it on my bed. I can't stop sobbing now, and Grace is calling my name.

"I'm fine. I'm fine," I whimper, but I'm not.

"Liz, I'm sorry."

I shake my head, as if she could see it. But it occurs to me that she has nothing to be sorry about. I am selfish. I am a brat.

Gran had the most amazing life, and my only adventure is that I went to college and got a job. I love my job, but I don't travel. I don't fly. I don't date. I don't live.

Gran left home for an adventure, and she never went back. She had affairs—great big affairs. She was in movies and plays, and on television. She wrote some of my favorite movies, and I didn't even know it. She kept Mark working when he could have just given it all up.

Mark.

The book was his to write, and it gave him purpose. I took that away from him.

I am a selfish brat.

"I have to go," I say, picking up my phone.

"Bitch, you'd better keep me on the line for at least another thirty minutes. You don't get to wake me up, give me all this information, and then cry and hang up. Oh, no. You get to hear about my getting sick and my new food cravings. And then, you're going to tell me intimate details about you sleeping with the house boy. Then, calmly, you're going to tell me about your grandmother being married to a prince, because, shit, Liz, you just don't hear that every day."

The tears are still flowing, but now I'm laughing. And the tears might just be from the laughter because it's coming out hard.

I love her. I love this woman who has put up with me all these years. And I'm going to spoil that baby rotten, because I don't want one of my own, so hers should be spoiled.

And when we're done here, I'm going to make things right with Mark. I owe it to him.

The Foreword

It's nearly three o'clock when I hear the door open. I'm getting more sun than I like, but I didn't want to chance missing Mark walk through, so I've been parked next to the pool for hours.

When the patio door opens, I hear Cosmo's refusal to go outside long before I see Mark.

He's standing at the door looking in my direction as if he hadn't considered I'd still be here.

His hair is mussed, and he has on the same clothes he left in.

I swing my legs to the side of the lounge and stand as Mark begins walking toward me. I take a breath to speak, but he holds up his hand.

"I don't have the energy, Liz," he says as he walks past me and straight to the pool house.

I take a breath to speak, and then let it out without words.

He deserves some down time in his own space. I need to be patient and giving. This isn't all about me.

It takes a few minutes before he opens his door and looks out over the pool at me. "What is this?" he asks, and I notice he's waving a paper in his hand.

I swallow hard, stand, and walk to his door.

His beard is coming in after not shaving for a few days. His eyes are hollow and dark.

"Explain this?" He's holding the paper out to me.

I lick my lips, not touching it. "It's the foreword to the book," I say.

"The foreword? The foreword to the book you threatened to sue me over? Real rich, Liz. Real rich."

"Let me explain, I—"

"No," he says, waving his hands. "No. You don't get to explain. I don't want to hear it. You don't want that book written with the information in it, then it's not written. In fact, I'm over it, Liz."

He rakes his fingers through his hair as he paces a small circle in the middle of the room.

"I was doing it for Betsy. Everything in my fucking life has been for Betsy—and why? Because she's the only one who ever gave a damn about me."

"That's not true," I counter.

"It is true. The only reason I'm alive and thriving is because of her. This was her last wish on my behalf, just like the trip was yours. But Betsy is yours, isn't she? She never was mine."

I blink hard and study him. "She was yours."

"You don't think so."

Again, I take a breath to speak, but nothing comes out. He's right.

"Mark, give me a moment to say something, please."

Resigned, he sits on the bed and scrubs his hands over his face. "What?"

"I was wrong," I say, and that has him looking up at me. "Grace keeps putting me in my place, and I think I need it."

I take a chance on his reaction by sitting down beside him. He doesn't argue, and instead he reaches for my hand and weaves our fingers together.

It calms me, and I know in that moment that I love this man, even if I can't keep him.

"Gran's story needs to be told the way she wanted it to be told."

Mark lifts his head so that he can look at me.

"Liz, if you don't want—"

"No. It's not about what I want. For the first time it needs to not be about me. I get that." I let out a slow breath. "Gran was never afraid to live. She has stories upon stories, and she's lived many different lives. I was reminded that I haven't lived yet," I say.

Mark's thumb brushes over my knuckles.

"You've lived a different life," he says.

"You're right. But from the time I was six, I lived it safely." I lick my lips as they've gone dry. "Mom and I almost died on that flight going home when I was little," I say and he nods as if he knew, but I continue. "It wasn't until I was much older that I learned that the engine had gone out on the plane, and that was why we crash landed."

I bat away new tears. "People were hurt. One man died because he had a heart attack. Mom and I walked away, but it kept us grounded. We would never travel again. Then she got sick. I had no one who could care for me like a parent should, and mind you, I understand why. I've always understood why. Then Gran showed up, and I was her whole world, but I lived scared. What if I left home and the plane crashed again? What if I did something big and then got sick and died? What if I wasn't right there for Gran?"

I sniff back the tears that had clogged up. "I've never lived even one half of one of the lives Gran did."

"You're young," he says.

I nod. "Then I'd better start living."

Now Mark takes a breath and I see his eyes clear a bit. "I mean it, Liz. If you don't want the book—"

"I do. Let's finish it."

The corner of his mouth turns up. "Okay."

Our hands grip tighter to one another, because he knows I'm not done with what I have to say.

"When we're done with it, we'll take Gran and scatter her."

He nods. "Okay."

"I'm going to take some of her home to Mom, but the rest I want left with your grandfather, and a little bit of her left in the ocean so she can still travel. Maybe all the way across the ocean."

Mark chuckles. "I like that."

"I have to sell the house," I say quickly so that I don't skip over it, and Mark's gaze dips from me to our hands.

He lets go of me and stands. "That's your call."

"I can't keep it. I have to go home."

He squeezes his eyes closed tight. "Okay."

"You can come with me," I say, though I hadn't planned to.

He opens his eyes and looks at me. "Mom," is all he says.

I hadn't even considered that.

Standing, I cross to him, reaching for him and he pulls me in. His arms come around me tightly, and he just holds me.

Everything inside of me is tight with the feeling that we were always a lost cause, yet we don't want to be. He said he loved me and I argued. I know that I love him, but I can't say it.

There is an expiration date on us, and now we both know it. This has to end when the book is done. I have to go home, and Mark has to stay to take care of his mother and live his life.

I wonder if Gran knew it would be so hard when she put us on the path to one another.

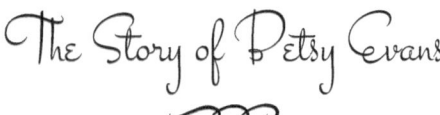

The Story of Betsy Evans

We become writing partners the day after Mark returns from Orlando, after I volunteer to take Joe to the recreation center for his physical therapy. Though, I think he is more than disappointed that my cute roommate is not the one to drive him.

The book that Gran and Mark had been working on for the better part of a decade was eighty-five percent finished. With the letters from O.Z., the timeline is complete.

Though all of our writing isn't on the book. I have deadlines and articles to write, and the next Constance Frost book is due to the editor in a week, so Mark is feverishly working on that. I'd like to think I give him some inspiration. Perhaps a bit of insight from a woman would only make the book that much better—or so I think.

Cosmo has taken it upon himself to decide when one of us has worked too hard. He equally distracts and loves on Mark as much as he does on me. I guess Cosmo will make the ultimate decision on who to stay with when it's time to go.

We haven't talked about me selling the house in over a week, and I suppose it will just be the thing that lingers between us and is unspoken.

Two weeks into the month that I promised Mark, and we haven't slept apart since the night he went to Orlando. In fact, I think since we both know our time together is limited, we spend every free moment taking in one another. I swear, every time with him is better than the last. Maybe we will have one of those relationships where we don't see one another for years, but we'll meet in New York and have an intimate night.

The thought has me grinning to myself.

"What are you thinking?" Mark asks from over the top of his laptop.

I look up over the top of mine and smile wider. "What if we're that couple that just randomly meets up every few years for a romantic night? I mean, it either needs to be close enough to Denver, or I'll need drive time."

"No winter interludes, I guess," he says.

"Why not?"

"I won't have you driving all over the country in the winter."

No, he wouldn't, because he cares about me—he loves me.

His computer chimes and he looks down at it. "Hot damn," he says and his eyes are wide.

"What's up?"

He looks back up at me. "The publisher reached out to the family of Omar Zaki for comments about the relationship he had with Genevieve Paige. We wanted permission to write it into the book, though we would have done so without their permission," he says. "But they agreed. After Zaki was assassinated," he says while reading, "his brother took over because Omar's children were too young, and all girls," he adds. "His brother reigned, and his son took over only in 2010. But, the affair was a secret that the family has kept under wraps for seventy years, and the new monarch thinks it should be part of the history of his uncle's legacy."

I narrow my gaze on him. "Legacy? Or does he want to tarnish the legacy?"

"I'm not sure." Mark chews his bottom lip. "We make it a point to write it so that Betsy comes out shiny. I mean, we only have one half of the relationship, right? From the sounds of it, she just went on with life, and took what was given to her, which was a fortune allowing her to buy a house where she would ultimately raise her daughter."

"Right," I agree.

He's in his thinking mode now. His eyes are wide, and they aren't focused on me, even though he's looking in my direction. "Yeah, we keep the prince in the story, but we make him as whiny as he seemed to be," he says before going back to work and his fingers flying over the keys on his laptop.

For the first time in three weeks, we haven't gotten out of bed at the same time.

When I roll over, Mark is gone. His suitcase is laying out on top of his dresser.

I manage myself out of bed and pull on the robe I had found in Gran's closet. It's only six o'clock, and Mark is not one to be up at six.

I walk past the pool and into the house where he has coffee brewed, but he's nowhere to be seen.

"I'll be there. Thanks, Jess," he says, and he's grinning wide looking down at his phone as he walks from the office to the kitchen. He jumps when he sees me standing there, but just as quickly, his face shifts back into that joy he'd had. "Hey," he says in that low whisper that always makes my knees weak.

"Jess?" I ask, and I try to keep any jealousy out of my tone, because, damn, it's my chest.

"Agent," he says as he moves to me and presses a kiss to my lips.

"Big day for the author," he says giving my rear a small slap as he moves to the coffee pot and fills the mug he had sitting there.

"Your suitcase is out?"

Mark pours the coffee and nods. "I have to go to New York. Jess and I have a meeting with the publisher about Betsy's book."

"That's good, right?"

"Great, actually. It so happens that the editor who is acquiring it, is a huge silver screen fan. She's published four of my other biographies, but she thinks this one is going to be much bigger."

"Why?"

Mark blinks hard as he stares at me. "Liz, she's Genevieve Paige and G.E. Paige. There's an Oscar sitting there, remember?"

I look toward the living room where the twin statues sit on the shelf. "Right."

"Anyway, now that the information on the prince is in there, she's beside herself. But, that wasn't the only news Jess had," he says, setting his mug on the counter and sweeping me into his arms. "Netflix wants Constance's last book."

"That's great," I say, genuinely happy for him.

"It is. Oh, baby, this is what I've waited for. Can you believe it?"

I keep my smile in place, because he deserves this. "I'm so happy for you."

"I mean, there's going to be a certain amount of work to keep Constance and I separate. I suppose someday that'll be out there, but..."

"But for now, this is great news."

"It is. I'm flying out in a few hours," he says stepping back and picking up his mug.

"When will you be back?"

"Few days, I guess. I don't know, actually. I'll have a few meetings and..." He stops and looks at me. "Go with me."

I shake my head. Now my pulse is quickening and I actually feel sick. "No. I can't. No."

"Liz, millions of people fly every day. There's like a one in a billion chance that something will happen. You should—"

"No," I say again and turn to walk back to the pool house.

I sit down on the bed and look at his suitcase. This is my reality. Mark is going to get everything he's ever wanted—because of Gran. Well, because of Gran and the fact that he's amazing with words and has a knack of adding romance to a story.

I'm grounded to my own space and I'll never have what he has.

He deserves this, I remind myself. And I swear I won't ruin it for him, but the old Liz wants to be petty over it.

He asked me to go, but my fear is keeping me right where I am.

The Wait

Joe must have decided that I wasn't such a bad companion. He's called me three times since Mark left for New York. I have taken him to the pharmacy, to the grocery store, and sock shopping at Walmart.

Joe, I have learned was a film director who ended up retiring in Palm Beach, in this eclectic neighborhood of old Hollywood royalty. And in the case of Gran, I guess actual royalty.

I've had a week to process that, and now I can laugh. Gran was married to a prince.

Mark has been gone for three days, and I've only exchanged a handful of texts with him. Biding my time in this house makes me realize that I can't live here—not even a little bit. The house is cold and impersonal. The air is much too thick for this Colorado girl. It's October, and it's still freaking hot.

I'm not sure Cosmo likes it either. He sleeps all the time.

I've talked to Grace for hours as I wander around the house, and wonder when Mark will return, because I miss him like crazy.

Are you home? Alone? Able to talk?

The text comes through just as I turn off the light and settle into Mark's bed.

Cosmo and I are in your bed. So I can't say I'm alone. Are you? I text, and then realize that it sounds horrible. So I add, *I can talk.*

My phone rings in my hand.

"Hey," he says softly, but I can hear a lot of noise behind him.

"Hey," I say. "Are you out on the town?"

He chuckles. "Sorta. I'm boarding a flight."

I sit up in the bed and Cosmo shifts on Mark's pillow as if I've disturbed him.

"You're coming home?"

"I'll be there in a few hours," he says. "I'll try not to wake you when I come in."

"Like hell," I nearly shout. "You'd better wake me."

Mark laughs. "I will. You might let Cosmo know I'm coming to claim my spot back."

I hate missing him. It's just a precursor to what's coming, and it's been miserable.

"Did it go well?" I ask.

"It did," he says, and I swear I can hear his smile in his words. "I'll talk to you soon."

"I'll be here, I say."

"I love you," he says, and then the call is disconnected.

I slowly let out the breath that I'm holding. He wasn't even going to give me a chance to say anything to that.

I can't just lay in bed and wait. I watch some TV in the living room. I do some writing. And I make a strong pot of coffee. I hope he's wired because I'm going to need to touch him, kiss him, and let him do all those things to me before I let him rest. I've missed him too much.

When lights flash through the front of the house, I know he's home.

I have never been so excited to see someone come through the door as I am waiting for Mark. Cosmo has finally joined me. I guess he felt the need to welcome him too.

When the door opens, Mark barely steps through before I'm lunging at him.

He gets the door closed before he's pressed to it and I'm wrapped around him.

He tastes like coffee and mints, and I can't get enough.

His hands are all over me, as if he's waited for this moment too. It's been four days in total, how could I have missed him so much—as if I might die if he hadn't returned when he did.

Hoisting me to his hips, I wrap my legs around him, and he carries me to the kitchen, where he plants me on the counter, but he doesn't move away. His hands are on my face, up into my hair, squeezing my breasts, and rubbing my thighs. Our mouths are open to one another, and breath is fought for.

"I fucking missed you," he growls, taking my face in his hands and again moving in, his tongue lapping at mine as if it's breath.

"I fucking missed you too," I manage as I begin to pull his shirt from his body.

Cosmo meows loudly, and we both look to see him sitting there looking up at us as if has been patient long enough and he's now demanding his hug.

Mark presses his forehead to mine.

"I have missed this cat," he says reaching down to pick him up and holding him between us. "I don't know how I'm going to survive when you go," he says, his voice balanced between sad and amused.

"Tell me you're not tired," I say.

Mark laughs. "I'm exhausted."

"That's too bad. I drank most of a pot of coffee waiting for you. I've written two articles. Watched TV, and had a long chat with Gran."

Rubbing Cosmo's back, Mark shifts a look between me and the cat. "You'll be up for a while, huh?"

"Yes."

"I'll have some more coffee and see how long I can last."

He steps back and I hop off the counter and move to the coffee pot. Taking down a mug, I watch him nuzzle his nose into the cat's fur. I should leave the cat with him, I think. No, I need that stupid cat.

"So, since we're up. Tell me what happened."

Mark and Cosmo move to a stool at the counter and sit down. Cosmo is in cat heaven on Mark's lap.

"I signed the contracts and turned over the book. She wants us to sign a release on the private photos we added to the book."

I nod. I'd expected that.

"She liked your foreword too," he adds.

"Does she know who I am to Betsy?"

Mark nods. "She wants me to ask you to reconsider your connection in the letter. She thinks that the fact that Betsy disappeared, and the reasons for which she did, it would mean a lot. Besides, what would it hurt with Betsy gone?"

I worry at my lip as I fill his mug and hand it to him. "I don't want anyone to think I'm trying to gain some notoriety because of Gran."

"Liz, you already have it. Why not own it?"

I hadn't thought about that. People will begin to put pieces together. Her obituary ran in the paper in Colorado, as it had to, and I already had one friend email me, asking questions. I hadn't returned the email. But Mark is right. Genevieve/G.E. became the Betsy Evans who left everything behind to raise her granddaughter.

I humor that the story would only be even funnier if we lived in a cabin in the forest where no one would ever find out who the true Betsy Evans was.

"I'll think about it," I say.

"I also want you to think about adding your name as a co-author."

My eyes are wide on him and I shake my head. "That project was yours. I just came in with the letters."

"No, you did much more than that."

"I didn't. I won't take any credit."

Mark reaches for my hand. "Just think about it. It could mean something for us. I mean, she's already talking about us doing the talk circuit, podcasts, morning shows…"

"Mark, I can't do that," I say resigned to it all. "I can't travel to make that happen. I just can't do it."

He draws in a breath. "I won't force you. But know that if you decide you want to try to fly again, I'd never leave your side. I'd hold you from the moment we got on that plane until we walk off —and we would walk off."

Just thinking about it makes me sick.

"Mark…"

He only nods and I know he'll never ask again.

Constance Frost

⁓⌒⌒⌒⌒

Since Mark has returned from New York, his head has been down and he's been working. Constance has one book being turned into a movie. He's finalizing edits on her next book, and he's been writing like a mad man on a new book he started after I arrived. He says I'm his muse, though I'm not sure what to think of that.

Brenda and gang have invited us over for dinner, but I'm really not feeling it. Though, she's called Mark three times today to make sure we're coming. Something tells me this isn't new. Mark gets so focused on his work that he easily forgets what time of day it is. Already I've had to remind him to eat, which makes me laugh. Grace has to make sure I eat or get up and walk around.

It makes me wonder if Brenda usually is that person for Mark.

That ugly sting of jealousy zips through me again, and I do everything in my power to shake it off as I walk toward him, sitting at the counter, and gently rest my hand on his back.

"If we're going to get to Brenda's even close to on time, we need to go."

He keeps working as if he can't feel me or hear me, but I know now he has to finish his thought or it'll disappear.

He continues to write and then hits the caps lock key and leaves himself a note in the middle of the manuscript.

SHE HAS TO GO BACK TO THE BANK. LOCKET IS IN HER POCKET. ONE SHOE IS RED ONE IS BLUE.

I grin at that. I can't wait to read this book.

Mark turns so that he's facing me, and with his hands on my hips, he pulls me to him. "Do we have to go?"

I wrap my arms around his neck. "I think I've been hogging you. Your friends are missing you."

He groans, resting his head to my chest. "I'm not lonely with you here. So, maybe I have been ignoring them."

"I guess we could stay here, turn off all the lights, and lock ourselves in your room. I'll have Grace call them and they can all commiserate on when we once were part of society."

He chuckles. "Give me ten minutes to catch a quick shower."

Brenda opens the door, her arms folded in front of her, and she shifts a gaze between us.

"I kind of thought if he had a keeper, he'd be on time," she says directly at Mark.

I'm not sure if she's kidding or not until she laughs and pulls Mark in for a hug.

"You're complicated," she says to him before kissing him on the cheek. Then she turns to me and pulls me in for a hug, which is strange since I've only been around this woman a few times. "I'm so glad you're here," she says to me, but it's more of an intimate conversation she's having with me, and it's not about just being at her house in that moment.

Brenda steps back and scans a look over Mark. "You're writing, aren't you?"

The corner of his mouth curls up, and he reaches back for my hand. When our fingers link, he nods.

"I have a muse," he says.

Brenda gives me a look and nods. "He doesn't even know what day it is, does he?"

"I'm not sure he does," I agree.

Brenda takes Mark's other hand and pulls him through the door. "Well, luckily no one has left yet. We can remind him."

As we walk into Brenda's small house, I notice that there are at least twenty people gathered between the living room and kitchen, and I can see others outside on the patio.

Finn and Jeff, the only other people I know in the house, come right for us.

"Holy shit, pal. Happy Birthday. You almost missed it," Finn says, pulling Mark in for a hug, and nearly taking me with him, since Mark hasn't let go of my hand.

Jeff slaps him on the shoulder when Finn moves. "Happy Birthday, man. I've almost finished all the beer I brought you."

Brenda studies Mark, and then looks at me. I'm sure my expression says a lot.

"Did you actually forget that it was your birthday?" she asks before looking at me again. "Did he tell you it was his birthday?"

I shake my head and Mark squeezes my hand.

"You're right. I forgot what day it was," he says, humored by the whole thing.

Brenda laughs and with both hands on his cheeks, she kisses him right on the mouth. Since he's still holding my hand, that jealousy bug doesn't even bite.

"It's a good thing you have a good woman to take care of you from now on. You'd better keep her happy. Don't let her go," Brenda says before walking toward the kitchen.

Finn and Jeff move into conversation with another guy who walks through, and Mark slips an arm around my waist and leans in close.

"By the way, today is my birthday," he says.

"You don't say?"

He shrugs. "I guess so."

That makes me laugh and I move into him, my arms looped around his neck, and his around my waist.

"Happy birthday," I whisper against his lips before I kiss him.

"Thanks," he says softly. "I did actually forget."

"I think Constance Frost is a problem," I tease.

"Like Brenda says, it's a good thing I have a good woman to take care of me from now on."

I can't argue. Not here. Not now. He doesn't need me to take care of him, and I don't need him to take care of me. We've both lived our lives without needing anyone. He will take care of his mother, just as he did for his grandfather. And I—well—a rush of grief hits me right in the stomach, and I feel sick. I took care of Gran. Now I guess I only have me to take care of.

I promised him a month, and I only have a week left. One more week to convince myself that when I leave him a part of me won't be destroyed. One more week before I drive home, back to my life. One more week before he moves on with Constance Frost's movie and work begins on the book about Gran. He'll be much too busy to remember me. It won't matter that I'm going to sell the house. He won't need it.

My breath is labored and I'm dizzy. Mark has turned to talk to someone, and even though he's still holding my hand, the room is fuzzy to me.

"Right?" he says turning to me.

I blink and he's smiling. I've created my own hell swirling around me.

I smile. "I'm sorry. What?"

"I was just telling Ed about your work, and how nice it is that you can do it from anywhere."

Oh, what is he doing?

I suck in a breath and smile at Ed—I guess that's who the man looking at me is. "Right. It's been a pleasure to get to work on the road," I say before I turn to Mark and lean in. "Where is the bathroom," I whisper in his ear.

"Down the hall," he says, finally letting go of my hand.

"I'll be right back," I say, before walking down the hall hoping for just a few moments to collect myself.

The surprise party for Mark's birthday seems to be as big a surprise for me too.

Surprise—I'm so in love with this man my heart is already breaking.

The Gift

Mark is pressed up behind me in bed, our bodies slicked with sweat.

"I think that was the best birthday gift I've ever had," Mark pants into my ear and I grin at that.

"Well, if I would have known, I could have planned a little something more," I tease trying to catch my breath. I roll to face him, his arms wrapping around me, keeping me close. "How in the hell do you forget that it's your birthday?"

He grins. "You might have gathered that the celebration of my birth was not important to either of my parents, or I might have remembered."

My heart breaks for him, and I realize that Grace would be the only one to remember my birthday now—and she'd remember.

Tears sting my eyes, and I quickly try to bat them away, but he notices.

"What's wrong?" he asks, lifting his thumb to my cheek to wipe away the tear that escaped.

"I don't have anyone but Grace who would remember my birthday either," I say and suck in the sob.

"April fourth. I'll never forget it," he says, because he's already committed it to memory.

I lick my lips. "You'll call me on my birthday?"

Something flashes in his eyes, and then settles. "I promise to call you."

It's all I can ask for and now, I'll wait for that call as if my life depends on it.

Mark finished his edits on Constance Frost's next book on Sunday afternoon, and then he wrote himself a contract and made me sign it as a witness.

I, Mark A. Watts will only write two thousand words a day, and will spend the rest of the time living in the moment.

He signs the paper and then passes it to me.

"You think this will fix your passion?" I ask before I sign the paper he has scrawled on.

"I don't break contracts," he says as I set down the pen and he gathers my hands. "Let's take a drive," he says. "I want to take you to see Grandpa."

I know that means we're going to a cemetery, but there is something about him wanting to take me to his grandfather that fills my heart.

"Should we take Gran?"

He shakes his head. "Not yet. Let's keep her with us until the last minute. And then we'll take her back."

I nod as Cosmo jumps up into my lap and I have to let go of Mark and hold on to the cat. "I think he wants to go with us."

Mark runs his hands over Cosmo's head. "Crazy cat. I've missed your antics."

I watch him with the cat, and again, I think I should leave Cosmo with him. I guess we'll discuss that.

We take off in Mark's car, because it's a convertible, and it's a beautiful October day. Of course, he stops by Joe's, checking on him first.

Then we head away from the coast. Mark reaches for my hand and links our fingers. We don't say much, but admittedly the silence is as comforting as conversation.

I let my head rest back, the wind blows the few strands of hair that have escaped from my ponytail, and I let myself live in the moment.

"How cold does it get here?" I ask.

Mark chuckles. "It gets chilly in February."

"And what do you consider being chilly?"

He shrugs. "It hovers around sixty."

I actually snort out a laugh. "Harsh."

"Not a selling point?"

"I like subzero temperatures and snow."

He shifts a look in my direction. "For real?"

I give it a moment of thought, then meet his eyes. "Yeah," I say knowing that I will always be a Colorado girl.

"I don't know if my below sea level blood could handle a Colorado winter."

We're teasing, but the truth is out there. We are from two different worlds, but we fit. We fit so well, it would make sense to stay together. But I can't stay here. I can't ask him to follow me and leave his mom. I can't travel with him, and he deserves all the success that's coming to him.

My phone chimes and I let go of Mark's hand to reach around Cosmo, who is extremely comfortable on my lap.

OMG I just showed the perfect house! I want this house.

Following the text is a string of pictures. It's a modest house, but by the first picture I know that it's exactly what Grace always wanted. There's a small porch on the front of the house, a formal dining room, and a gorgeous kitchen. There are three bedrooms and an amazing master suite. There is a small backyard for her kids to play in.

It's perfect, I reply.

It's only fifteen minutes from your house. Thirty from your Gran's. So no matter where you land, we'd be close to Auntie Liz.

I read Grace's text over and over. It's not just Grace anymore. She's giving me an entire family to love—well, she's starting to.

"Everything okay?" Mark asks.

"Yeah. Grace showed a house she fell in love with. She sent me pictures."

"I would think that be a job hazard."

I grin down at my phone. "Usually she sends me decorating tips. She only sends photos if a house is staged for sale. She never sends pictures if someone is living there."

"And it never gives you a desire to move?"

I shake my head. "My condo is all me. I've done everything inside of it, chose all the items in it. I'm comfortable there. And now, I have to decide if I'll stay there or go to Gran's—my mom's."

"What do you think you'll do?"

I shrug. "I don't know. I have a lot to do when I get back." I let my head fall back against the seat again. "I still have a lot to do here," I sigh.

Mark reaches for my hand again. "I'll help."

I turn my head to look at him. "I know you will, but I don't..."

"You don't want to hurt me with what you have to do."

I chew on my bottom lip. "Yes."

"I know you have to sell the house, Liz. You don't belong here. You're not comfortable here."

I swallow hard because there's a lump in my throat. "How do you know all that?"

He gives my hand a gentle squeeze. "Because I know you."

The Grandfather

Mark pulls into the cemetery, driving until he comes to a large tree, where he parks the car. He puts the top up and cranks up the air conditioning for Cosmo's benefit.

"Grandpa didn't want to be cremated," he says. "He wanted the viewing, the funeral, grave side services, and a reception after."

"That's not so strange."

Mark shrugs. "Sure as hell isn't what I want. I'd rather do it Betsy's way."

"Gran didn't want to leave a corpse," I say with some humor, and Mark's lips turn up into a smile.

"That doesn't surprise me." He lets out a breath and looks out the window. "C'mon, I want to introduce you to my grandfather."

He opens his door and steps out of the car, and I follow. Mark waits for me to come to his side before he takes my hand and we walk toward the large tree.

"He liked the shade. This reminded him of picnics as a child and it wasn't near any of the streets that border the cemetery. Less noise," he says.

"He gave it a lot of thought."

"That he did," Mark says as he stops in front of a large headstone.

THOMAS A. WATTS

The name is big and bold, as I assume the man was. Mark is silent looking down at it.

"Do you come here often?" I ask.

"Every few weeks. I used to come more often, but I guess after the first few years, you realize they're not here." He presses his hand to his heart. "They're here."

I bat my eyes, because of course, tears are welling. I guess Gran won't have a place like this. She didn't want this. I have nowhere to go and sit with her—or without her as it is.

I blink again and let the tears run their course. No, she didn't want to be laid to rest where people came to remember and mourn. She wanted to be remembered in a million different ways.

A small chuckle escapes me on what should have been a sob and it chokes me. Mark turns to look at me.

"Are you alright?"

I nod, smile, and cover my mouth with my hand. "Sorry."

"Don't be sorry. What are you thinking?"

"How Gran never wanted this. She didn't want a corpse. She didn't want a religious funeral, or to be buried where I'd have to go to be with her." Now I'm laughing and crying. "She wanted to be everywhere, and she wanted to make sure I was everywhere."

Mark steps to me, his hands on my waist as I'm wiping away tears.

"You're living her dream, Liz. She lived well, and she wants you to live it too. She did all her extravagant living before she was thirty.

You have a whole life ahead of you to give to the adventure of living," he says. "Live this life to its fullest. Cherish it."

I nod, because standing in the cemetery, where I'm eventually going to leave some of Gran, I get it.

Mark's mouth turns up into that grin that makes my knees weak. "If you sell the house, seven million dollars will go a long way in living a life well." He raises his brows to emphasize his point.

"I could also give you the house and your mother could come live with you."

His smile fades. "I only live in the house because Betsy asked me to." He steps in even closer until our bodies are touching, and he wraps his arms around me. "I'd only stay in the house if you stayed with me."

My breath sticks in my lungs and I hold it as he shakes his head.

"You can't stay. I can't go. I get it," he says. "I understand it. But, I'm not afraid to fly, Liz. We can—"

I press a finger to his lips. "I don't want to talk about it. I'm not good with relationships. I can't plan for a relationship based on promises of visits."

He nods and then looks down at the headstone. "For the record, I'm the blood of this man. This man understood how to make a long-distance relationship work."

"Did he? Wouldn't I have known about it if it worked?"

Mark shakes his head. "Betsy didn't want you to know. And what Betsy wanted—"

"Betsy always got."

The grin is back. "You're having an adventure, right?"

I bite down on my bottom lip and study him. Those blue eyes scan my face, and I know him so well. I know the slope of his nose, the softness of his lips, the texture of his hair wrapped in my fingers. There's a scar on his shoulder from hitting a rock in a river after letting go of a rope swing. He clicks his tongue when he's deep in thought while writing. The toothpaste in his bathroom is squeezed from the end and folded.

I thought that he was the adventure. But he's not.

I drove across the country, mostly alone, with the cat. I had to find my great-grandfather in the house—well Grace found him. I had to accept that my dear, old, sweet Gran wasn't always the person I knew. I took some side trips and learned about my family. I met a guy—this guy. The guy that is reminding me to live beyond this moment.

I look into those blue eyes and smile. "Yeah, I am having an adventure, and I like it."

"There's more to be had. And, when you can, or want to, I'd love to be part of your adventures."

Well, that's something to consider.

I give Mark a few moments with his grandfather as I go back to the car. Cosmo is in my seat looking up through the window at me. I tap the pads of my fingers to the window, playing with him, and he raises his paw to touch the window where my fingers were.

There have been a few times where that silly cat has gotten on my nerves, but I love him. I love that he sits with me and keeps me company. I love that he loved Gran. I love that he came from Mark.

When Cosmo sits back down, I open the door and pick him up.

"You're a good sport," I say to him, nuzzling my nose into his fur. "I love you, you silly cat."

I hear Mark's shoes on the gravel and I look up. He's smiling at me, and I'm lost in him.

"Is he okay?" he asks, nodding to Cosmo.

"Yes. I'm just loving on him."

"He's a lucky guy."

I can't help but question everything in this moment. I want to stay. I want this man and I want this cat. My home is in Colorado

—my best friend, my job, and that new baby, whose life I get to be part of.

I have to go home. I have to finish everything Gran had there. Adventures have to end, right? Just like a long vacation, I have to go back to my life.

"What do you say to a drive down the coast?" he asks as he pulls open his door.

"I think I would love that adventure."

It's Time

We both have been writing nonstop for the past two days. I gave Mark a reprieve on his contract since I, Mark's muse, gave him something to write about. I'm not sure what Constance Frost is making people do with that muse, but it will always be fun to know that I put that sparkle in his eye—well, *after* I put that sparkle in his eye. I grin behind my computer screen just thinking about what's going on in his mind.

I've turned in two more articles, and Julie is thrilled with them. I had also asked Grace if she had contact with any real estate agents in Florida, whom I could trust and she had one email me.

"Do you have time to talk?" I look up at Mark, who is busy typing.

He holds up a finger. He's mid-thought. I know when he hits that caps lock key and is leaving himself a note. He gives himself a nod and then smiles at me from over the top of his screen.

"What's up?" he asks.

"I just heard from a real estate agent who wants to come by to talk about listing the house."

His throat works and he clenches his jaw, but his eyes remain light.

Mark closes his laptop and reaches his hand out. I stand, and walk to him. He pulls me down on his lap and wraps his arms around me.

"Okay, what do we need to do?"

I take a moment to gather my thoughts. "She'll come look at it and let us know what we can get for it. Then I guess we'll stage it and get it on the market."

He nods and looks around. "I suppose it's staged enough." Then he winces. "Maybe we should do something to the bedroom Betsy set up for you though."

I wrinkle my nose. "We could sell the house as a time capsule. Between the decor of my bedroom and the office," I tease and he agrees with a wink. But a sobering feeling takes over. "I'll give you the house if—"

He presses a finger to my lips. "I'll help you get it ready. That's part of my mission, right?"

Pamela Roth walked slowly through the house taking notes on her phone. I'm grateful to Mark because he knows everything about the house that up until a month ago, I didn't even know existed.

"Houses like this sometimes sit on the market for quite a while. The price point is high, but normal for this neighborhood. And then sometimes, these neighborhoods are so hard to get into, there's a buyer just waiting to jump. With your grandmother and grandfather's reputation, that might help if we name-drop," Pamela says.

I exchange glances with Mark, who has pressed his knee to mine under the table in a stance of solidarity.

"I don't see what it would hurt," I say, knowing that when his book is released, everyone will know all about my gran.

"Let me get some things worked up. I'll send you the contract via email, and we'll get started." She gathers her laptop, phone, and planner. "Will someone be living in the house while it's on the market?"

I take a breath to answer, but Mark answers before me.

"No. The house will be void of residents in two weeks."

Pamela gives him a nod. "But you'll be close by?"

"I'll be available," he says, resting his hand on my thigh.

We take the rest of the day to do nothing but lounge in the pool. Having heard him say that the house would be empty within the next two weeks hit me hard. I'll leave next week, and his entire life will be rocked the next.

I keep going back and forth over keeping the house, but it just doesn't make sense.

Mark makes another lap in the pool and then swims up to me, gathering me to him.

"You're thinking too much for an afternoon we decided to take off," he says, grinning at me.

"Where are you going to live?"

He runs his hand over his wet hair and studies me. "I'll go to Mom's for a bit, and I'll find a place. I'm a grown man, I can do this."

"I think we should leave some of Gran here too," I say, tracing my finger over the scar on his shoulder. "I think the house needs her."

Mark grins at me. "I think that's a great idea. In fact," he says easing me against the side of the pool and pressing against me. "We should replace that tree I had taken out in the front yard. We can leave some of her there. It'll be Betsy's tree."

There's a lump in my throat that I can't swallow down. "I like it."

"Tomorrow we'll make some calls and get us a tree." He skims his lips over mine. "Any other business that you can't keep your mind off of?"

"Everything," I say on a sigh.

"I'll bet I can make you stop thinking about everything else for just a bit." His lips move to my jaw and down my neck.

"I'm going to miss this," I say on a heavy sigh.

"I'll deliver it to you," he promises.

I want to argue and tell him that I don't expect him to wait out his life for me. When I go, I should just go. He should go on with his life too.

Then again, didn't we have a relationship before we ever actually met, as adults that is.

Mark eases the strap to my swimsuit off my shoulder and trails kisses where his finger has just brushed.

"You said you weren't going to wear a swimsuit," he reminds me and I let out a little giggle as his fingers feather over my skin and it sends a shiver through me.

"I did say that."

"And yet, here you are." He eases back from me. "I'm happy to peel you out of it."

"I can tell," I say, raising my brows.

"No secrets here, baby." His mouth moves to my neck. "I've never been skiing," he says.

I push him back, laughing now. "What in the hell?"

He gives me that grin and grips my bottom. "I'm just saying, we've fooled around in the pool in hot weather. I'm thinking a hot tub in a snowy cabin would be nice too."

"I don't ski."

He shrugs. "We could just vacation in the snow then."

"I live in the snow. That's not a vacation," I argue.

"You're missing my point, baby," he says pressing his erection against me and I let my head ease back as his lips are back on my throat. "I really don't plan to be in the snow. I just know, I'll never get enough of you."

"I just don't see how it'll—"

"I have another week with you. Don't harsh my mellow."

I sigh as he eases down the top of my swimsuit. For one more week I can pretend like nothing is going to change.

"You'd better take me to your room," I whisper in his ear. "We have a lot to pack into this next week."

Mark groans in my ear. "I'll make sure you never forget me," he says, hoisting me around his hips and heading for the stairs.

Doesn't he know that he's already made sure I'll never forget him? That's part of my problem.

♪

Gran's Final Wishes

I suppose name-dropping Betsy Evans and Tom Watts to the right people helps in getting things done quickly. We'd met with the real estate agent on Thursday, and I'm spending Saturday morning standing on the driveway watching arborists replace the tree which Mark had taken out.

Mark's arm is wrapped around my waist as we watch.

"I can feel her here," I say as they lower the tree in place, atop the small pile of Gran's ashes that we'd put in the ground. "It's as if we put her in there and her spirit was free."

Mark nudges me with his hip. "She had a lot of that great life in this house. I think it was the right thing to do."

I turn into him. "Do you think it'll feel the same when we leave some of her with your grandfather?"

"I wouldn't be surprised if there's some kind of instant rainbow or something," he says grinning at me.

"They were in love, right? I mean, the kind that if you just saw them, you knew?"

"Most certainly," he says without hesitation. "When one of them would talk to someone, the other would watch them intently and smile. You know, they each hung on every word as if they were proud to be with the other. Even when one of them was scolding me, the other one backed them up—even if later they'd let me off the hook."

I laugh, resting my head on his shoulder. "Your grandfather would scold you and Gran would later bring you ice cream or something, right?"

"Yep."

"She'd do the same to me. She'd have to discipline me for this or that and then she'd cave."

"What did you ever do so bad that she had to discipline you?"

I eased back to look up at him. "*Sins of My Lover*," I say and Mark purses his lips.

"Most risqué book I've ever read," he admits.

"I was thirteen."

"You read that when you were thirteen? God, did you need therapy for that after?"

I laughed. "I'll admit, it skewed what I thought sex was all about."

"Most definitely."

"But when she heard my friends were passing it around, she forbade me from reading it."

"You scoundrel. You read it?"

I winced. "I stole it from a local bookstore."

"Bad ass," he teases.

"She didn't find out about that until she found out I had it under my pillow. It was dog-eared and highlighted."

He laughs and I can feel my face grow hot.

"Please tell me more," he begs.

"We had a long talk about sex, which was weird. She forbade me from having that too," I chuckle. "Then she took me to the store, where I had to admit what I did. I had to pay for the book and then help the owner, on a Sunday, clean the store."

"That's all?"

I shrug. "The owner was so impressed that I had owned up to

it all and helped, she hired me when I was sixteen. But, she also gave me the other three books in the series after I told her I'd annotated the first book."

That had Mark laughing harder. "They were worse than the first one."

"Yeah, but Esther McQueen, who owned the store, was a great woman, a free spirit, if you will. She thought I should know how it all ended."

"It had a happily ever after."

"It did."

"And what happened to your dog-eared, annotated copy?"

I shrug. "I'm worried I'll find it in Gran's things."

"Well, that's not so bad."

"With what I know now, I just hope she didn't highlight anything else or make notes."

Mark snorts at that, and I think we both know that it's totally possible.

The urn that carries Gran is lighter now. I left some of her in St. Louis, and now there is some of her left at the house she bought with the *love money* from the prince.

I can't help but grin as I hold her close as Mark drives back out to the cemetery. In the backseat is a bag of garden tools to bury part of Gran with Tom, making the job easier than it was when I left her with her family.

"Are you doing okay?" Mark asks as he turns into the cemetery.

"I am."

"You're smiling. I didn't expect that."

I chuckle and roll my head to look at him. "I didn't expect it either. But knowing we're doing what she wanted us to do, I feel at ease."

"It's okay if that changes."

I nod. "I know that now. It's okay if I fall apart and it's okay to celebrate her in the grandest ways. I know it will make her eternally here with your grandfather."

"I would like to think so."

He parks the car, gathers Cosmo up, and slips on the harness we had bought for him. Mark had assured me that the cat needs to be there when we leave Gran with Tom, and I agree.

With Gran, her cat, and a bag of gardening tools, we walk toward Tom A. Watts's grave, where we sit down and Cosmo follows along.

"How do we do this?" Mark asked.

"You saw how I did it with her father. I just dug a moat. Of course, that's all I could do with what I had."

Mark looks around, just as I had in St. Louis. And, just as it was in St. Louis, there is no one around. He takes the trowel from the bag of tools and begins to dig a similar moat to the one I dug for my great-grandfather. When it's long enough and deep enough, Mark puts down the trowel and picks up the cat so that he doesn't go treading in the moat, or get in my way.

I take the lid off the urn, and let out a slow breath.

I thought I was going to make it through this without crying, but I'm not. Tears well in my eyes, and I can't even see what I'm doing. So I take a moment to let the emotions settle before I wipe my eyes.

"Well, Gran, I wish you had shared Tom with me. I think I would have liked him. Yes, I know I met him, but you know I don't remember any of that," I say as if no one else is listening. "I've learned that the love you had for each other was very special. I don't know why you felt like you had to hide that from me."

Mark's hand comes to my shoulder, and I know I've started down a path that will just anger me. Gran's not here to give me the answers to the questions I have, or to explain to me why she did what she did.

But Mark is here—and I know her purpose was to give me him, even for the short time we'd get to be together.

Carefully, I pour some of the ashes from the urn into the moat that Mark dug. While he holds Cosmo, I look inside the urn and decide a little more of her needs to stay with Tom.

I put the top back on the urn and set it to the side, then I take the trowel and replace the grass that Mark had dug up.

Sitting back on my heels, I look at the ground where I've left part of Gran.

"This is what she wanted," I say.

"It is," Mark agrees as he lets Cosmo down and the cat moves to the area where I'd replaced the grass. He circles and then lays there, as if he too is taking his last moments with her—with them.

"Where do you want to be buried?" I ask, keeping my attention on Cosmo.

"I don't think I want to be buried. I like Betsy's plan."

I shift so that I sit flat on the ground with Gran's urn to my side. "I like it too," I say, but my body trembles. "But I won't have anyone to scatter me along the way." My voice breaks as the sob takes over. "I'll just be someone's responsibility—maybe someone I don't even know."

Mark moves to sit next to me. "It doesn't need to be that way."

I choke out a laugh. "Am I supposed to just have a kid to bury me? I don't want that. I don't want kids. I have nothing to offer a child. But, seriously, do I just assume that Grace's child has to take care of that for me?"

His arm comes around my shoulders and he pulls me to him.

"Maybe we make a plan. Whichever of us goes first, the other one scatters the other in designated places."

"Oh, great idea. What happens to the other one?"

"Grace's kid deals with it," he says and that breaks me. I begin to laugh through my tears.

"This kid is screwed."

Mark moves his arm and turns to me, taking my hands in his. "Liz Evans, will you be buried with me?"

I stare at him. I have no idea what the hell he's talking about. "What?"

"Seriously, will you be buried with me? No matter what happens after next week when you drive away, let's make a plan. We'll leave letters, just as your grandmother did. Whoever is in charge of granting our final wishes can scatter us in the same places. We'll be together forever, after all of this."

I blink hard. "Really?"

"Why not? It's something you're worried about. It's something we're thinking about. What do you say?"

I pull my lips between my teeth to keep them from trembling or to keep me from smiling. "You'd spend eternity scattered with me?"

"I can't think of anyone I'd rather be scattered with."

"I may never see you again after next week."

A line forms between his brows. "I hate to think that's the case, but even if it is, we'll have this pact."

"Right here with Gran and Tom?" I ask.

"Some of us." He lifts my fingers to his lips and kisses them. "Let's say a little with our mothers, we'll add that we want a little bit with the tree at the house," he says smiling. "They'll have to trespass, but it'll give them an adventure."

I choke on my half laugh, half sob.

He kisses my wrists and then leans in and presses a gentle kiss to my lips. "And the rest can be left here with Betsy and Grandpa."

I study the sincerity in his face. No matter what happens, I'll have eternity with him. That's enough for now, I think.

"I'd be honored to be scattered with you," I say.

"Good. We'll write it out when we get home."

My Final Wishes

Just as Mark had said at the cemetery, when we got home, we sat down and began to write letters that would give our final wishes to whoever would be in charge of them.

"Are you going to let me read yours?" he asks.

I shake my head. "I don't think so."

He narrows his gaze on me. "Did you cut me out of it?"

"No."

"Fine," he says, folding his letter and sitting back in his chair. "Then I won't let you read mine."

"Did you cut me out of yours?"

His eyes went serious and dark. "I'd never cut you out of my life, or my death."

Leaving my letter on the table, I stand and walk to him. Reaching for his hands, I pull him from his chair and drape my arms around his neck. Mark's arms come around me and he pulls me to him.

"You know how I feel about you," he says and I nod.

"I'm going to miss you so much it's going to hurt," I admit.

"We can—"

"We can live in this moment and then go our separate ways. I want to see you, but I don't want promises of it."

"Why?"

"Because promises are always broken."

"I don't break promises," he says, and I know that to be true. Wasn't he fully capable of owning his own house, but he promised Gran to stay in her house until I came? And here he is.

"No, but they get broken. It just happens." I lay my head to his chest, and his arms tighten around me. "We'll just continue like we started. Texts. Calls."

"Visits?"

I ease back from him. "Your life is taking you in a new direction. Movies. New book deals. Talk show circuits. None of that will land you in Denver."

"You don't know that."

"Let's just take it day by day, okay?" I look up into those blue eyes that sparkle when they look at me.

Mark's hands move to my cheeks, and I rest my hands on his chest. "I don't want you to say anything. Okay?" I nod in agreement. "I love you," he says, and then presses his thumbs against my lips when I take a breath. Easing, I pucker my lips so I don't speak. "When I promise I'll visit, I will. I know you won't fly, and you certainly don't want to make that drive again, but you're important. Important enough that I'll make the effort."

Again, I take a breath to speak, but he silences me with his mouth on mine.

"Don't say anything," he says, his lips still touching mine. "There's nothing more to say."

Joe has moving boxes. Though I wonder how long they've been in his garage.

"I knew they'd come in handy," he says as he walks us to them.

I'll admit, I'm completely surprised to find a brand new, flat stack of Home Depot boxes. I expected a collection of old Amazon boxes.

"How much do you want for them?" I ask.

"Are you kidding me? Take what you need. Mark here has taken care of me for years. And since you've been here, you've done your share," he says.

"Thank you."

"No, thank you." Joe takes my hand between his and gives it a little pat. "Having you here has been like having Betsy back. You have her spirit in you."

With what I've learned about her, I'm not so sure. "I appreciate that," I say.

"It's too bad you can't live in the house, but there's a great big world out there to explore. Maybe you'll head back this way when you're old and retired. I'll be gone, but..." He smiles at me and lets go of my hands. "Heading up to your mama's?" he asks Mark.

"Until I get settled."

Joe's brows draw in. "She doing okay?"

"She still struggles to get out of the house. She might tire of me, or maybe it'll help."

Joe gives Mark a slow nod. "You let her know I have a mother-in-law's apartment in my pool house and she can live there. Then she can visit her daddy once in a while."

Mark blinks hard, and I know that Joe's offer has meant something to him. "I'll let her know."

"Well," Joe adjusts his grip on his walker. "If you two need anything else, you let me know."

Mark holds out his hand and Joe shakes it. "We appreciate it."

"And, if that Oscar is too heavy to move, you can keep it on my shelf."

That makes us both laugh.

I lean in and kiss Joe on the cheek. I will miss him.

Before I can pull back, he takes my arm and whispers in my ear. "I'm an ordained minister. From the internet," he says. "In case you ever need me."

When I ease back, he winks.

The office looks much like Gran's room back in Denver. I've started cleaning it out, but at the moment it looks as if I've torn through everything.

When I look up from the pile on the floor, which I'm sitting cross-legged in front of, I see Mark leaned against the doorjamb, his arms crossed in front of him and his legs crossed at the ankles. He's grinning, and it makes my heart melt.

"What are you doing?" he asks.

"Sorting."

He nods slowly. "Why?"

I look around at my piles. "Some of this is Gran's and some of this is obviously your grandfather's."

"After you sort it, then what?"

I blink hard. "Well, I guess I'll take hers and you can take his."

"It's just stuff, Liz. Is any of it important?"

"Do you want me to just throw it all away?"

He shrugs. "Would it matter?"

My shoulders drop and I look around. Some of the scripts I found have Gran's handwriting on them. Shouldn't that be preserved? Then again, I have lots of things with her handwriting. The note she wrote telling me what to do when she died, for instance. Does it matter that she left notes on script pages for Tom?

There are playbills and receipts. I did find one of Mark's old report cards, wouldn't he like to have that?

Mark walks toward where I sit and he squats down, picking up one of the scripts and leafing through it.

"This never got made," he says. "They worked on it for years."

"Why didn't it get made?"

He scans a few more pages. "My guess is that it was never to be made. This was one of the last ones they worked on together. He'd send Betsy pages in the mail and she'd send them back. He refused to use email until I came to take care of him," he chuckles. "I think this just kept Betsy in his life."

"Maybe you can rewrite it into a book," I suggest.

Mark nods. "Maybe." He sets it back on the pile. "Maybe I can send you pages in the mail and you can add your notes."

He's smiling at me. And even though I want to cry at the thought of just tossing everything, his smile calms me. Since I figured who WATTS was, he's offered me calm.

"I did find this," I say, reaching for a small stack of newspaper articles and handing them to him.

Mark sits on the floor and looks at them. "The plane crash."

I nod.

Mark reads the articles of the first moment that changed who I am now. I'd been surprised when I'd read the article that I hadn't cried or become unnecessarily panicked.

"Is this you?" Mark asks, pointing to one of the pictures in the article.

"Yes. My mother was being interviewed. I clung to her coat. It wasn't until a few weeks later that the impact of what had happened hit me. After that, I wouldn't sleep alone. When I did sleep, I'd wake up screaming."

"Shock?"

"I guess so."

He studies the papers again. "Liz, planes don't crash."

I motion to the paper. "They do."

Mark hands me the newspaper and looks around, but he doesn't say anything.

Tucking the news article back into the pile it was in, I look around. "Don't think I'm some packrat, but I want to take this all with me."

"I would never think that. All of this is new to you. It's good that you're here to go through it. To me, it was Betsy and Tom's life that we lived together."

My heart breaks at that. "I'll never get over all the lives she lived," I say.

"Well, I think her final wish has been granted."

I look up at him. "How?"

"You're seeing life differently," he says. "Nothing will ever be the same."

May the Waves Carry You

We have our first showing of the house on Saturday afternoon. Mark and I decide that we'll drive down the coast and send Gran off into the waves.

I have to take a sweatshirt with me today as we drive with the top down. The temperature, though still warm, is cooler than it has been. Cosmo is snuggled up between my feet and seems to be happy with the rumble of the car beneath him.

We've been silent on our drive, and Mark hasn't reached for my hand. In the month we've spent together, I know this mood. It's a little bit carefree, a little bit creative mind at work, and a little bit broody.

His moods certainly aren't as volatile as mine. I'm happy, sad, crying or laughing. When I'm angry, I slam doors and throw things. When I'm happy I laugh. I pick fights when I'm uncomfortable, and I wallow when my mood affects his. But when I'm with Mark, I'm usually happy.

One thing is for sure, I'll never forget the views I've taken in on this trip. From fields that offered me hours of what I thought was boring vastness, but now appreciate in hindsight, to the rivers I crossed, to the cities I strolled, and small stores I went into. I'll never tire of the view of the ocean, even if I'd rather have a large mountain range outside my window.

Mark was right, Gran did give me something with this journey.

I turn and study him as he drives. His dark sunglasses shielding eyes that I know so well now. His unshaven face which makes him sexier somehow, and yet when he shaves, I can't get enough of touching his face.

In the past month we've explored one another with patience and in haste. He's given me experiences I've never had, and I don't even mean just in bed.

And he's told me he loves me.

My heart is so full it could burst, and at the same time, it aches so badly I think I could easily die from the pain.

When Mark pulls over and parks the car, I know he's found a spot he thinks will honor Gran as we set more of her out into the ocean.

He turns off the engine and stares out the windshield.

"Betsy and I drove out here once when she and Grandpa were in a fight." The corner of his mouth curled up. "She wanted me to know that they'd fix whatever was wrong. I don't remember what the fight was about, but she knew that not all kids understood grown up fights. And, should anything happen to their relationship, I was to know how much she loved me. She wanted me to understand that no matter where we ever landed in this great big world, no one could ever take away what I meant to her."

He could hardly get out the last words before he choked on a sob, and lifted his fist to his mouth to cover it.

I don't know what to say to him. I just wish Gran had loved him enough to share him with me—and then my breath catches. She did.

Before I can reach for him, Cosmo jumps up into my lap and walks across me to get to Mark.

He laughs through his tears and holds the cat against him. "God, you're smart," he says, holding Cosmo close.

"I wish we had grown up together," I say.

Mark kisses the cat and turns his head to look at me. "Six years is a long time in kid years. It would have been different. And, let's consider one thing. If we had grown up together, we wouldn't be here now—I mean, well, you know," he says, and I can actually see his cheeks darken with color.

"I love you," I say, unaware that I was going to say it.

He sits quiet for a moment before pushing his sunglasses to the top of his head. His eyes are red and damp.

He licks his lips. "You do?"

I swallow hard. "I do."

With Cosmo still held against him, he reaches for my hand. "That will carry me until someone reads those letters we wrote." He smiles. "No matter where we go from here, I will always love you, Liz."

Hand in hand, with me holding Gran's urn and Mark holding her cat, we walk toward the ocean. Cosmo curls into Mark's arm, and I wonder if Mark is being clawed, but he doesn't let go of my hand.

Once the water covers our feet, we stop.

I look out at the never-ending horizon. When we let Gran go, she can travel the globe from here.

I swallow the tears that clog my throat, and turn to Mark. "Hand me the cat and you take Gran."

"Why?"

I wait until he takes the urn, and I pull Cosmo from him and he clings to me, his claws digging into my shirt. I nuzzle my face into his fur, wrapping both of my arms around him to calm him.

Looking up at Mark, I take in the moment.

"You send her off this time. It's your turn to say goodbye to her," I say.

"Liz," he says, shaking his head.

"I mean it. Have your moment, on this beach, your beach with Gran. Just save me enough to take home to Mom."

Mark nods as he steps to me and gently kisses me.

Stepping back out of the water, hoping to calm Cosmo, I watch as Mark stands there, the water lapping at his ankles. He's silent, as if maybe he's praying, or silently talking to Gran. He slides his glasses back onto his face, then lifts them to wipe at his eyes, before adjusting them back into place.

Cosmo settles in my arms and watches, as if he too knows what Mark is about to do.

A moment later, Mark removes the lid to the urn and then he sends Gran out into the water.

Tears slide down my cheeks before I even realize I'm crying. Watching the specks of Gran carry out on the water, I think of her adventures, her loves, her personality that attracted everyone to her. I miss her even more than I did a few days ago, and I just can't imagine what it's going to feel like when I get home.

I watch as Mark puts the lid back on the urn, but he doesn't turn away from the water. He's taking it in. I still can't believe she didn't tell me about these people she loved just so she could give me all of her attention.

I suck in a heavy breath. I'd never thought of it that way.

She loved me so much, she gave me all her attention.

Mark wipes his cheeks before he turns back to me. Without a word, I know we both understand that we stand there broken, but together. There's a lot more to mourn than just Gran's absence.

He walks back toward us, kisses me on the cheek, and we walk back silently to the car.

I open the door and slide in, holding on to Cosmo until the door is closed, and then he settles in by my feet again. Since the top is down on the car, Mark hands me Gran's urn, before he walks to the other side of the car. Before he climbs in, he reaches into his pocket, pulls something out, and holds it in his fist.

Sliding into the car he sits for a moment before turning toward me.

"I want to give you something," he says as he looks down at his closed hand.

"Mark—"

He shakes his head. "I hope you don't mind that I did this, but I wanted this to be special."

I have no idea what it is that he's talking about, or what he has in his hand. Sweat breaks out on the back of my neck, and I swear I'm getting dizzy.

Again, he lifts his sunglasses to the top of his head. When he looks at me, his eyes are soft and full of that love he professes.

Mark opens his hand, and in his palm is a necklace with a silver cylinder pendant.

"This is for you. Inside the pendant are your grandmother's ashes. I didn't ask, so I hope you don't mind."

I cover my mouth, and because we are both emotional wrecks, the sobs begin.

"You did that for me?"

He nods. "You gave her back to all the people and places that meant something to her. And you'll finish the job when you get back home. But, you need her with you too, Liz. You were Betsy's greatest adventure. Remember that."

Mark has seen me at my worst, and seriously, this has to be it.

My face is hot, and tears pour from my eyes. As hard as I try to bat them away, it's no use.

I wipe the back of my hand under my nose and hold Gran's urn a little tighter.

I can hardly breathe.

I need to speak, and I don't know if I can.

Mark's eyes scan over me. When I cry like this, my eyes swell and my freckles get darker. I know I'm an absolute mess.

Mark worries his lip. "If you're upset that I did this. I can empty it."

I shake my head and cover his palm with mine.

After taking in a few breaths, I wonder if I can even talk.

"This is the most precious gift I've ever been given," I say, but it comes out in a heavy whisper.

"Really?"

I nod. "Thank you."

Mark holds up the necklace, unclasps it, and leans into me. He fastens it around my neck and lets his fingers skim over the chain and down the pendant that rests at the top of the valley between my breasts.

Looking back up at me, he eases back slightly, and pulls out a matching necklace from under the neck of his shirt.

"I wanted a bit of her too. I hope you don't mind," he says.

Mimicking his movements, I reach my hand to his necklace, run my finger over the chain, and then touch the pendant.

"I don't mind," I say, raising my eyes back to meet his. "She loved you."

"She did," he agrees.

I lift my hand to his cheek. "I love you too. Always remember that."

Last Days

We only pack a few hours a day, and only the personal effects that we want to keep. Mark has a few boxes of his grandfather's items in the pool house, and I have an enormous stack at the front door.

We have a trailer rented and will pick it up tomorrow. The Oscar did get his own box, and is wrapped up in almost every one of Gran's towels to keep him safe. The lid is also taped on so hard that I may never ever see that silly gold statue again, because I may never be able to get him out of the box.

I have three days before I head home, but we're not talking about it. I assume on Thursday morning I'll drive away a wreck and alone. Mark hasn't asked to go with me, and I don't expect him to. I know he's needed in New York next week, and there was talk that they want him in California to help work on the script for the Constance Frost movie.

His life needs him. My life needs me.

I need to finish going through Gran's things, and then I need to sell one of the houses. Then, focus can be put on Grace and her baby. Where one life ends another begins.

I walk in the house from the patio and close the sliding door.

Mark has two glasses of wine poured, music is playing, and he's stirring something at the stove.

"I have wine for you," he says, nodding to the fullest glass.

"What are you making?"

He wrinkles his nose. "Goulash. Do you like goulash?"

"A Betsy Evans staple," I laugh as I reached for my wine.

"It is. So I wasn't sure if you'd have liked it and it was a good thing, or if it would be something you'd never want to eat again."

"Well, she was no culinary genius, but she had six meals she could do well," I say still laughing.

"Grandpa loved to grill," he says. "I'm guessing I might have eaten better than you did."

I take a sip of my wine and grin at him from behind my glass. "I'm thinking you did."

"Betsy was never my PTA president though."

"You missed quite a show," I say moving to stand right next to him, our arms brushing. We're still not discussing the piles of boxes by the door, or the trailer we're going to pick up tomorrow. There is no talk about me getting on the road as early as possible.

Through emails and texts, within the same house, and sometimes at the same table, we've mapped out my trip, but backward. Yet, we're both living these next two days in denial.

Mark sets the spoon he's stirring with on the spoon holder and turns to me. He touches the pendant he gave me and then lifts his eyes to gaze into mine.

"How do you feel about phone sex?" he asks, and instantly I choke out a laugh.

"I did not see that coming," I say, lifting my wine, and take a long drink.

Mark takes my glass as I lower it and takes a drink from it before setting it on the counter.

"You didn't answer my question either." He lifts his hand into my hair and I lean into his palm.

"I've never had phone sex."

"We've had a lot of firsts between us." He brushes his lips over mine. "It could be another."

I realize this is as close as we've gotten to discussing me leaving and what will happen after.

I pick up my wine. "I'm going to need more of this before I consider phone sex," I say smiling, then drinking down the rest of the wine.

Mark kisses the tip of my nose and turns back to the stove, just as his phone rings in his pocket.

He hands me the spoon and steps back, answering his phone.

"This is Mark Watts," he says and then listens.

I set the spoon down and notice that he's leaned against the adjacent counter and his hand is pressed to his forehead.

"She's okay?" he asks, and at that point I turn off the stove. "How did this..." He listens and then looks at his watch. "I'm three hours out. I'll head that way," he says before disconnecting the call.

Mark sets his phone on the counter and scrubs his hands down his face.

I take a step toward him, but stop. His expression isn't one I know now.

"Mark..."

With his hands still covering his face, he draws in a deep breath before letting it out.

"Mom overdosed on one of her prescriptions," he says as if he's letting it resonate. "Fuck."

I touch his arm and even though I've spoken to him, he looks up as if he's only now noticing that I'm there.

"How is she?"

He shrugs. "I don't know. I mean, they've given her stuff to help. I don't even know what the fuck he said to me," he says looking at the phone on the counter. "She's alive."

"I'll go pack us a bag," I say turning from him, but he reaches for my hand.

"You're not going."

"I'll drive you up there. I'll keep you company. She's going to need—"

"You need to go home. I'll head up there. I just don't know if, or when I'll get back."

I look where he's still gripping my arm. "I don't have to hurry home. I can..."

"Liz," he says my name before he shifts his eyes to me. "I don't want you to be part of this."

"Why?"

He rubs his fingers over his forehead. "Listen, this is why I can't just pick up and go. She's done this twice before. She'll probably die doing it again if I don't..."

Mark steps away from me.

"I don't understand. I love you. I want to help."

"There is no help," he's shouting now, but I don't think he means to. "I have to get to her."

"Please let me—"

This time he turns back to me. He cups my face. "Oh, Liz. I love you so much that I can't even think about you leaving. But I love you so much, I can't include you in this. I don't even have time to worry about it. I have to go."

He drops his hands and a moment later heads toward the pool house.

It's twenty minutes before Mark returns to the house with the duffle bag he'd had in Nashville. His phone is pressed to his ear, and he's talking as he walks through the door.

"Can you make it happen or not?" he's asking. "Thanks. This isn't how I wanted this to go."

Mark drops his bag and disconnects the call before looking up and realizing I'm standing there watching him. His face wears a mask of panic, and I understand that. What I don't understand is why he won't let me join him.

"I've talked to her. They have her stable," he says.

I press my hand to my heart. "That's good."

Mark nods and slips his phone into the pocket of his shorts, then runs his hands over his head.

"Liz, I didn't anticipate anything like this—"

"You couldn't have," I say, taking one little step to move to him, but I linger, not sure what else has happened between us, and remembering this moment isn't about us. "You're heading out then?"

He lifts his sad eyes to meet mine. "I am."

"I can go with you," I say one more time, and he shakes his head.

"Your adventure ends with the need to tend to Betsy. Tending to Tammy Watts, that wasn't in your list of duties."

I take a breath to protest, but his attention on me is already gone. He walks through the kitchen, finds his keys, and pulls a bottle of water from the refrigerator, setting them on the table, he then turns back.

He moves to me and pulls me to him.

I hold on tight. This is the last I'll see of Mark A. Watts, and this wasn't how I'd intended to say goodbye. It's not how he'd intended it either.

"I have had the most amazing time with you," he says with his lips pressed to my ear. "No matter what ever happens, where we ever go, wherever we land, I will always love you Elizabeth Evans."

That breaks me, and I sob against him.

He kisses my temple and steps back. His mind is now on his journey as he picks up his keys, the water, and his duffle bag.

"Keep in touch on your drive home, and be careful," he says, not even looking at me before he walks out the front door.

As soon as the door closes, my knees give out on me, and I slide to the floor. And, because he's the most intuitive cat in the world, Cosmo comes out from wherever he's been napping and curls up on my lap.

I hold him close to me as if he's my lifeline, and I cry into his fur. Once again, it's just me and this cat—and my heart is broken.

Goodbye Palm Beach

Finn and Brenda stand in the driveway next to my car. It had been Finn that Mark was talking to when he'd come into the house. Mark had asked him to get the trailer and help me put it on. He asked him to check my car and make sure everything was running okay too, just as Ashton had done before I'd set out on the first leg of this journey.

I'd been so sad about losing Mark, I hadn't even realized, until today, he was making sure I was taken care of.

My phone dings in my hand and I look down to see Grace's name.

Did you leave yet? Don't forget to tell me when you leave. I can fly out and meet you on the route.

I chuckle. I have missed her so much, and right now, she's my driving force to get home safely. I need her. I need her to tell me that everything is going to be okay. I need her to help me sort through Gran's things and list the house—that's what I've decided I need to do. I need Grace, and I will always need Grace.

Heading out in a few. Just saying goodbye to new friends.

I respond before slipping my phone into my back pocket.

I tuck my hair behind my ear. It'll be up in a ponytail in the next hour, I'm sure, but for now, I just felt the need to let it be free.

I walk toward Finn and Brenda. "I can't thank you both enough for helping me load up."

Finn steps in and hugs me. "He'd have done it himself, you know."

I nod as he releases me. "I know."

Brenda pulls me to her next and holds me so tight I can barely breathe.

"Don't give up on him. He loves you," she whispers in my ear and her words squeeze in my chest.

I purse my lips as I step back, again, warding off tears. I seriously have to be void of tears by now. I've spent the last month and a half doing nothing but crying.

Cosmo meows from the car. I didn't even put him in his crate. He's earned my trust.

I take one last look at the house. The house built with money given to Gran by a lover she didn't take all that seriously, I muse. The prince had been only one of her adventures.

"Oh, good. I didn't miss you," I hear the voice from behind me and turn to see Joe walking up the driveway with his walker and a young man behind him.

I walk toward him and he holds out his arms so that I move right into them.

"You were a breath of fresh air, darling. I'll miss you."

I sniff back more tears. "I'll call."

"Of course you will. It's the least you could do," he says and I laugh as I step back. Joe leans in. "Do you like my new eye candy?" He nods toward the young man that walked up behind him.

"Very nice. You behave," I say.

Joe laughs. "Oh, honey. Haven't you learned it's not worth behaving. Live big and don't regret," he says, as he lifts a wave to Finn and Brenda before walking away.

I feel Gran surrounding me in this place, and with Joe's words. "I get it," I whisper into the still warm air.

I can't leave this place with regrets, she didn't. She gave all of this up for me, so the least I can do is respect it. She walked away from the love of her life to be with me in my time of need. Now I have to walk away from the love of my life too, he needs me to.

Where are you? Are you driving okay with the trailer on? Grace texts and I answer her when I pull off the road to get yet another cup of coffee.

I'm doing just fine with the trailer, though parking is going to be interesting. I text back.

Just stopping for coffee.

I will drive right through Orlando, and everything inside of me says I should stop. Then the trailer behind me tells me that would be a bad idea.

I've only heard from Mark a few times, and they were quick texts.

Mom is stable and doing fine.

Make sure the lights are connected on the trailer. Have Finn check.

Be safe on the road - I love you.

It's what I can have of him in this moment. It would be selfish of me to think he could offer more. We had our time together. We mourned Gran together, and now we wear matching necklaces that tie the three of us together.

I cry as I pass the first exit in Orlando, and I drive until I get to Valdosta.

Julie calls when Cosmo and I are in our first hotel and tells me that the articles I've submitted are exactly what she wanted. She's glad to hear that I'm headed back to Denver, and she wants to take me to lunch next week and discuss upcoming articles she'd like me to write.

Grace calls as Cosmo and I have our dinner, which we had DoorDashed from a local restaurant.

"Is that cat behaving?" Grace asks as I drag a corn chip through the dollop of guacamole.

"I have a whole new respect for this cat."

"You must. You didn't call him a stupid cat."

I let out a chuckle. "He's anything but. I'm sure the only reason Mark didn't fight me for him is because, well…" I let it roll in the silence.

"Have you talked to him?" she asks.

"Not really. Miscellaneous texts."

"He'll call when he can," Grace assures me, but her tone, though calm, isn't reassuring.

"Yeah, when he gets a chance," I say as nonchalantly as possible while taking another chip, but there's a heaviness inside me.

"Okay, turning the attention to me. I want you to hear something," she says. For a moment I hear her jostling her phone. "Now, just listen."

Grace's end of the line goes silent for a moment and then I wonder if our connection has gone bad. There is a whirring sound with a constant beat.

"What am I listening to?" I ask.

"Liz, that was the baby's heartbeat," she beams through the phone.

I drop the chip in my hand and cover my mouth. "Oh, Grace."

"The most beautiful sound in the whole world." She's crying, and now so am I.

"I already love that baby of yours," I say with a hiccup of tears in my voice.

"Liz, it's going to be so wonderful. We're going to have so much fun with her, or him," she corrects with a giggle.

I close my eyes and press my hand to my forehead. I don't regret this trip and falling in love with Mark. But I would regret not being there with Grace through this. I can't wait to get home.

Hey. Did you make it to Valdosta?

The text stirs me awake. It's from Mark and it's just shy of midnight.

Yeah, we're here, I respond, and then adjust myself on my bed while Cosmo sleeps away next to me.

Good. I'm glad you're safe.

I don't respond because those little bubbles dance at the bottom of the screen telling me he's typing something else. Then, the bubbles disappear.

Was that all he had to say? Was I supposed to text him back?

My phone rings in my hand, and I pull my lips in through my teeth.

"Hey," I say, just as I would when we first started talking after Gran died.

"Hey," he says back in that easy tone that had me falling for him. "Did I wake you?"

"I sleep light," I say, and he laughs softly.

"I don't think so," he says. "I just had to hear your voice."

"I'm glad."

"I miss you, Liz and it's only been a few days."

I don't know what to say to that. Not having seen him or talk to him makes me miserable.

"Mom came home from the hospital today," he says. "It's a good thing I'm here. Her place is a mess."

"I could come back and..."

"Keep going, Liz. It's an adventure going back too."

I hate that he can be positive about it.

"You're settled at your Mom's?"

"As much as I can be. We'll figure it out though. She's going to need people around."

"You're a good son," I say.

"I'll do what I can for her."

We fall into a silence and my eyelids begin to grow heavy.

"Liz," he says my name softly, as if he too teeters on sleep.

"Yeah?"

"I love you."

Home Quiet Home

I do what I'd been asked not to do, I drive through Atlanta, not stopping at the theater as I'd wanted to. Then, I just keep going and never stop in Nashville at all. Twelve hours later, and exhausted, I'm in St. Louis.

I couldn't stay in Nashville without him. I didn't want to stay in Nashville without him. At least a part of Gran was still in St. Louis, as stupid as that really sounds.

And my trusty pal Cosmo, never once gives me a problem. I think he wants to get home as quickly as possible too.

After leaving St. Louis, where I make a stop at the cemetery, I drive to Topeka, mostly crying. I hadn't heard from Mark all day yesterday. Not even one text asking if I was okay.

He has a lot going on in his life, and I can't get wrapped up in worrying about why he didn't even reach out. I was the one that chose to go home. I could have stayed in the house with Mark forever. I could have given up my comfort for once, but no, I chose to go home where I know I won't go on any more adventures. I won't leave my house often enough. I won't take neighbors to appointments, play pickleball at the community center, or just sit and listen to the waves roll out in the ocean. I will do what I always do. I will work. Head down, fingers on a keyboard, I will work until Grace shows up and makes me leave the house.

But I'm going home to be part of her new adventure.

Cosmo meows from the passenger seat. I think he worries that I'm not paying attention to the road. Maybe he's right.

In Kit Carson, I order food and sit with Cosmo at a picnic table in a local park and eat. I don't take any time on my trip home to notice the scenery or enjoy local culture. My only purpose is to run from Florida as fast as I can.

I run my hand over Cosmo's back. "Do you think he's worried about us?" I ask him.

Then, as if Mark knows I can't scrub him from my mind, my phone chimes.

Where are you? Are you making good time? Did you stop anywhere? I miss you.

I let out a long breath and read the text over and over.

We're having lunch in Kit Carson before making the final leg into Denver, I type back, wanting desperately to tell him I made a mistake and I'll come back.

My phone rings in my hand.

"You're already in Colorado? That wasn't the plan," he begins the moment the call is connected.

"Yes," I say calmly, though I'm not calm at all. "I drove straight from Valdosta to St. Louis."

"Liz," he begins, but I interrupt.

"I'm fine. I was fine. I just couldn't stay in Nashville, alone," I say.

He doesn't say anything for a long moment. "I put Mom in a hospital," he says and his voice is soft. "She needs a little more support than I can give her right now. She'll be there a few weeks, and then we can assess if she can go back home."

Everything in me deflates. This is why I couldn't let him promise me that he'd visit. He can't now. Tammy needs her son more than I do, I convince myself.

"Keep in touch though. Let me know how she's doing," I say.

"I will." There is another long pause, and I can imagine him sitting there as lost as I am. "The real estate agent called and has another showing," he says.

"That's good."

"Yeah. Finn and Jeff are going to move my stuff out of the house. Joe said I could store it in his garage for now."

"I already miss Joe," I admit.

"I'll miss him too," he says. "Liz, I'm sorry it all came down to this. I would have packed up and moved with you if it weren't for Mom."

I'm batting my eyes trying to ward off the tears. I'm about to drive straight through to Denver, and I can't have tears bothering me.

"She needs you. You're doing the right thing," I say.

"I love you," he says, his voice soft.

"I love you, too."

"Call me when you get there, okay?"

I nod, but only because in that very moment, I find it hard to talk. "Okay."

Though I've lived in Denver my whole life, I've never much cared for the lights. I mean, it's never dark or peaceful. It's not like sitting in the pool at Gran's Florida house.

But tonight when I drive into Denver, her lights welcome me. I have to get off the highway, because of course I start to cry. Cosmo paces around the car as if he too knows we are almost home.

I contemplate driving right to Gran's, but instead, I drive home—to my home, which has all but been forgotten since Gran passed.

The moment I pull into my driveway, I text Grace.

I'm home.

It isn't even thirty seconds later that I get a string of happy emojis.

I'm coming over first thing in the morning for breakfast. I'll bring everything. I know for a fact you don't have any food, because I cleaned out your refrigerator.

That makes me laugh. And I remember this is why I came home.

Hey, the text came in at midnight, which means that it's two o'clock in Florida.

I rub my eyes, turn on the lamp, and look at the simple word that turns me soft.

Hey, I reply.

I'm heading to New York tomorrow. Just wanted you to know. I might be MIA for a bit.

I adjust the pillow behind me.

You're leaving your mom?

She's in good hands at the hospital right now. It's a good time to go, he adds. *Sorry if I woke you. I just needed to tell you goodnight.*

A few days ago, those words were spoken sweetly and followed with a kiss. Now they will forever be just platonic and empty.

Goodnight.

Goodnight, I say. *Cosmo and I hope you have a good trip.*

Give Cosmo a snuggle for me.

There is a pause before I can reply, and he adds, *I love you.*

Back to My Normal Life

Grace is at my door with breakfast just as promised. She has a bag of bagels and two large cups of coffee.

The moment she sets down the items in her hands, I pull her in and hug her. God, I've missed her.

"You look good," she says to me, and I laugh. "I mean it."

"I feel like a walking hot mess."

"You deserve to be a hot mess. You're mourning your grandmother, who sent you on a wicked adventure, which gave you a man, and now you're home alone."

"I have Cosmo," I add and she laughs.

"I'm glad he came back with you."

I look at the cat, sleeping in the sun coming through the window. I'm glad he came back with me too, but I know Mark would have loved his company.

We take the bags Grace brought and set up the bagels and cream cheese on the table. I add a splash of cream to my coffee, which she also brought, and I study her.

"How are you feeling?" I ask.

Grace tears off a piece of her bagel and pops it in her mouth.

"I'm excited. I'm so happy I can't see straight. But, to be honest, I feel like constant shit. Morning sickness is no joke."

I laugh, but there is some gratefulness in knowing that I'll never go through that. I want to be here for Grace and her children, but there is nothing that makes me want to go through what she's going through.

Grace sits back in her chair and kicks her feet up. "Okay, so come clean," she says.

I sip my coffee. "About what?"

"Why did you come home?"

"It was time," I say.

"That's not what I mean. I mean, why? Why didn't you stay there—with him?"

I set my coffee on the table and stand. I move to the refrigerator, pull it open, and remember that it's completely empty, because my best friend cleaned it out.

I close the door, but keep my hand on the handle.

"I'm not cut out for Florida living," I say, but immediately Joe comes to my mind, and then Brenda, Finn, and Jeff. "I wanted to be back here with you."

She nods. "And you're going to sell your Gran's house here?"

That's what I'd told her. "I think so. I can't keep both houses."

She raises a brow. "Liz, with what you've told me, you could keep all three."

I purse my lips and sit back down at the table. "The house in Florida didn't hold any meaning for me. I mean, I never remembered being there."

Grace rests her hand on my arm. "Why didn't you stay with him?"

My chest is heavy just thinking about leaving Mark. "I had to come back to you."

She shakes her head. "Liz, I'm not afraid to fly. I would have visited you all the time. Don't get me wrong, I want you to be part of my baby's life. You're one of the most important people in the world to me, but the world is accessible."

"I need to be home. What Mark and I had was nice, but I need to be here."

She smiles and eases back. "Well, I'm glad you're home." Grace picks up her phone and begins to scroll through it. "I have a showing at three, and tomorrow I have a closing and a showing. I'll meet you at your gran's tomorrow after my last showing. What else do you need to do?"

"I need to close out her accounts and finalize insurances."

"All of your mail is on my counter. So, tomorrow after we work at your gran's, you'll have dinner at our house and we'll go through everything. We'll make a spreadsheet, and start ticking off boxes," she says.

This is why I came home. Grace and her organization is just what I need. I need her more than a lover, or so I try to convince myself.

Grace wipes off her hands and takes a sip of her decaffeinated coffee. "Okay, so where are the boxes you brought back from Florida? I want to see the Oscar."

I have my own stack of flat Home Depot moving boxes leaned up against the wall in Gran's hallway. I decide to disassemble my old bedroom first.

I know that millions of people go through this every year, having to pack up someone's life. But that equally means clearing out my old life too.

Rolling up the few posters that are still on my walls, I place them in a box. The picture collage of Grace and I gets wrapped up and put into a box. It'll have a new prestigious place in my home, and always should have.

I start in the dresser drawer which I know is nothing but trinkets that I dumped out of my backpacks and purses over the years. Picking through old movie tickets, mints that are beyond expired, pencils and pens in varied colors, I realize this drawer doesn't hold any treasures.

I'm thankful when my phone rings. It's easy to be grateful for any distraction.

"Hello," I answer the call without ever looking at the ID.

"Hey," the voice on the other end is silky, and my knees go weak.

I drop down on my bed. "Hey."

"What are you doing?" he asks.

"Currently I'm disassembling my old bedroom."

"What treasures have you found?"

I look around the room. "I haven't gotten in too far," I say as I scan a look over my bookshelf. "Oh, yes I did." I laugh as I move and pull the book *Sins of My Lover* off the shelf.

"What did you find?" he asks, his voice light and humored.

"That dog-eared, stolen book."

"No kidding? You had it all along, huh?"

I flip through the book. "I'm not sure I did. This made an appearance some time later, I think." I let out a sigh. "I can't believe she kept it."

"So you're packing up her house?"

I look around the room where I grew up under both of my guardians. "I am. I think it's time to let this house go."

"That's a big decision."

I lay back on the bed and grasp the pendant on my necklace feeling closer to him and Gran while doing it. "What are you doing?"

"I'm in New York. It's snowing and I'm ill-prepared for this."

I want to smile, imagining that he's a fish out of water in the snow, just as I was in the humidity. But I find that all I want to do is run to him with a heavy coat.

"How are things going?"

"They have the cover art for Betsy's book. It'll be nearly a year before it comes out, but they'll start sending out early copies for reviews."

"I still don't know what to think about it all."

"Think about it as a gift to Betsy. She'll never, ever be forgotten."

"You're right." I rest my hand flat on my stomach and wish that random phone calls weren't all we had left. "How is your mom?"

He lets out a low hum. "She's doing good. They're happy with her progress."

"That's good."

"It is." He pauses for a moment. "In more interesting news, my dad called."

That had me sitting up. "Really?"

"It seems like there is a certain age in which the nomad life isn't as easy anymore."

"Did he only call you for money?" I'm appalled by this man.

Mark laughs. "No. Nothing like that. He was never present in my life, but he was never a trouble-maker like that. He's relocated to Orlando, to stay, and wants to get to know me."

"Wow. And what did you tell him?"

"That I was out of town," he says, his voice filled with humor. "But I told him when I got back, we could sit down and feel it out."

A pang of jealousy moves through me. He has both of his parents in his life—in Orlando. I look around the room I'm disassembling and I miss him terribly.

"Liz!" Grace's voice rings through the house.

"I'm in my room," I say. "Now the cleaning is about to get serious," I say to Mark, taking the dig at Grace.

"She's the commander?" he asks.

"She is. Completely organized," I say smiling at Grace who is now standing at the door.

"I'll let you get back to it," he says. "I miss you, Liz."

I swallow hard. "I miss you too."

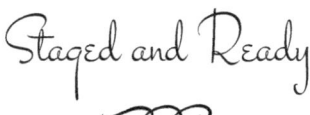

Staged and Ready

I didn't consider the holidays without Gran. I was used to having Thanksgiving with Grace and her family, but Gran had always been there too. This year, there was a big hole in the conversations.

Grace's mother did everything she could to make me feel comfortable, but it was hard to find joy, or be thankful.

And now, Gran's house is void of any personal items. Her movie poster now hangs in my bedroom, and her keepsakes are stored in my garage until I find homes for them.

Grace has the house staged, and designed to sell. It no longer holds memories of Mom and Gran. It's just a nice little house that will be a good place for another family.

Perhaps it helps. I don't feel anything looking around the house where I was raised—the house that was mine, and no one pulled me from it for their own comfort to raise me.

"You're sure you want to do this?" Grace asks as I stand in the living room of Gran's house taking in the sight of the house in this new state.

"I am. I have to move on without them, without Mom and Gran. This is step one."

"I want to warn you, I think this will sell fast."

I steady myself with a breath. "I'm still sure."

Grace studies me. "Are you okay? And I don't mean about just selling the house."

I smile and nod. "I'm fine."

"I mean, don't get me wrong. I understand that you're mourning, but it just seems deeper. Can't he come visit?"

"Grace, I'm okay," I say as I tuck my hands into the pockets of my jeans. "He has a lot going on. He has to be there. I have to be here. It's how it has to be."

"You don't have to stay here, Liz. You have the whole world."

"I have as much of the world as I can drive to. For me, this is where I have to be."

She shakes her head. "I know you don't want to fly, but..."

"I can't," I remind her. "I wish I could, but I can't."

Grace pulls me into her arms. "I love you. I'm proud of you. You making that trip was huge. And the adventure isn't over, even if you stay here."

"Keep saying it. I think I'll need to be reassured of it."

Gran's Christmas tree sits in the corner of my house and twinkles at me. It's a small tree, on a table, and I'm more than surprised that Cosmo isn't interested in it. How did she train him to leave it alone? I guess it doesn't matter why he doesn't jump up to the tree, I'm just grateful that he doesn't.

I've been working on another grief article for Julie. This one focuses on those first holidays. Thanksgiving, Christmas, and in February I'll celebrate Gran's birthday without her. I know it's okay to feel the grief I'm writing about, but tonight it's hitting hard.

Tonight I don't just miss Gran and Mom, I'm missing Mark.

I turned down an invitation to join Grace and Ashton at her company Christmas party. Actually, I'm surprised she let me. She knows I'm just going to sit in front of my TV, work on my article, and eat candy cane ice cream with Magic Shell on it.

It's been a week since Mark and I had a full conversation. It just so happened that each time we'd try to text, we'd each have something going on. But I miss him terribly. I mean my heart actually aches each time I think about what we had when I was at Gran's in Florida.

How is it possible to fall in love with someone and leave them? I did that. I left.

I look at Gran's urn which sits on a high shelf in my living room. I haven't gone to Mom's grave yet to spread Gran's ashes. There's some comfort in her being with me, in my house.

I close my laptop and set it on the coffee table. Picking up my phone, I scroll through my pictures. I'm tormenting myself by looking at pictures from my drive out, and those I took after Mark joined me, and Cosmo. The pictures of Gran's house, and Mark. The pictures of the beach, and Mark. In one month with the man, I took more pictures of him than I have of any other subject in a very long time. Not only that, I took selfies of us. I never take selfies. I hate looking at myself in photos. But in photos with Mark, I'm happy.

The tears begin, and I just let them fall.

Until Mark came into my life, I didn't know I was lonely.

I drop my phone in my lap and cover my mouth with my hands.

I'm lonely.

God, I'm lonely.

And the only reason I know I'm lonely is because I'm in love.

I stand, wiping the tears from my cheeks. I need to be with him. I need to spend my Christmas with the man I love—the man Gran sent me to.

Mark is my adventure.

Grace had called, texted, and emailed. When I didn't answer, she walked through my front door.

"If you're alive, you answer my damn calls," she shouts, and Cosmo hisses at her, before returning to his sleeping spot on my feet.

"I'm fine," I bite out the words.

"You're a mess," she says, looking at me in the clothes I had on yesterday. "Have you slept?"

"I'm fine," I repeat, not answering her question.

Grace walks to the coffee pot, picks it up, and studies it. "How old is this?"

"What time is it?"

"Eleven o'clock in the morning."

"Old," I tell her.

She pours the coffee down the drain and makes a new pot. "If you're only drinking coffee, and you've been up all night, you're working."

I shrug. I have done some work, because when I started looking at websites and travel blogs, inspiration for articles began to flood my head.

While the coffee brews, Grace walks up and stands behind me. "That's a website for an airline," she says.

I nod. "It's one of the busiest travel seasons. The cost for airfare is—"

"Liz," she interrupts me. "What are you doing?"

"I'd have to fly on 476,000 flights to be on one that has an issue. I've already been on one. So, I figure I can fly 475,999 more times before something bad happens," I say, but my rapid words nearly choke me.

"You're going to fly to him? You're going?" Grace's voice rises with excitement.

"I have to. I have to be with him. I'm sick not being with him." I scrub my hands over my face. "I can't live there. I need to be here. I want to be here. But I want to be with him. He needs to be with his mom and he has so many things going on in his life. I just need to get over this."

Grace wraps her arms around me from behind, pressing her head to mine. "I've never been so excited for you in all my life. Let me help you navigate this. Do you need me to go with you?"

"I have to leave tomorrow. His schedule is too crazy right now. If I don't go now, then..."

"I get it." She moves to the chair next to me, pulls it out, and sits. "I can't leave tomorrow. I have a showing, but I can drive you to the airport."

I purse my lips and tuck my hands under me because they've started to shake. "What if I freak out?"

"Maybe take a few more days to plan this and get someone to prescribe you something to calm you."

I shake my head. "It has to be tomorrow."

Grace rests her hand on my thigh. "Okay. We'll get you a flight. We'll get you packed. And we'll figure out some tools for you to use to calm yourself, but in the end, you'll be with him, and that's all that matters, right?"

"Right." At the end of it all, I'll be with Mark.

Life Changing Decision

Grace never left my side all day. She helped me book airline tickets. She helped me clean my kitchen. And at some point, she made me lunch and encouraged me to take a nap—and I slept all night.

Now, Grace is standing in my kitchen with tears in her eyes as I wheel my suitcase out of my room.

"I feel as if you're headed off to college or something stupid," she says.

"I don't think you're supposed to be crying. I'm supposed to be crying, right?"

"Are you going to cry?"

I let out a nervous laugh. "Actually, I think I'm going to throw up."

Grace steadies herself with a deep breath. "You talked to him? He knows you're coming?"

I wince at that. "I did talk to him. He's in Orlando right now."

She eyes me coolly. "He doesn't know you're coming?"

"If I'm going to do this, I want it to be a surprise. I also don't want him to get too excited. What if I get to the airport and can't even get out of the car? What if I get on the plane and have a meltdown and they have to kick me off?"

Grace takes my hands. "You're going to be just fine. Liz, remember you have 500,000 flights to take."

I snort out another laugh. "475,999 to be exact."

She laughs. "We'll worry about it when you get close to hitting that mark." She kisses my fingers. "Okay, let's go. I have to get you out there and hurry back for a showing."

"I can take the train if—"

"I wouldn't give up the chance to drive you to the airport, and I'm going to cry all the way home," she says.

"Why?"

"One, I'm hormonal. But, two, I'm so freaking proud of you, I could burst. Seriously, Liz, this is huge."

"I don't know if I can do it."

She laughs again, and this time I can hear the tears in it. "But you've never even considered it. Flying was just off limits. You're considering it. You're researching it. You bought a ticket! You'll do anything to get to the man you love. God, this is amazing." She takes a breath and just grins at me. "You can get to him from the airport?"

"You know, I have taken an Uber before."

"Right. Uber, yes. Airplane, no. I never did understand that."

I pull her into me. Yes, I'm going to do this. I drove across country to meet a man I didn't know and live with him. And I did all of that with my cat in tow, and my grandmother.

I can do this.

I can't do this.

I have bitten down my nails and now I'm hyperventilating on the drive to the airport. I'm going to throw up.

Last night when Mark called he wanted to FaceTime, but I

held him off. In fact, I managed to get him off the phone in less than ten minutes because I knew if I talked to him I would crack.

The house in Florida is under contract, and he's moved everything to his mom's, except what is in Joe's garage. The longer I let him talk about that, the better off I was.

"If you don't start breathing right, you're going to pass out," Grace says as we get closer to the huge white teepeed canopy of Denver International Airport.

"I can't do this."

"Like hell you can't. You are Elizabeth Evans. You are fucking Betsy Evans' granddaughter. You are on an adventure to live a life with no regrets and if you don't get on that fucking plane, you'll regret it."

I stare at Grace and blink hard.

"You're right. I am Betsy Evans' fucking granddaughter," I restate and Grace laughs as she drums on the steering wheel.

As we pull up to the drop off, I feel that surge of sickness wash through me again. I can tell you for sure, I will never be pregnant. Nerves are bad enough. I can't imagine being pregnant on purpose.

Grace puts the car in park and we sit in silence for a few minutes. I grip the pendant around my neck. Gran is with me. Wherever Gran is, I'm safe—that was always the case.

"Everything is electronic," Grace tells me. "Do you have your ticket on your phone?"

"Yes."

"Do you have your driver's license close?"

"Yes."

"And you're carrying on your suitcase, right?"

"Yes," I say with a laugh because actually she has me more freaked out than I was.

"Your flight isn't for four more hours, but once you're beyond security, you're committed."

I turn to her. "I couldn't leave?"

Now she laughs. "Well, you could—I guess."

"I'm going," I say gripping my purse to me. "I'm going. I'm going," I repeat and Grace finally gets out of the car and walks around to the other side.

I open my door and step out into her waiting arms.

"Have a drink or two to calm yourself. And then, get on that plane, fall asleep for four hours. It'll make the flight go faster. And when you get to him, stay. Make this only one leg in your many travels, Liz. Live that life your gran wanted you to live. See the world. Have sex in amazing locations. Love a man who loves you back."

I hold her longer than I should. This is why I'll come back home. This is the love I'm used to. And, yes, if I can start to fly, the whole world is my playground, and Mark's too. But I can always come home.

When Grace eases out of my arms, I'm not sure I can stand, let alone walk and maneuver a bag through an airport. A part of me wants to get back in that car and throw a fit until Grace takes me home. But a warmth from my pendant reminds me that there is a big fat life to live beyond these doors. I can do this. I can fly for four hours and be there with the man I love.

I take in a deep breath and let it out slowly.

Here I go. Another adventure I never saw coming.

Maneuvering through the airport is an acquired skill. I don't have that skill. South TSA check point. North TSA check point. Terminal A TSA check point.

I'm assured that the south side is where I need to be, but there have to be two thousand people in front of me. Aren't we in between holiday travel? And, there isn't even a big storm outside.

I keep breathing as if it's me having a baby and not Grace getting ready to have one. I'm dizzy. I'm thirsty. I'm getting hungry, and yet I'm sure if I ate I would throw up.

The line moves quickly, and I just follow what everyone else does. I take off my shoes. I unload my liquids. I panic that my extra pair of underwear in my personal carryon is going to fall out.

Once I make it through TSA, I find that I'm delivered to a train platform. Seriously, how big is this place?

On the train to my terminal, my phone rings and it's Mark. The announcements on the train will give away my position. So I text him instead.

Hey! Can't talk right now. In a meeting. I'll call you when I'm done, I type.

As soon as I exit the train, I'm swept up in a mass of people going up an escalator and then moving to another escalator. I feel like I'm being herded. If every airport is this big, driving would be faster, not to mention that the airport is an hour out of town.

Once I'm at the top of the escalators, I can move to the side and figure out which direction to go for my gate. I'm so turned around. Luckily, I still have three hours.

I'm headed into a meeting of my own, he texts back. *Text me when you're out of yours. I'll text you when I'm out of mine.*

Will do, I reply.

And, Liz, I love you.

I'm almost there, I think. In three hours, plus four flying, and another to get to him, I'm almost there.

Battling the crowds going both directions, I find my gate, and as luck would have it, there is a sit-down hamburger bar right next to it. I'm going to take this time to sit, eat some lunch, and have that drink Grace said I should have.

I scan the menu on my phone, then order. I check my tickets and make sure the apps for entertainment are downloaded. I know where the airplane mode is and I wonder if I should turn it on now. Cell phones make planes crash, right?

As I'm sitting in the restaurant, I press the pendant around my neck against me. I know I need Gran on this trip.

"Gran, if this isn't an adventure, I don't know what is. I just hope you're proud of me."

Now Boarding

After an hour of sitting in the restaurant, I decide to walk around and stretch out my legs. I've settled into the fact that there are thousands of people milling around in this central area. I now understand why it's such a big deal when travelers get stuck here. I mean, what would I do if I had to charge my phone? I see people sitting on the floors just to be near outlets. There are a few people who seem to be as lost as I am. That's comforting. And I wonder if their knees are shaking too. Seriously, I'm considering having to ask someone to wheel me to the plane, unsure if I can walk.

I'm about to get on a plane, and I'm scared to death.

And, a new article comes to my mind in all of this. *A Newbie Travelers Guide to DIA.* I laugh at the very thought of it. Maybe, if this goes well and sparks a new fire in me, I can write about other airports.

Still laughing, I wander into a store full of Colorado trinkets and look around. Would Mark enjoy a fashionable Colorado T-shirt? As Coloradans, we are proud of our flag and its symbol. We put it on everything.

I decide that's exactly what he needs. I mean, I can't show up empty-handed, right?

After I buy the shirt, I head to the gate and wait. It's still too noisy to call Mark. I guess the element of surprise is only enhanced by hours of silence.

I'm mesmerized by the airplanes parking and backing out of the gates. The plane I'm about to board is unloading passengers, and I now can't tell if I have to go to the bathroom, or if it's just nerves. I'm going to bank on the latter and hope I'm not wrong.

I have come this far. I don't want to turn around.

Okay, that's a lie. I do want to turn around. I want to go home —but I want Mark more.

Once the plane is unloaded, and the staff begins to assemble, they announce that we'll be boarding soon. It's been hours since I heard from Mark and I am surprised that Grace hasn't checked on me. I guess they know I'm going to do this. I have to prove to them, and myself, that I can.

I take my phone from my pocket to pull up my ticket. Will my ticket work if I'm in airplane mode? Do I turn that on now? Do I wait until they tell me to do that?

I look at my phone and study the settings.

I am in airplane mode. Did it just know? Why would it turn it on for me?

Wait, I did that in the restaurant.

I turn off the airplane mode, and the moment I do, my phone begins to ding and chime. I have text messages. I have voice messages.

One from Mark. One from Grace. Three more from Grace. A call from Mark. Three calls from Grace.

I don't even get through the first few texts from Mark that say, *Can you talk yet? Liz? I have something I need to tell you. Where are you?*, when my phone rings in my hand.

"Grace?" I say without a hello.

"Oh, my, God! Did you fucking turn off your phone? I have been calling you for hours."

"What's wrong? What happened?"

"Don't get on that plane," she says frantically, just as they call for the first group to board.

"Excuse me?" Seriously? She's telling me not to get on the plane? I don't want to get on the plane. What does she know that I don't know? "Grace, what's wrong?"

"Don't get on the plane."

I look out the window at the plane that's sitting there. My hands shake. Sickness moves through me again. I knew this was a bad idea.

"Grace, it's boarding. I have to get on the plane if I'm going to do this."

"Mark isn't in Orlando!" she shouts through the phone.

I press my fingers to my forehead. "He's not in Orlando?"

"No, I'm not, because I needed to be here with you," his voice comes from behind me, shaking and breathless.

Lowering the phone, I slowly turn around.

He's standing right there—with me.

I blink hard, lifting the phone back to my ear. "I have to call you back," I say to Grace and then disconnect the call.

The corner of Mark's mouth turns up into that sexy grin, and it does its job on me. Now I'm shaking for an entirely different reason. He's here.

"You're here," I say, my voice breathy and soft.

He reaches his hand to my face and just looks at me. "I'm here," he says, his breathing hard as if he'd run through the airport to find me.

"Why are you here?" I ask and we're pushed closer together when the area grows more crowded as people move to the gate.

"Your mom—your meetings," I'm stammering out words.

"I couldn't not be with you." He eases in closer. "Where are you going?"

"To see you," I say looking up into those mesmerizing blue eyes that hold me.

"You were going to fly?"

I nod. "According to statistics, I have 475,999 more flights to take before I'm on another plane that crashes."

"Is that all?" he teases, still gazing at me.

"I couldn't stand it any longer. I can't be without you. It was worth the anxiety."

His grin widens. "You must really love me," he says wrapping his arms around me and holding me closer. "Tell me, Liz. Do you love me?"

"You know I love you."

"Just say it."

"I love you."

He lets out a sigh. "I love you too. That's why I'm here. I was Grace's showing."

I feel my jaw go slack as I stare up at him. "You were looking at a house?"

"I was. I need to be here, because you're here. I don't want to live without you. I don't want to do long distance. You have a big fat life to live, and I want to be part of it."

I chuckle at his use of Gran's words.

He touches my pendant. "She didn't put us in one another's paths for a moment, Liz. She knew what she was doing. I can't be without you."

"I don't want to be without you either. But your mom..."

"Crazy thing. So my dad is back. I mentioned that?" he asks and I nod. "It appears that the attraction they had some thirty-six years ago is still a thing. He's given up roaming the country and wants to settle down. It just so happens that she has a spare room and likes his company."

I swallow hard. "Your dad is taking care of your mom?"

"Yeah, and vice versa."

As they begin boarding the plane, I look at the door. "How are you here? I mean, you got through security?"

He chuckles. "You wouldn't answer your phone. I had to buy a ticket."

I wince. "I'm sorry."

"It's worth every penny." He lifts his hand to my cheek again and searches my eyes. "Stay here with me, Liz. We can fly back together when we're ready."

"I only want to be wherever you are."

"Good, because I never want to leave you again. I've never been so broken."

"Really?"

"Really." He dips down to press a soft kiss to my lips. "You are my adventure, Liz. Betsy sent you to me."

Grace hadn't known that Mark was her showing. He'd made the appointment as Constance Frost, but the moment he climbed out of the car, Grace knew who he was.

According to Mark, she'd all but thrown him into her car and raced toward the airport. It had only become a frantic race when I hadn't answered my phone.

Mark stayed, just as he'd promised to, and now, on Christmas Day, we stand over my mother's grave, looking down at it.

"I can't even tell you how many hours I have sat here. Sometimes, I bring a blanket and read her a book, or listen to music she would have liked," I say kneeling down in front of her headstone, running my fingers over her name. "She's been gone twice as long as I had her with me, but I always feel her."

Mark kneels down next to me. "Betsy was devastated when your mom died," he says. "When she got the call that your mom wasn't going to make it, Betsy changed in that moment. I'll never forget it."

"I'll always feel guilty that she gave everything up for me, especially your grandfather and you."

Mark shakes his head. "Oh, Liz, you were her whole world. No one holds a grudge."

I press my hand to the pendant that lays against my chest, and I feel Gran with us, and I know she's happy that we're together.

Cosmo prances around Mom's headstone, unsure of the snow on his paws. I feel as if he knows what we're doing, since he's been part of it multiple times.

Mark takes the trowel from his coat pocket and digs a hole. "Is this deep enough? The ground is frozen."

That makes me laugh. "Are you sure you'll be okay to live here in the cold?"

"Baby, I'm warm. I have the woman I love with me every day. You'll never hear me complain."

Taking Gran's urn, I open the top. This is it. She will have been left everywhere I've had my adventure. It was exactly what she wanted for me.

I pour the rest of her ashes in the hole next to Mom's headstone. When the urn is empty, Mark covers the hole with the dirt he'd taken out, and I put the lid back on the urn.

"Gran, you and Mom will always be together." I let out a little chuckle. "You'll always be with your family, with the man you loved, with the house loved, and of course, on the waves being carried to the prince you loved." I touch the pendant again. "And you'll always be with Mark and me."

Mark reaches for my hand, and I lean toward him and kiss him softly. I miss Gran and Mom so much, but I'm happy. I'm so happy.

Epilogue

HAPPILY EVER AFTER

Seven Months Later

Grace had been right. The house, which had started as Mom's and where Gran lived out her life, sold within weeks, and we got more than the asking price.

The house in Florida had taken much longer to sell, but when it sold, it was worth more than seven million, and Grace convinced me to talk with Julie about being completely remote for the magazine, because there is no need for me to actually work now, except that I love what I do.

I did get on an airplane after the new year, and I cried every time we had turbulence and when we landed, but Mark held me the entire time. I survived, and an entire world was opened up to me.

After that initial flight to Florida, where I met Mark's father, and we spent the day driving Joe around, as if we'd never left, we drove by Gran's house slowly just to feel her as we passed.

Since then, we've attended Mark's meetings in New York, together. His agent is interested in my work and has suggested that

I consider writing a book. I don't know what I'd write about. Maybe I could write a story about a woman who learned a lot about herself when her dead grandmother sent her on an adventure.

From there, we flew cross-country to California where they were finalizing the script and details for Constance Frost's book.

Now, in our own tiny backyard, we sit on the couch on the patio reading in the warmth of summer. Cosmo is zooming around the back yard. I don't know what he's found, but I hope he doesn't bring me any gifts that wiggle.

We bought the house Mark had originally scheduled to look at with Grace. We liked the open floor plan, like Gran's house in Florida. The kitchen is updated, and there is an amazing display alcove where the pair of Oscars sit.

My legs are draped over Mark's lap as I lounge back. The sun is beginning to slip behind the mountains, and Mark puts down his book.

"I'll never get tired of that sight," he says watching the hues of orange light up the Rocky Mountains.

I put down my book and watch the sight with new appreciation.

"I never noticed just how beautiful our sunsets were until you came here."

He gives my thigh a squeeze. "Then it's a good thing I showed up," he says with that half smile.

"Oh, it's such a good thing," I say, dropping my feet and scooting up next to him. "I suppose we should decide what we're going to eat for dinner."

He nods slowly just as my phone buzzes on the table. I pick it up, read the text, and jump to my feet.

Mark laughs. "Whoa! What's up?"

"We have to go. I have to go. Now. We have to go," I say frantically, looking around as if the things I need to leave the house will be outside on the patio.

Mark's brows draw in and he stands, taking hold of my arms and making me focus on him.

"You're freaking me out now," he says.

I lift my eyes to his. "Baby! Grace. Ashton." I can't seem to say entire sentences.

"Grace is having her baby?" he asks. I nod. He laughs. "Okay, we'll get there. But, baby, we're not the ones having the baby. We have nothing but time."

"I have to be there."

"You will be," he promises as he pulls me into him. "I wouldn't dream of you missing this."

"This is big," I say.

"It is. Grace is going to be so excited to show you her baby. But she's going to have some time. Let's gather our things and head to the hospital—calmly," he adds.

"Fine. But if we're late—"

"Have you ever known a baby that came that fast?"

"I've never known a baby. This baby is everything. I'll get to be his or her auntie. I can help Grace anytime."

He laughs again. "You're sure you don't want your own baby?"

I blink hard. I take a breath to argue that he knows how I feel, but in that brief moment, I'm not so sure.

When I had made that decision, I didn't have Mark—or even the promise of Mark.

"I've never been around a baby," I remind him.

"Me either," he says.

"I guess we could see how it goes as babysitters, right?"

"Absolutely."

Lifting my hands to his face, I study his eyes. "I've never wanted kids of my own."

"I know."

"So why am I thinking about it in this instance?"

"Because I'm here forever," he says.

Licking my lips, I consider that. "Forever?"

"Forever. You can't get rid of me. And don't forget, we have letters written to whomever we leave behind, letting them know we need to be buried together—or scattered in the same places."

"I thought I was going to be lonely for the rest of my life," I say. "I had no idea that my well-lived grandmother could give me such a gift after she was gone."

"Well," he pulls me in closer, and I let my arms wrap around him. "I think since we are living our own big fat lives, we should see how the babysitting goes. Maybe flying all over the world isn't the biggest adventure we're supposed to have."

"Maybe it is," I argue.

Mark chuckles. "Maybe it is. But, Liz, I already know that whether that adventure is travel, books, movies, a family—I know that we'll have that adventure together. That's the most important part."

"A life well-lived with no regrets."

"No regrets." He leans in and kisses me softly. "Now, let's go meet Grace's next adventure."

The Rom Com Movie Club

We hope that you liked this release from 5 Prince Publishing, LLC. Please enjoy the following excerpt, available now at 5PrinceBooks.com.

The Rom Com Movie Club - Book One

The Rom Com Movie Club

BOOK ONE

There was a ritual, and no one strayed from the ritual.

Pajama pants. Check.

College T-shirts. Check.

No makeup so that a face mask, acquired by the hostess, could be worn at some time during the evening. Check.

Popcorn. M&Ms. Diet soda. Wine. Pizza.

Check. Check. Check. Check. And check.

Lisa looked around the small living room right off the even tinier kitchen, and decided she had everything in order. It was only four in the afternoon and she looked as if she were staying in for a slumber party, but that was what Rom Com Movie Night was all about.

They'd created the monthly viewing "club" after having watched *Grease* in the dorms, and Lisa mentioning that she'd never had, or been to, a slumber party. And though it was never intended to be a slumber party, sometimes it just happened.

Usually, movie night was the second Saturday of the month, but Tina's sister had planned Tina's bridal shower for that afternoon, and Lisa couldn't help but wonder if that was on purpose. Cicely was a wonderful woman, she really was. A younger sister to them all, but there had always been some resentment toward Tina's besties. Cicely didn't have a core base of friends like her sister did, and that was too bad, she could have used her own posse.

So, without a word about it, Rom Com Movie Night was simply moved to the first Saturday in May.

Lisa never much cared for being the hostess, and luckily it was only once every four months. Her condo was the smallest of all the houses where the besties lived.

Ruby's apartment was also a two bedroom, but with a bigger floor plan, and she usually had a roommate. Though, she didn't tend to keep any one roommate for long.

Mindy had a house with a yard, a gazebo, and a fountain. It had been her grandmother's house and she'd inherited it after college graduation. Everyone agreed that they'd be happy to do movie night there every month, even though the house was extremely outdated, but fair was fair, and they all took their turns.

Tina was currently living with her future in-laws because weddings were freaking expensive. As soon as she and Aaron were married, they were moving out—or so she'd said.

Lisa turned on the oven for the pizzas. She'd premade the pizzas and created a video for her YouTube channel, which was all about food. She thought homemade was better than someone running out in the middle of the movie to get them or risk some eighteen-year-old college kid toking up in his car with their pizza in the passenger seat.

The doorbell rang just after four. There was no surprise in finding Tina standing at the door, a bottle of wine in hand, and her favorite Snoopy pajama pants on.

She had her blonde hair pulled up into two ponytails, like Chrissy from *Three's Company*, a sitcom Lisa used to watch re-runs of after school with Mama Rose.

"I'm going to drink this entire bottle of wine by myself. Put my name on it," Tina growled through gritted teeth.

THE ROM COM MOVIE CLUB

Lisa took the bottle and smiled at her friend who barely stood five feet tall. "Future in-law drama?"

Tina groaned as she walked into Lisa's condo and plopped right down on the sofa. She had on a T-shirt from the first college her fiancé attended, the University of Maryland, and she'd worn fuzzy slippers instead of shoes.

"His mother wants those stupid almonds on the tables at the reception. Seriously? Do you know my mother broke her tooth on one of those once? It's a liability and a cost I don't want to have. And, now her best-friend's sister wants to come to the wedding. I don't know that woman. We have all the invitations out and RSVPs coming back. This is my wedding."

Lisa took the corkscrew she'd laid out on the counter, and opened the bottle of wine that Tina had brought. Filling one of the wine glasses she'd had at the ready, Lisa poured Tina a full glass of wine and carried it to her as Tina scooped up a handful of M&Ms and began to pop them into her mouth one by one.

"What does Aaron say to all of this?" Lisa asked.

Tina took the wine glass and sipped. "He thinks I should just be calm. His mother has a lot going on right now."

"And you don't?"

Tina's eyes went wide at the validation. "Right?" She sipped again. "They went from empty nesters to us moving in. Temporarily," she demanded. "And now Aaron's brother has moved back in because the company he worked for just sold and there are like a thousand employees being moved around the country or getting laid off."

Lisa sat on the arm of the sofa. "And which is he?"

"Undecided. They have an office here in Denver, but he's not sure."

"I've never met his brother. What's his name?"

"Ryan." Tina finished the M&Ms in her hand, set down the glass of wine, and pulled her phone from where she'd tucked it in her bra. She scrolled through her Facebook feed and then handed Lisa the phone.

"Where has he been hiding?" Lisa swooned.

Tina's brow rose as she picked up her glass of wine. "In Illinois."

"But he's coming here?"

Tina laughed. "I warn you against him."

"Why?"

"Because I live with his mother too."

Lisa laughed, but she couldn't help but let her finger scroll over the pictures on his Facebook feed. Tall, dark, handsome—he fit the bill.

In a photo with Aaron, he stood at least four inches taller than his brother. And in a photo on a boat—fishing—he was a well-defined specimen of man.

Lisa's mouth went dry. "Is he seeing anyone?"

Tina was mid sip of wine as she looked up at Lisa. "No. He used to date some woman in Chicago, but they've been off again more than they were on."

"Tragedy."

"You're not hooking up with my new brother-in-law."

"Who said hooking up? I'm thinking I could fall in love with this guy and keep him."

Tina snorted out a laugh. "Keep dreaming."

Lisa thought she just might keep dreaming. And to think, Mr. Tall-Dark-Handsome would be around a lot soon. They'd be at dinners together. Rehearsals. Parties. Weddings. Receptions. Oh, yes. Ryan Blair was in her sights now.

When the doorbell rang, Lisa stood, Tina's phone still in her hand.

On the front step, Ruby and Mindy stood in pajama bottoms and college T-shirts, bare-faced, hair up, and each of them had something to drink in their hands.

"What are we watching?" Ruby asked as she strolled into the condo.

"*While You Were Sleeping*," Lisa replied.

Mindy's eyes went wide. "Bill Pullman. Yummy."

Ruby turned back to her and winced. "Over Peter Gallagher?"

"Too many eyebrows," Mindy snorted a laugh and then looked at the phone in Lisa's hand. "Who is that?"

Lisa looked down at the picture she'd landed on of Ryan in ski gear. "The future Mr. Palmer, of course," she teased and Tina groaned.

"It's my future brother-in-law, and Lisa's horny," Tina called out from the couch.

Ruby laughed a thunderous laugh, while Mindy blushed at the comment.

Ruby shrugged. "Just think. You and Tina could compare notes."

"Oh-my-God!" Tina took a large sip of her wine and handed her glass back to Lisa. "More. I'm going to need a lot more."

Please Review

We hope you enjoyed *Liz's Road Trip*
by Bernadette Marie.
If you did, we would ask that you please
rate and review this title.
Every review helps our authors.

Rate and Review: Liz's Road Trip

Meet The Author

Bestselling Author Bernadette Marie writes contemporary romances and believes in Happily Ever After. The married mother of five believes in love at first sight, quick love, and second chances. An avid martial artist, Bernadette Marie is a certified instructor and holds a second degree black belt in Tang Soo Do. She loves Tai Chi, traveling to Disney parks, and having lunch with friends. When not writing, or running her own publishing house, Bernadette is probably immersed in a Rom Com, from which she will often quote one-liners.

Other Titles from 5 Prince Publishing